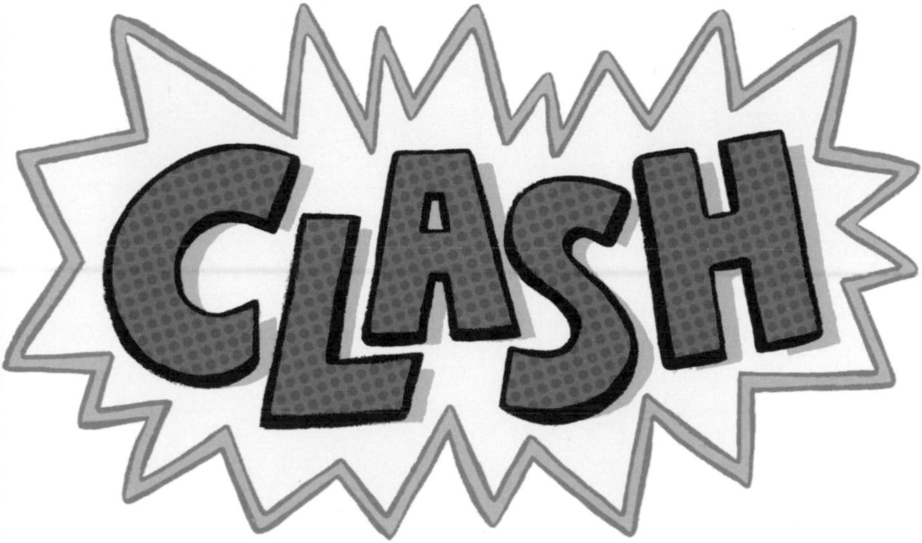
CLASH

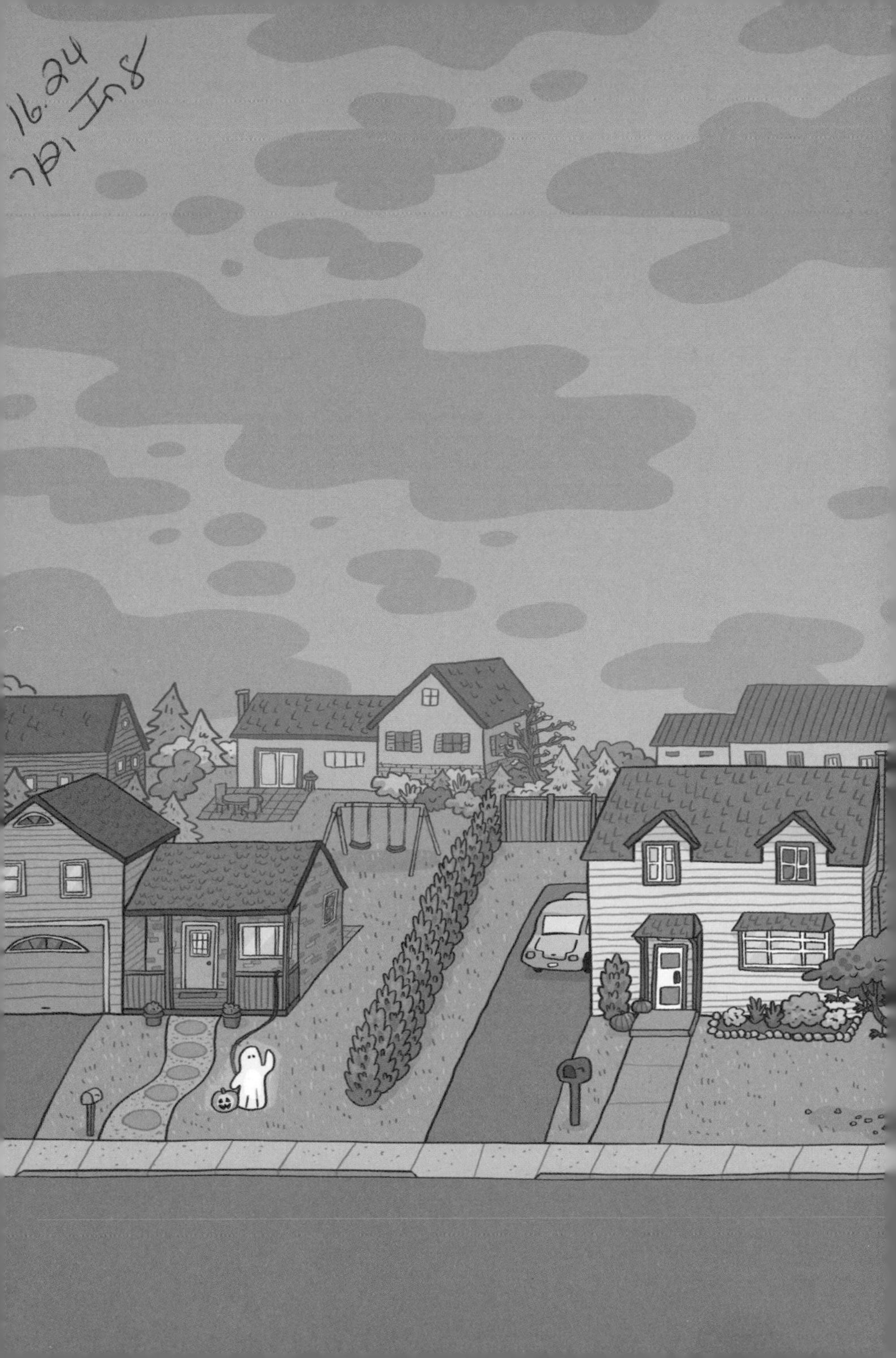

CLASH

BY KAYLA MILLER

ETCH
HOUGHTON MIFFLIN HARCOURT
BOSTON   NEW YORK

COLOR BY JESS LOME
LETTERING BY MICAH MYERS

Etch is an imprint of Houghton Mifflin Harcourt Publishing Company.

hmhbooks.com

The illustrations in this book were done using inks and digital color.

Design by Andrea Miller

ISBN: 978-0-358-24220-8 hardcover
ISBN: 978-0-358-24219-2 paperback

Manufactured in China
SCP 10 9 8 7 6 5 4 3 2 1
4500820332

FOR ANYONE WHO NEEDS
A LITTLE UNDERSTANDING -KM

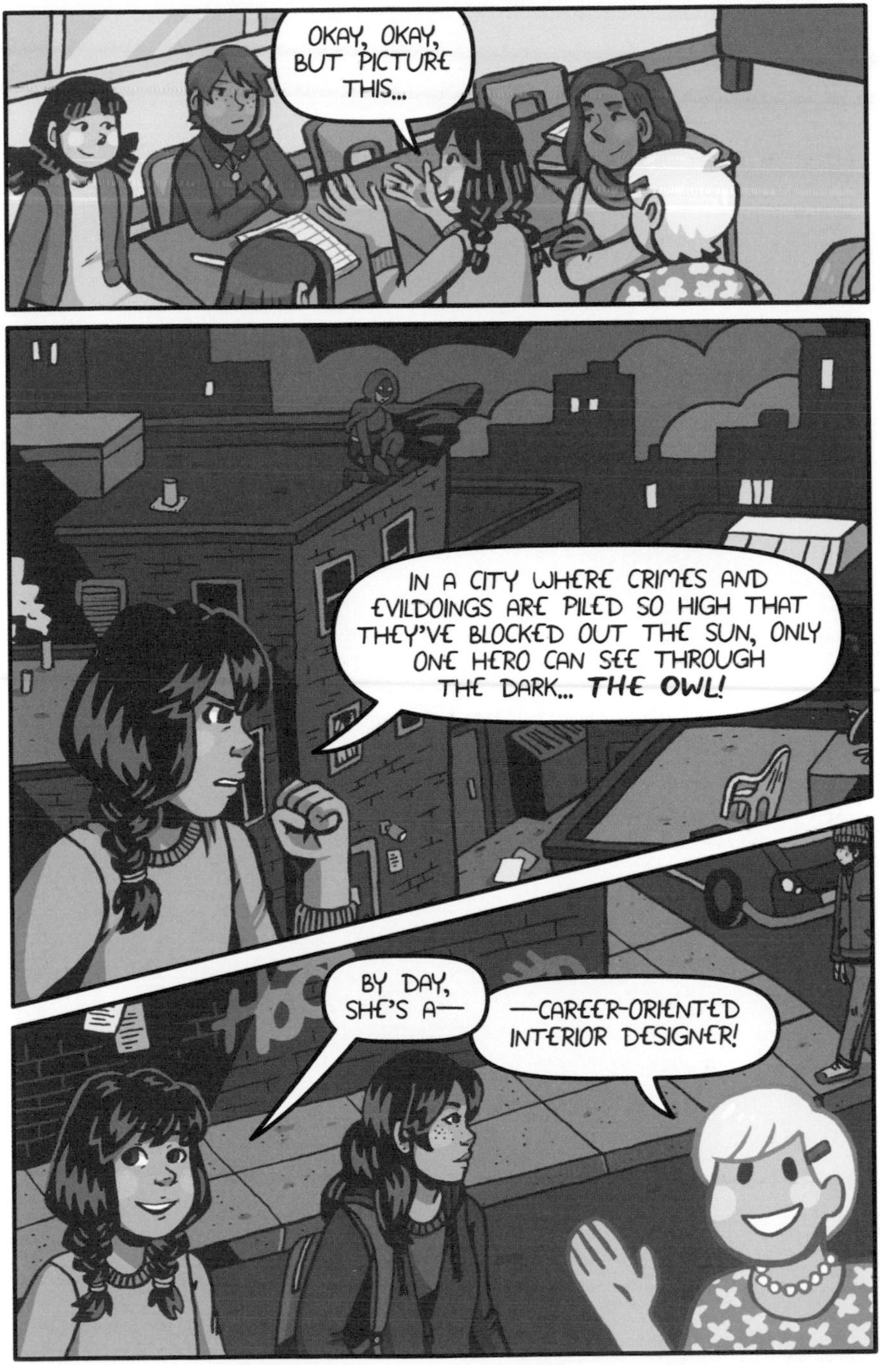
OKAY, OKAY, BUT PICTURE THIS...
IN A CITY WHERE CRIMES AND EVILDOINGS ARE PILED SO HIGH THAT THEY'VE BLOCKED OUT THE SUN, ONLY ONE HERO CAN SEE THROUGH THE DARK... **THE OWL!**
BY DAY, SHE'S A—
—CAREER-ORIENTED INTERIOR DESIGNER!

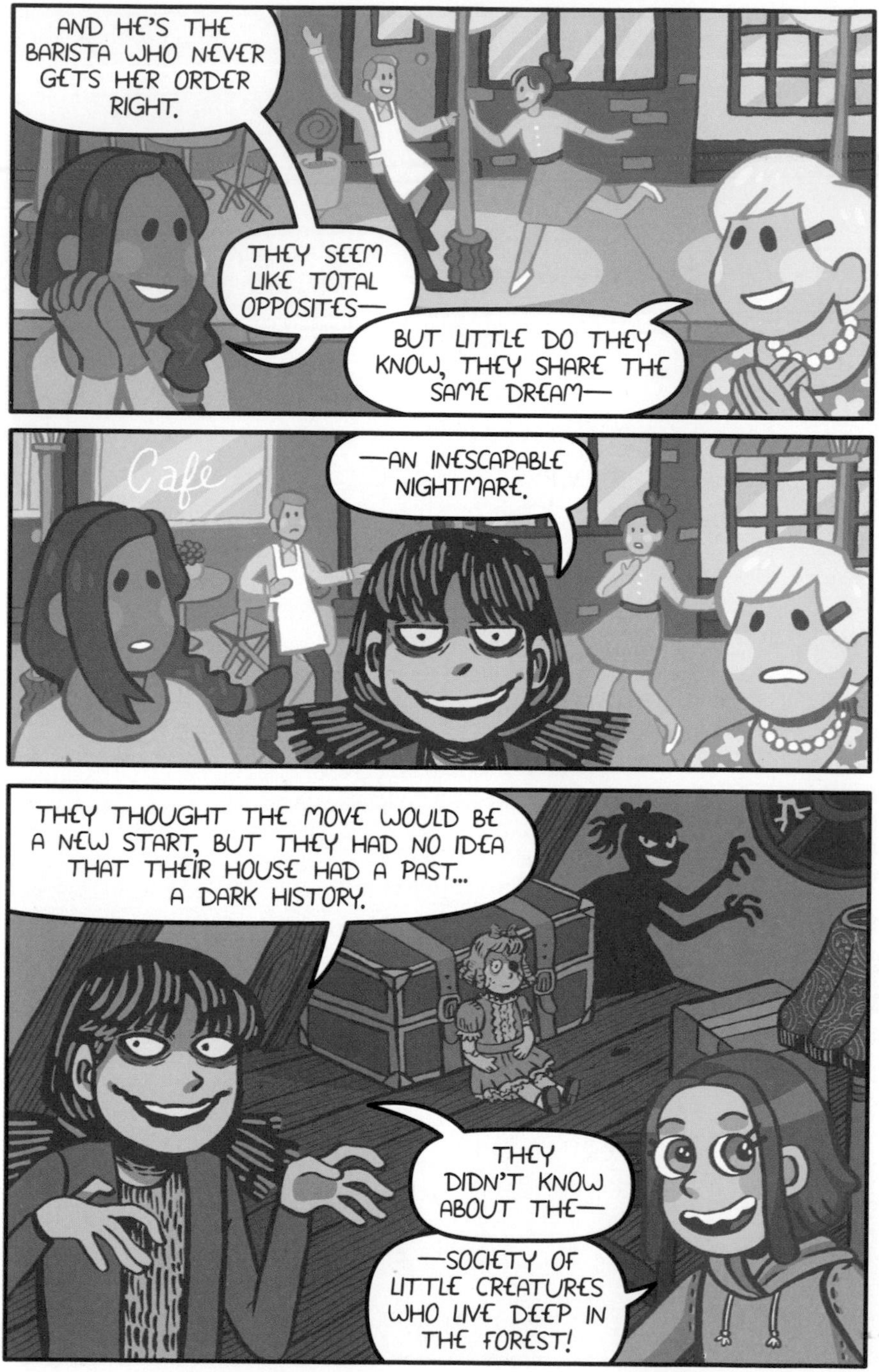
AND HE'S THE BARISTA WHO NEVER GETS HER ORDER RIGHT.
THEY SEEM LIKE TOTAL OPPOSITES—
BUT LITTLE DO THEY KNOW, THEY SHARE THE SAME DREAM—
—AN INESCAPABLE NIGHTMARE.
Café
THEY THOUGHT THE MOVE WOULD BE A NEW START, BUT THEY HAD NO IDEA THAT THEIR HOUSE HAD A PAST... A DARK HISTORY.
THEY DIDN'T KNOW ABOUT THE—
—SOCIETY OF LITTLE CREATURES WHO LIVE DEEP IN THE FOREST!

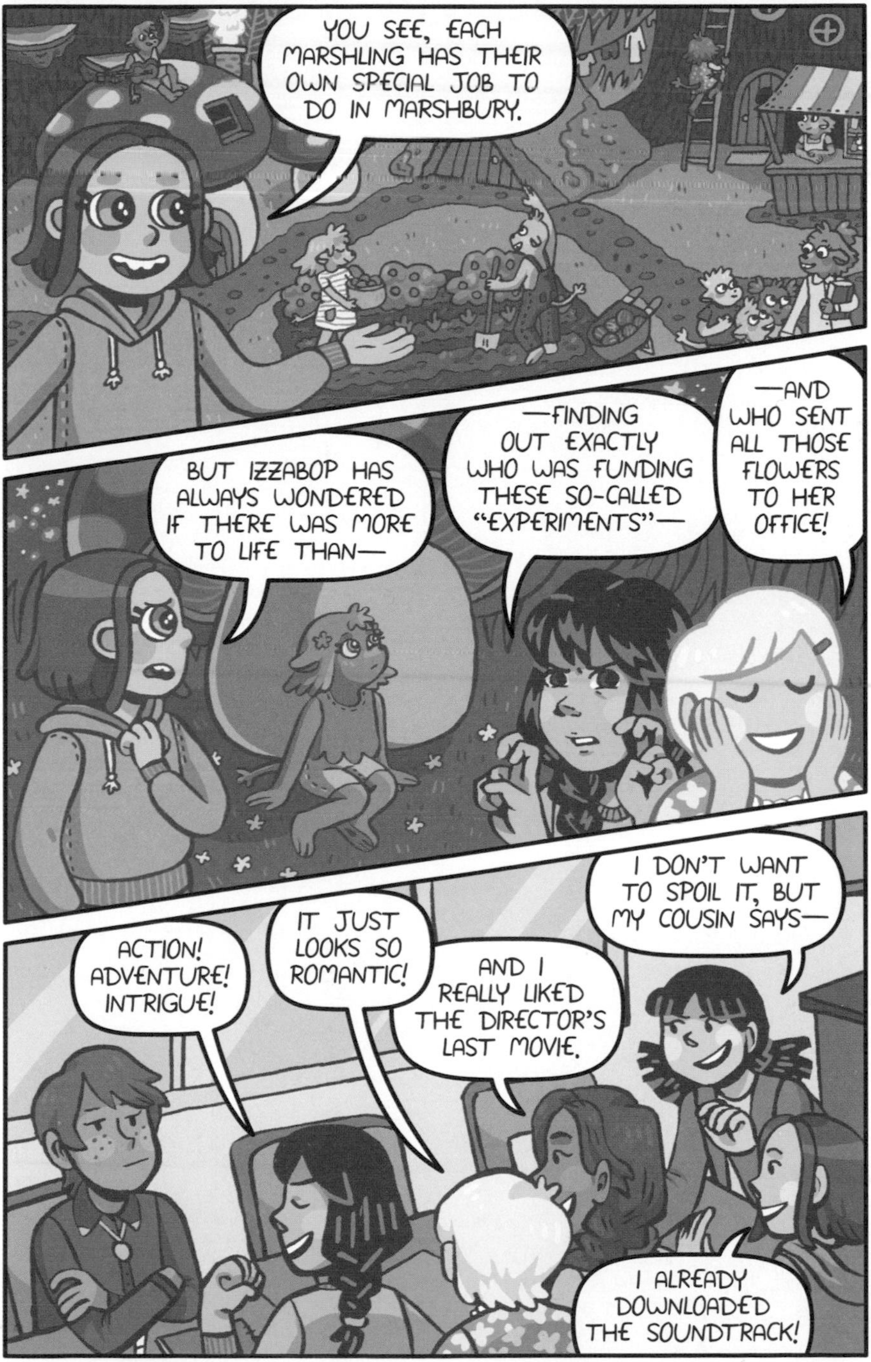
YOU SEE, EACH MARSHLING HAS THEIR OWN SPECIAL JOB TO DO IN MARSHBURY.
BUT IZZABOP HAS ALWAYS WONDERED IF THERE WAS MORE TO LIFE THAN—
—FINDING OUT EXACTLY WHO WAS FUNDING THESE SO-CALLED "EXPERIMENTS"—
—AND WHO SENT ALL THOSE FLOWERS TO HER OFFICE!
ACTION! ADVENTURE! INTRIGUE!
IT JUST LOOKS SO ROMANTIC!
AND I REALLY LIKED THE DIRECTOR'S LAST MOVIE.
I DON'T WANT TO SPOIL IT, BUT MY COUSIN SAYS—
I ALREADY DOWNLOADED THE SOUNDTRACK!

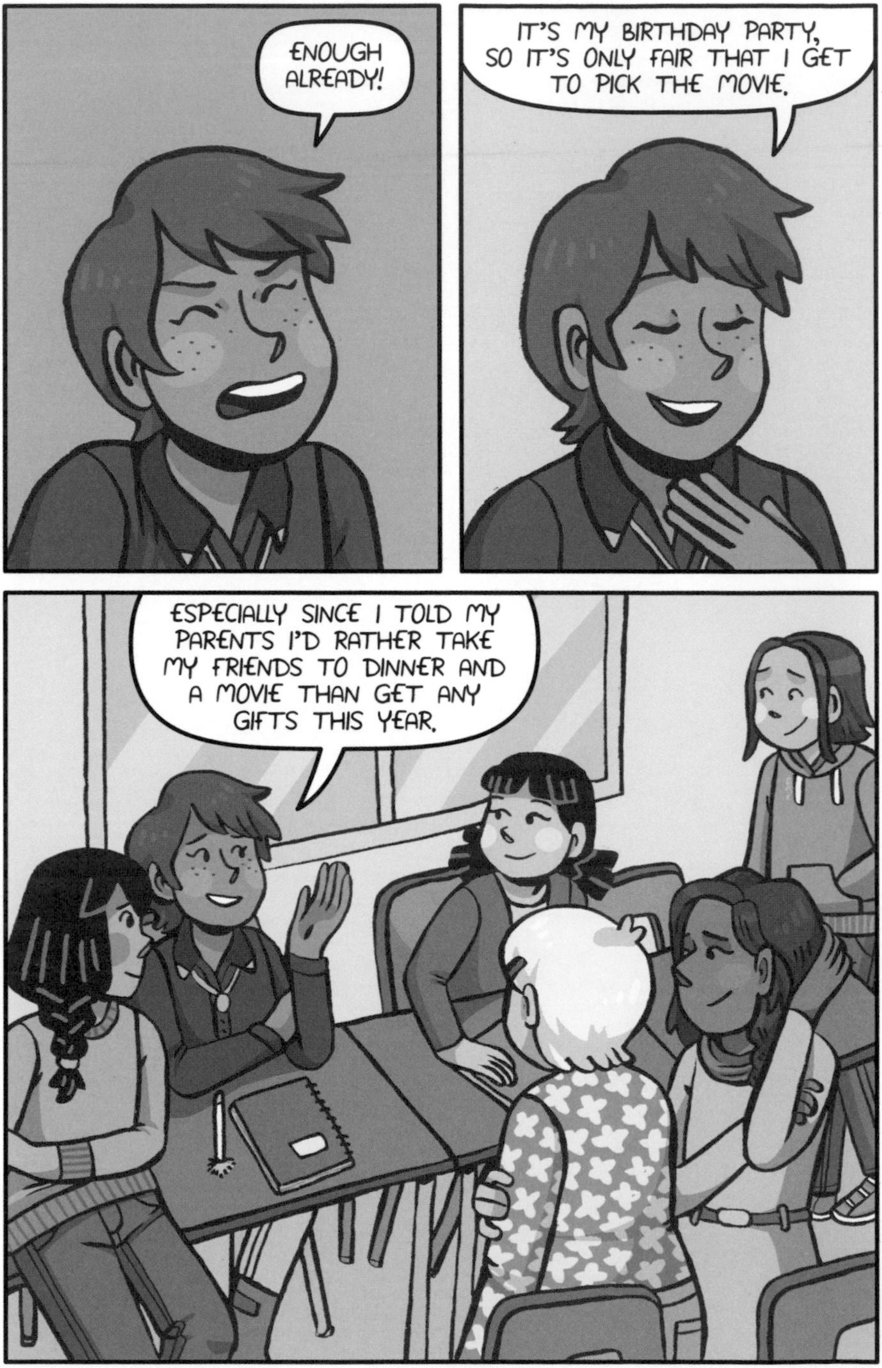
ENOUGH ALREADY!
IT'S MY BIRTHDAY PARTY, SO IT'S ONLY FAIR THAT I GET TO PICK THE MOVIE.
ESPECIALLY SINCE I TOLD MY PARENTS I'D RATHER TAKE MY FRIENDS TO DINNER AND A MOVIE THAN GET ANY GIFTS THIS YEAR.

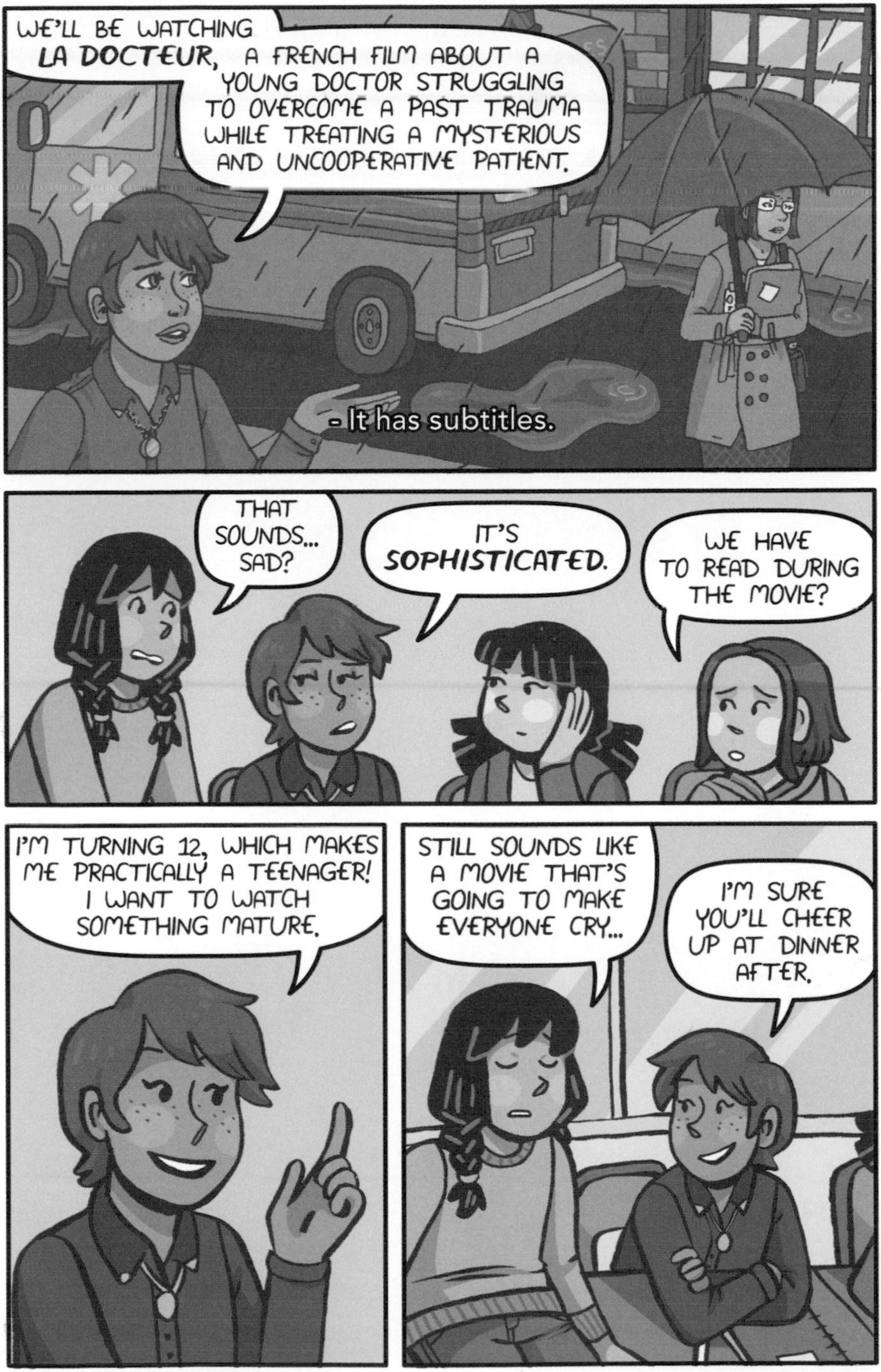
WE'LL BE WATCHING **LA DOCTEUR**, A FRENCH FILM ABOUT A YOUNG DOCTOR STRUGGLING TO OVERCOME A PAST TRAUMA WHILE TREATING A MYSTERIOUS AND UNCOOPERATIVE PATIENT.
- It has subtitles.
THAT SOUNDS... SAD?
IT'S **SOPHISTICATED.**
WE HAVE TO READ DURING THE MOVIE?
I'M TURNING 12, WHICH MAKES ME PRACTICALLY A TEENAGER! I WANT TO WATCH SOMETHING MATURE.
STILL SOUNDS LIKE A MOVIE THAT'S GOING TO MAKE EVERYONE CRY...
I'M SURE YOU'LL CHEER UP AT DINNER AFTER.

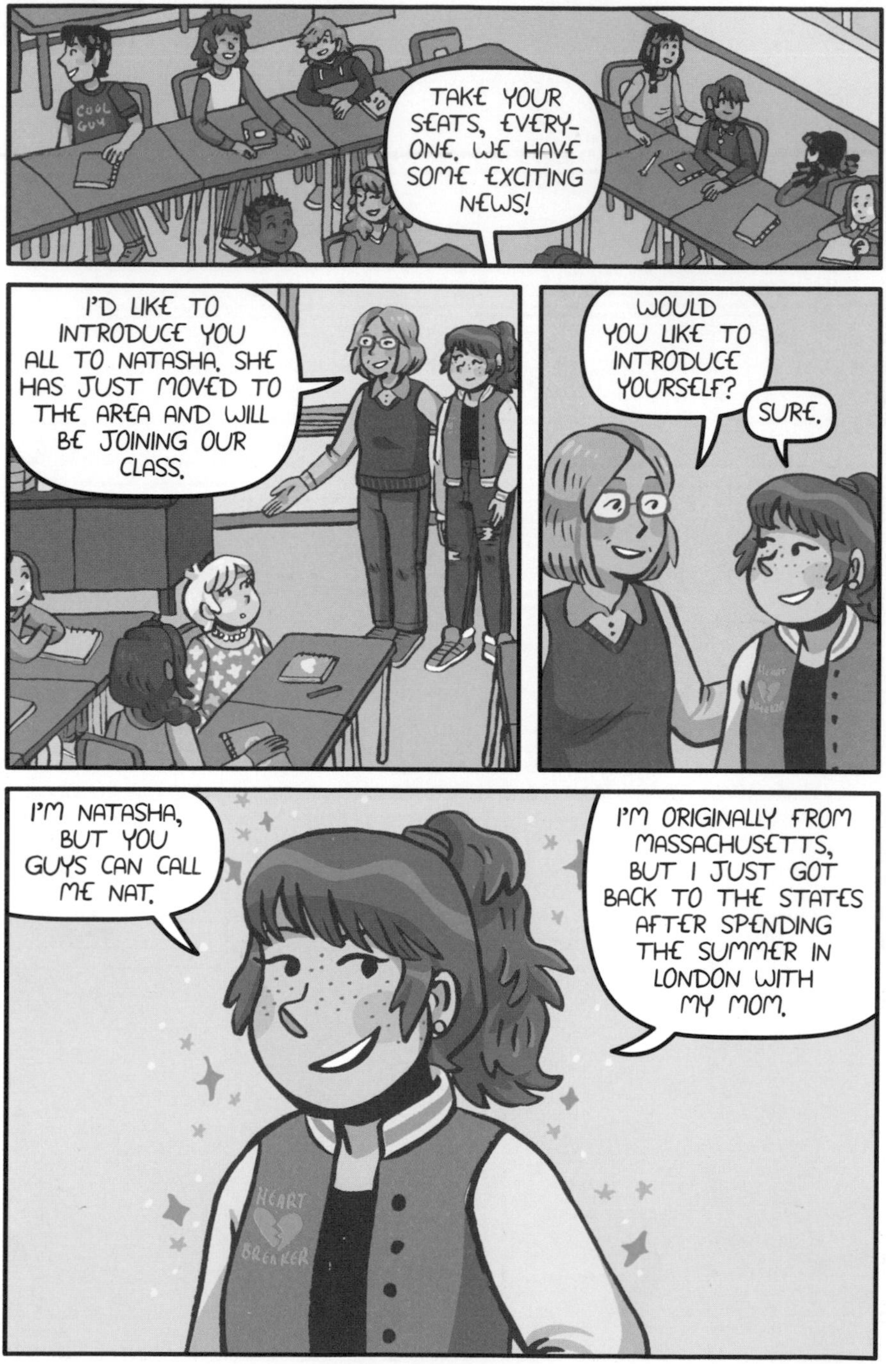

TAKE YOUR SEATS, EVERYONE. WE HAVE SOME EXCITING NEWS!
COOL GUY
I'D LIKE TO INTRODUCE YOU ALL TO NATASHA. SHE HAS JUST MOVED TO THE AREA AND WILL BE JOINING OUR CLASS.
WOULD YOU LIKE TO INTRODUCE YOURSELF?
SURE.
I'M NATASHA, BUT YOU GUYS CAN CALL ME NAT.
I'M ORIGINALLY FROM MASSACHUSETTS, BUT I JUST GOT BACK TO THE STATES AFTER SPENDING THE SUMMER IN LONDON WITH MY MOM.
HEART BREAKER

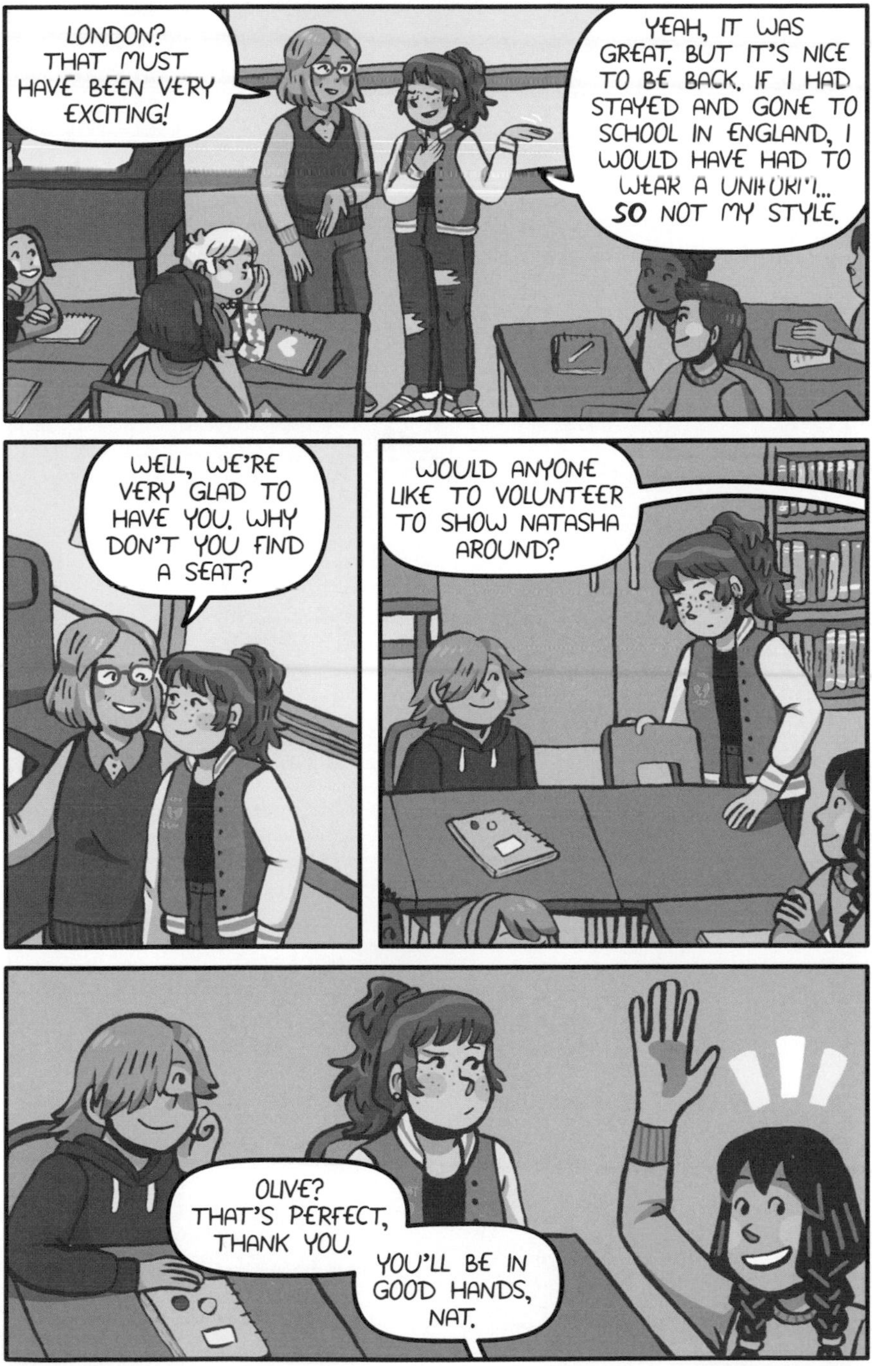
LONDON? THAT MUST HAVE BEEN VERY EXCITING!
YEAH, IT WAS GREAT. BUT IT'S NICE TO BE BACK. IF I HAD STAYED AND GONE TO SCHOOL IN ENGLAND, I WOULD HAVE HAD TO WEAR A UNIFORM... **SO** NOT MY STYLE.
WELL, WE'RE VERY GLAD TO HAVE YOU. WHY DON'T YOU FIND A SEAT?
WOULD ANYONE LIKE TO VOLUNTEER TO SHOW NATASHA AROUND?
OLIVE? THAT'S PERFECT, THANK YOU.
YOU'LL BE IN GOOD HANDS, NAT.

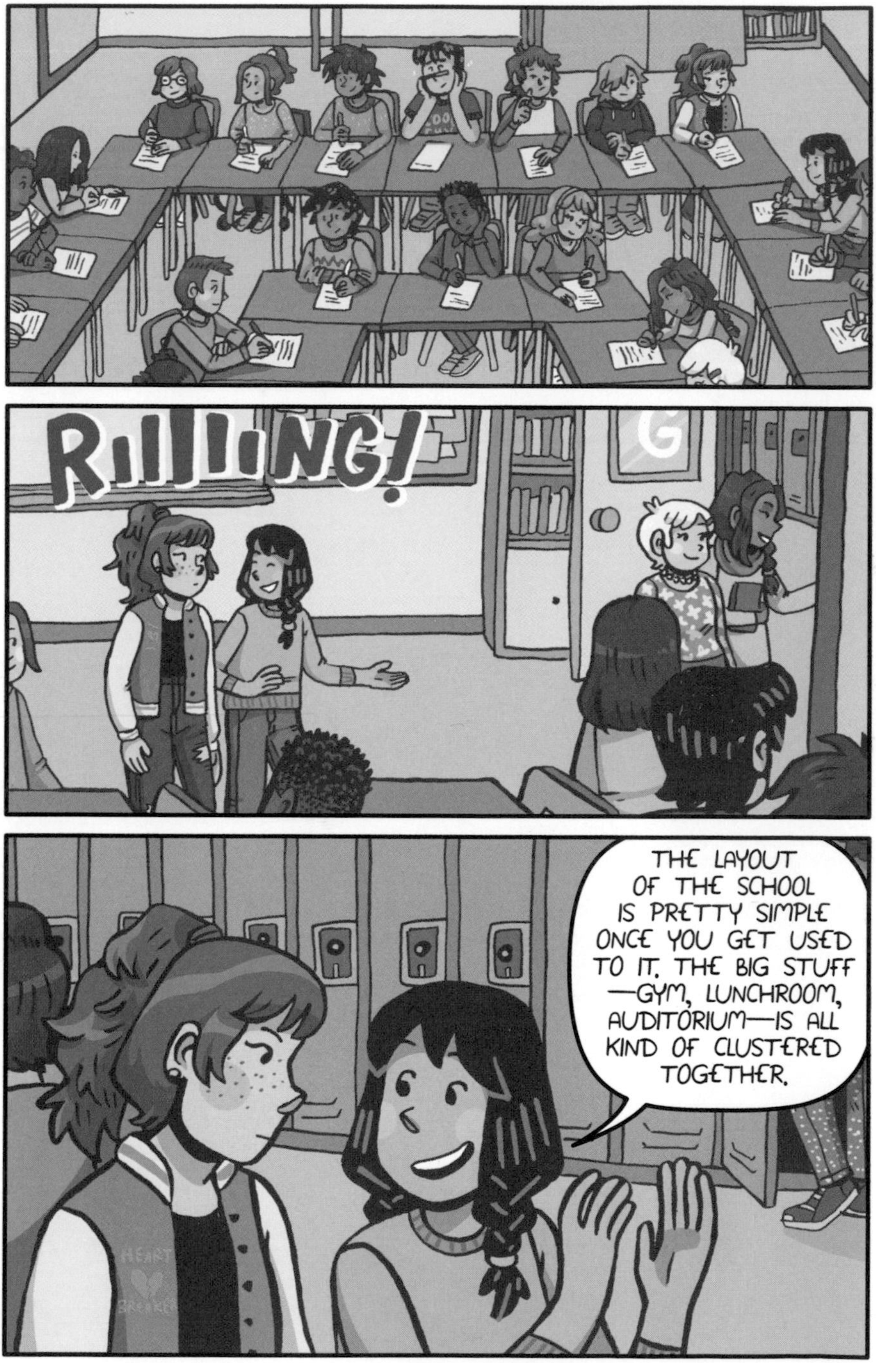
RIIIIING!
THE LAYOUT OF THE SCHOOL IS PRETTY SIMPLE ONCE YOU GET USED TO IT. THE BIG STUFF—GYM, LUNCHROOM, AUDITORIUM—IS ALL KIND OF CLUSTERED TOGETHER.

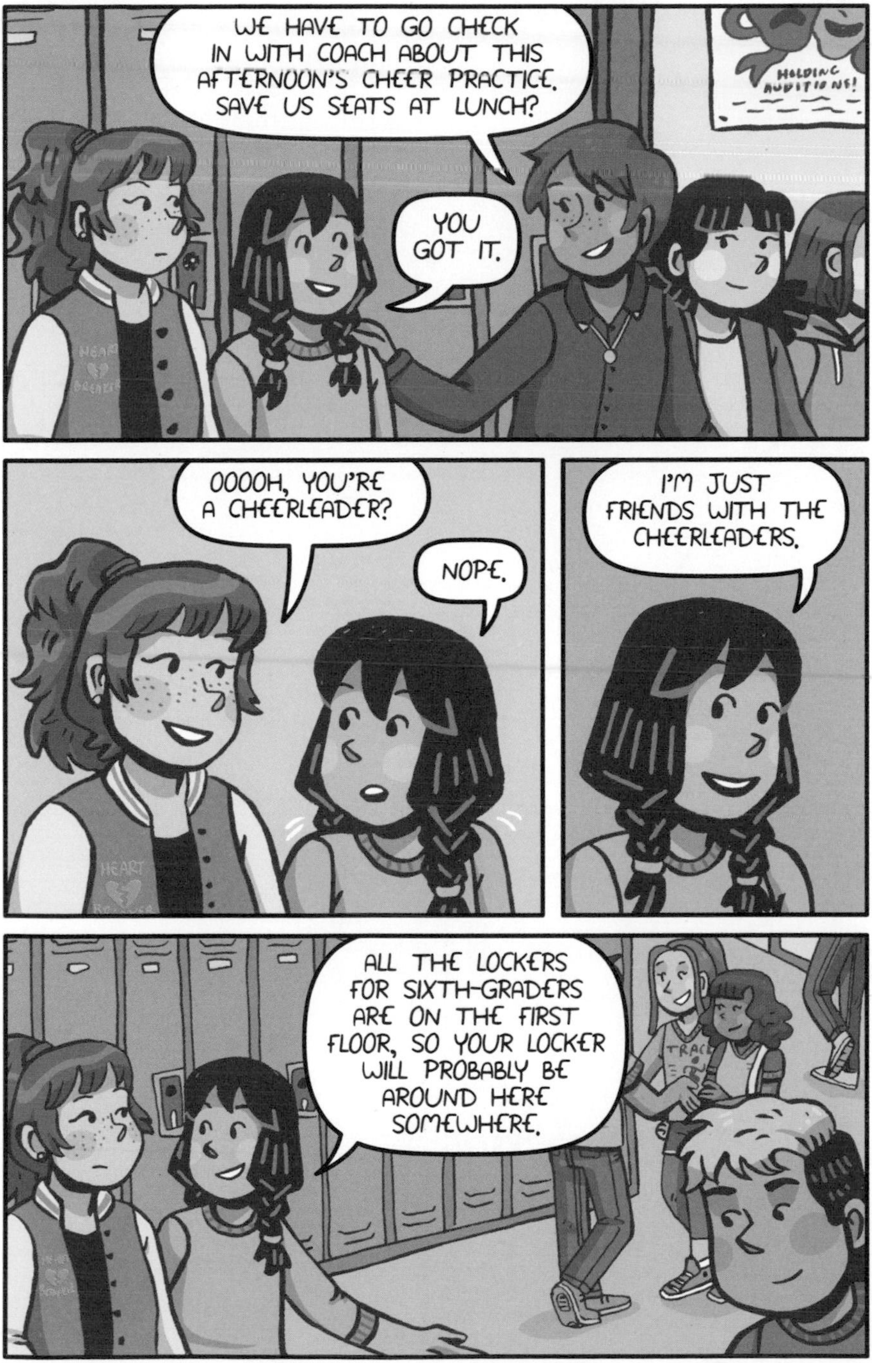
WE HAVE TO GO CHECK IN WITH COACH ABOUT THIS AFTERNOON'S CHEER PRACTICE. SAVE US SEATS AT LUNCH?
HOLDING AUDITIONS!
YOU GOT IT.
OOOOH, YOU'RE A CHEERLEADER?
NOPE.
I'M JUST FRIENDS WITH THE CHEERLEADERS.
ALL THE LOCKERS FOR SIXTH-GRADERS ARE ON THE FIRST FLOOR, SO YOUR LOCKER WILL PROBABLY BE AROUND HERE SOMEWHERE.

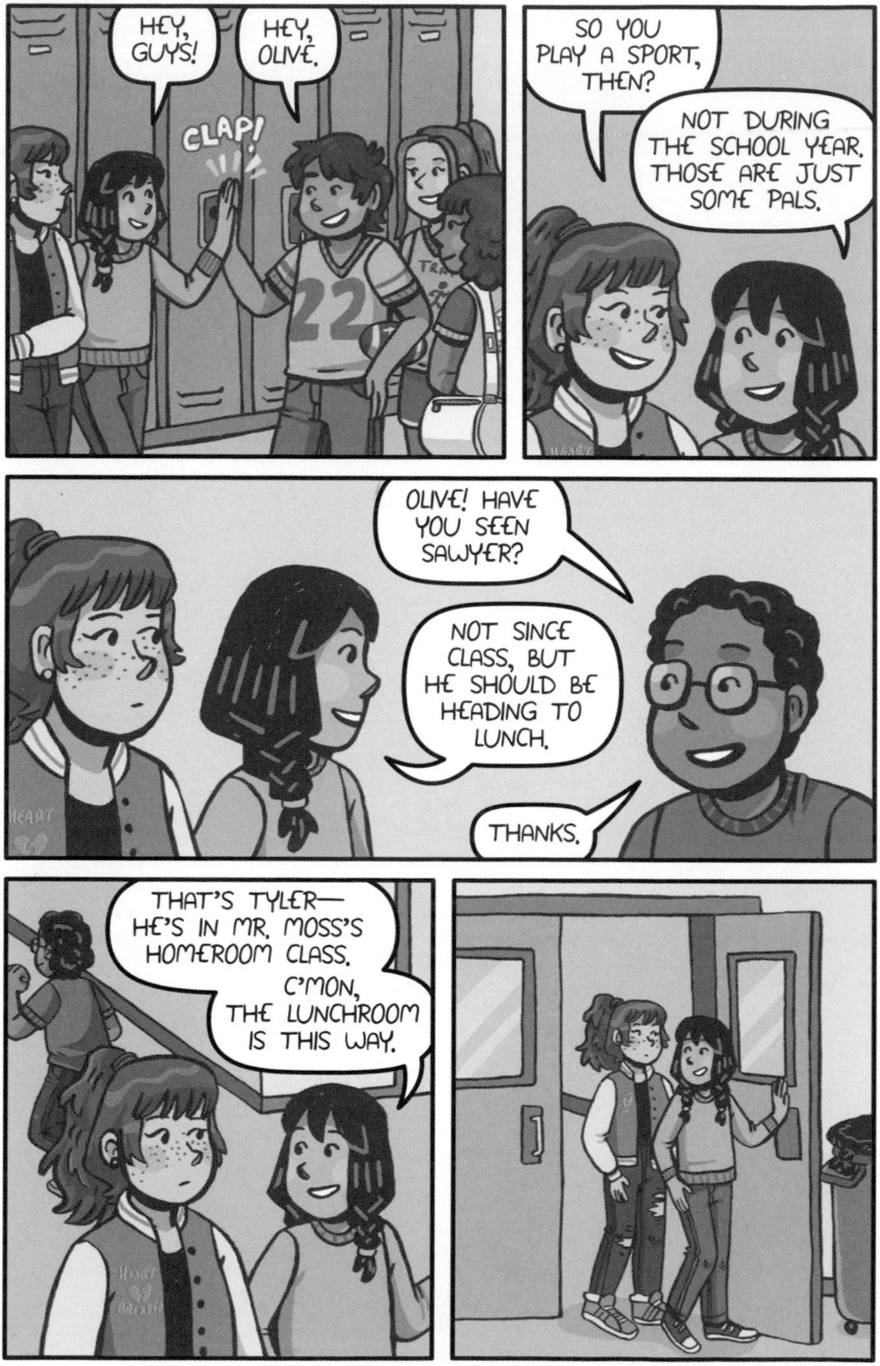
HEY, GUYS!
HEY, OLIVE.
CLAP!
SO YOU PLAY A SPORT, THEN?
NOT DURING THE SCHOOL YEAR. THOSE ARE JUST SOME PALS.
OLIVE! HAVE YOU SEEN SAWYER?
NOT SINCE CLASS, BUT HE SHOULD BE HEADING TO LUNCH.
THANKS.
THAT'S TYLER— HE'S IN MR. MOSS'S HOMEROOM CLASS.
C'MON, THE LUNCHROOM IS THIS WAY.

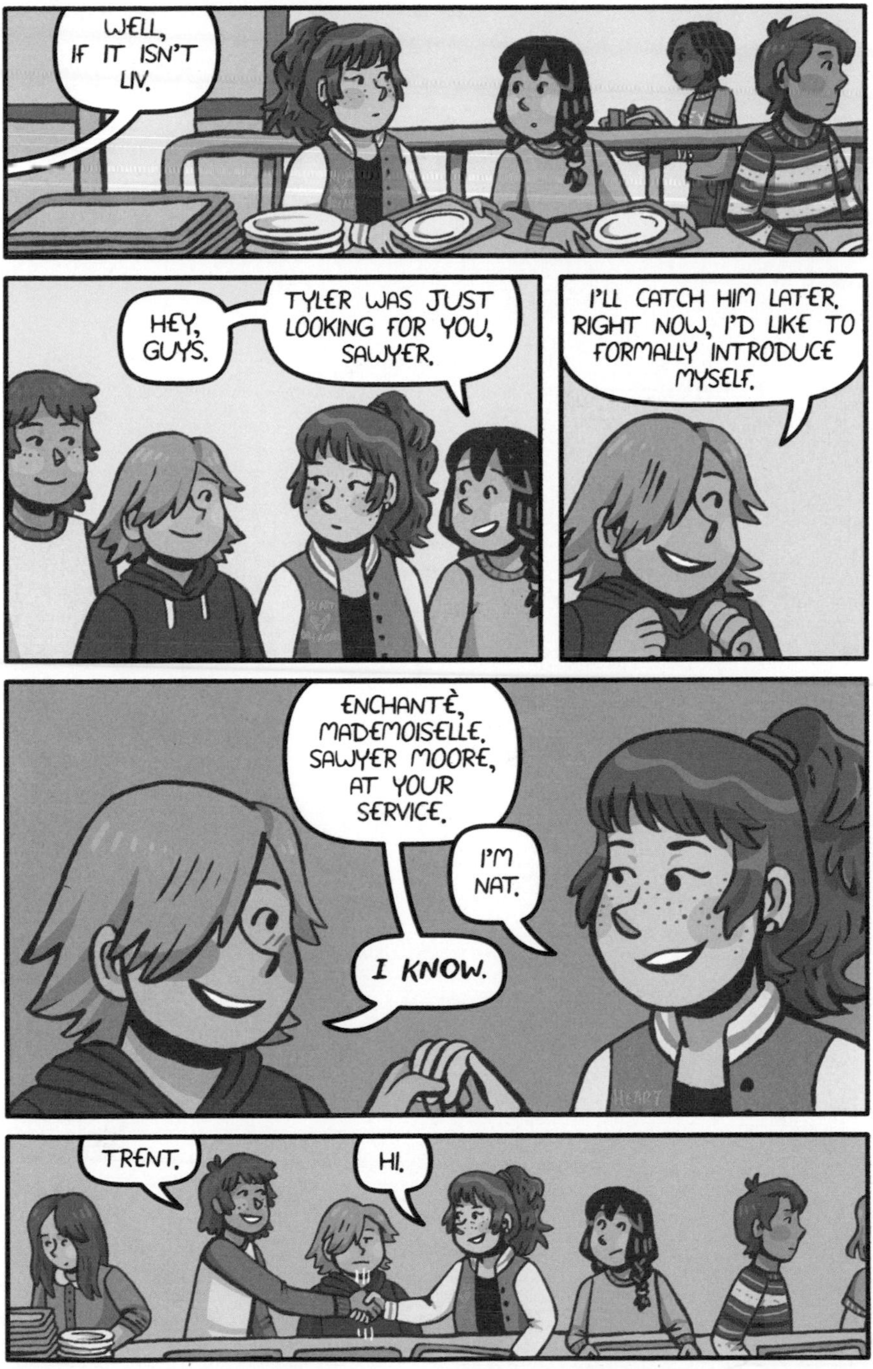
WELL, IF IT ISN'T LIV.
HEY, GUYS.
TYLER WAS JUST LOOKING FOR YOU, SAWYER.
I'LL CATCH HIM LATER. RIGHT NOW, I'D LIKE TO FORMALLY INTRODUCE MYSELF.
ENCHANTÈ, MADEMOISELLE. SAWYER MOORE, AT YOUR SERVICE.
I'M NAT.
I KNOW.
TRENT.
HI.

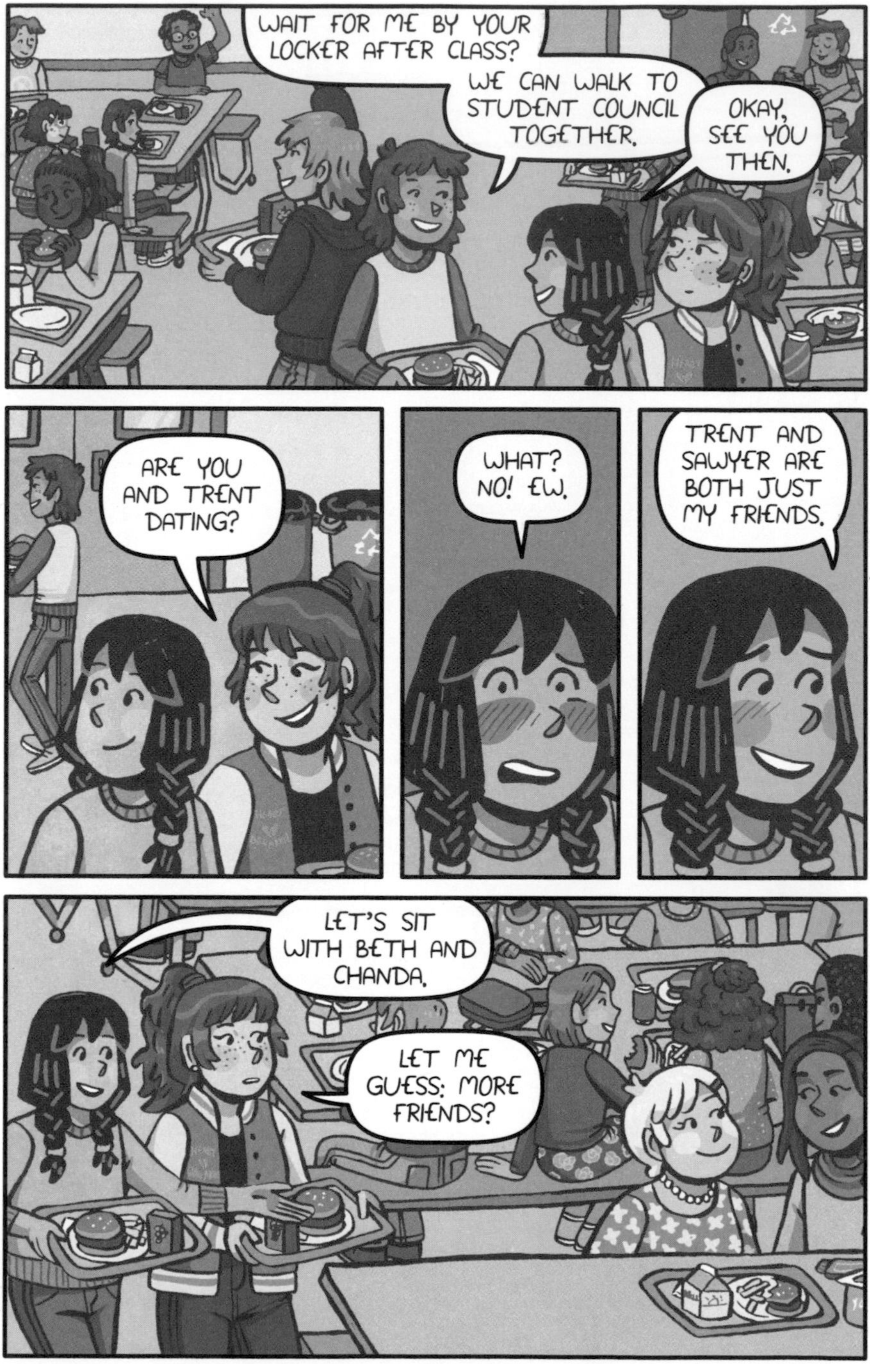
WAIT FOR ME BY YOUR LOCKER AFTER CLASS?
WE CAN WALK TO STUDENT COUNCIL TOGETHER.
OKAY, SEE YOU THEN.
ARE YOU AND TRENT DATING?
WHAT? NO! EW.
TRENT AND SAWYER ARE BOTH JUST MY FRIENDS.
LET'S SIT WITH BETH AND CHANDA.
LET ME GUESS: MORE FRIENDS?

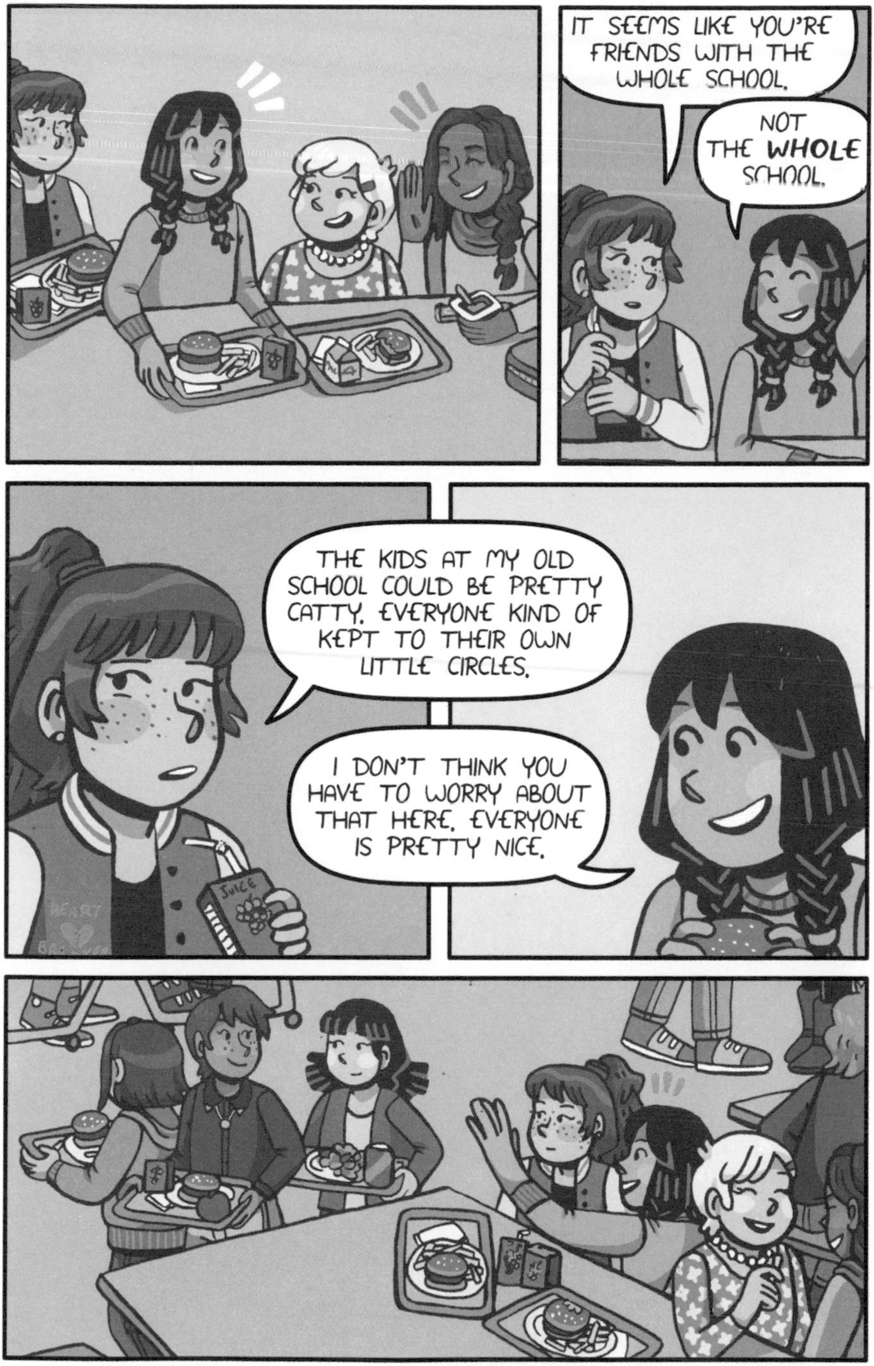
IT SEEMS LIKE YOU'RE FRIENDS WITH THE WHOLE SCHOOL.
NOT THE **WHOLE** SCHOOL.
THE KIDS AT MY OLD SCHOOL COULD BE PRETTY CATTY. EVERYONE KIND OF KEPT TO THEIR OWN LITTLE CIRCLES.
I DON'T THINK YOU HAVE TO WORRY ABOUT THAT HERE. EVERYONE IS PRETTY NICE.
JUICE

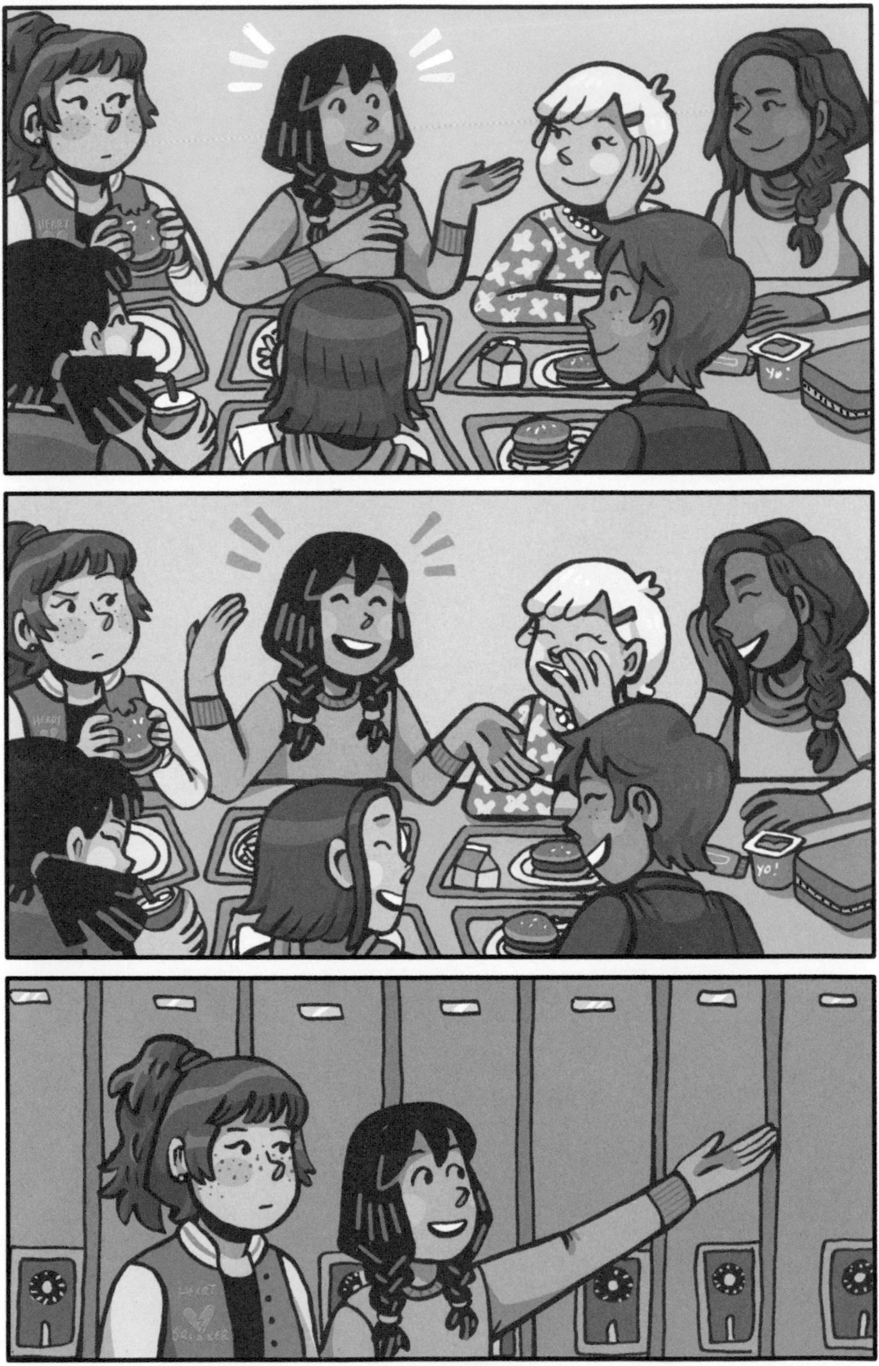
YO!

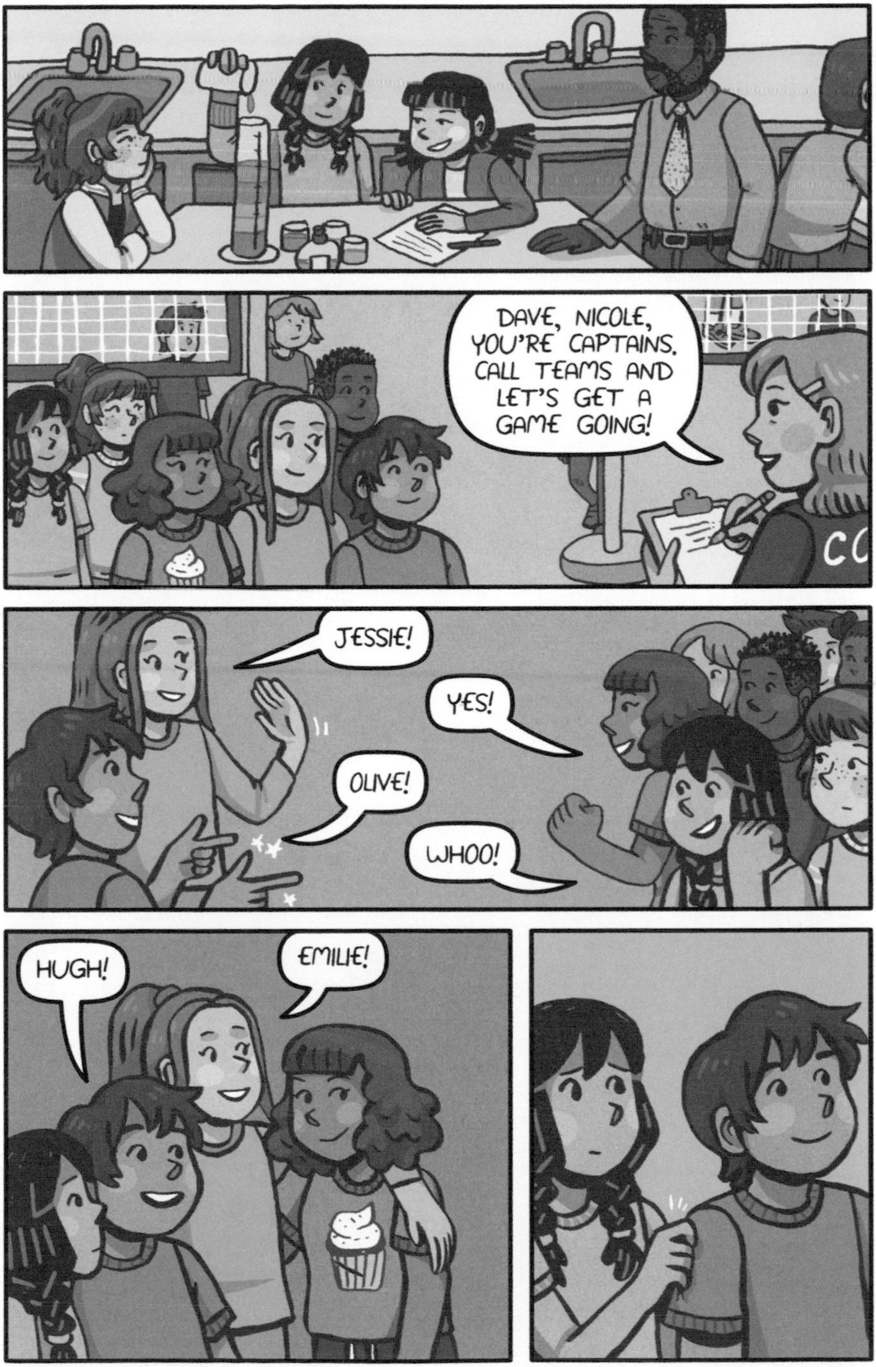
DAVE, NICOLE, YOU'RE CAPTAINS. CALL TEAMS AND LET'S GET A GAME GOING!
JESSIE!
YES!
OLIVE!
WHOO!
HUGH!
EMILIE!

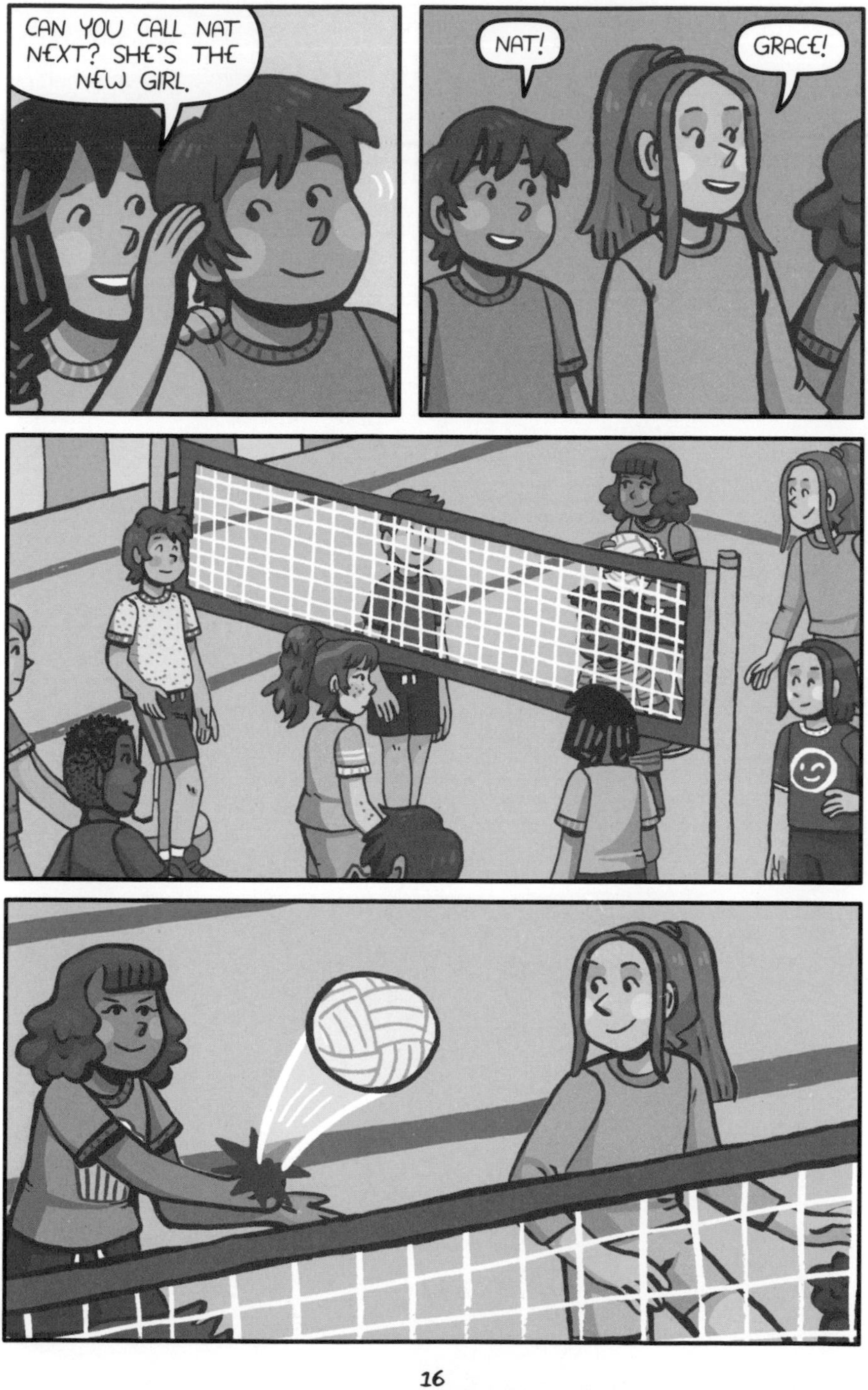
CAN YOU CALL NAT NEXT? SHE'S THE NEW GIRL.
NAT!
GRACE!

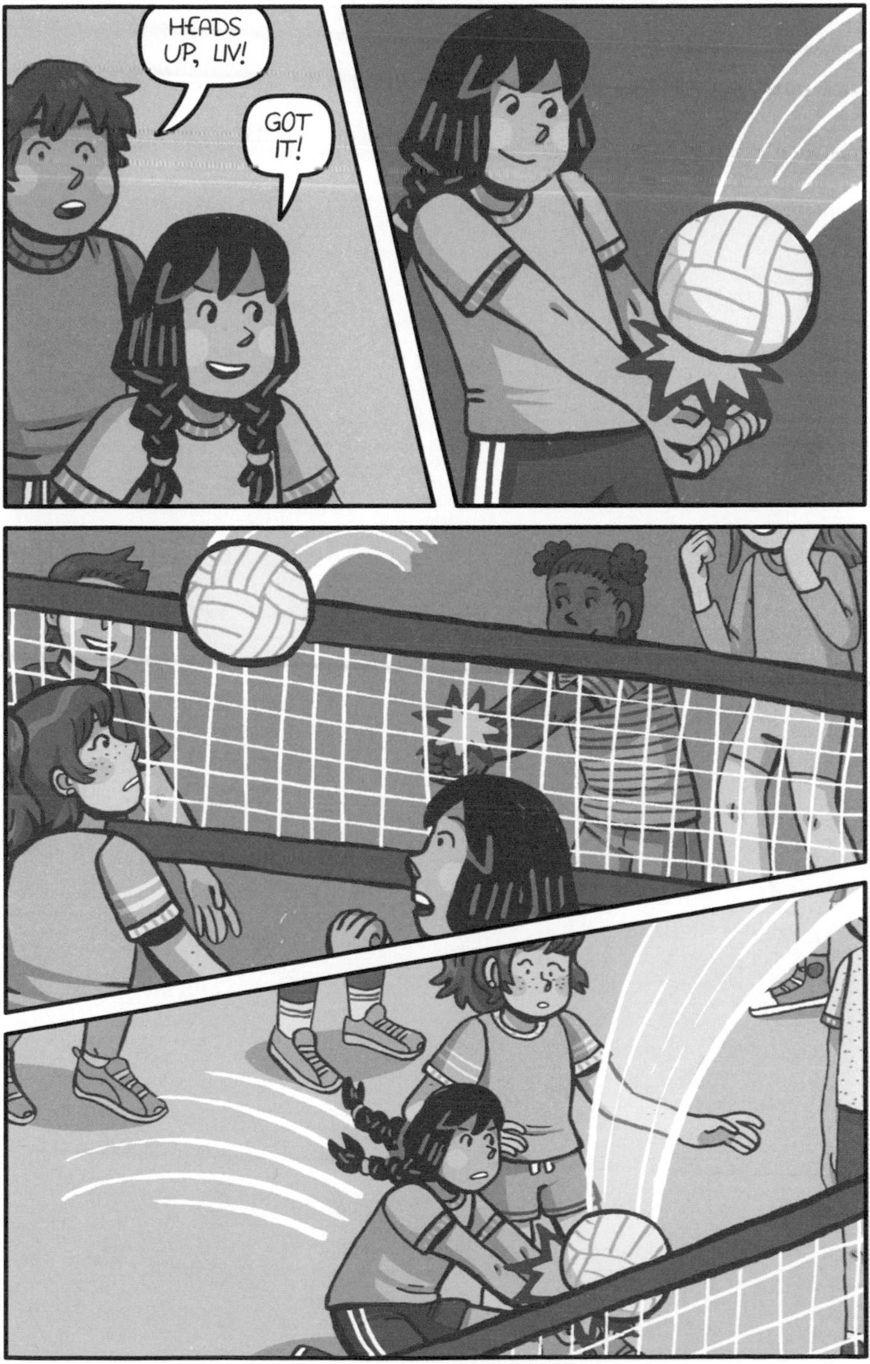
HEADS UP, LIV!
GOT IT!

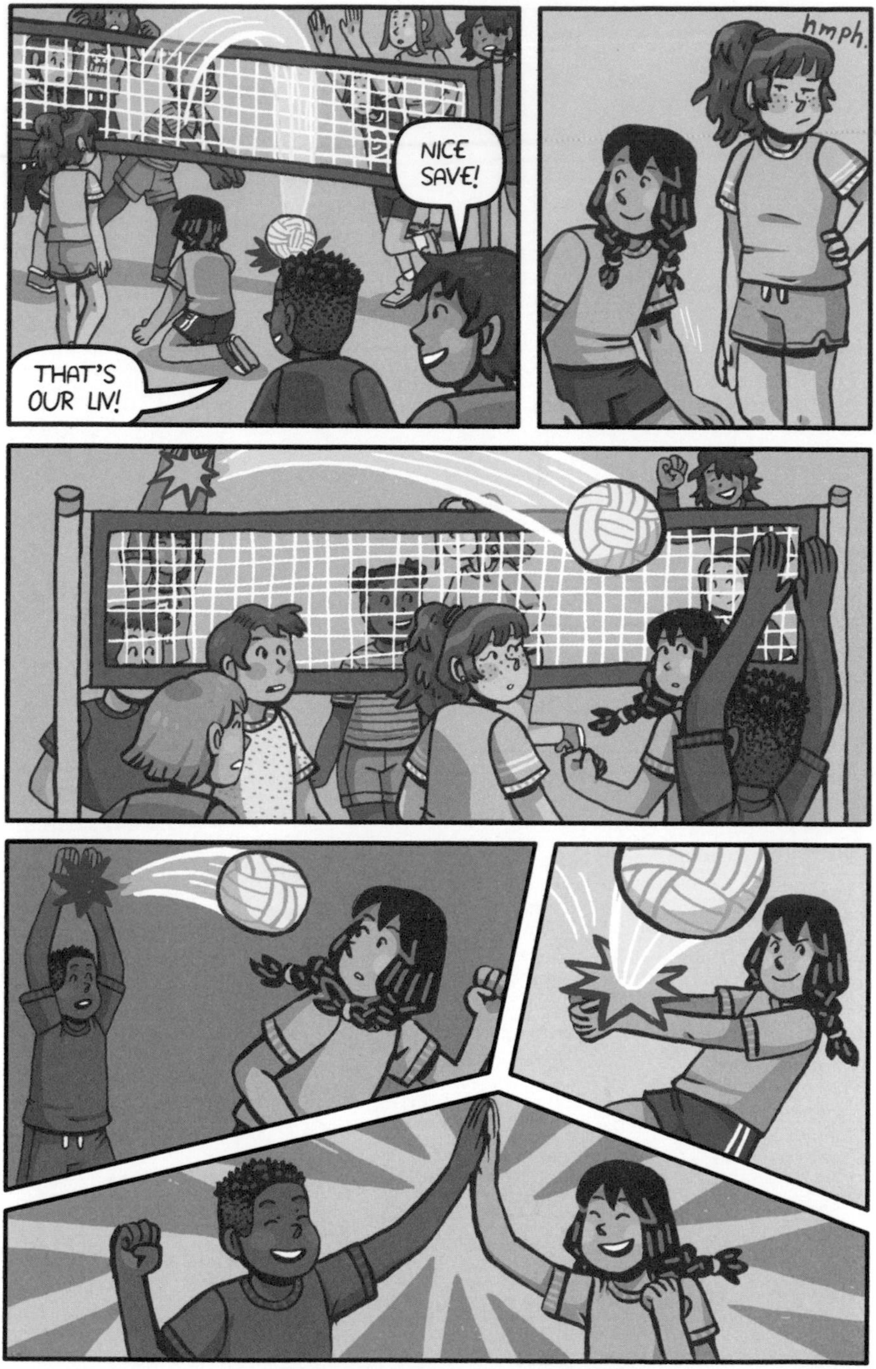
NICE SAVE!
THAT'S OUR LIV!
hmph.

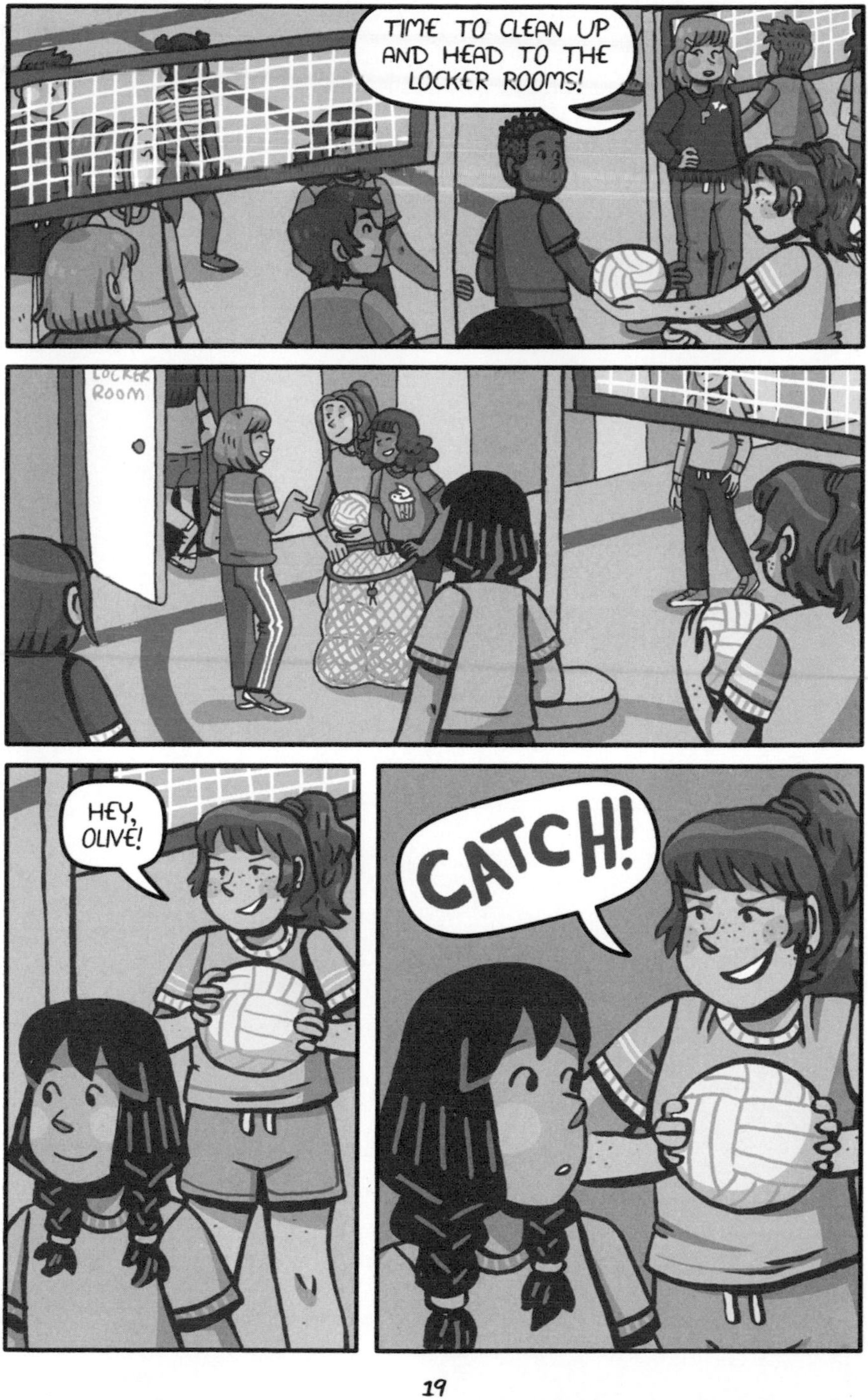
TIME TO CLEAN UP AND HEAD TO THE LOCKER ROOMS!
LOCKER ROOM
HEY, OLIVE!
CATCH!

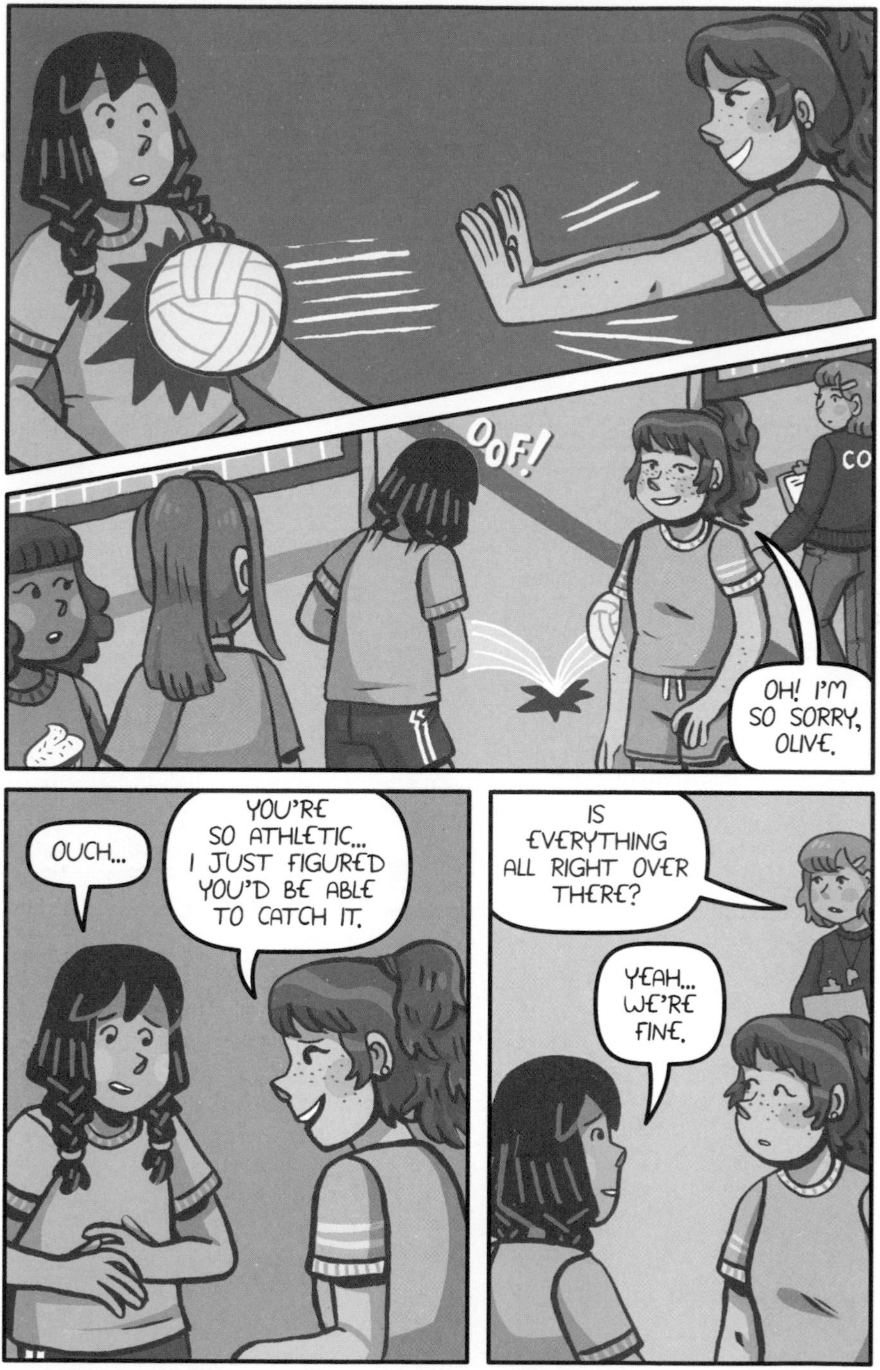
OOF!
CO
OH! I'M SO SORRY, OLIVE.
OUCH...
YOU'RE SO ATHLETIC... I JUST FIGURED YOU'D BE ABLE TO CATCH IT.
IS EVERYTHING ALL RIGHT OVER THERE?
YEAH... WE'RE FINE.

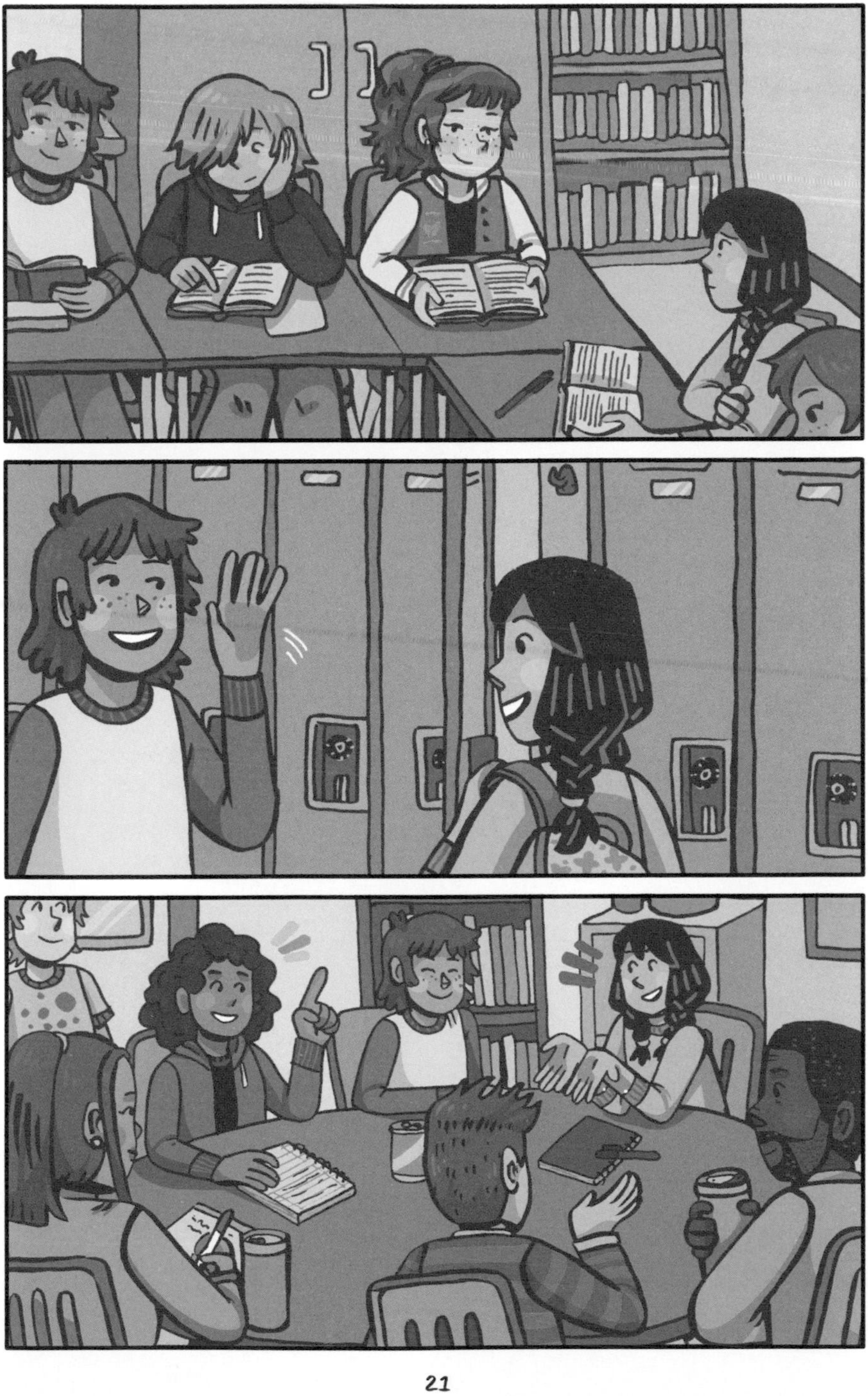

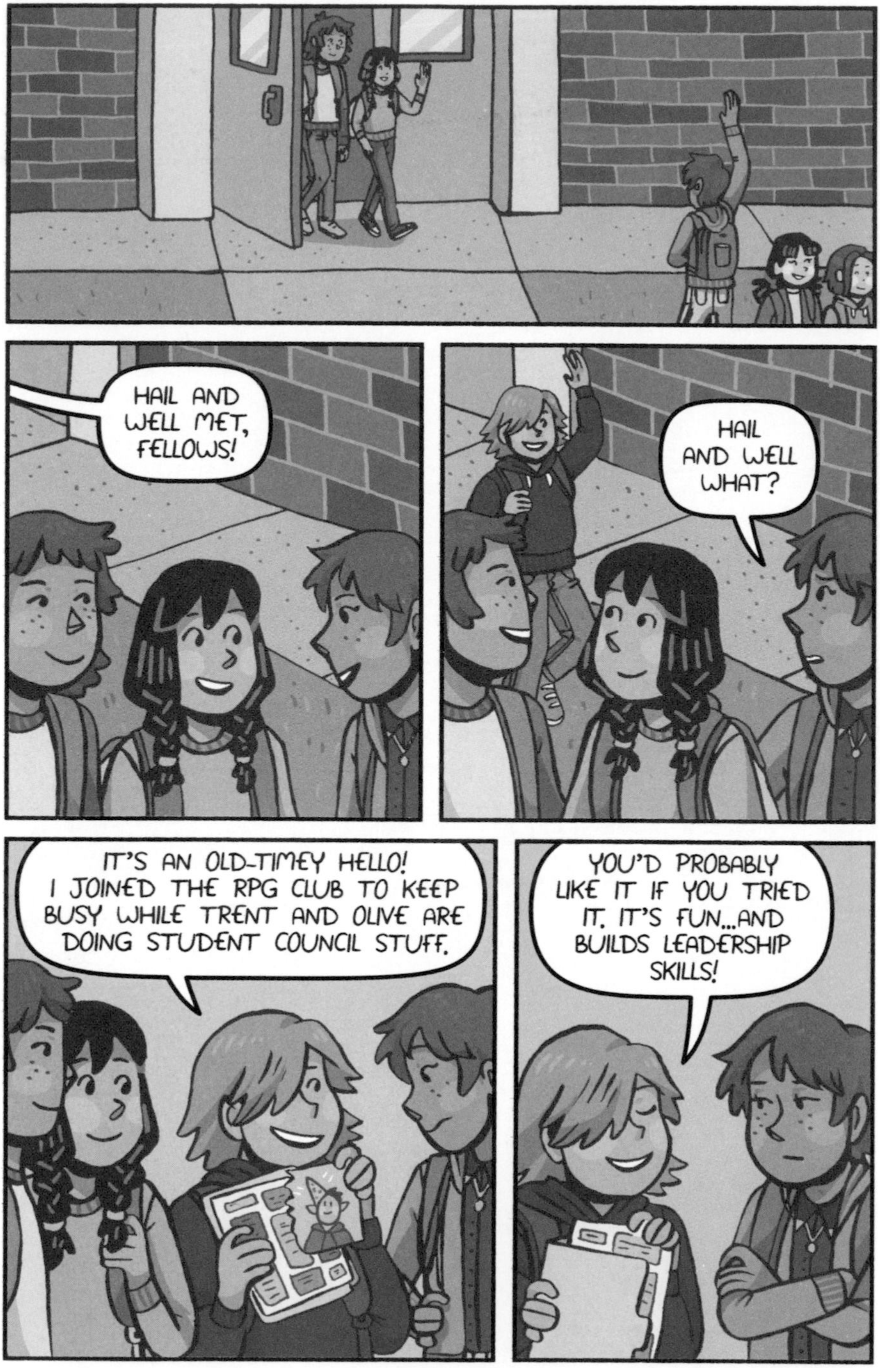
HAIL AND WELL MET, FELLOWS!
HAIL AND WELL WHAT?
IT'S AN OLD-TIMEY HELLO! I JOINED THE RPG CLUB TO KEEP BUSY WHILE TRENT AND OLIVE ARE DOING STUDENT COUNCIL STUFF.
YOU'D PROBABLY LIKE IT IF YOU TRIED IT. IT'S FUN...AND BUILDS LEADERSHIP SKILLS!

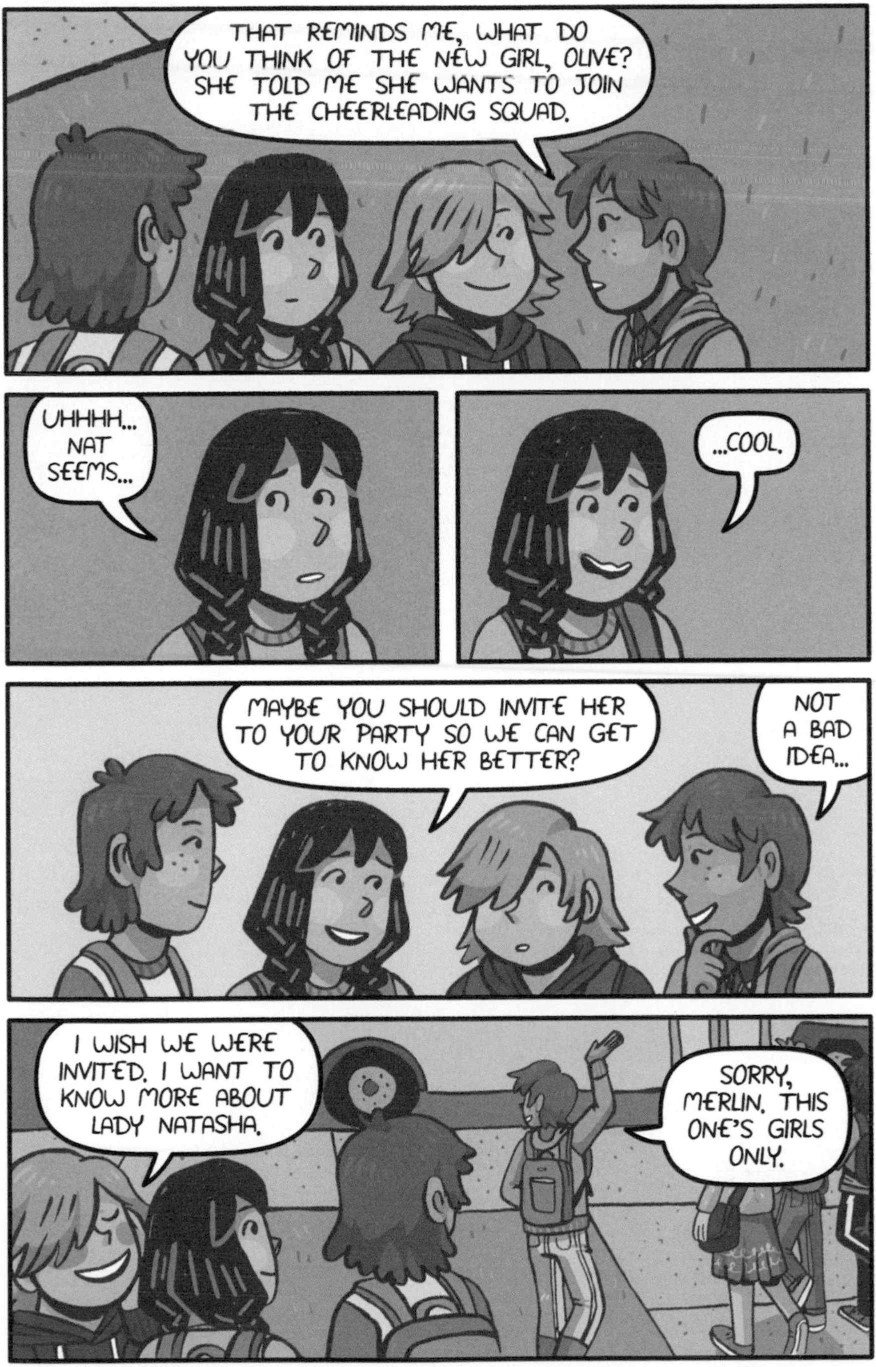
THAT REMINDS ME, WHAT DO YOU THINK OF THE NEW GIRL, OLIVE? SHE TOLD ME SHE WANTS TO JOIN THE CHEERLEADING SQUAD.
UHHHH... NAT SEEMS...
...COOL.
MAYBE YOU SHOULD INVITE HER TO YOUR PARTY SO WE CAN GET TO KNOW HER BETTER?
NOT A BAD IDEA...
I WISH WE WERE INVITED. I WANT TO KNOW MORE ABOUT LADY NATASHA.
SORRY, MERLIN. THIS ONE'S GIRLS ONLY.

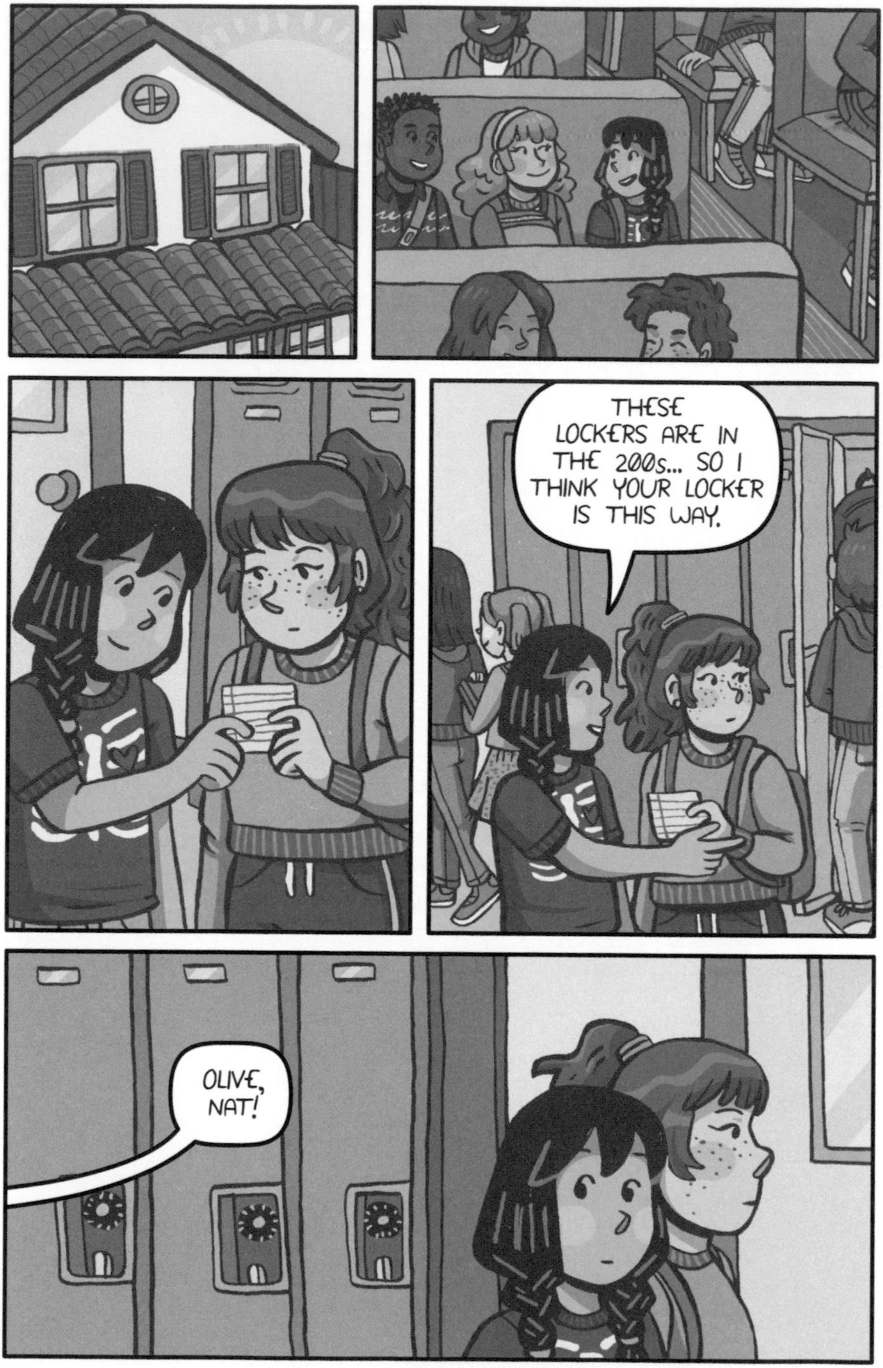
THESE LOCKERS ARE IN THE 200s... SO I THINK YOUR LOCKER IS THIS WAY.
OLIVE, NAT!

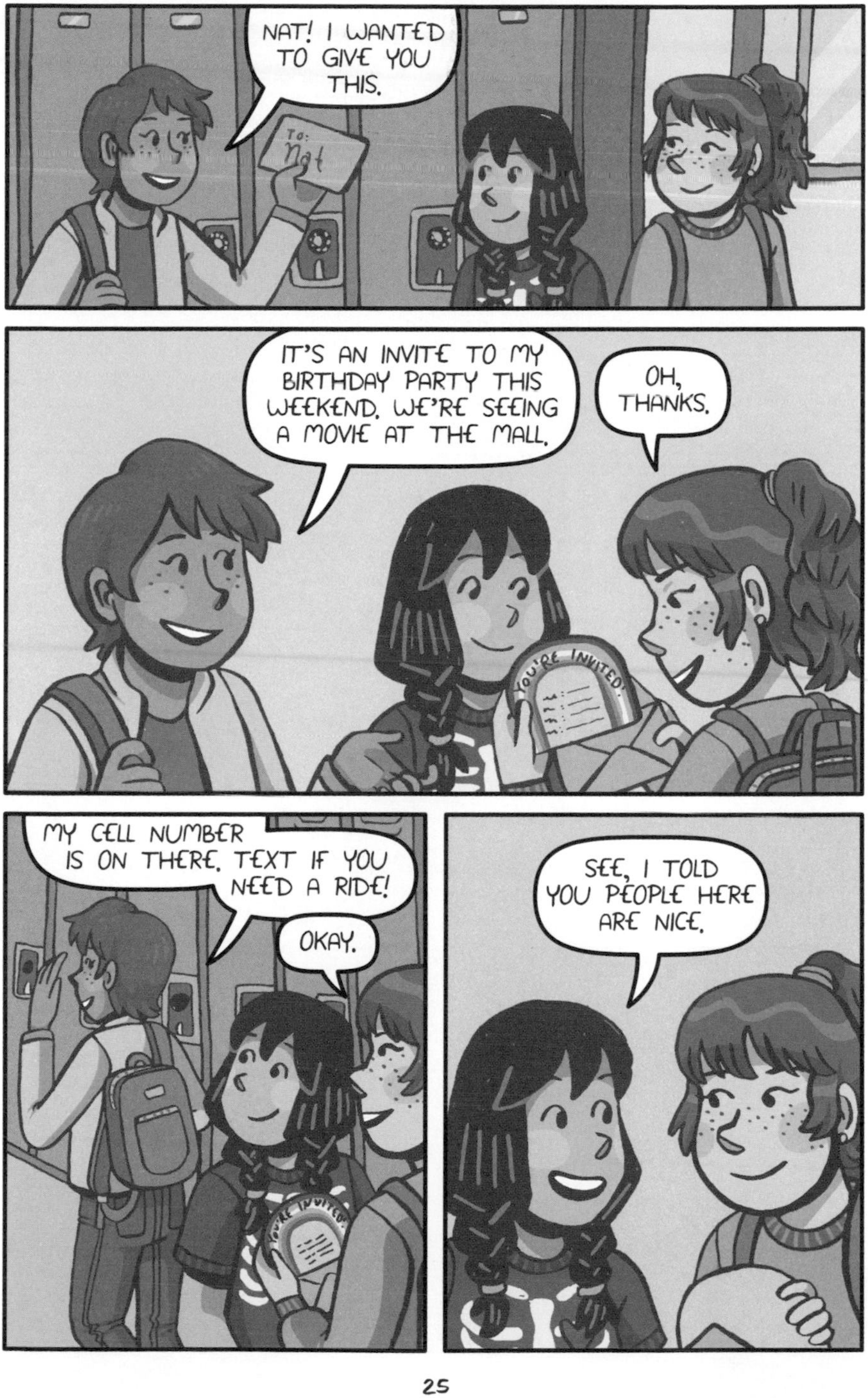
NAT! I WANTED TO GIVE YOU THIS.
To: Nat
IT'S AN INVITE TO MY BIRTHDAY PARTY THIS WEEKEND. WE'RE SEEING A MOVIE AT THE MALL.
OH, THANKS.
YOU'RE INVITED!
MY CELL NUMBER IS ON THERE. TEXT IF YOU NEED A RIDE!
OKAY.
SEE, I TOLD YOU PEOPLE HERE ARE NICE.

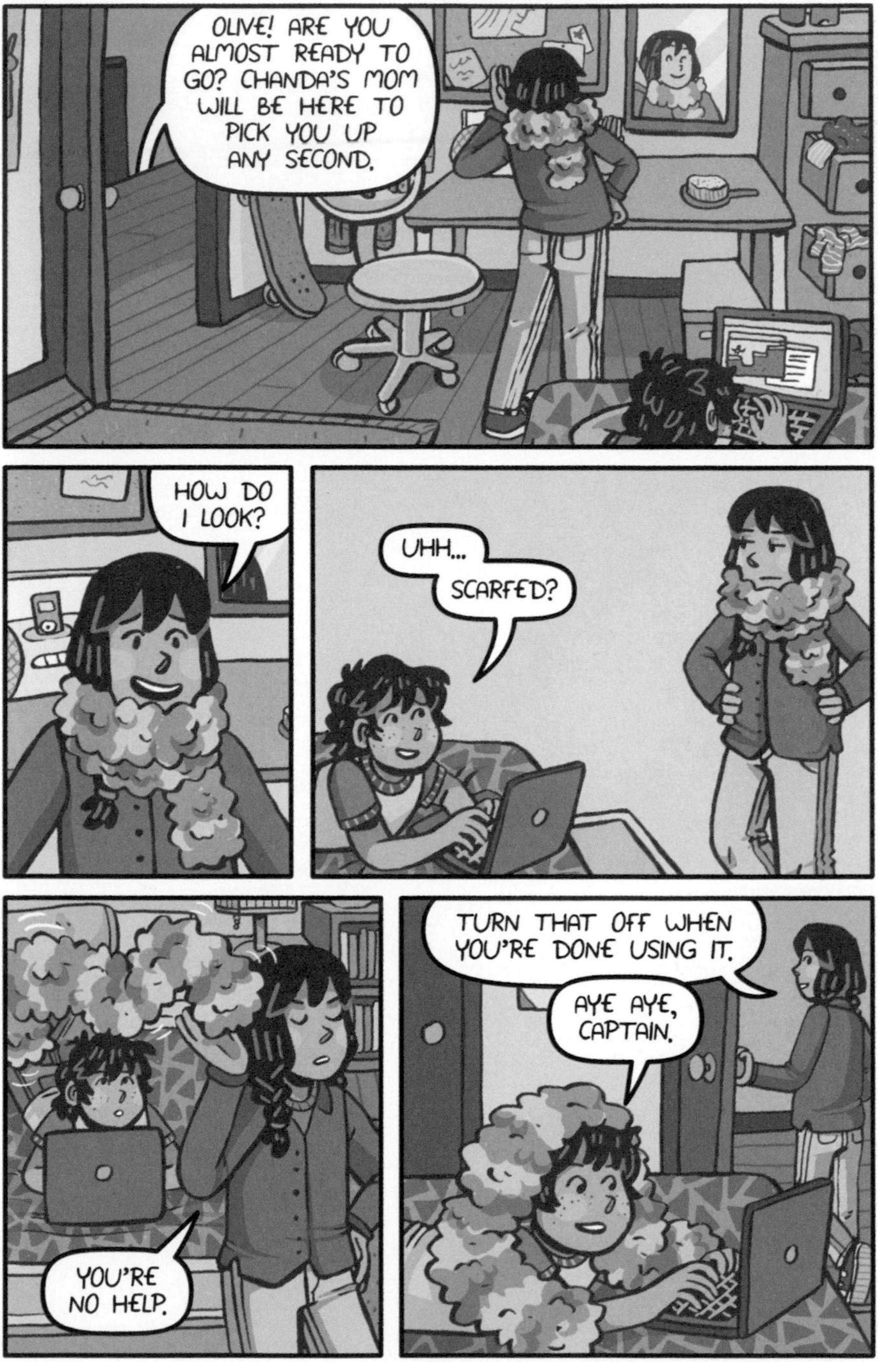
OLIVE! ARE YOU ALMOST READY TO GO? CHANDA'S MOM WILL BE HERE TO PICK YOU UP ANY SECOND.
HOW DO I LOOK?
UHH...
SCARFED?
YOU'RE NO HELP.
TURN THAT OFF WHEN YOU'RE DONE USING IT.
AYE AYE, CAPTAIN.

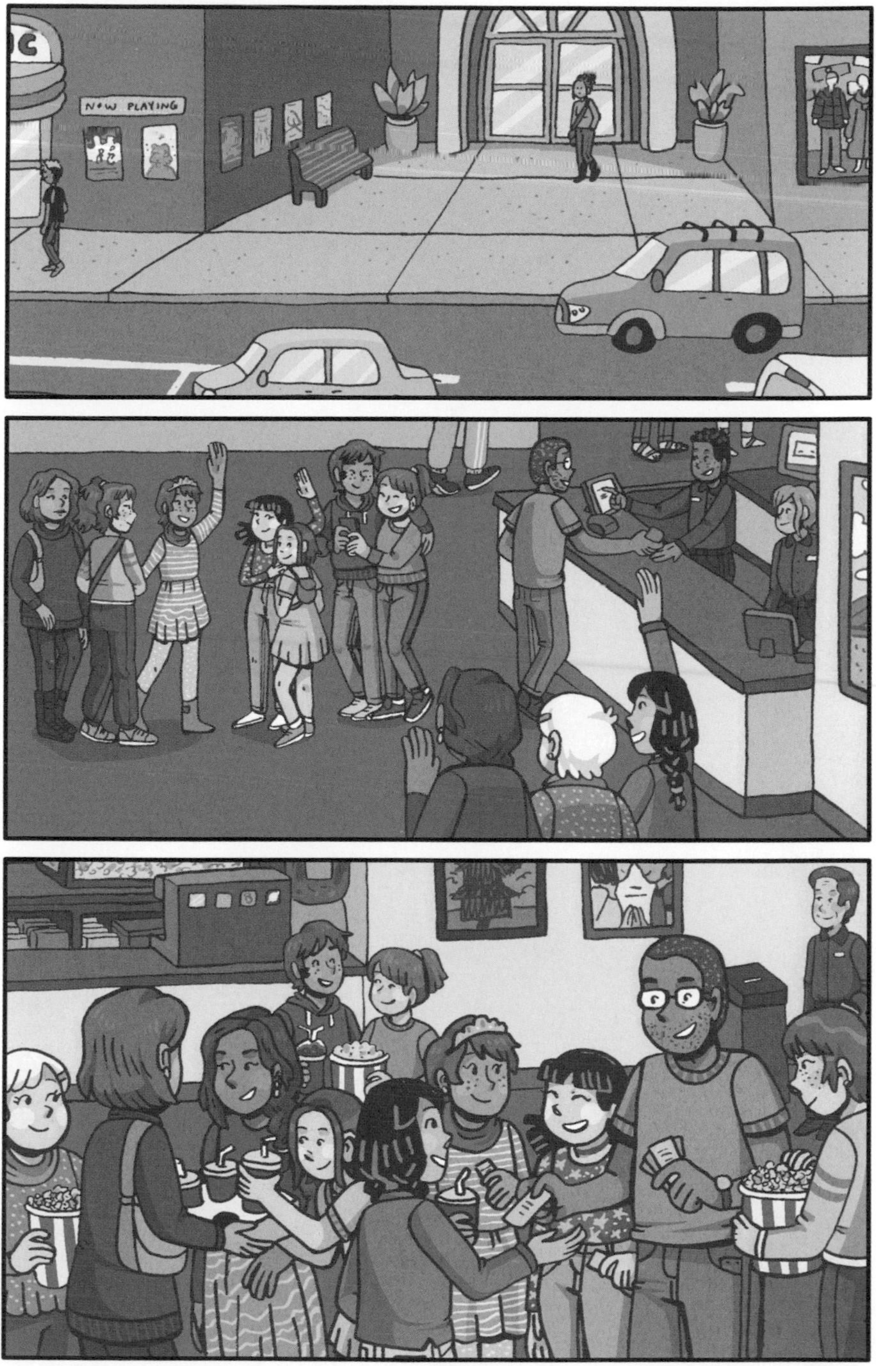
NOW PLAYING

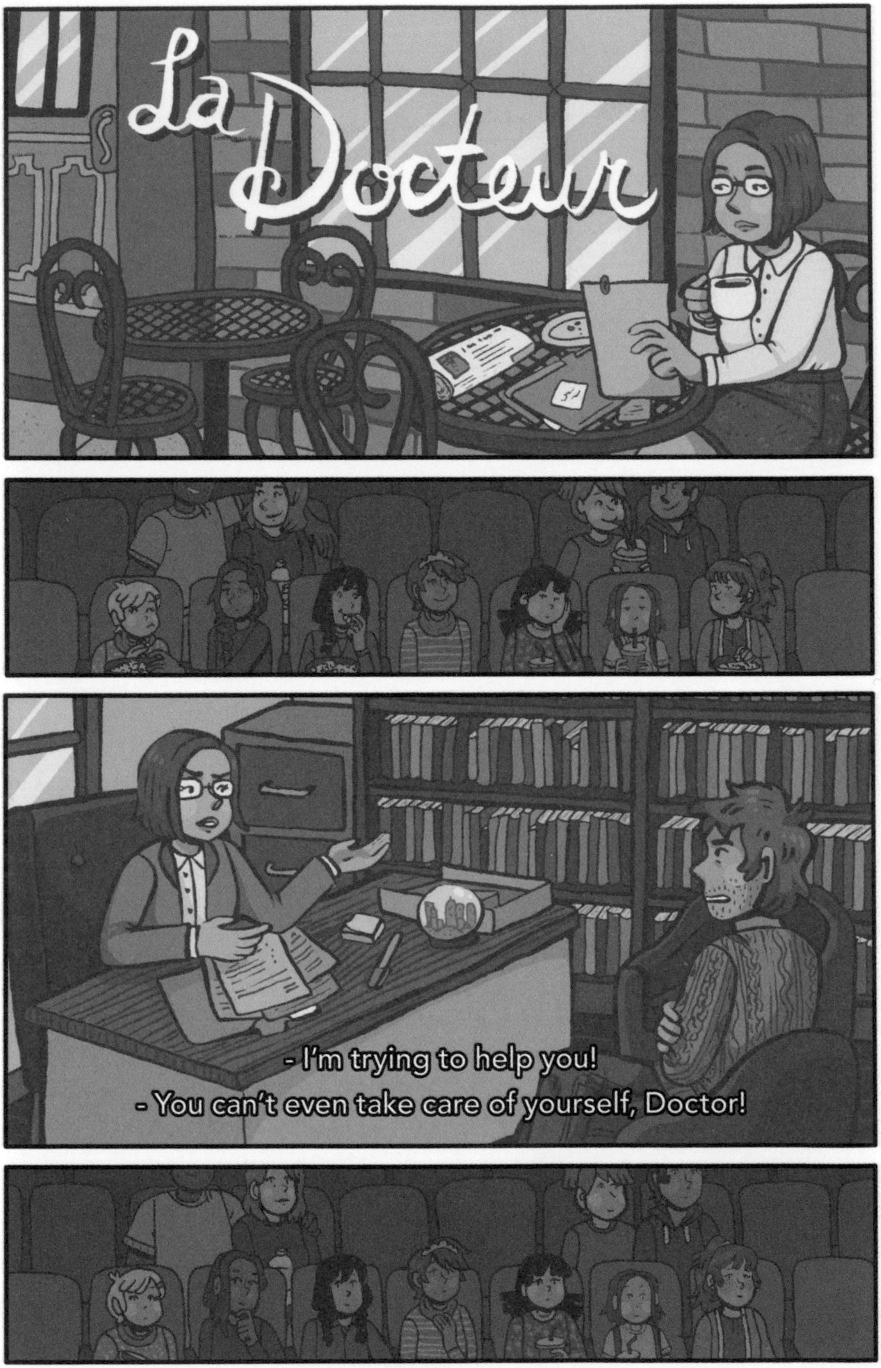
La Docteur
- I'm trying to help you!
- You can't even take care of yourself, Doctor!

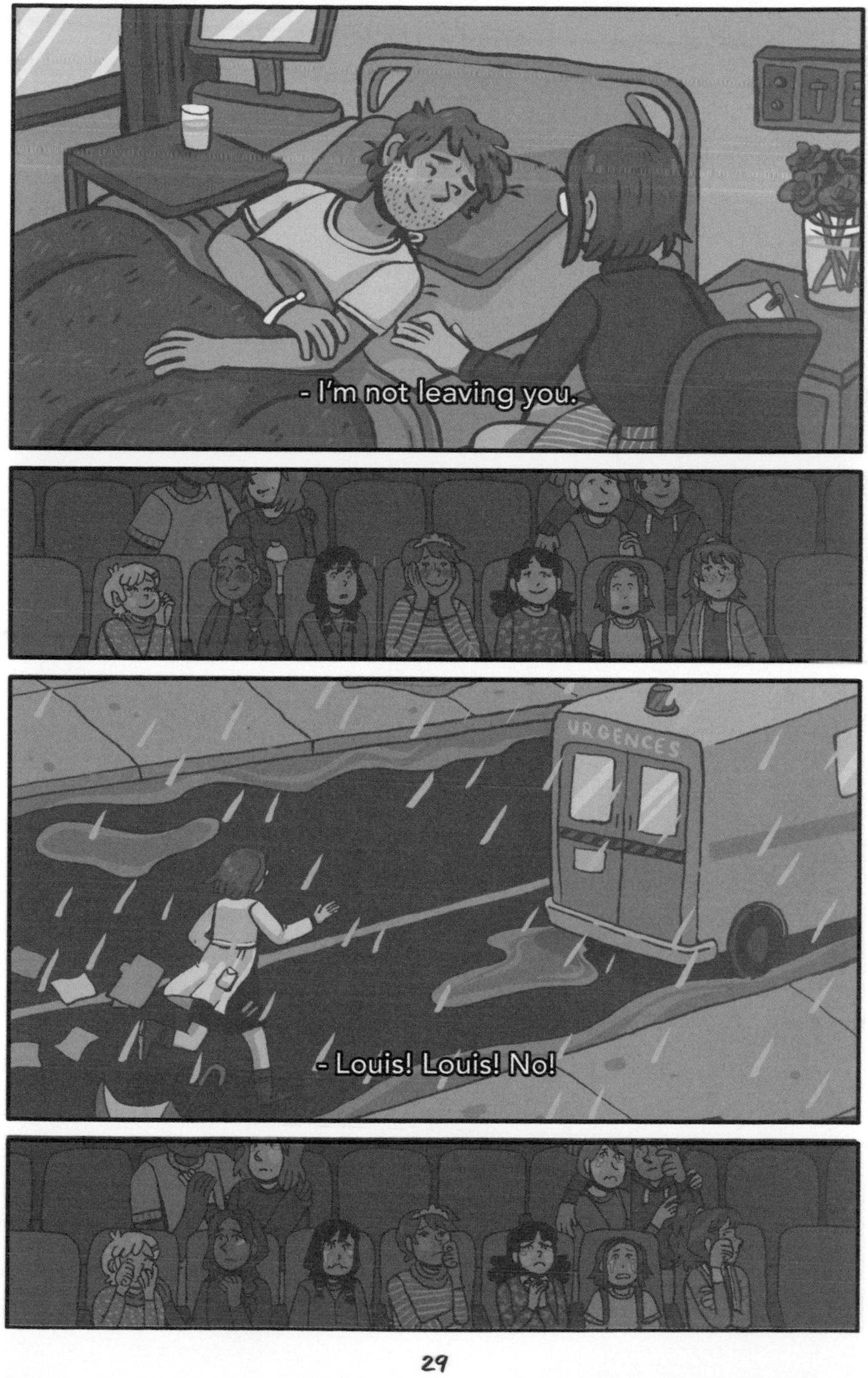
- I'm not leaving you.
URGENCES
- Louis! Louis! No!

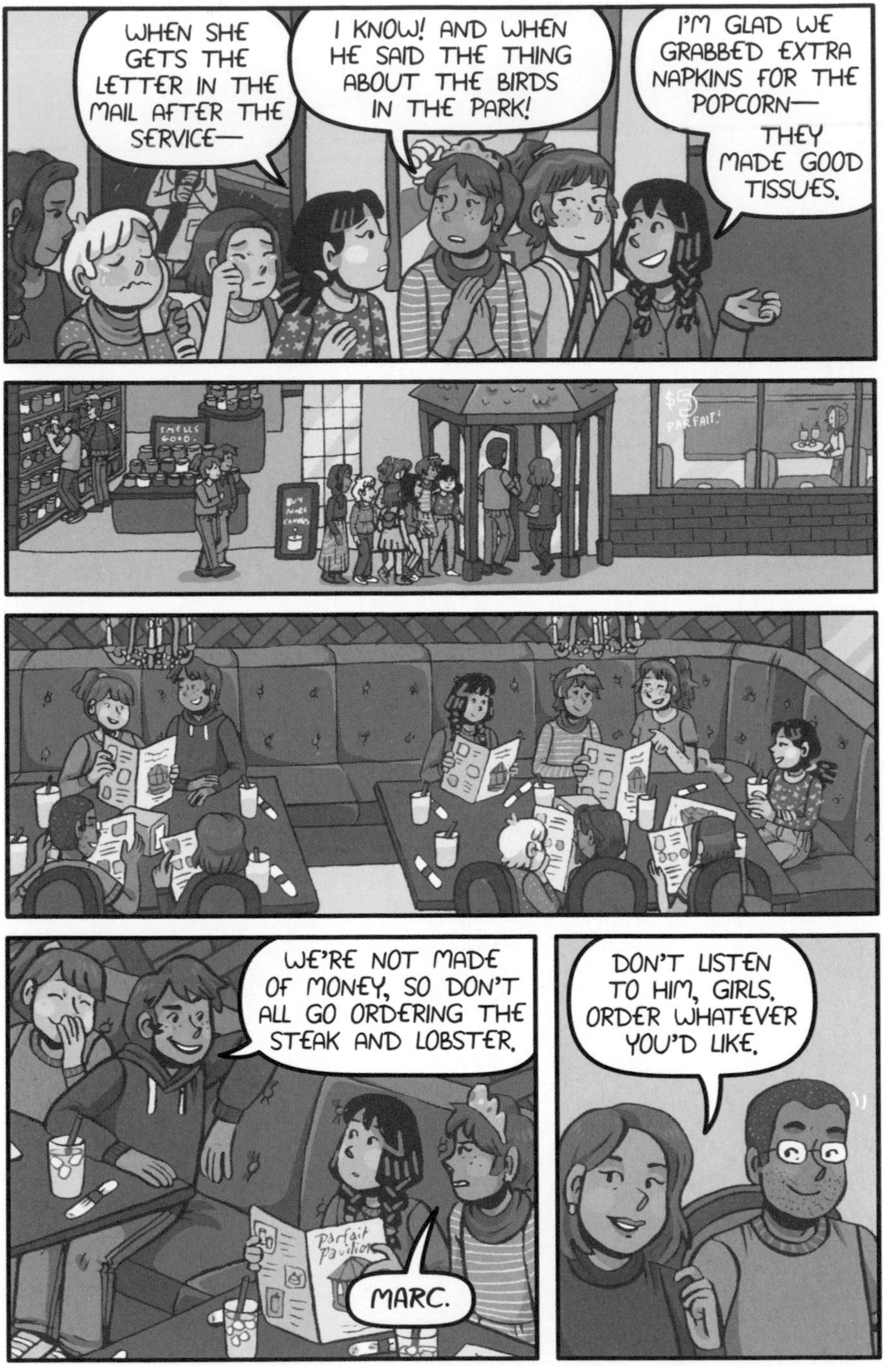
WHEN SHE GETS THE LETTER IN THE MAIL AFTER THE SERVICE—
I KNOW! AND WHEN HE SAID THE THING ABOUT THE BIRDS IN THE PARK!
I'M GLAD WE GRABBED EXTRA NAPKINS FOR THE POPCORN—
THEY MADE GOOD TISSUES.
$5 PARFAIT!
WE'RE NOT MADE OF MONEY, SO DON'T ALL GO ORDERING THE STEAK AND LOBSTER.
Parfait Pavilion
MARC.
DON'T LISTEN TO HIM, GIRLS. ORDER WHATEVER YOU'D LIKE.

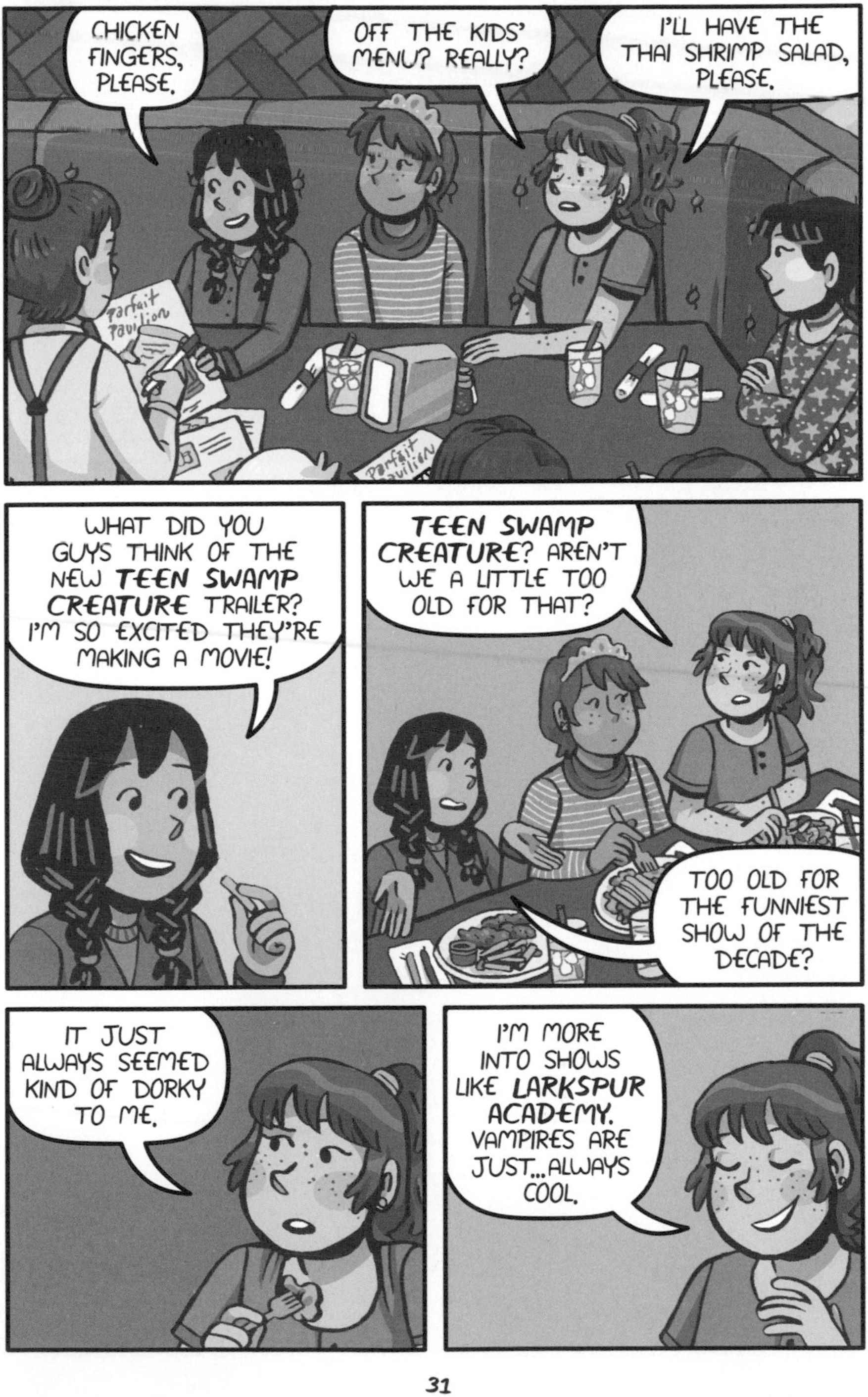
CHICKEN FINGERS, PLEASE.
OFF THE KIDS' MENU? REALLY?
I'LL HAVE THE THAI SHRIMP SALAD, PLEASE.
Parfait Pavilion
Parfait Pavilion
WHAT DID YOU GUYS THINK OF THE NEW TEEN SWAMP CREATURE TRAILER? I'M SO EXCITED THEY'RE MAKING A MOVIE!
TEEN SWAMP CREATURE? AREN'T WE A LITTLE TOO OLD FOR THAT?
TOO OLD FOR THE FUNNIEST SHOW OF THE DECADE?
IT JUST ALWAYS SEEMED KIND OF DORKY TO ME.
I'M MORE INTO SHOWS LIKE LARKSPUR ACADEMY. VAMPIRES ARE JUST...ALWAYS COOL.

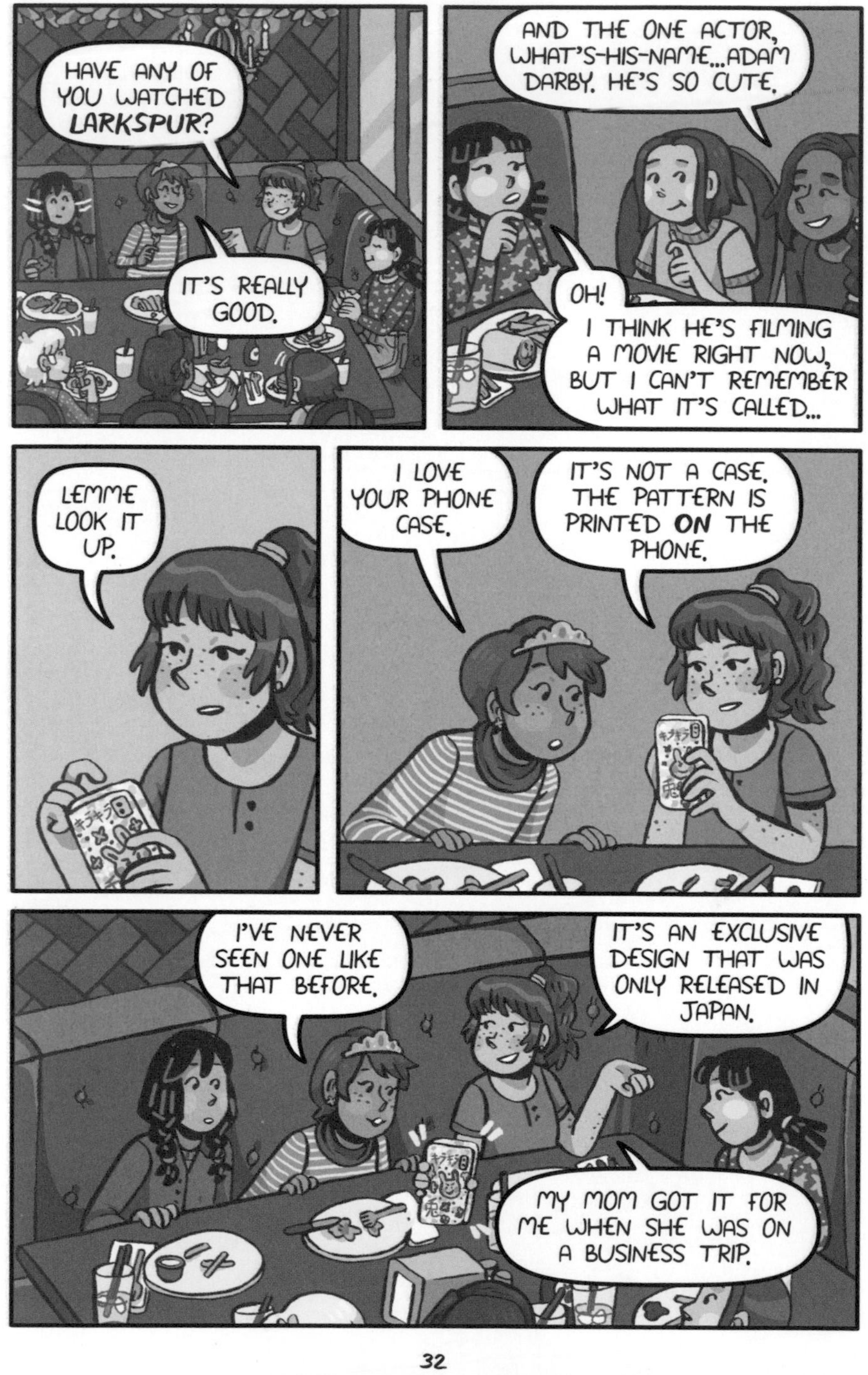
HAVE ANY OF YOU WATCHED **LARKSPUR**?
IT'S REALLY GOOD.
AND THE ONE ACTOR, WHAT'S-HIS-NAME...ADAM DARBY. HE'S SO CUTE.
OH!
I THINK HE'S FILMING A MOVIE RIGHT NOW, BUT I CAN'T REMEMBER WHAT IT'S CALLED...
LEMME LOOK IT UP.
I LOVE YOUR PHONE CASE.
IT'S NOT A CASE. THE PATTERN IS PRINTED **ON** THE PHONE.
I'VE NEVER SEEN ONE LIKE THAT BEFORE.
IT'S AN EXCLUSIVE DESIGN THAT WAS ONLY RELEASED IN JAPAN.
MY MOM GOT IT FOR ME WHEN SHE WAS ON A BUSINESS TRIP.

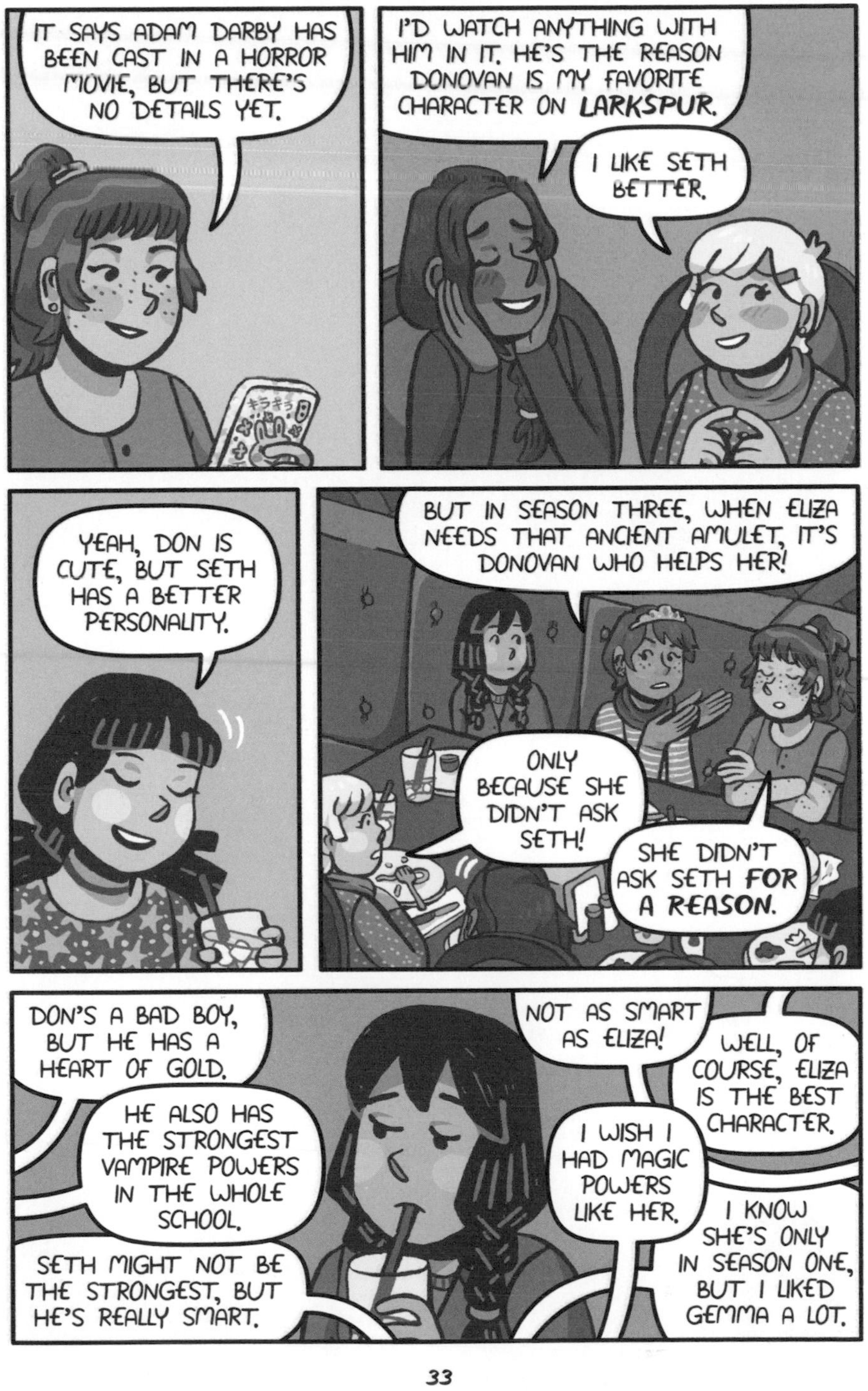
IT SAYS ADAM DARBY HAS BEEN CAST IN A HORROR MOVIE, BUT THERE'S NO DETAILS YET.
I'D WATCH ANYTHING WITH HIM IN IT. HE'S THE REASON DONOVAN IS MY FAVORITE CHARACTER ON LARKSPUR.
I LIKE SETH BETTER.
YEAH, DON IS CUTE, BUT SETH HAS A BETTER PERSONALITY.
BUT IN SEASON THREE, WHEN ELIZA NEEDS THAT ANCIENT AMULET, IT'S DONOVAN WHO HELPS HER!
ONLY BECAUSE SHE DIDN'T ASK SETH!
SHE DIDN'T ASK SETH FOR A REASON.
DON'S A BAD BOY, BUT HE HAS A HEART OF GOLD.
HE ALSO HAS THE STRONGEST VAMPIRE POWERS IN THE WHOLE SCHOOL.
SETH MIGHT NOT BE THE STRONGEST, BUT HE'S REALLY SMART.
NOT AS SMART AS ELIZA!
WELL, OF COURSE, ELIZA IS THE BEST CHARACTER.
I WISH I HAD MAGIC POWERS LIKE HER.
I KNOW SHE'S ONLY IN SEASON ONE, BUT I LIKED GEMMA A LOT.

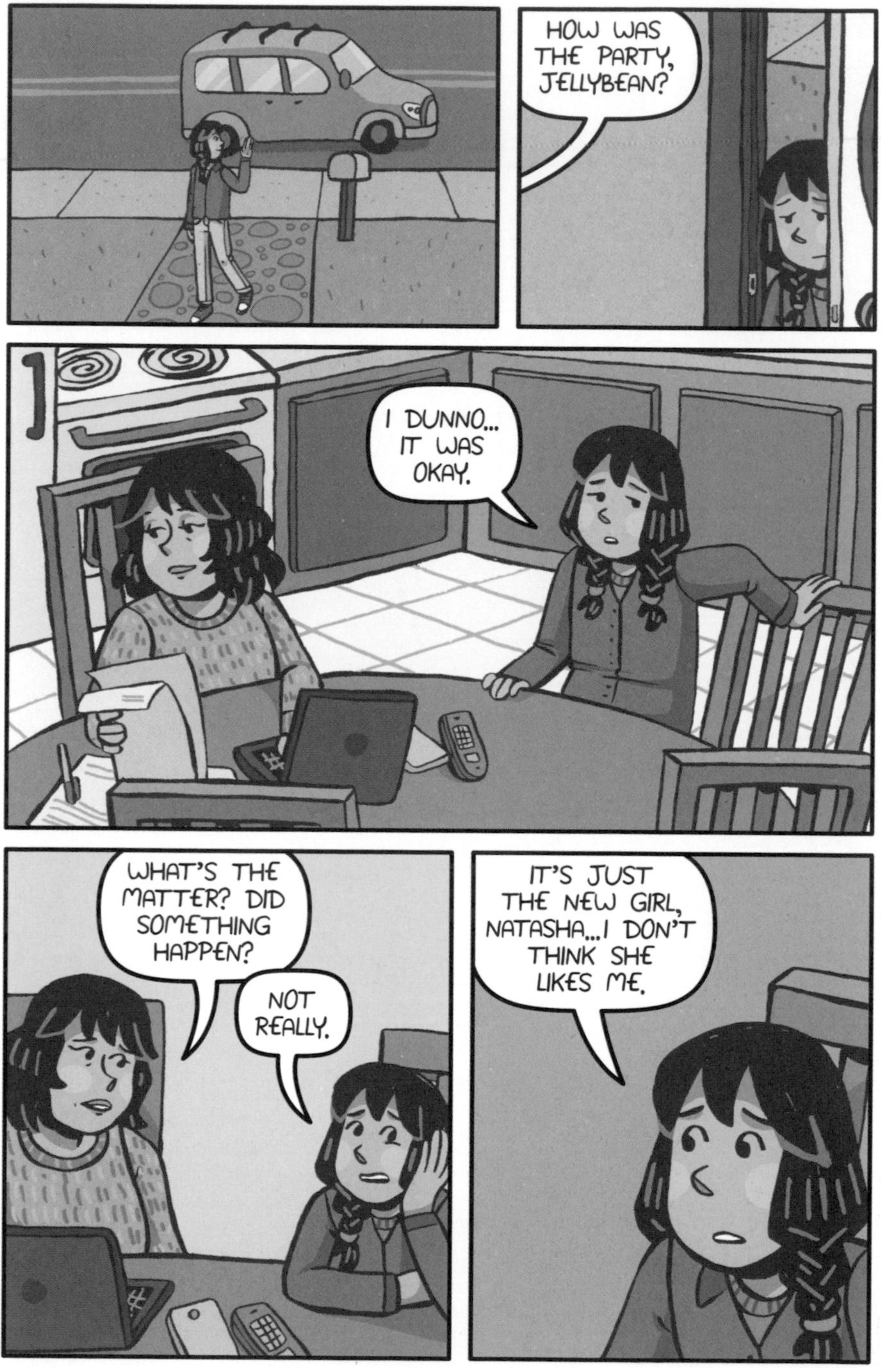
HOW WAS THE PARTY, JELLYBEAN?
I DUNNO... IT WAS OKAY.
WHAT'S THE MATTER? DID SOMETHING HAPPEN?
NOT REALLY.
IT'S JUST THE NEW GIRL, NATASHA...I DON'T THINK SHE LIKES ME.

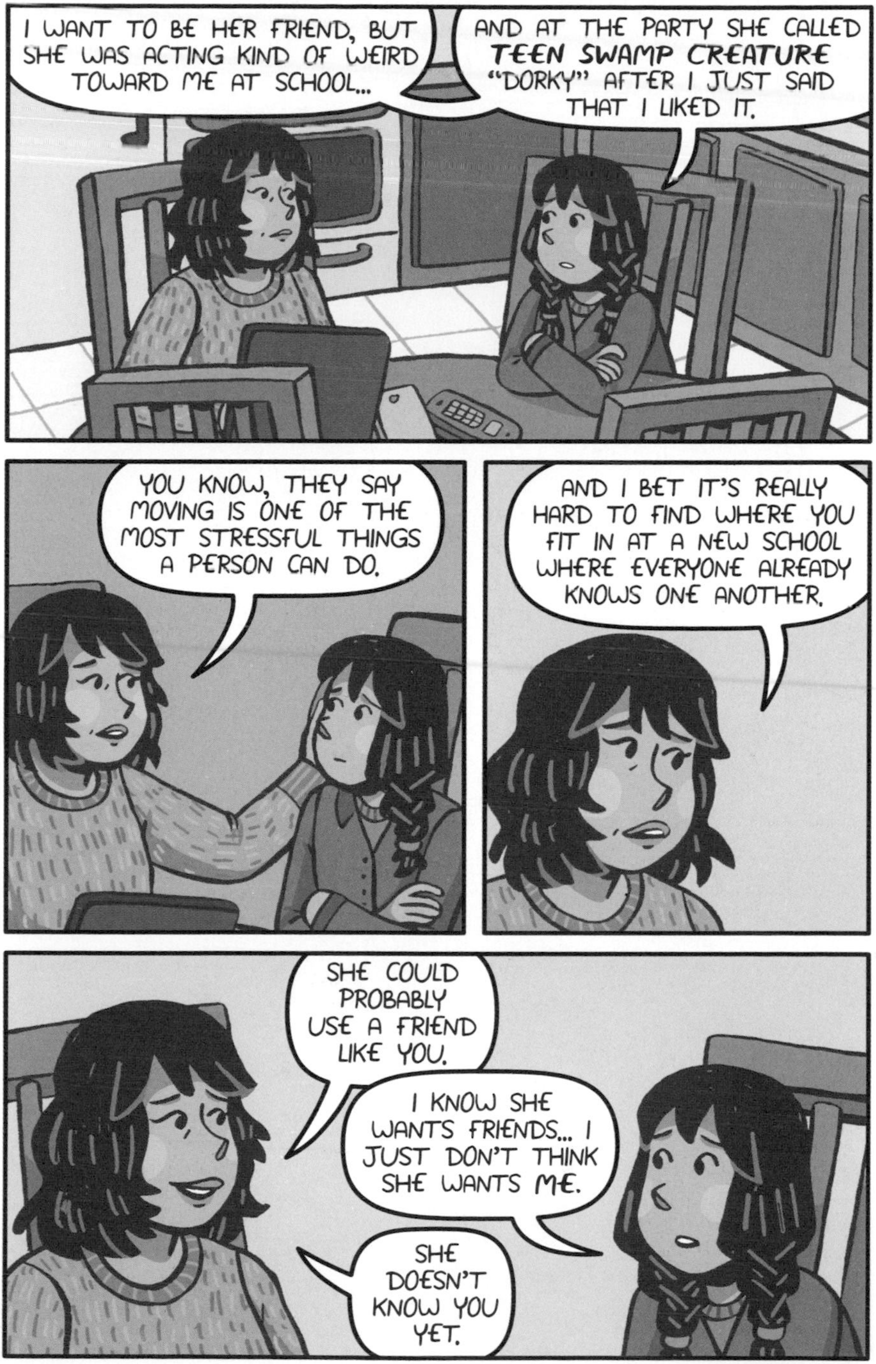
I WANT TO BE HER FRIEND, BUT SHE WAS ACTING KIND OF WEIRD TOWARD ME AT SCHOOL...
AND AT THE PARTY SHE CALLED **TEEN SWAMP CREATURE** "DORKY" AFTER I JUST SAID THAT I LIKED IT.
YOU KNOW, THEY SAY MOVING IS ONE OF THE MOST STRESSFUL THINGS A PERSON CAN DO.
AND I BET IT'S REALLY HARD TO FIND WHERE YOU FIT IN AT A NEW SCHOOL WHERE EVERYONE ALREADY KNOWS ONE ANOTHER.
SHE COULD PROBABLY USE A FRIEND LIKE YOU.
I KNOW SHE WANTS FRIENDS... I JUST DON'T THINK SHE WANTS *ME*.
SHE DOESN'T KNOW YOU YET.

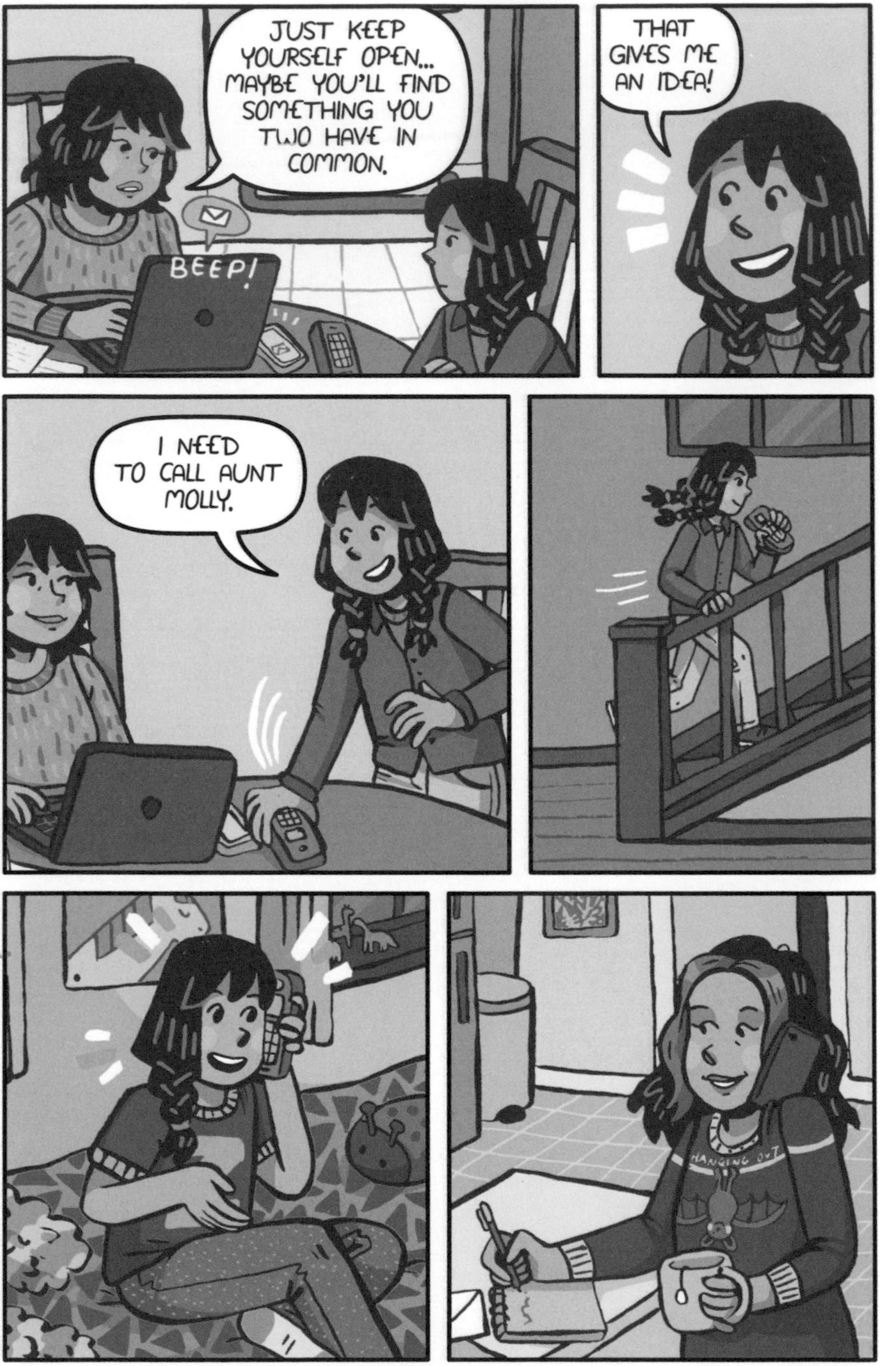
JUST KEEP YOURSELF OPEN... MAYBE YOU'LL FIND SOMETHING YOU TWO HAVE IN COMMON.
BEEP!
THAT GIVES ME AN IDEA!
I NEED TO CALL AUNT MOLLY.
HANGING OUT

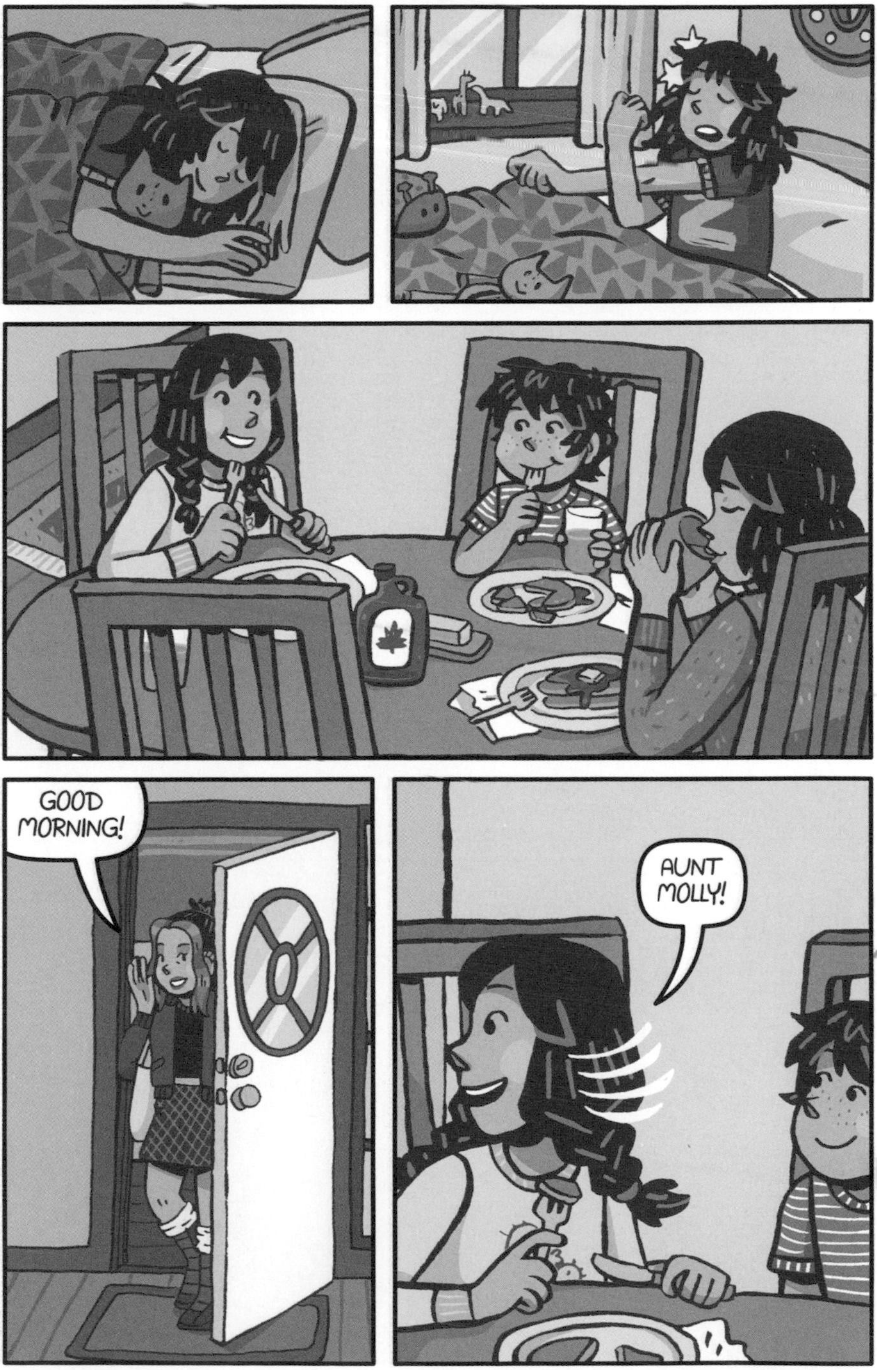
GOOD MORNING!
AUNT MOLLY!

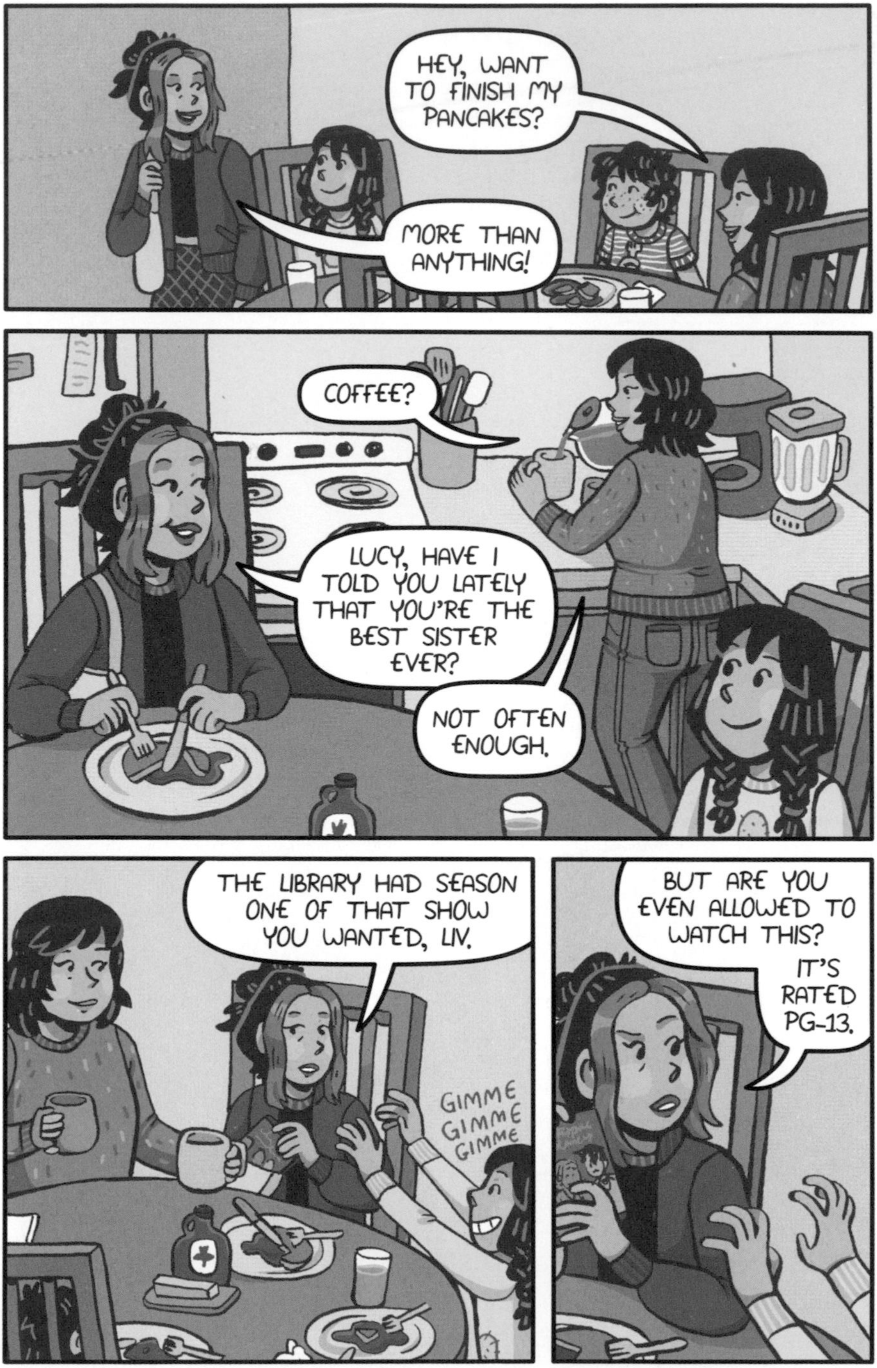
HEY, WANT TO FINISH MY PANCAKES?
MORE THAN ANYTHING!
COFFEE?
LUCY, HAVE I TOLD YOU LATELY THAT YOU'RE THE BEST SISTER EVER?
NOT OFTEN ENOUGH.
THE LIBRARY HAD SEASON ONE OF THAT SHOW YOU WANTED, LIV.
GIMME GIMME GIMME
BUT ARE YOU EVEN ALLOWED TO WATCH THIS?
IT'S RATED PG-13.

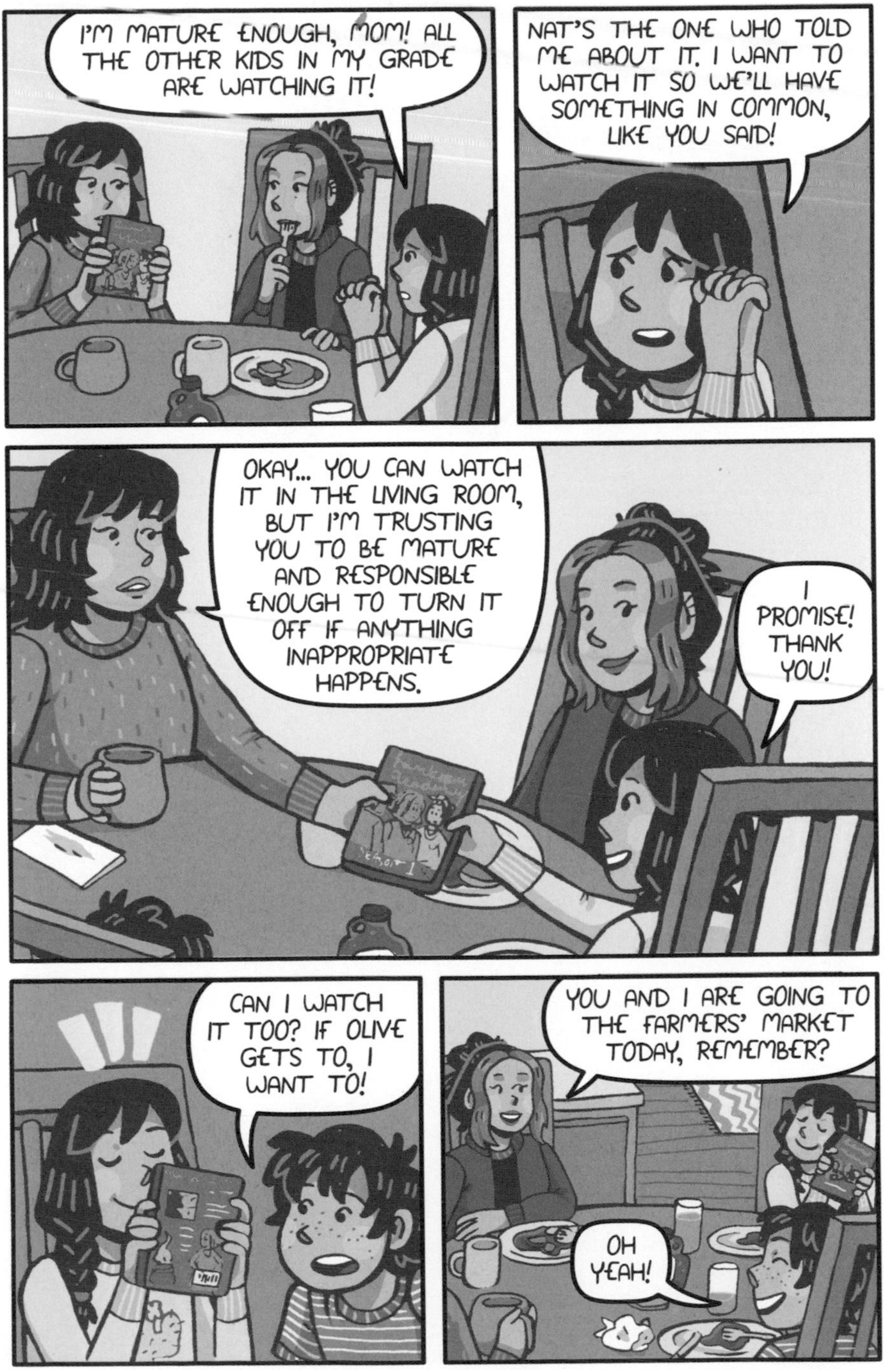
I'M MATURE ENOUGH, MOM! ALL THE OTHER KIDS IN MY GRADE ARE WATCHING IT!
NAT'S THE ONE WHO TOLD ME ABOUT IT. I WANT TO WATCH IT SO WE'LL HAVE SOMETHING IN COMMON, LIKE YOU SAID!
OKAY... YOU CAN WATCH IT IN THE LIVING ROOM, BUT I'M TRUSTING YOU TO BE MATURE AND RESPONSIBLE ENOUGH TO TURN IT OFF IF ANYTHING INAPPROPRIATE HAPPENS.
I PROMISE! THANK YOU!
CAN I WATCH IT TOO? IF OLIVE GETS TO, I WANT TO!
YOU AND I ARE GOING TO THE FARMERS' MARKET TODAY, REMEMBER?
OH YEAH!

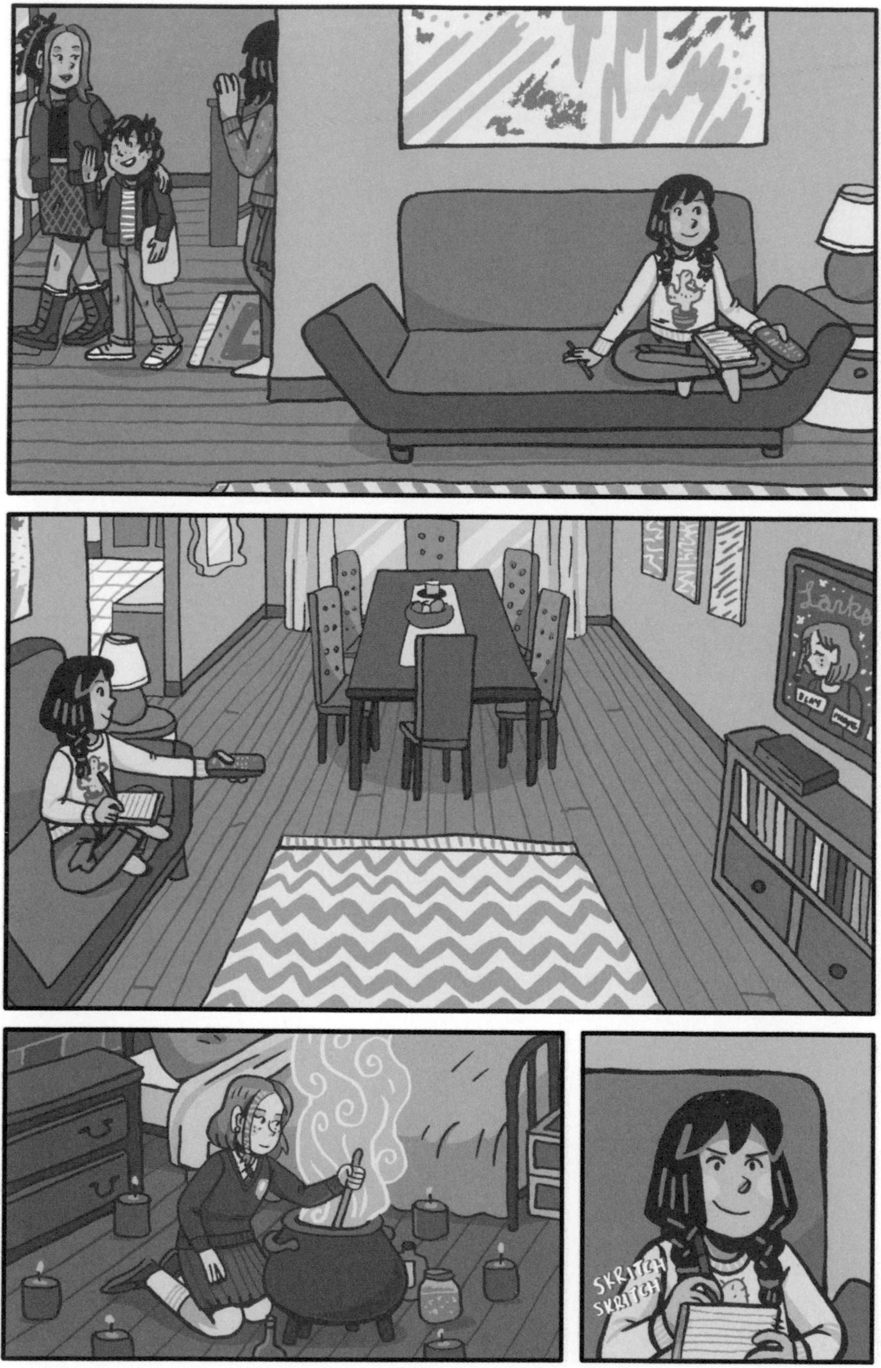
SKRITCH
SKRITCH

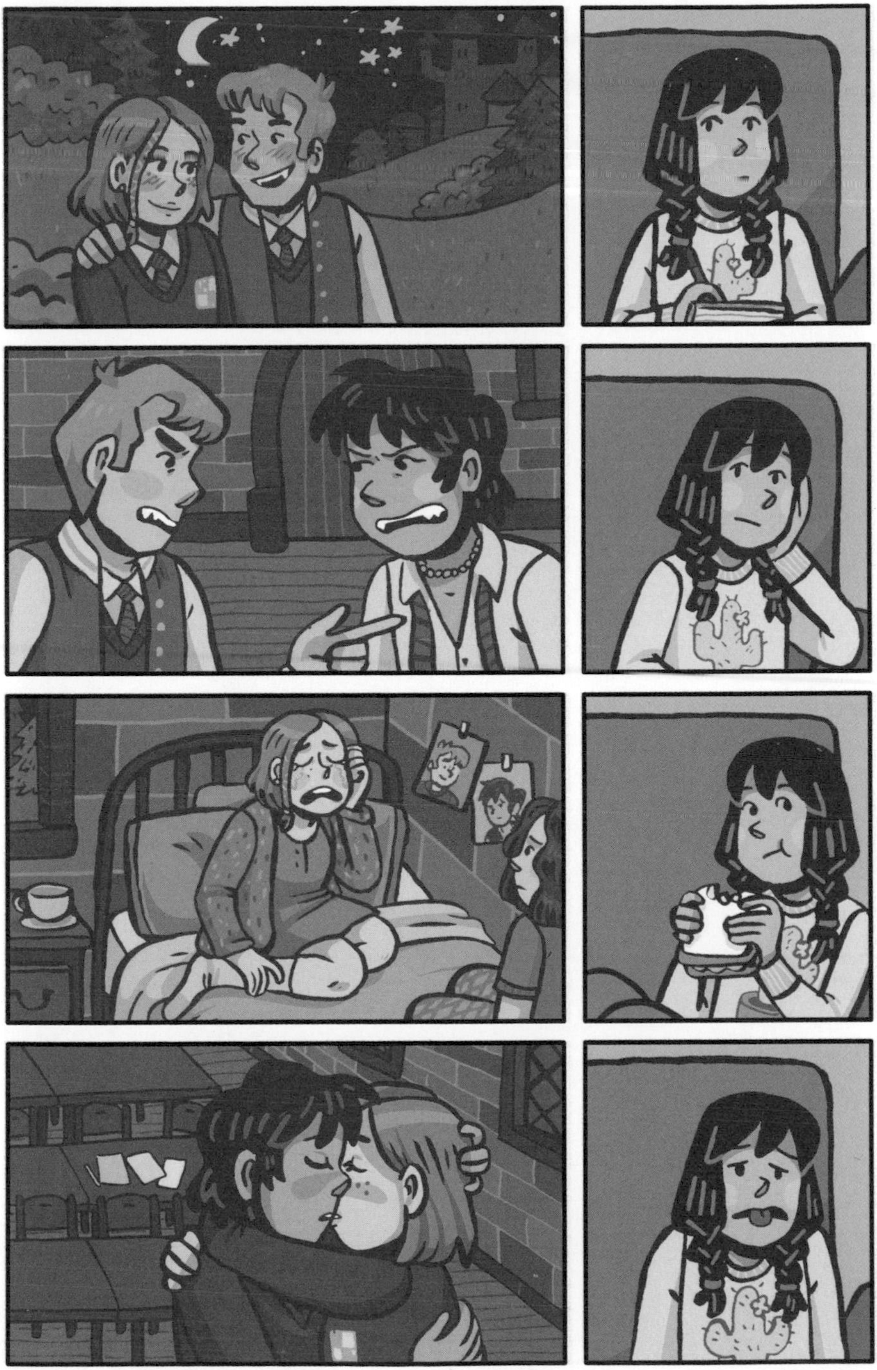

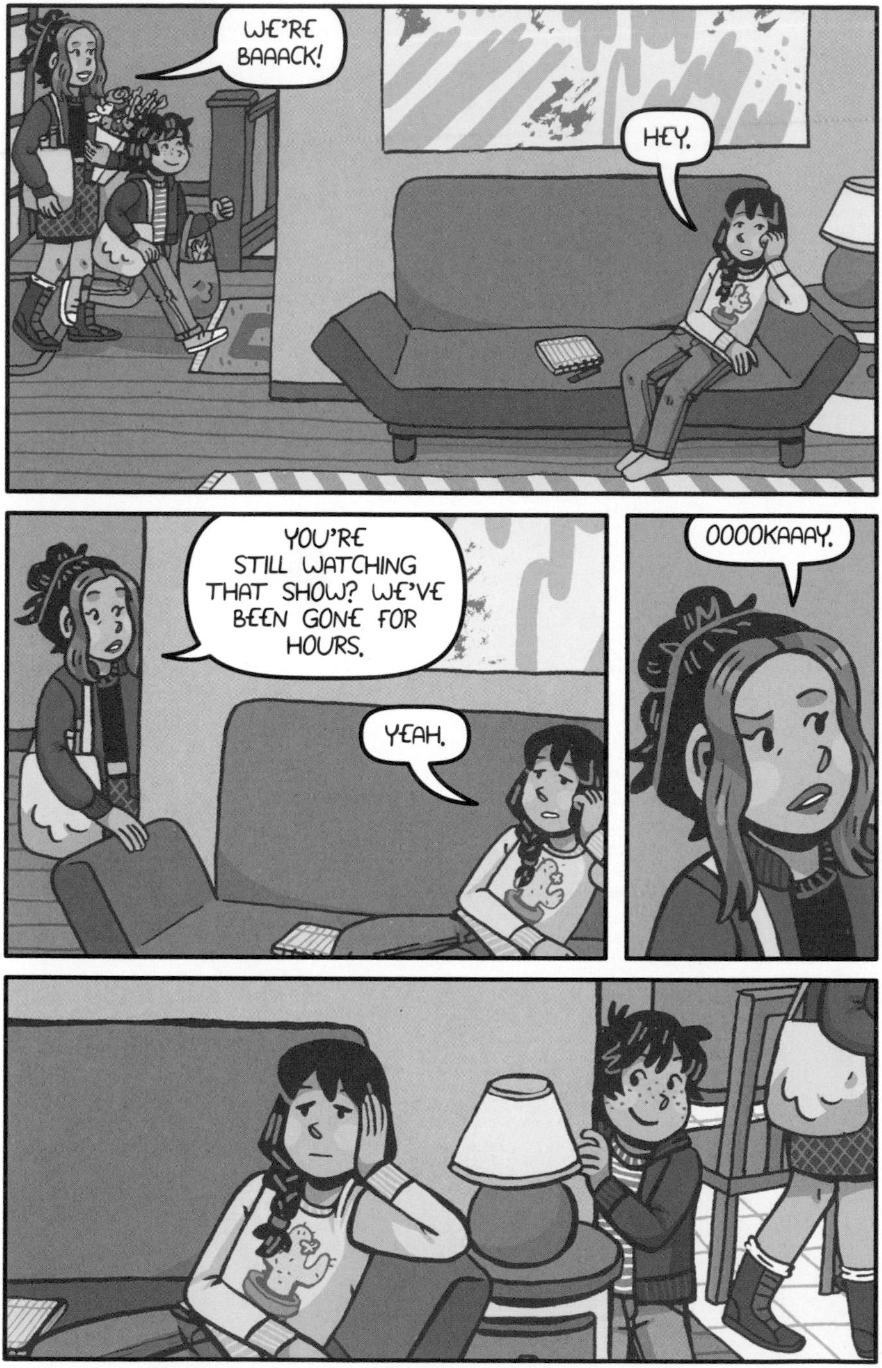
WE'RE BAAACK!
HEY.
YOU'RE STILL WATCHING THAT SHOW? WE'VE BEEN GONE FOR HOURS.
YEAH.
OOOOKAAAY.

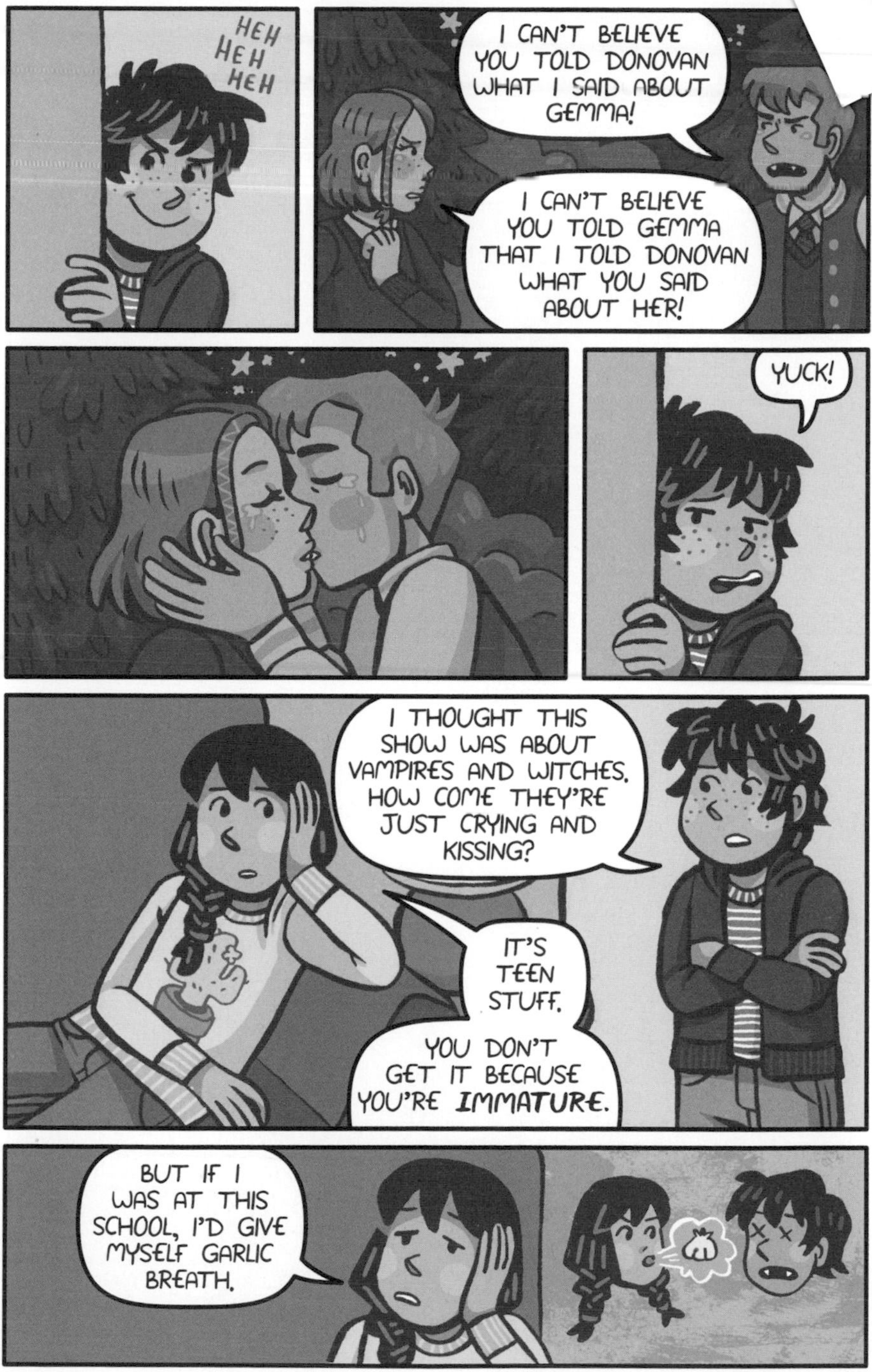
HEH
HEH
HEH
I CAN'T BELIEVE YOU TOLD DONOVAN WHAT I SAID ABOUT GEMMA!
I CAN'T BELIEVE YOU TOLD GEMMA THAT I TOLD DONOVAN WHAT YOU SAID ABOUT HER!
YUCK!
I THOUGHT THIS SHOW WAS ABOUT VAMPIRES AND WITCHES. HOW COME THEY'RE JUST CRYING AND KISSING?
IT'S TEEN STUFF.
YOU DON'T GET IT BECAUSE YOU'RE **IMMATURE**.
BUT IF I WAS AT THIS SCHOOL, I'D GIVE MYSELF GARLIC BREATH.

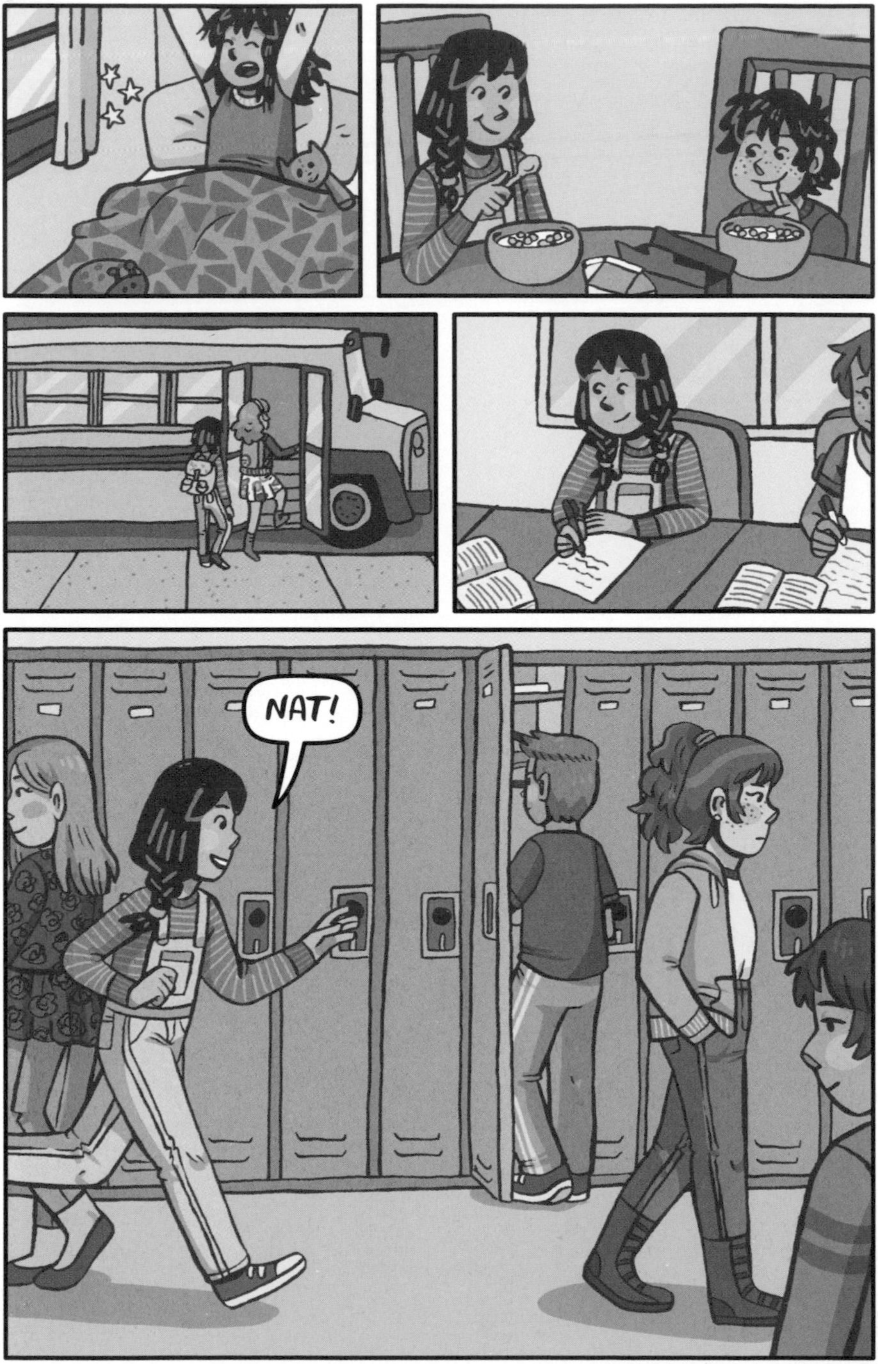
NAT!

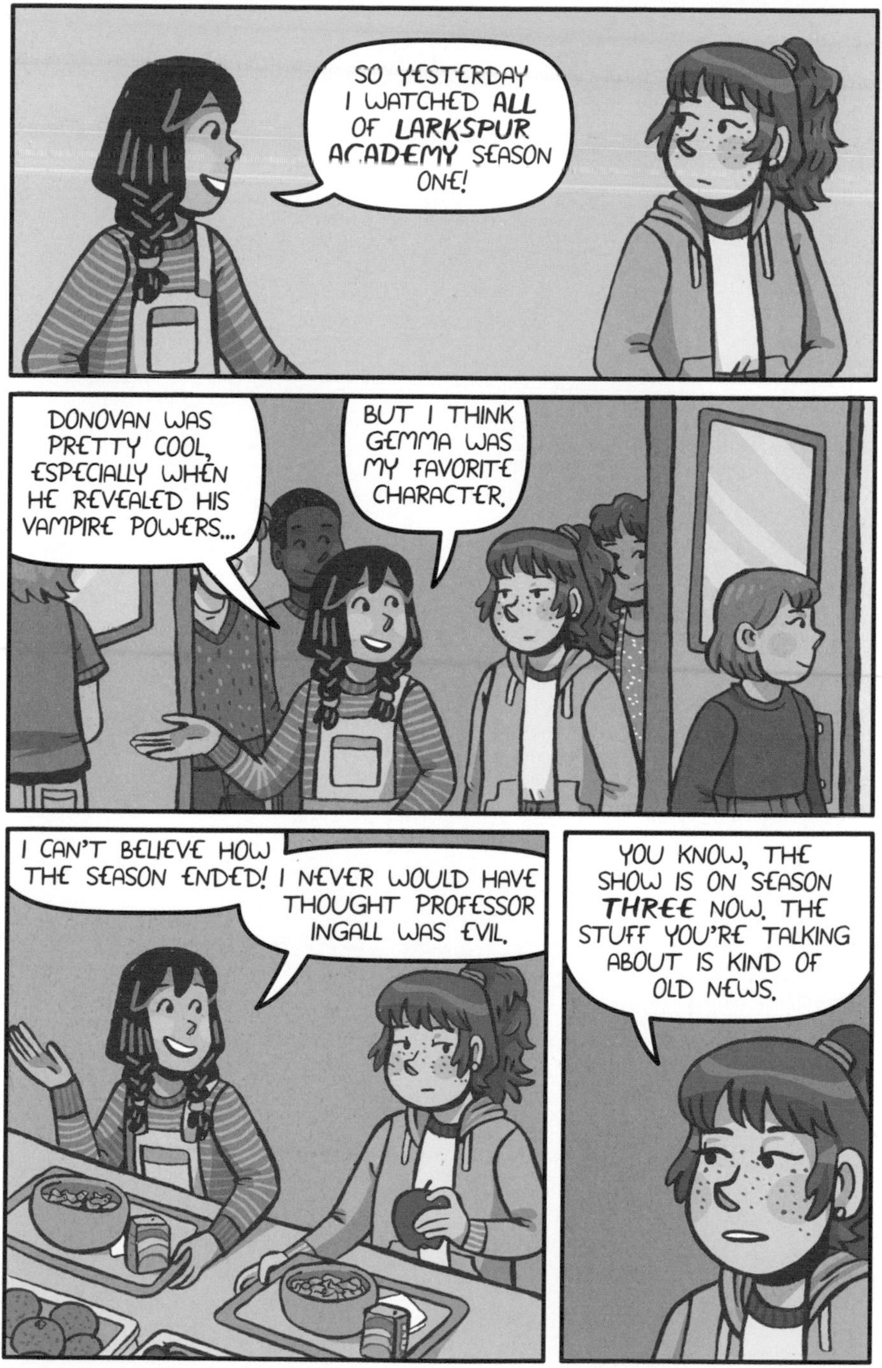
SO YESTERDAY I WATCHED ALL OF LARKSPUR ACADEMY SEASON ONE!
DONOVAN WAS PRETTY COOL, ESPECIALLY WHEN HE REVEALED HIS VAMPIRE POWERS...
BUT I THINK GEMMA WAS MY FAVORITE CHARACTER.
I CAN'T BELIEVE HOW THE SEASON ENDED! I NEVER WOULD HAVE THOUGHT PROFESSOR INGALL WAS EVIL.
YOU KNOW, THE SHOW IS ON SEASON THREE NOW. THE STUFF YOU'RE TALKING ABOUT IS KIND OF OLD NEWS.

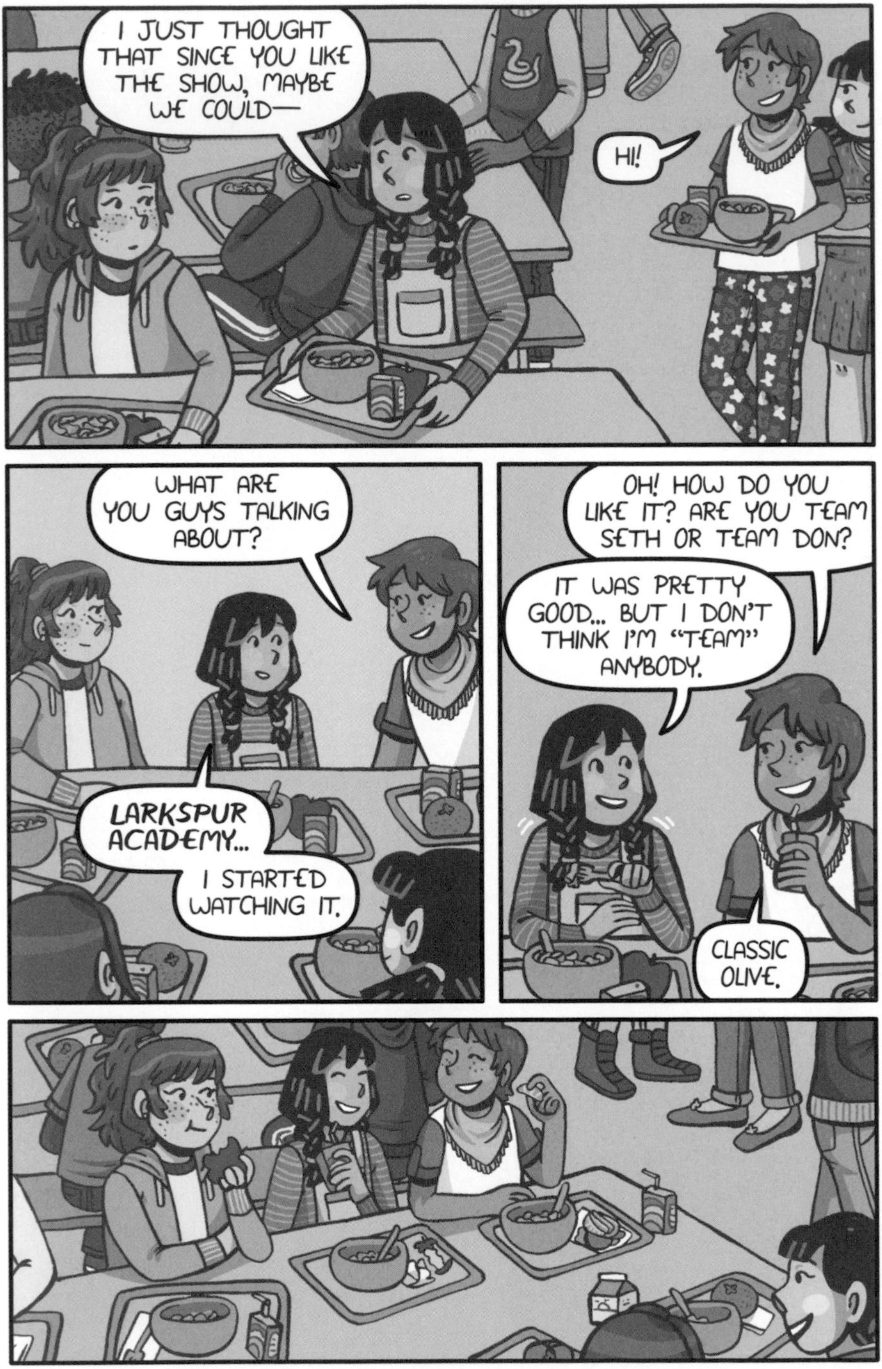
I JUST THOUGHT THAT SINCE YOU LIKE THE SHOW, MAYBE WE COULD—
HI!
WHAT ARE YOU GUYS TALKING ABOUT?
LARKSPUR ACADEMY...
I STARTED WATCHING IT.
OH! HOW DO YOU LIKE IT? ARE YOU TEAM SETH OR TEAM DON?
IT WAS PRETTY GOOD... BUT I DON'T THINK I'M "TEAM" ANYBODY.
CLASSIC OLIVE.

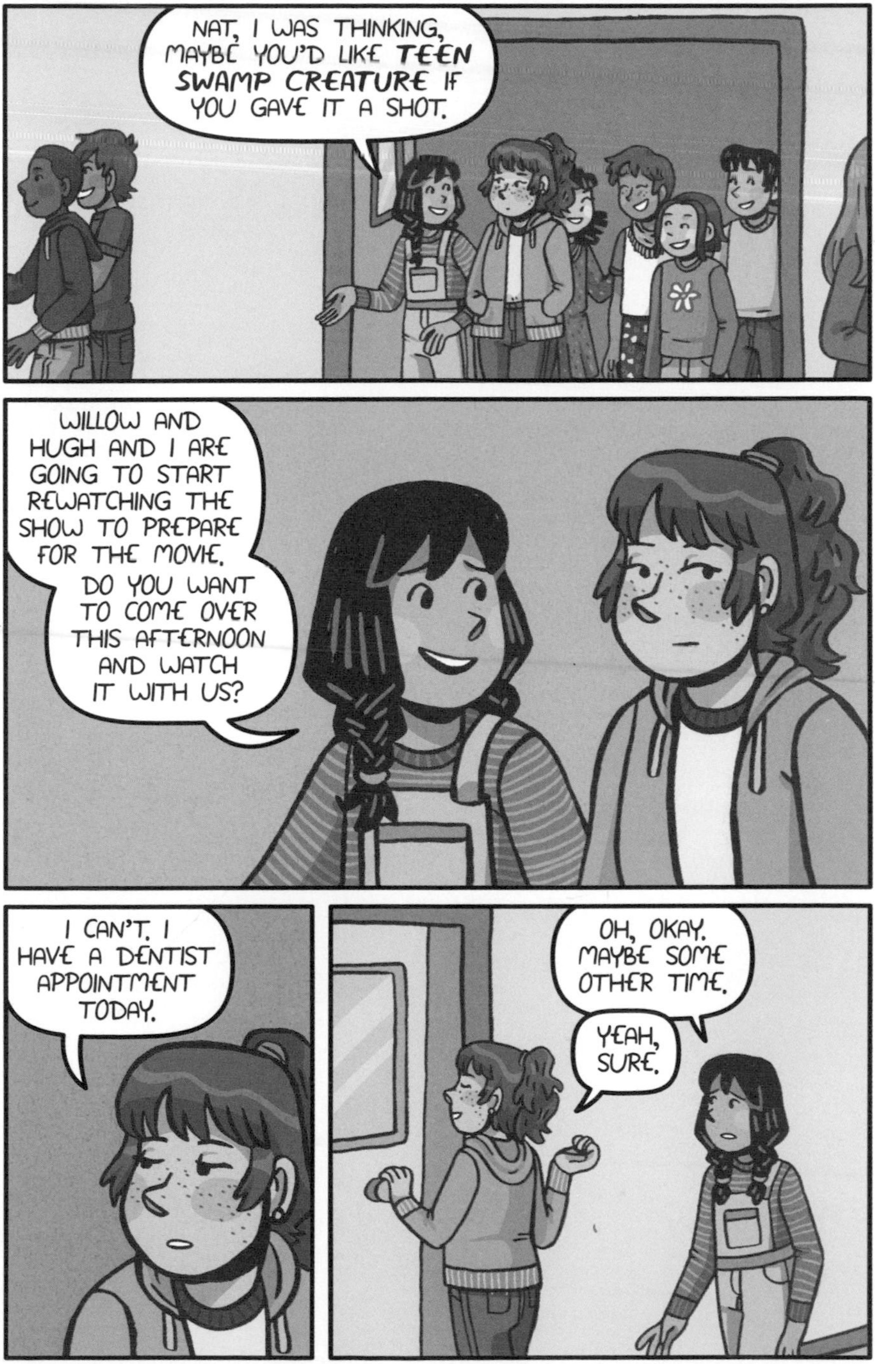
NAT, I WAS THINKING, MAYBE YOU'D LIKE **TEEN SWAMP CREATURE** IF YOU GAVE IT A SHOT.
WILLOW AND HUGH AND I ARE GOING TO START REWATCHING THE SHOW TO PREPARE FOR THE MOVIE.
DO YOU WANT TO COME OVER THIS AFTERNOON AND WATCH IT WITH US?
I CAN'T. I HAVE A DENTIST APPOINTMENT TODAY.
OH, OKAY. MAYBE SOME OTHER TIME.
YEAH, SURE.

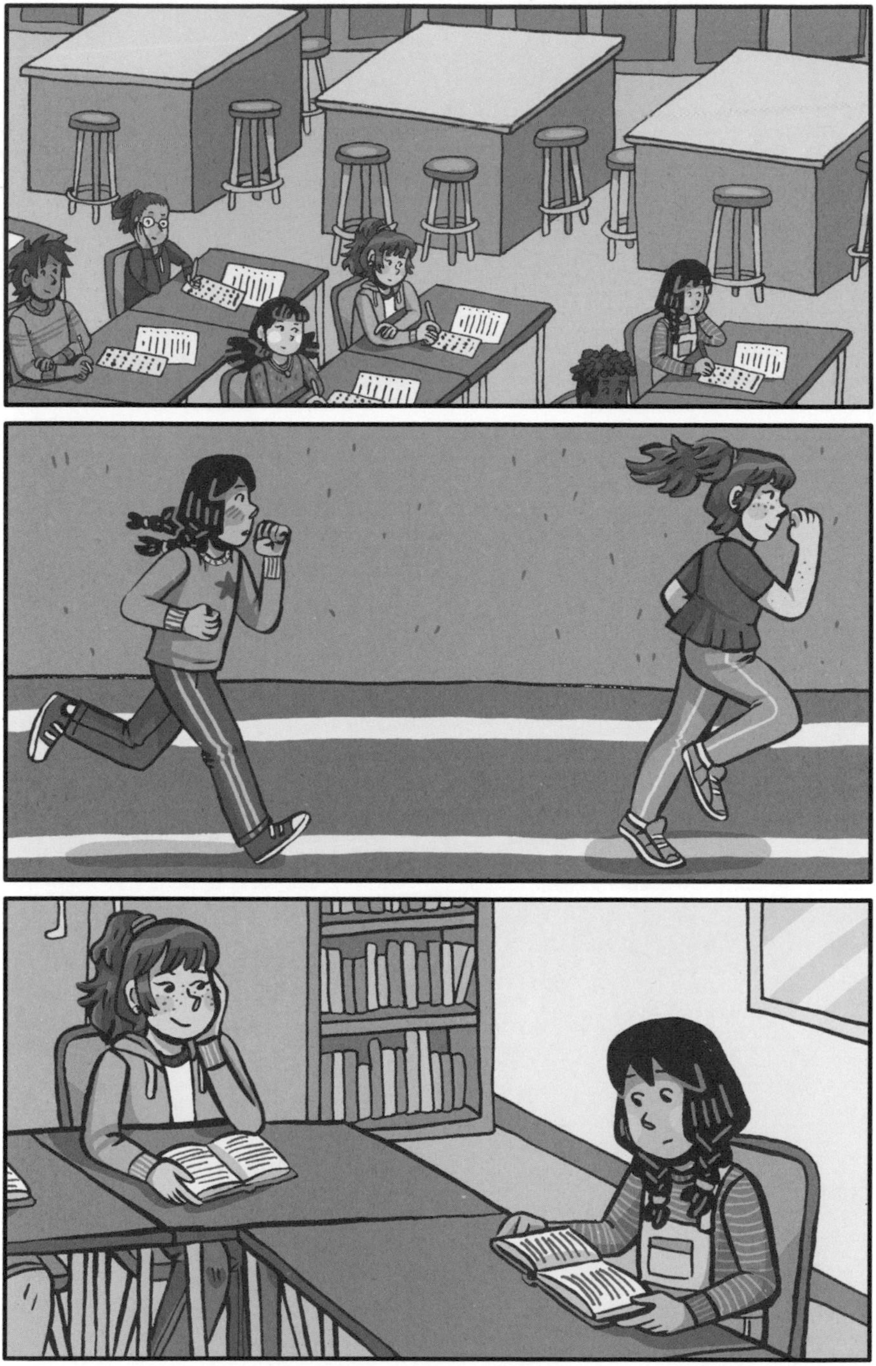

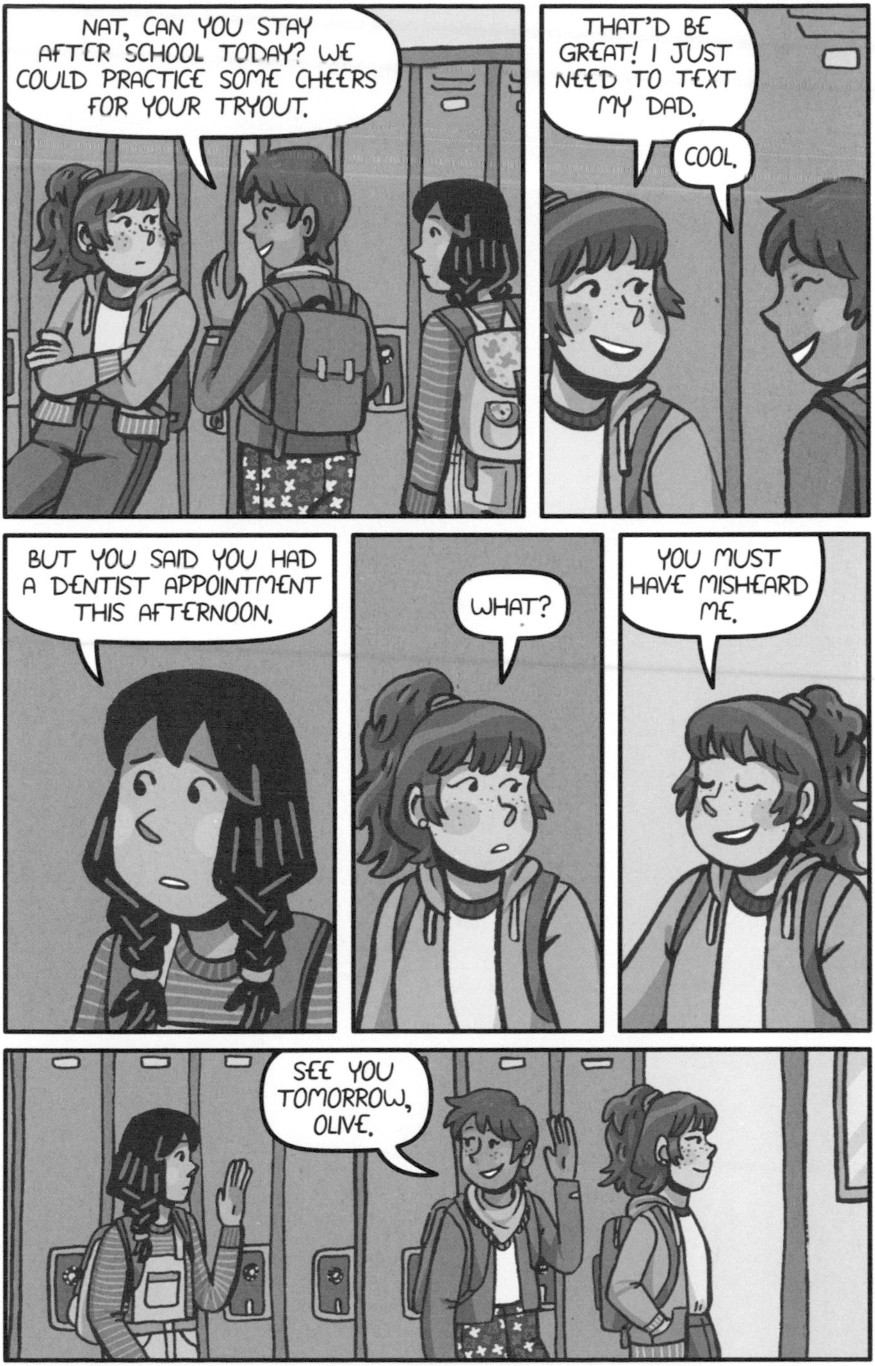
NAT, CAN YOU STAY AFTER SCHOOL TODAY? WE COULD PRACTICE SOME CHEERS FOR YOUR TRYOUT.
THAT'D BE GREAT! I JUST NEED TO TEXT MY DAD.
COOL.
BUT YOU SAID YOU HAD A DENTIST APPOINTMENT THIS AFTERNOON.
WHAT?
YOU MUST HAVE MISHEARD ME.
SEE YOU TOMORROW, OLIVE.

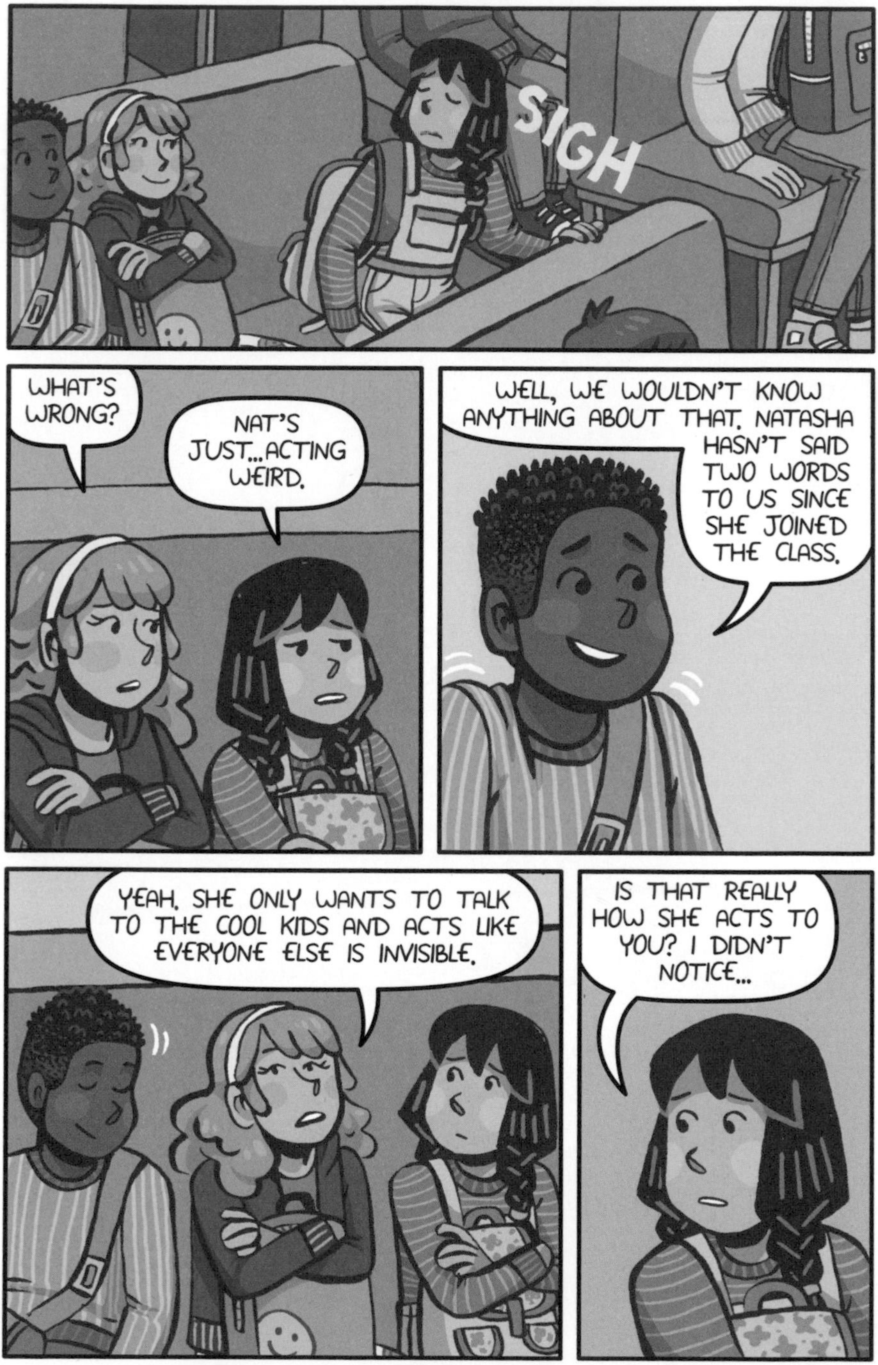
SIGH
WHAT'S WRONG?
NAT'S JUST...ACTING WEIRD.
WELL, WE WOULDN'T KNOW ANYTHING ABOUT THAT. NATASHA HASN'T SAID TWO WORDS TO US SINCE SHE JOINED THE CLASS.
YEAH, SHE ONLY WANTS TO TALK TO THE COOL KIDS AND ACTS LIKE EVERYONE ELSE IS INVISIBLE.
IS THAT REALLY HOW SHE ACTS TO YOU? I DIDN'T NOTICE...

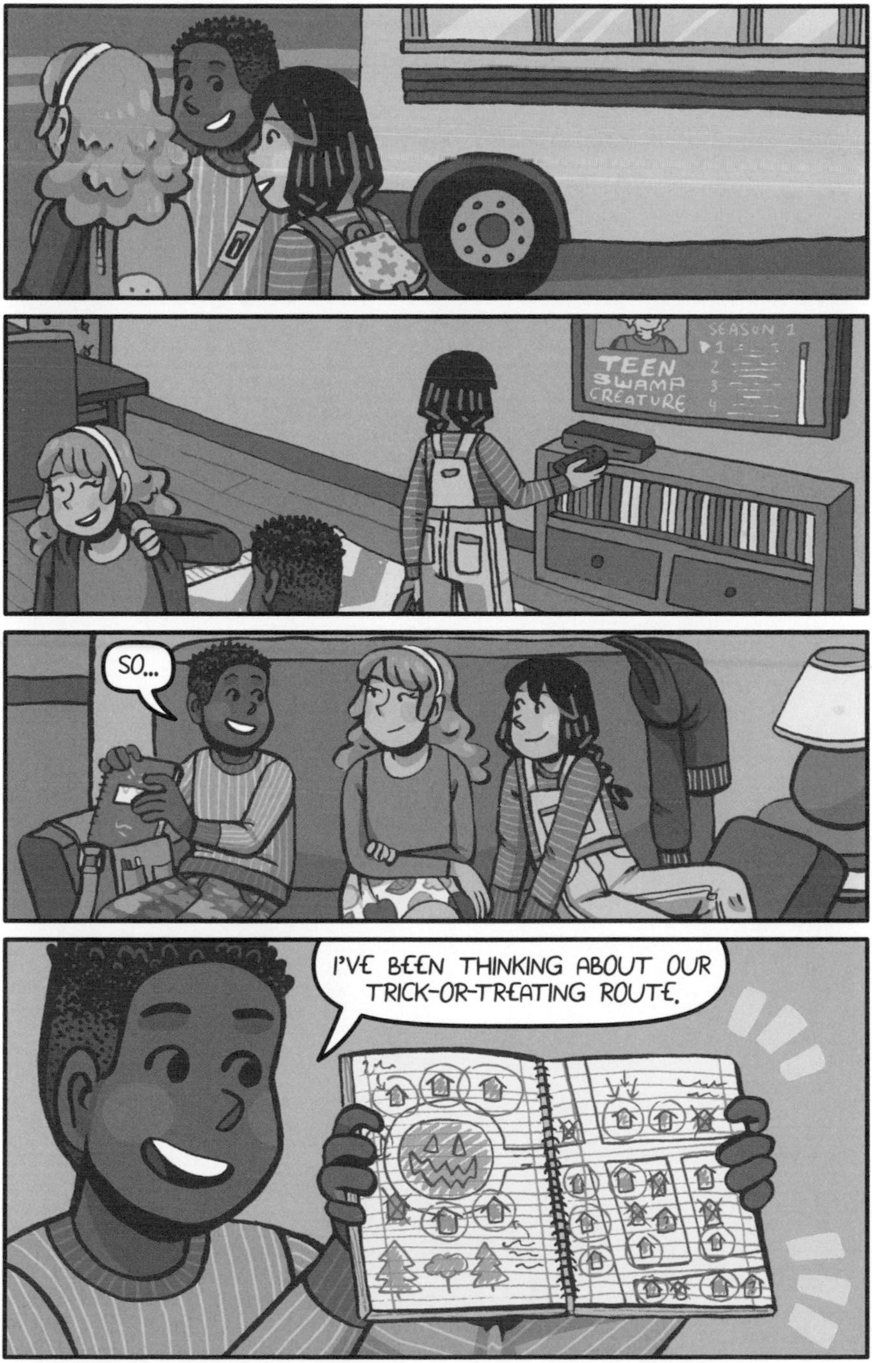
SEASON 1
TEEN SWAMP CREATURE
SO...
I'VE BEEN THINKING ABOUT OUR TRICK-OR-TREATING ROUTE.

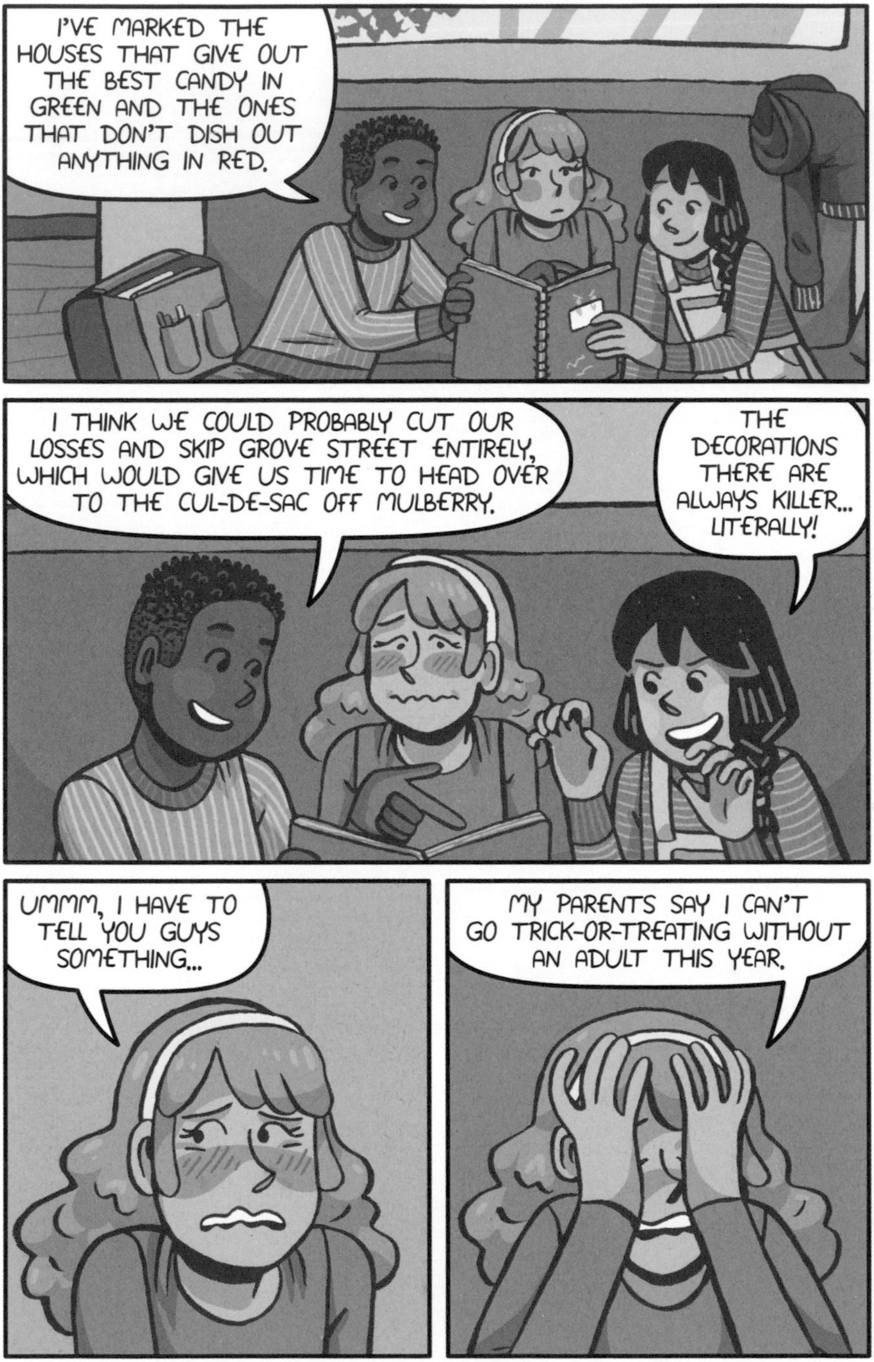
I'VE MARKED THE HOUSES THAT GIVE OUT THE BEST CANDY IN GREEN AND THE ONES THAT DON'T DISH OUT ANYTHING IN RED.
I THINK WE COULD PROBABLY CUT OUR LOSSES AND SKIP GROVE STREET ENTIRELY, WHICH WOULD GIVE US TIME TO HEAD OVER TO THE CUL-DE-SAC OFF MULBERRY.
THE DECORATIONS THERE ARE ALWAYS KILLER... LITERALLY!
UMMM, I HAVE TO TELL YOU GUYS SOMETHING...
MY PARENTS SAY I CAN'T GO TRICK-OR-TREATING WITHOUT AN ADULT THIS YEAR.

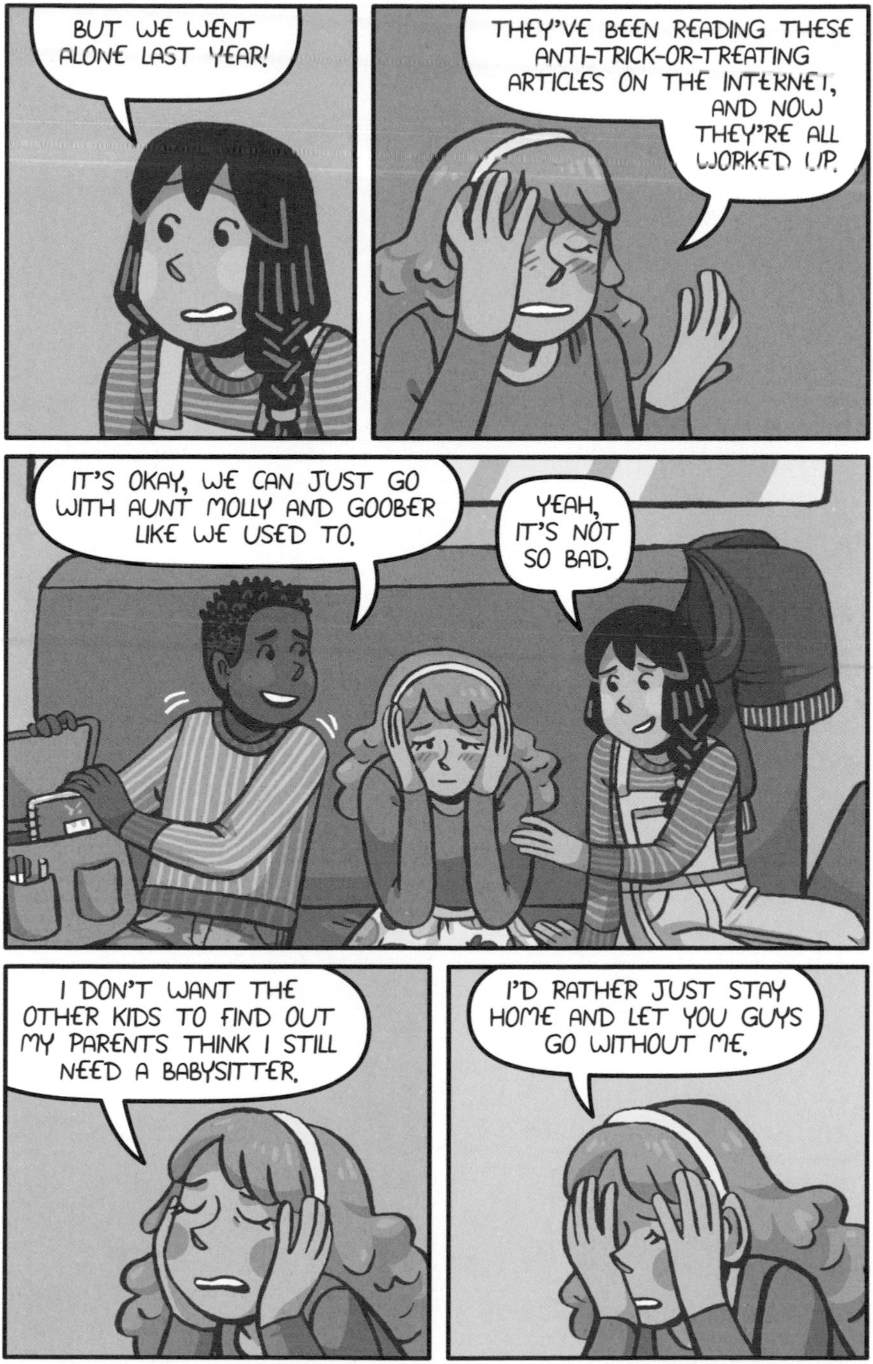
BUT WE WENT ALONE LAST YEAR!
THEY'VE BEEN READING THESE ANTI-TRICK-OR-TREATING ARTICLES ON THE INTERNET, AND NOW THEY'RE ALL WORKED UP.
IT'S OKAY, WE CAN JUST GO WITH AUNT MOLLY AND GOOBER LIKE WE USED TO.
YEAH, IT'S NOT SO BAD.
I DON'T WANT THE OTHER KIDS TO FIND OUT MY PARENTS THINK I STILL NEED A BABYSITTER.
I'D RATHER JUST STAY HOME AND LET YOU GUYS GO WITHOUT ME.

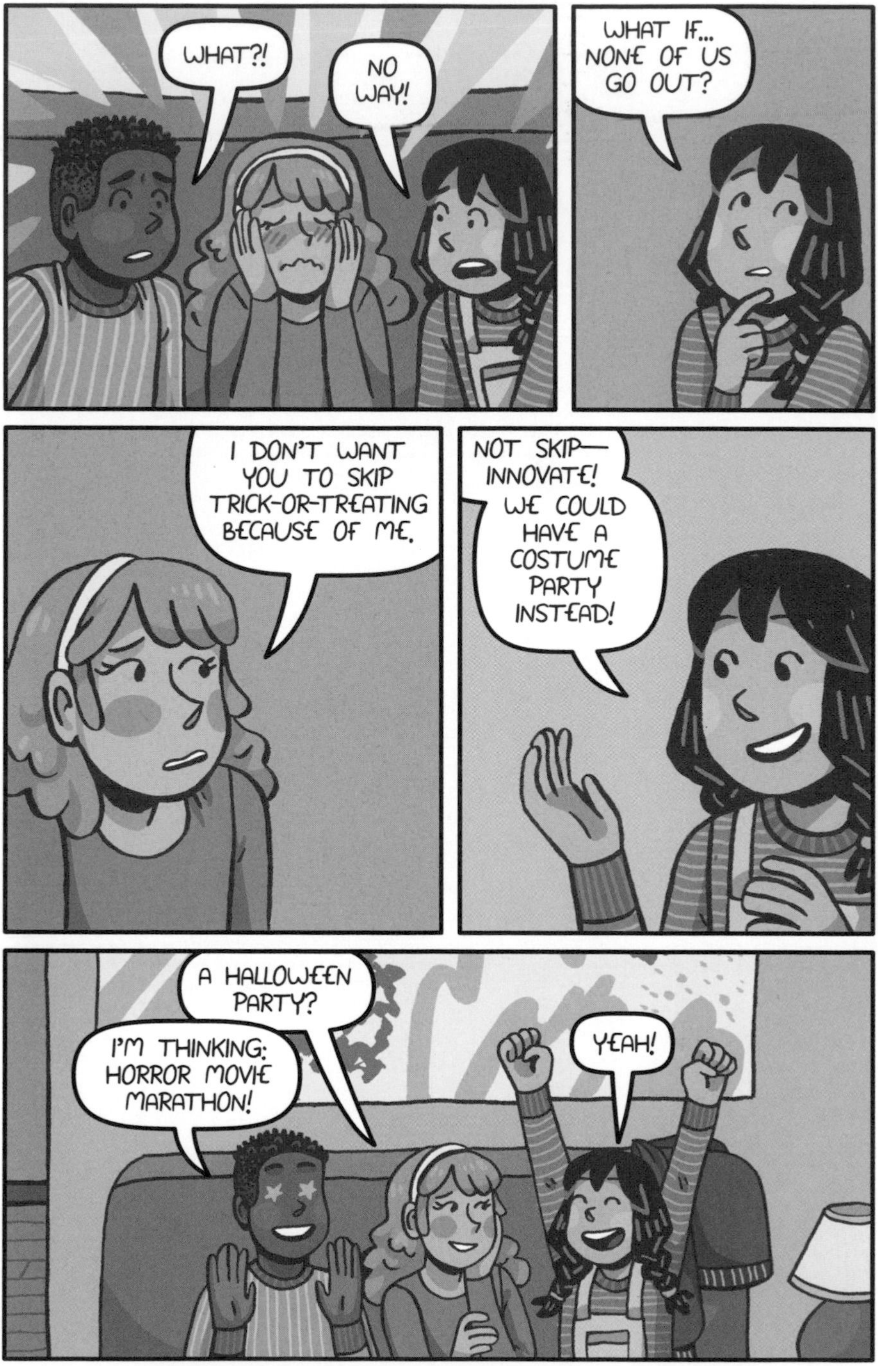
WHAT?!
NO WAY!
WHAT IF... NONE OF US GO OUT?
I DON'T WANT YOU TO SKIP TRICK-OR-TREATING BECAUSE OF ME.
NOT SKIP— INNOVATE! WE COULD HAVE A COSTUME PARTY INSTEAD!
A HALLOWEEN PARTY?
I'M THINKING: HORROR MOVIE MARATHON!
YEAH!

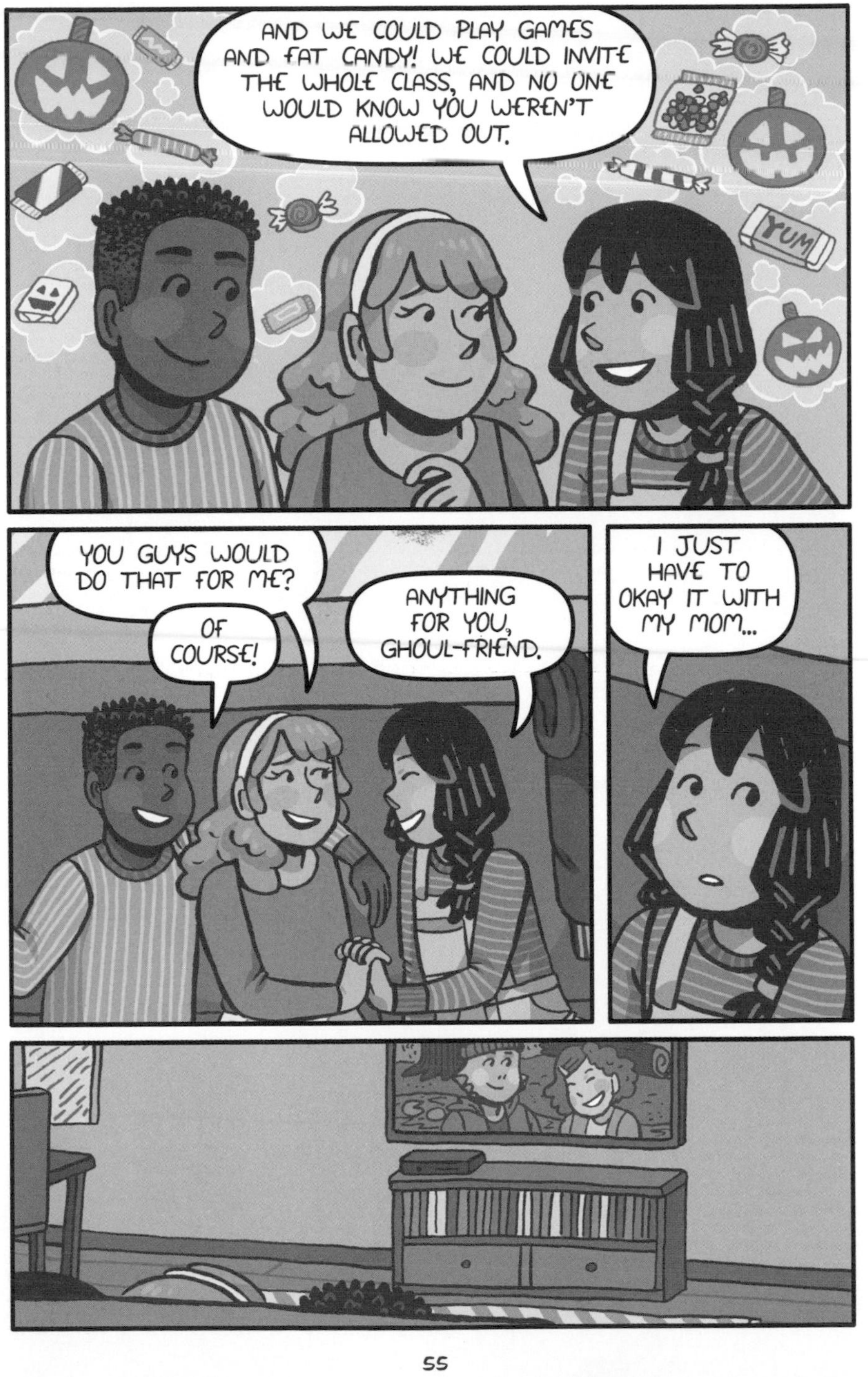
AND WE COULD PLAY GAMES AND EAT CANDY! WE COULD INVITE THE WHOLE CLASS, AND NO ONE WOULD KNOW YOU WEREN'T ALLOWED OUT.
YUM
YOU GUYS WOULD DO THAT FOR ME?
OF COURSE!
ANYTHING FOR YOU, GHOUL-FRIEND.
I JUST HAVE TO OKAY IT WITH MY MOM...

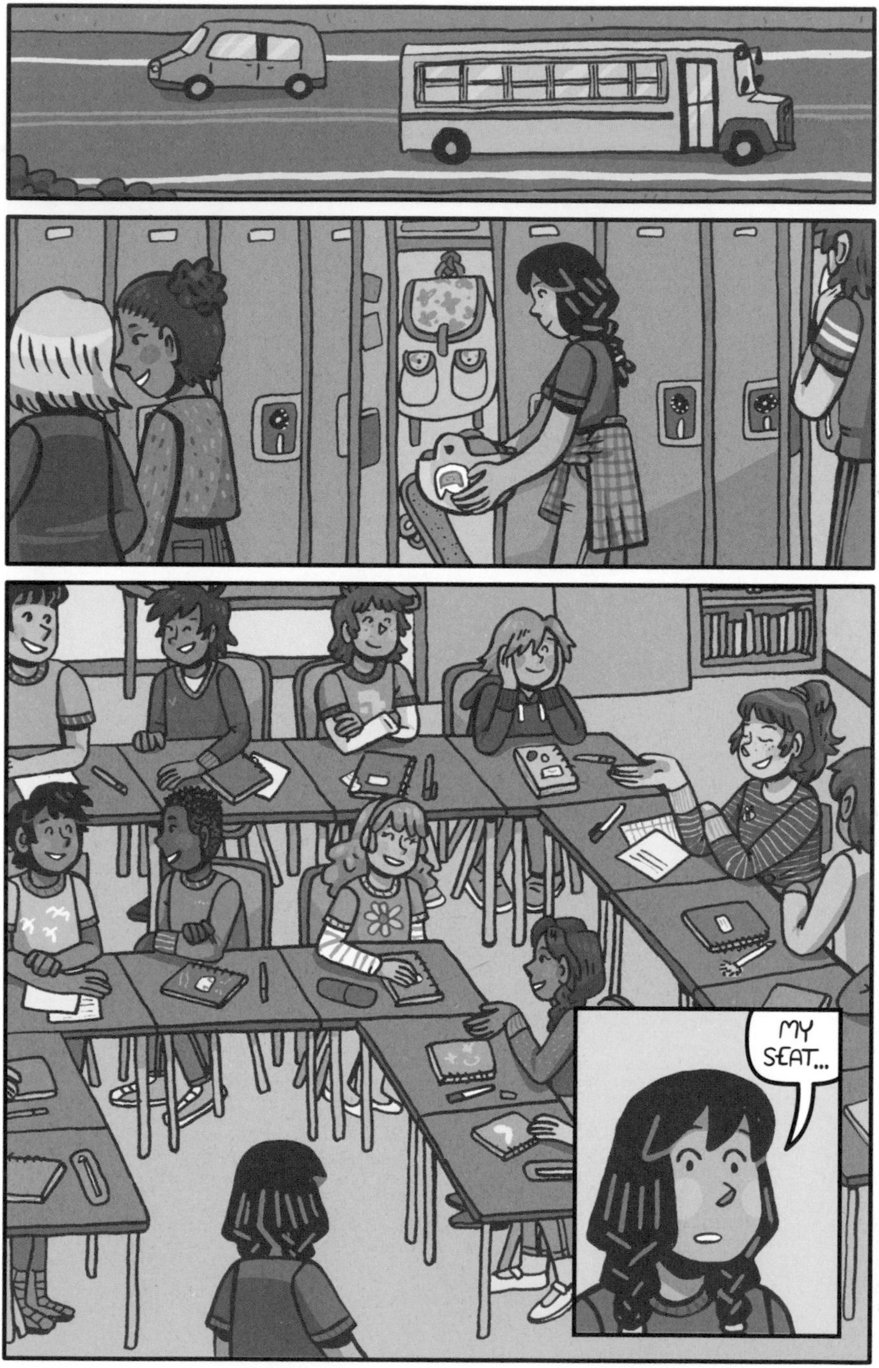
MY SEAT...

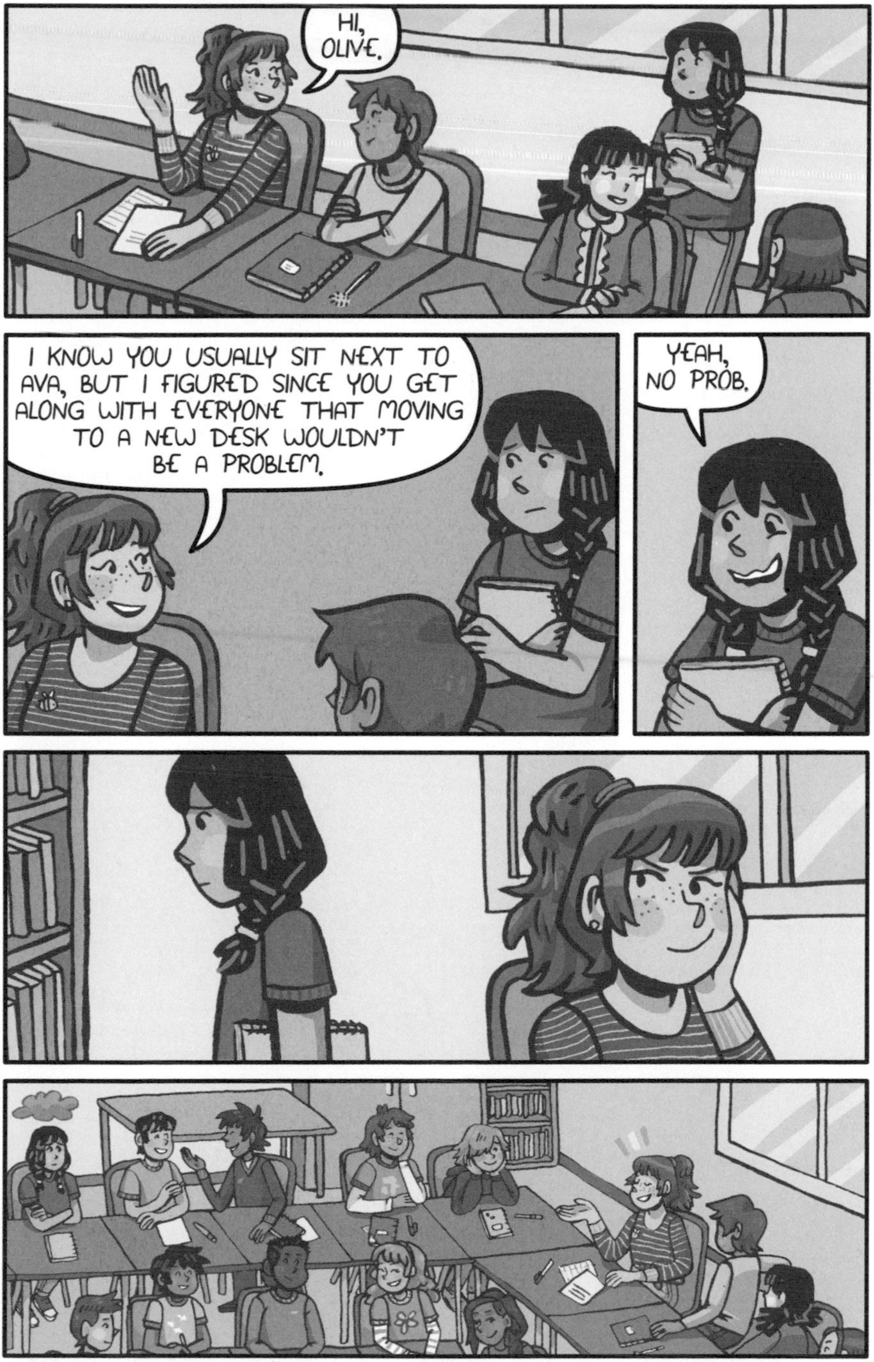
HI, OLIVE.
I KNOW YOU USUALLY SIT NEXT TO AVA, BUT I FIGURED SINCE YOU GET ALONG WITH EVERYONE THAT MOVING TO A NEW DESK WOULDN'T BE A PROBLEM.
YEAH, NO PROB.

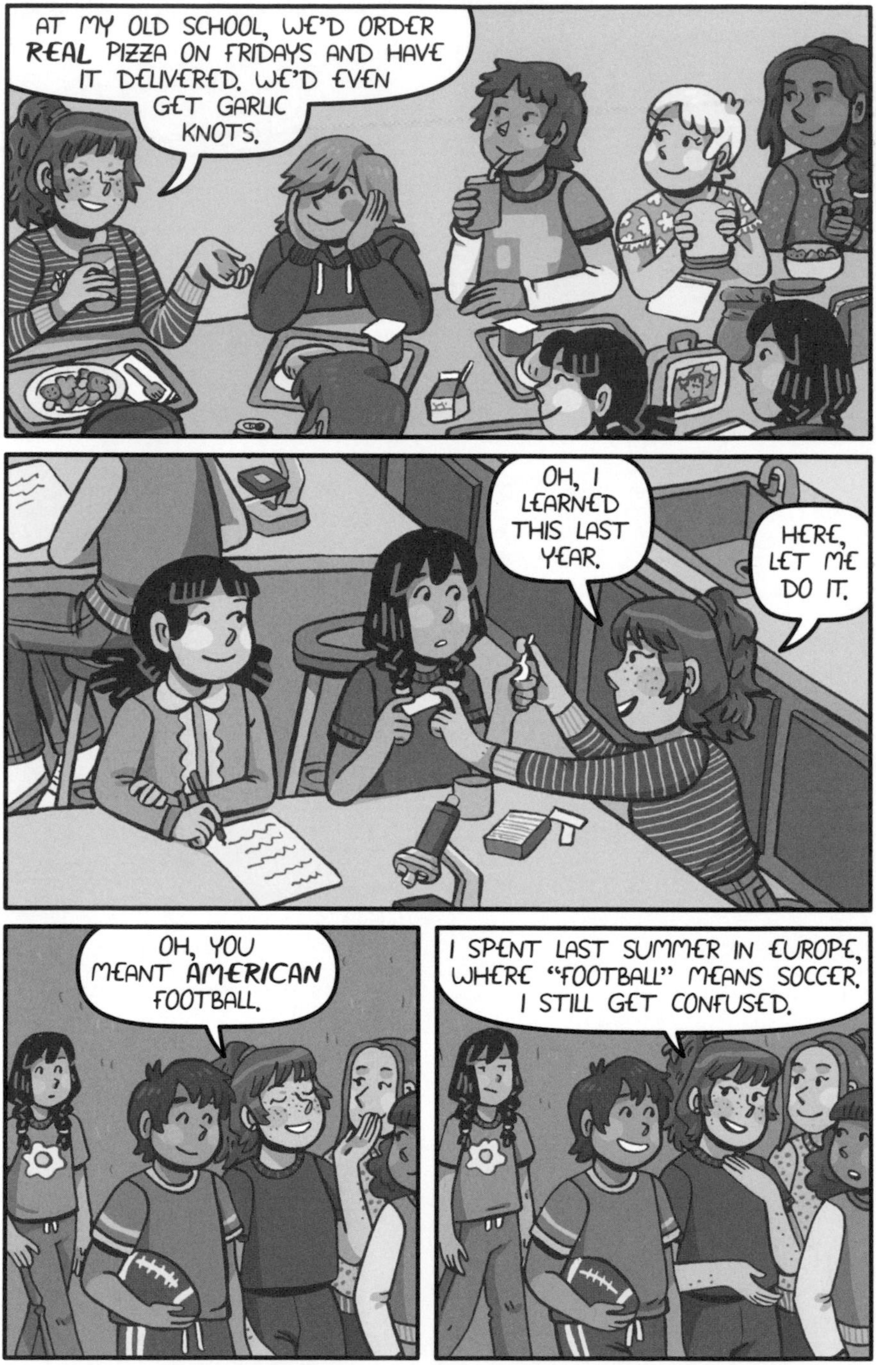
AT MY OLD SCHOOL, WE'D ORDER **REAL** PIZZA ON FRIDAYS AND HAVE IT DELIVERED. WE'D EVEN GET GARLIC KNOTS.
OH, I LEARNED THIS LAST YEAR.
HERE, LET ME DO IT.
OH, YOU MEANT **AMERICAN** FOOTBALL.
I SPENT LAST SUMMER IN EUROPE, WHERE "FOOTBALL" MEANS SOCCER. I STILL GET CONFUSED.

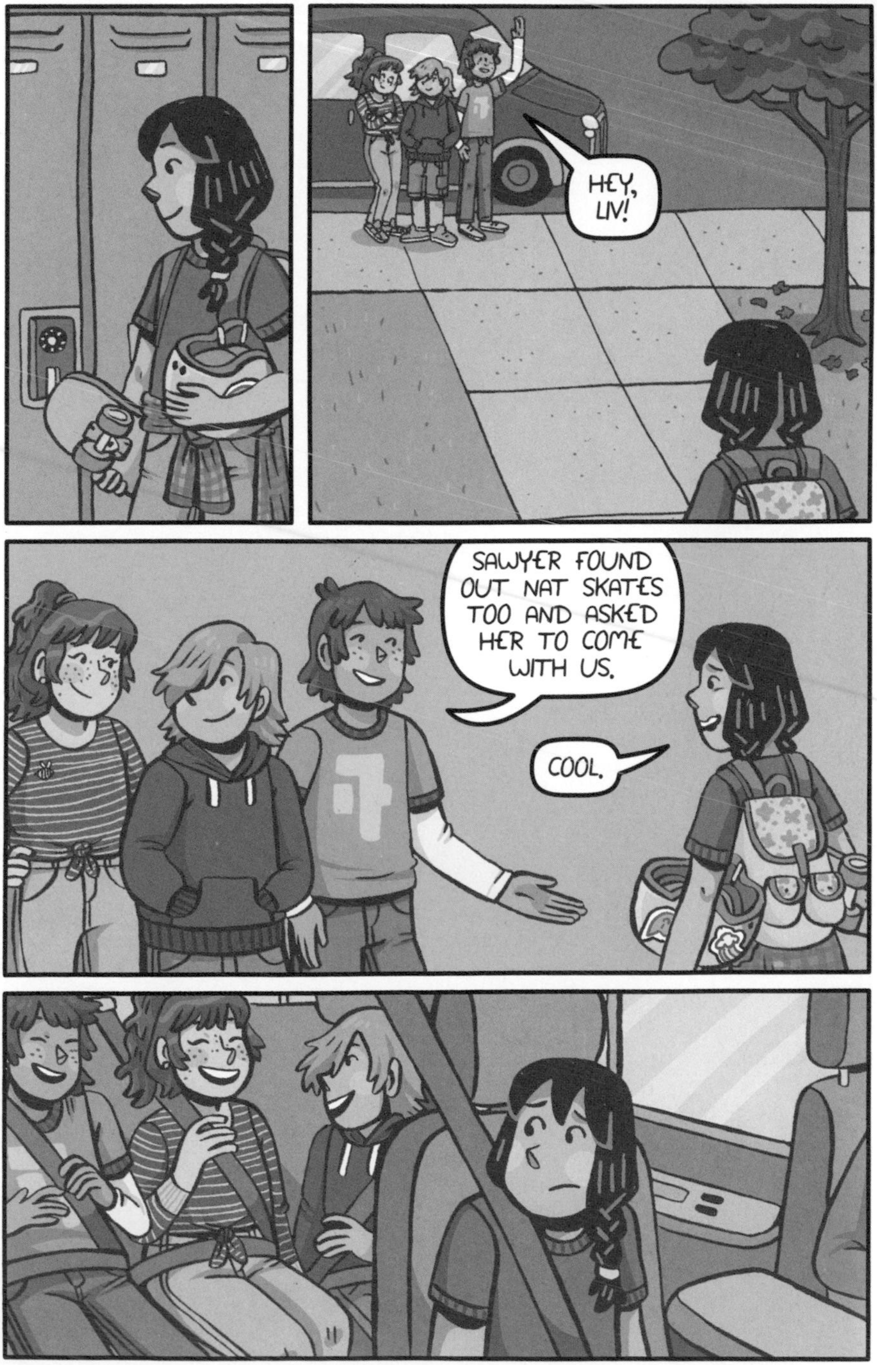
HEY, LIV!
SAWYER FOUND OUT NAT SKATES TOO AND ASKED HER TO COME WITH US.
COOL.

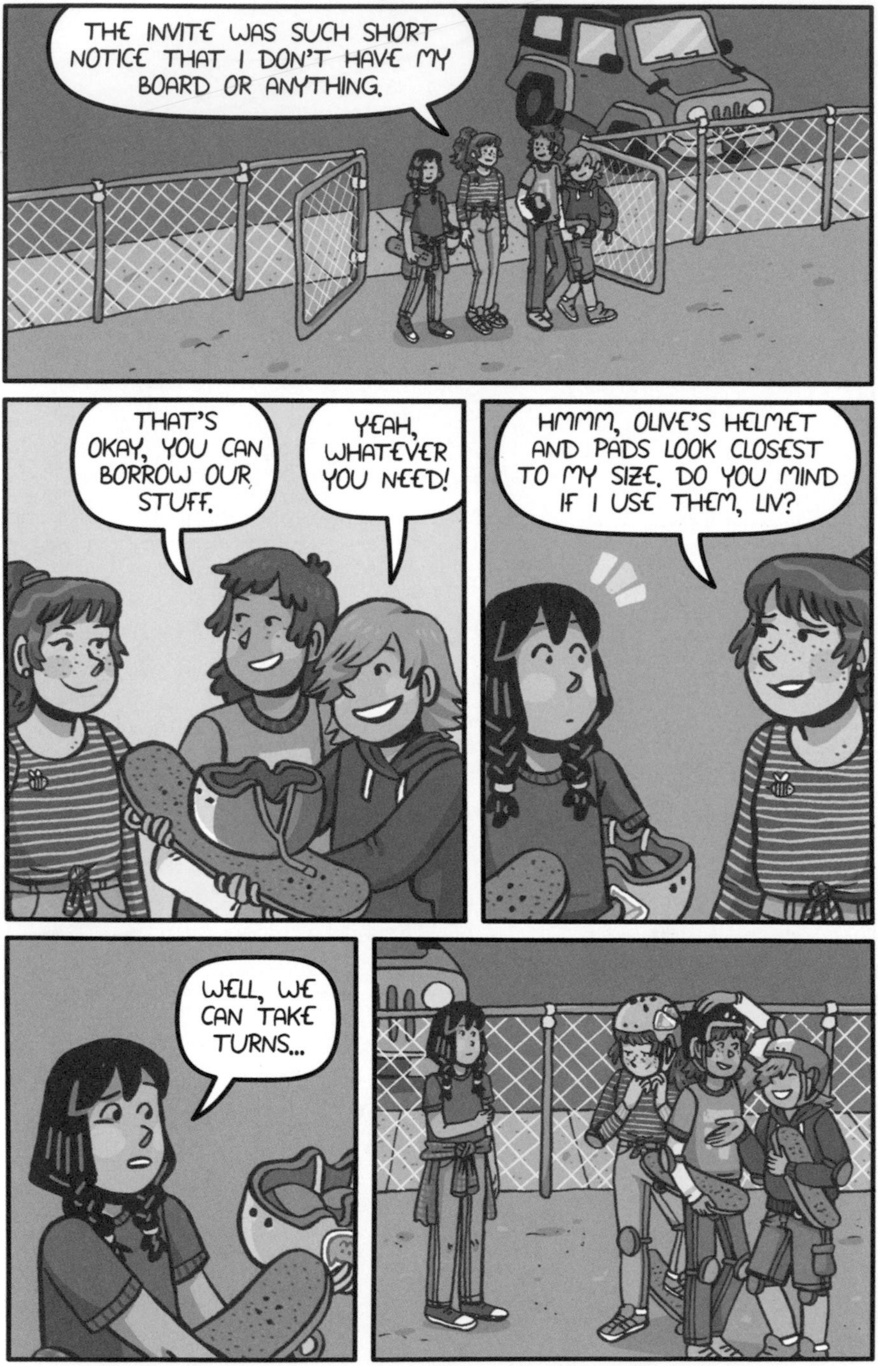
THE INVITE WAS SUCH SHORT NOTICE THAT I DON'T HAVE MY BOARD OR ANYTHING.
THAT'S OKAY, YOU CAN BORROW OUR STUFF.
YEAH, WHATEVER YOU NEED!
HMMM, OLIVE'S HELMET AND PADS LOOK CLOSEST TO MY SIZE. DO YOU MIND IF I USE THEM, LIV?
WELL, WE CAN TAKE TURNS...

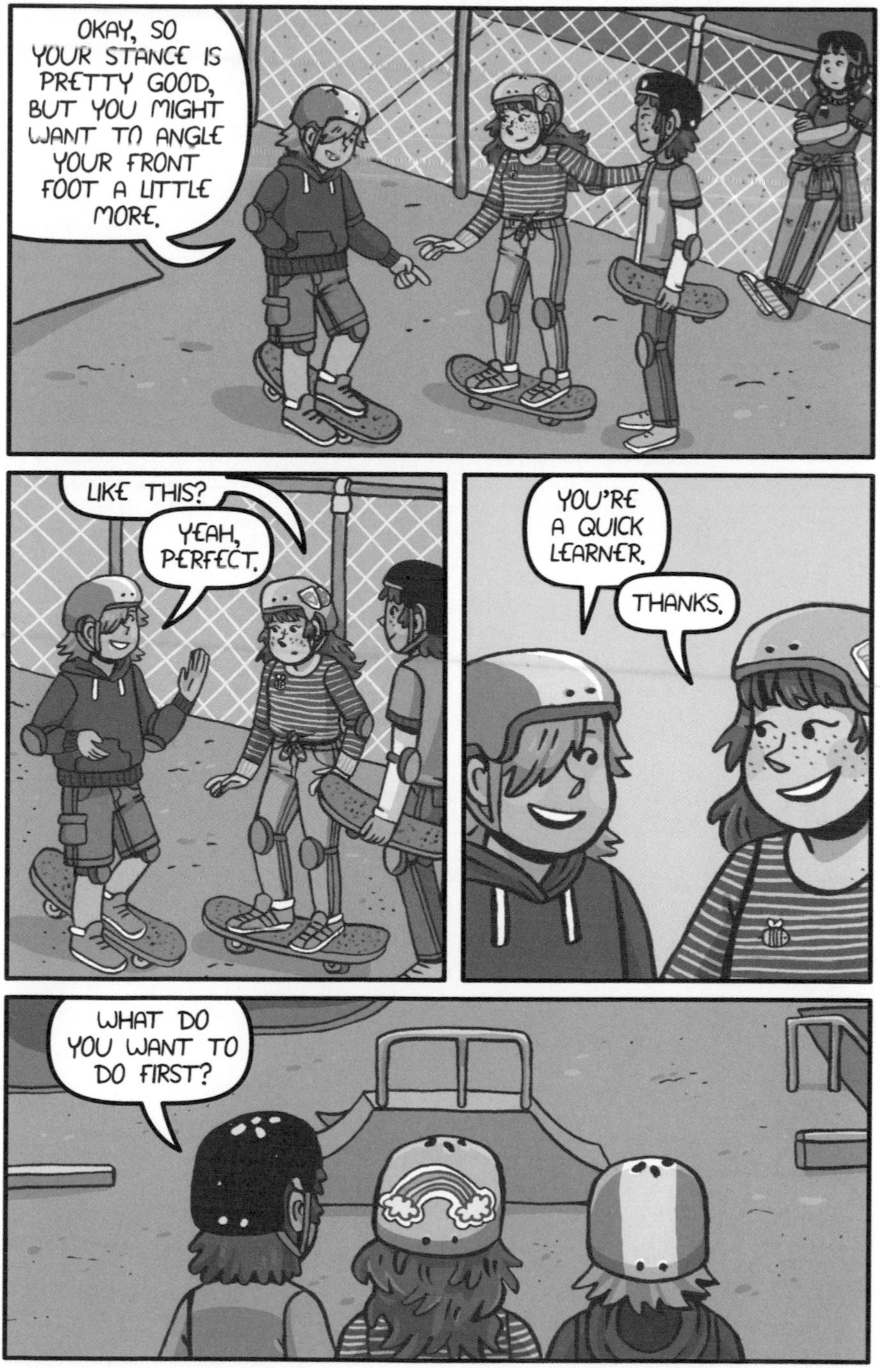
OKAY, SO YOUR STANCE IS PRETTY GOOD, BUT YOU MIGHT WANT TO ANGLE YOUR FRONT FOOT A LITTLE MORE.
LIKE THIS?
YEAH, PERFECT.
YOU'RE A QUICK LEARNER.
THANKS.
WHAT DO YOU WANT TO DO FIRST?

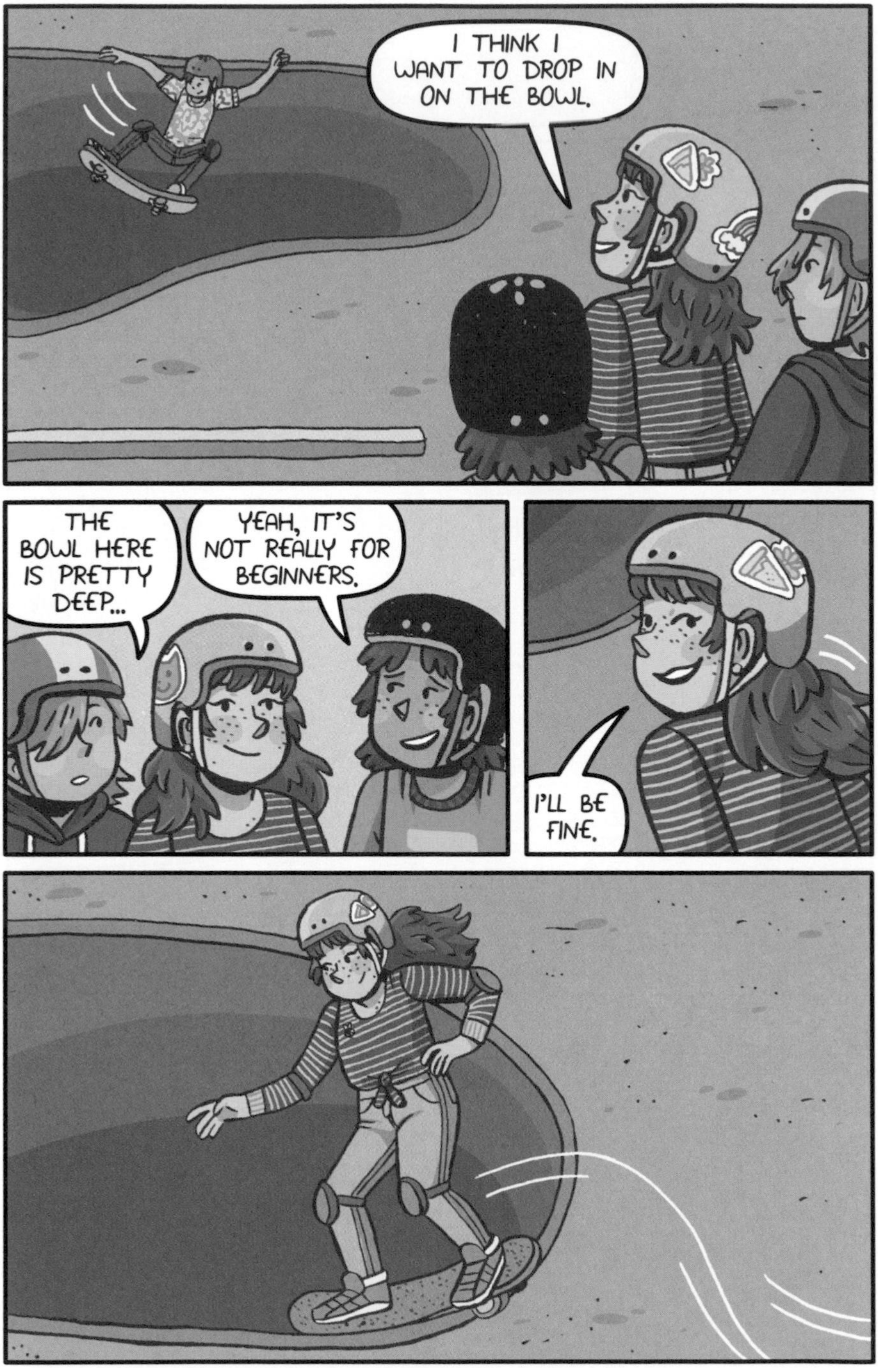
I THINK I WANT TO DROP IN ON THE BOWL.
THE BOWL HERE IS PRETTY DEEP...
YEAH, IT'S NOT REALLY FOR BEGINNERS.
I'LL BE FINE.

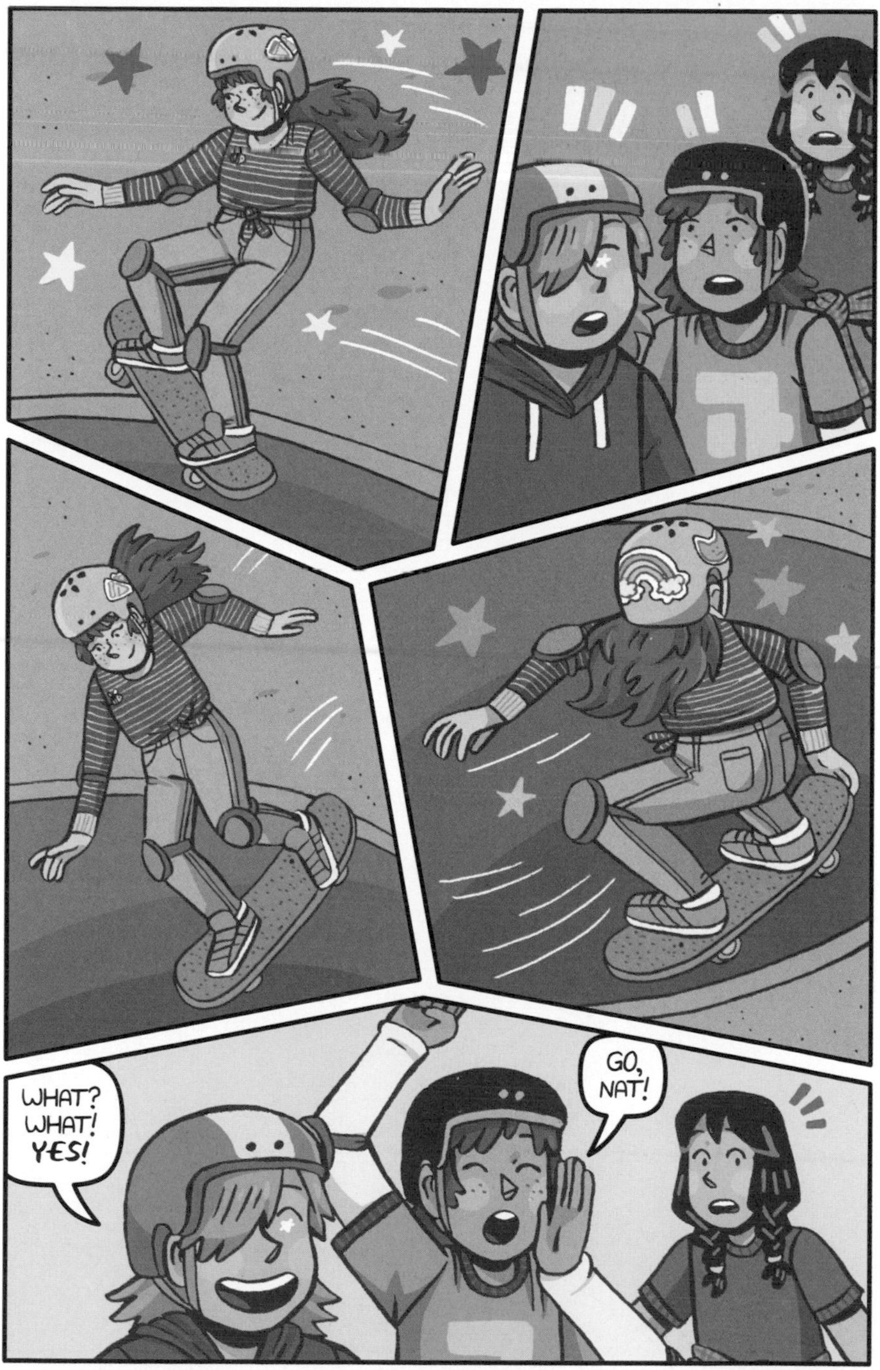
WHAT?
WHAT!
YES!
GO,
NAT!

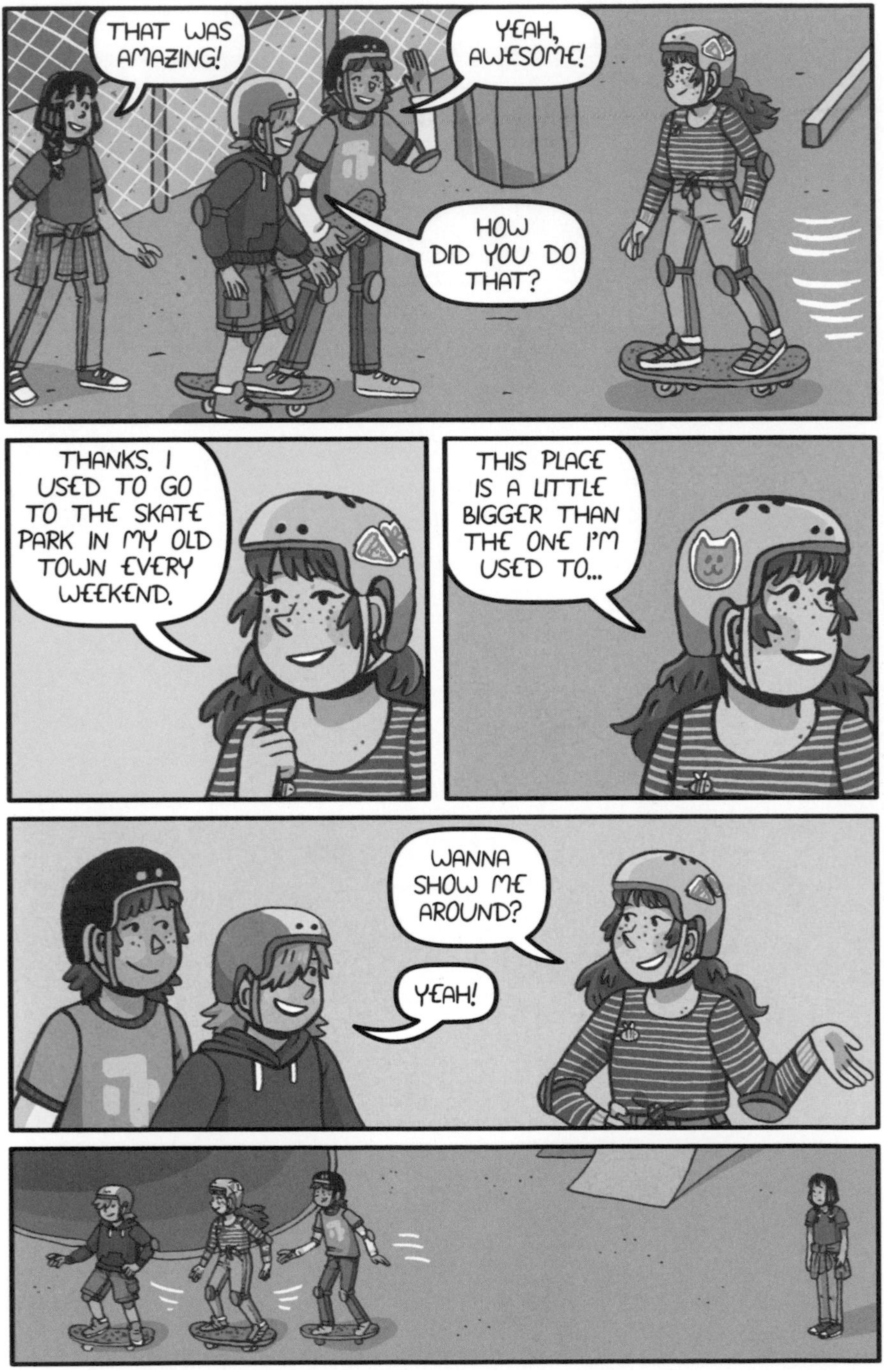
THAT WAS AMAZING!
YEAH, AWESOME!
HOW DID YOU DO THAT?
THANKS. I USED TO GO TO THE SKATE PARK IN MY OLD TOWN EVERY WEEKEND.
THIS PLACE IS A LITTLE BIGGER THAN THE ONE I'M USED TO...
WANNA SHOW ME AROUND?
YEAH!

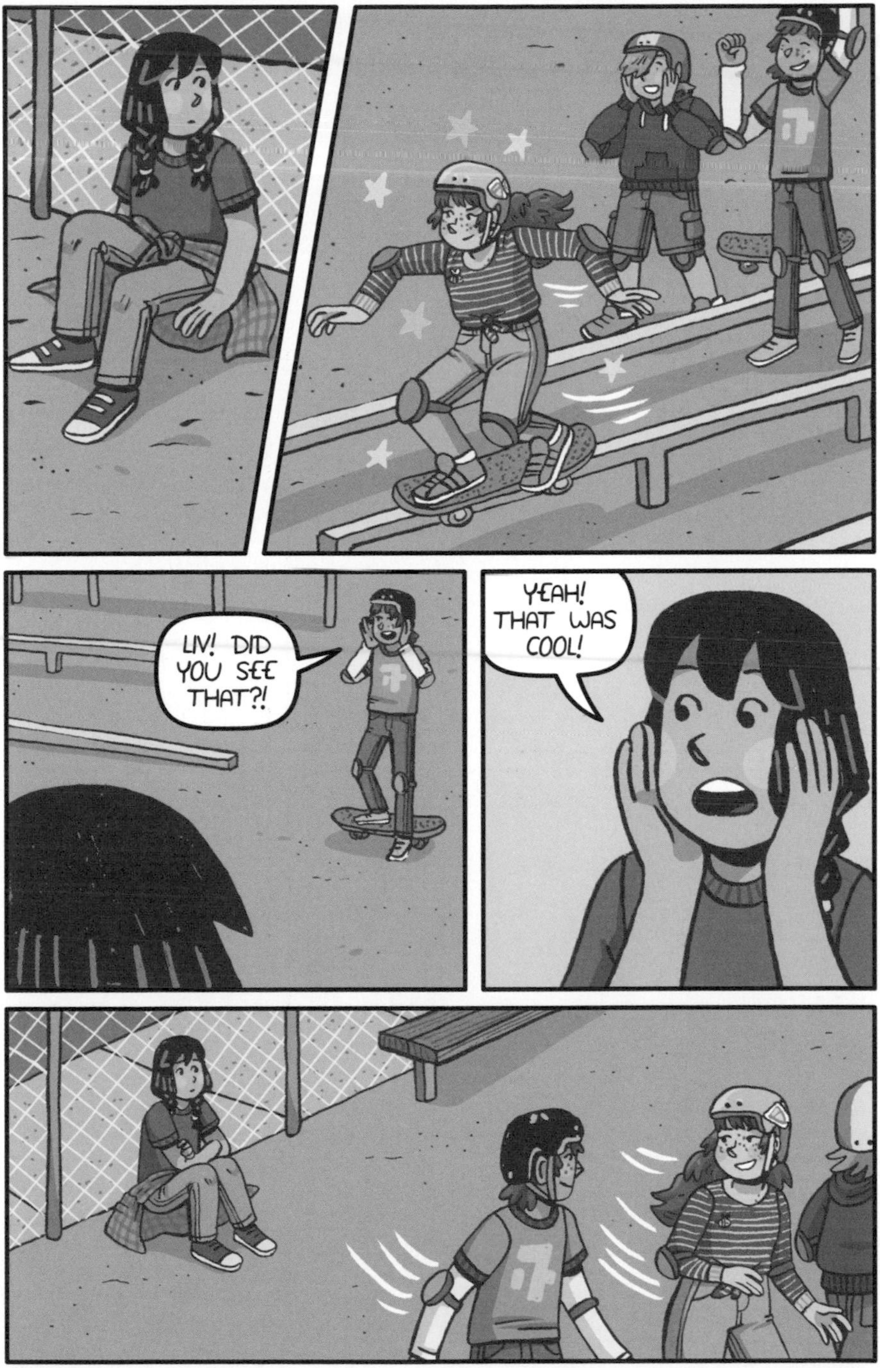
LIV! DID YOU SEE THAT?!
YEAH! THAT WAS COOL!

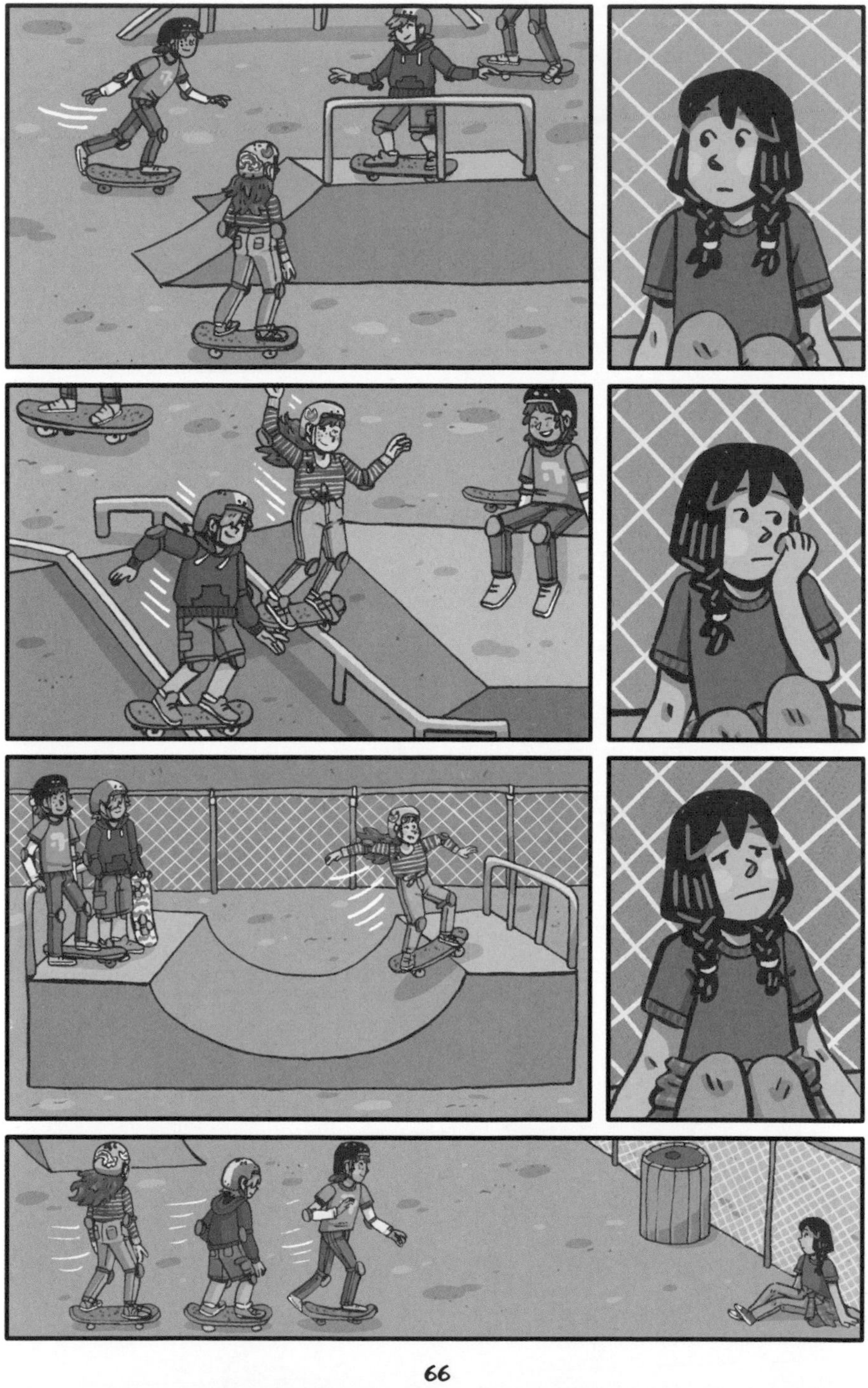

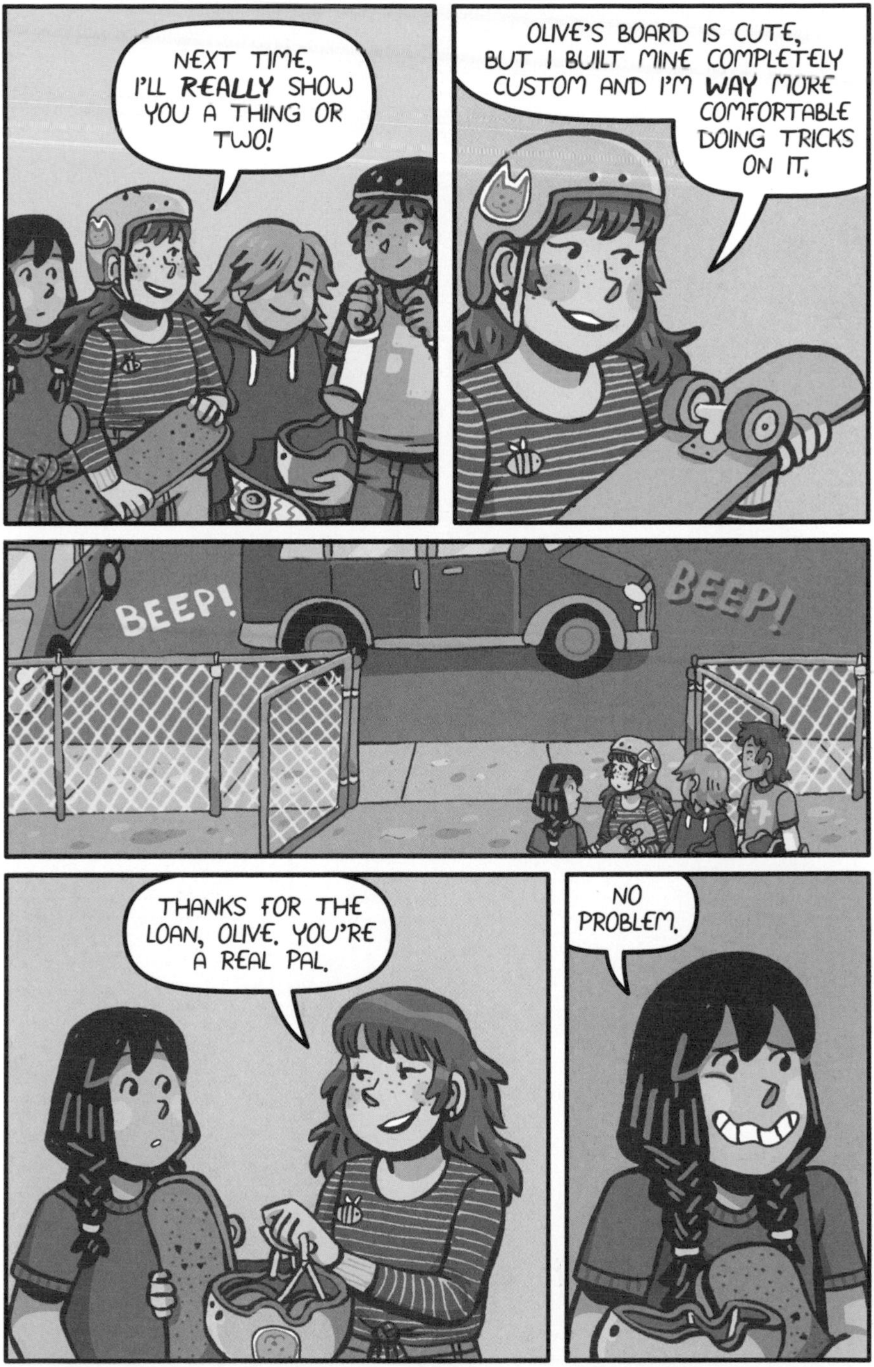
NEXT TIME, I'LL REALLY SHOW YOU A THING OR TWO!
OLIVE'S BOARD IS CUTE, BUT I BUILT MINE COMPLETELY CUSTOM AND I'M WAY MORE COMFORTABLE DOING TRICKS ON IT.
BEEP!
BEEP!
THANKS FOR THE LOAN, OLIVE. YOU'RE A REAL PAL.
NO PROBLEM.

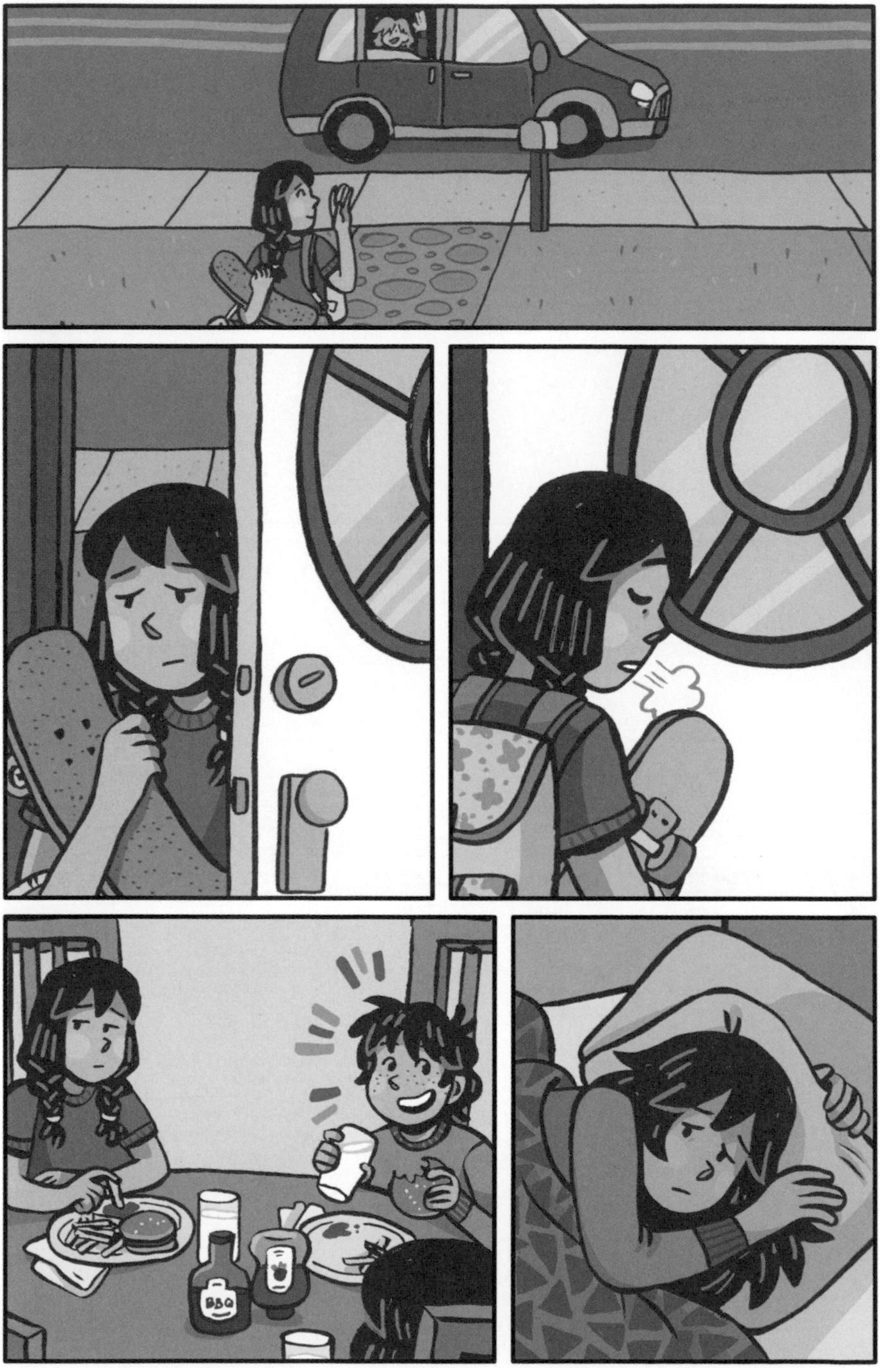
BBQ

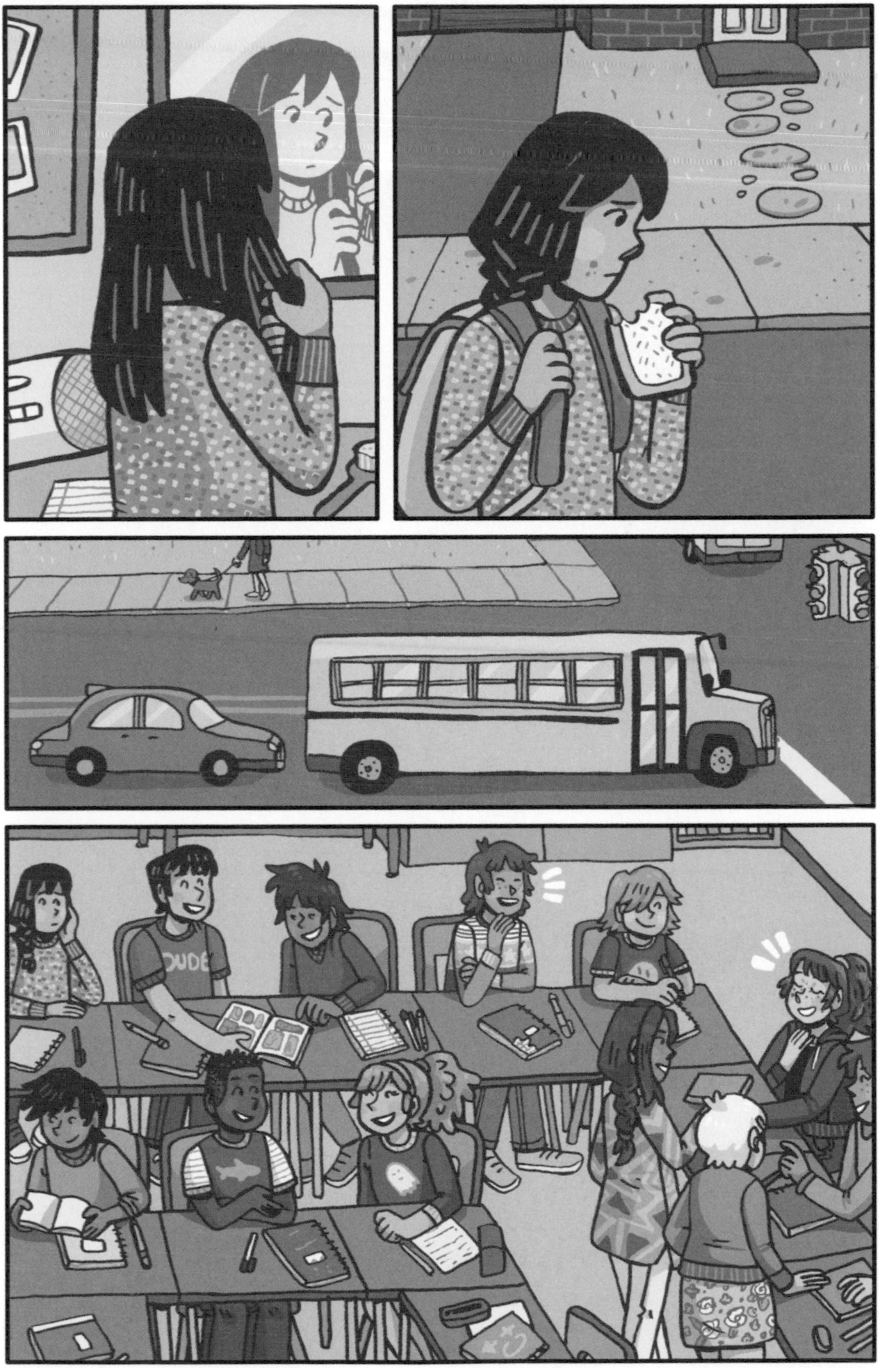
DUDE

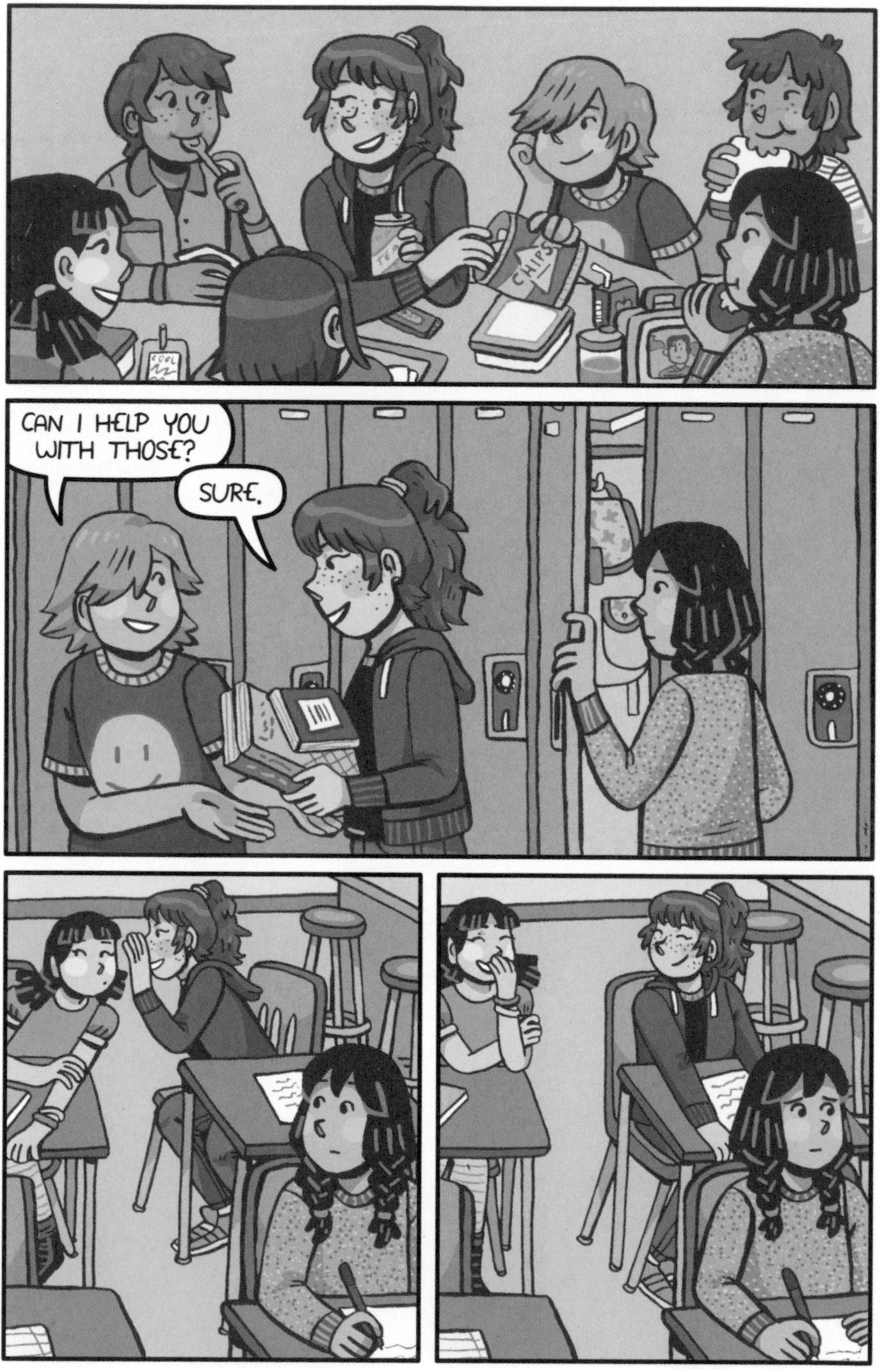
CHIPS
CAN I HELP YOU WITH THOSE?
SURE.

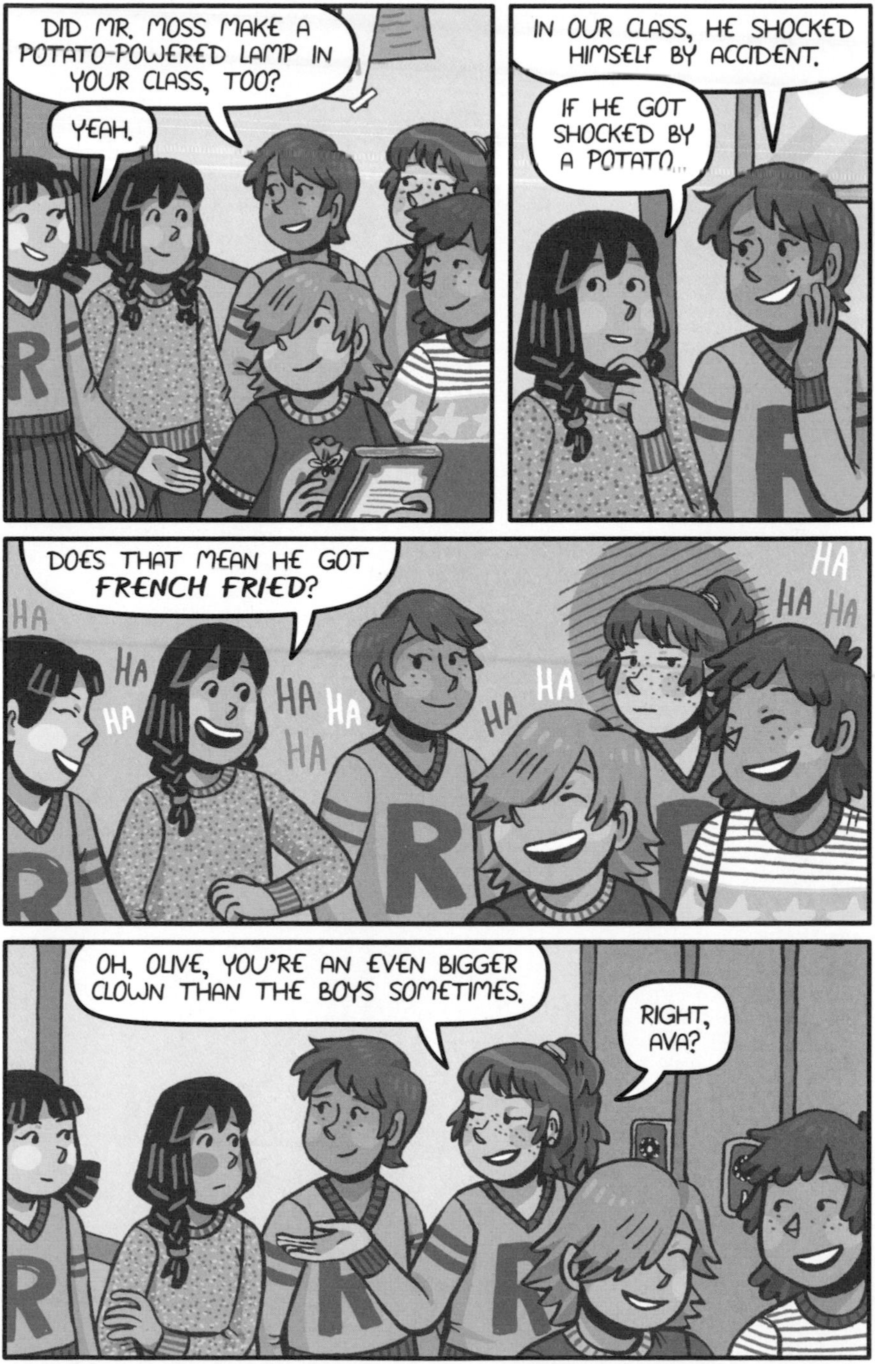
DID MR. MOSS MAKE A POTATO-POWERED LAMP IN YOUR CLASS, TOO?
YEAH.
IN OUR CLASS, HE SHOCKED HIMSELF BY ACCIDENT.
IF HE GOT SHOCKED BY A POTATO...
DOES THAT MEAN HE GOT **FRENCH FRIED**?
HA HA HA HA HA HA HA HA HA HA HA HA
OH, OLIVE, YOU'RE AN EVEN BIGGER CLOWN THAN THE BOYS SOMETIMES.
RIGHT, AVA?

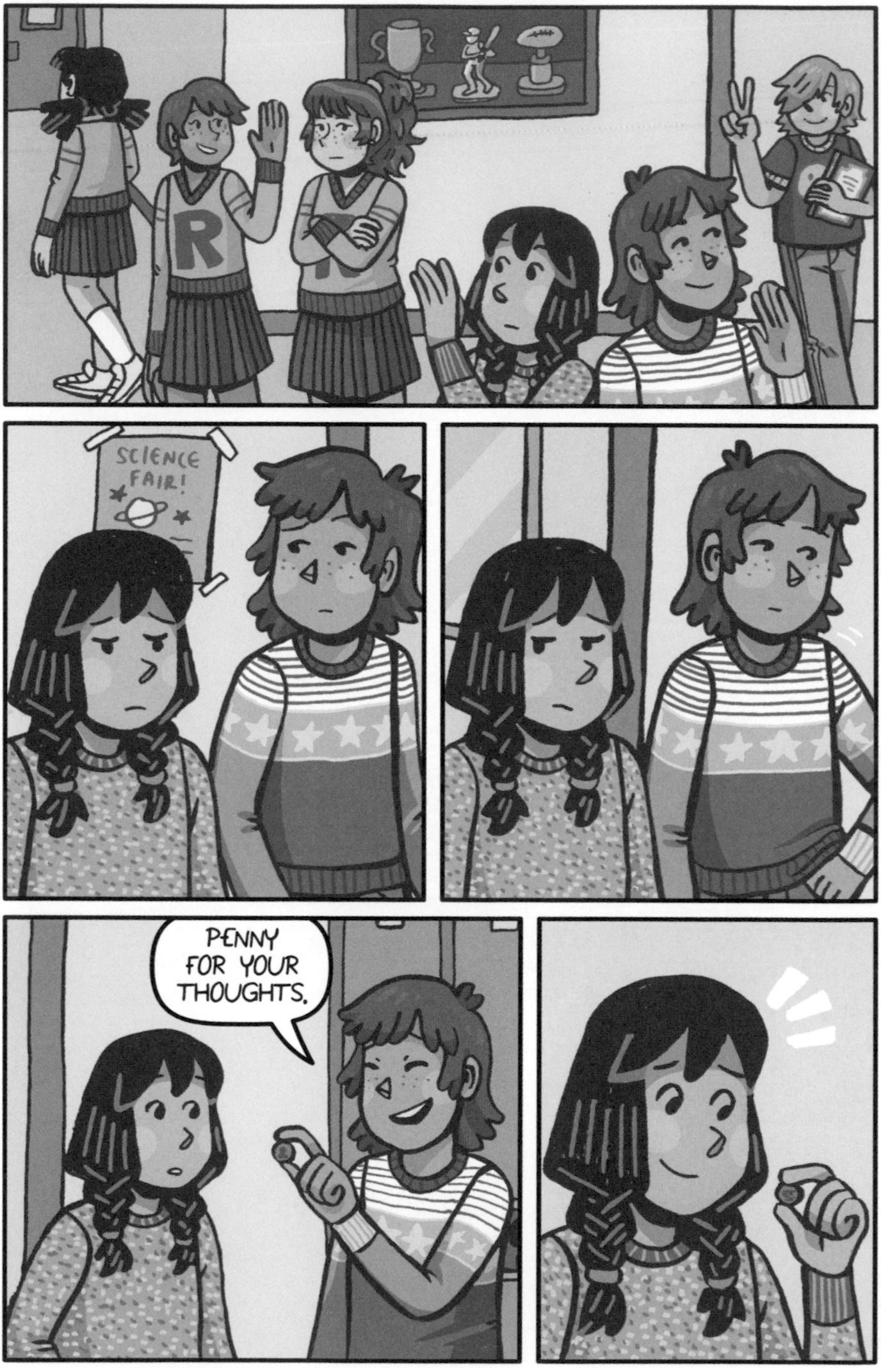
SCIENCE FAIR!
PENNY FOR YOUR THOUGHTS.

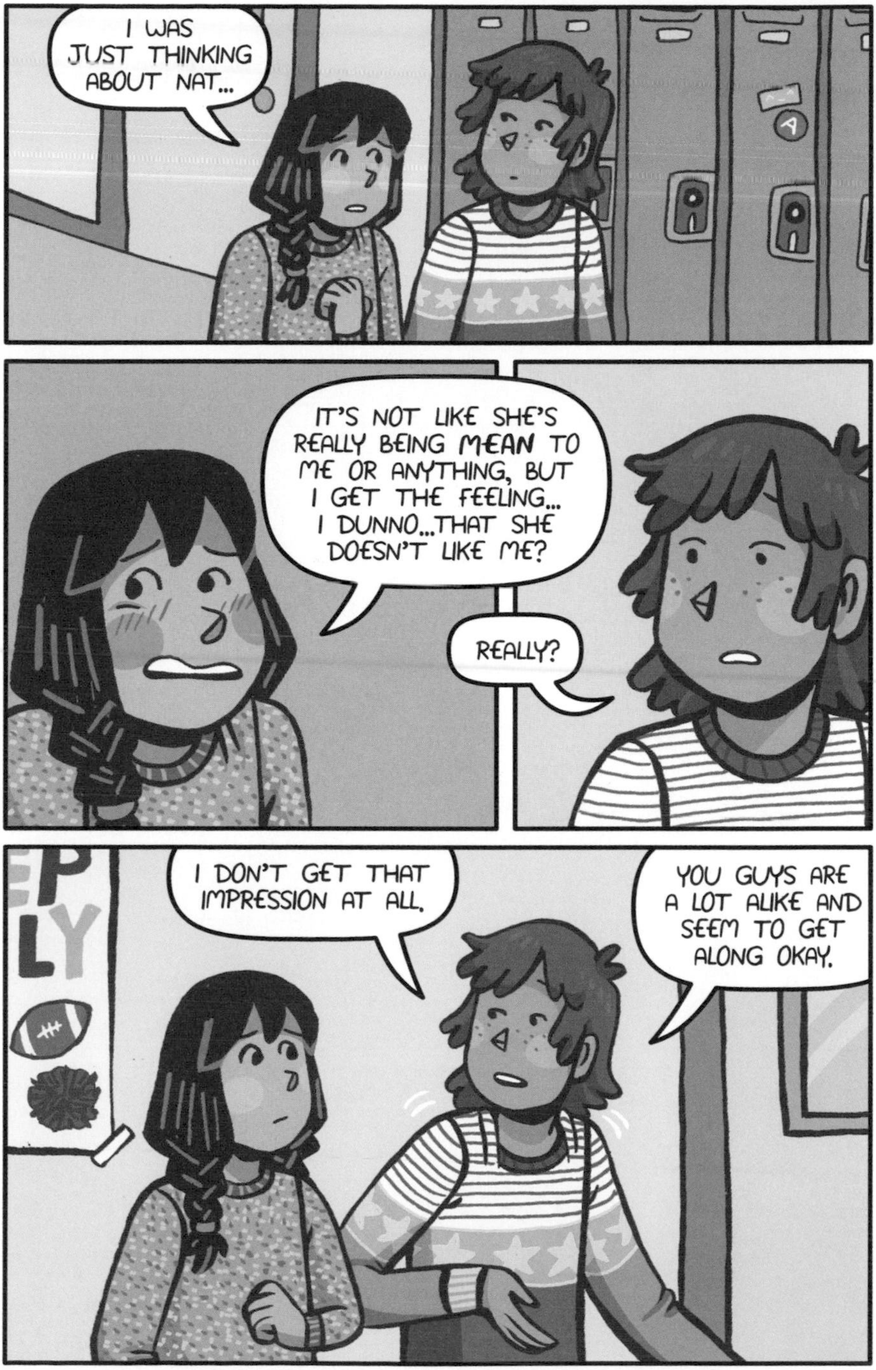

I WAS JUST THINKING ABOUT NAT...
IT'S NOT LIKE SHE'S REALLY BEING MEAN TO ME OR ANYTHING, BUT I GET THE FEELING... I DUNNO...THAT SHE DOESN'T LIKE ME?
REALLY?
I DON'T GET THAT IMPRESSION AT ALL.
YOU GUYS ARE A LOT ALIKE AND SEEM TO GET ALONG OKAY.

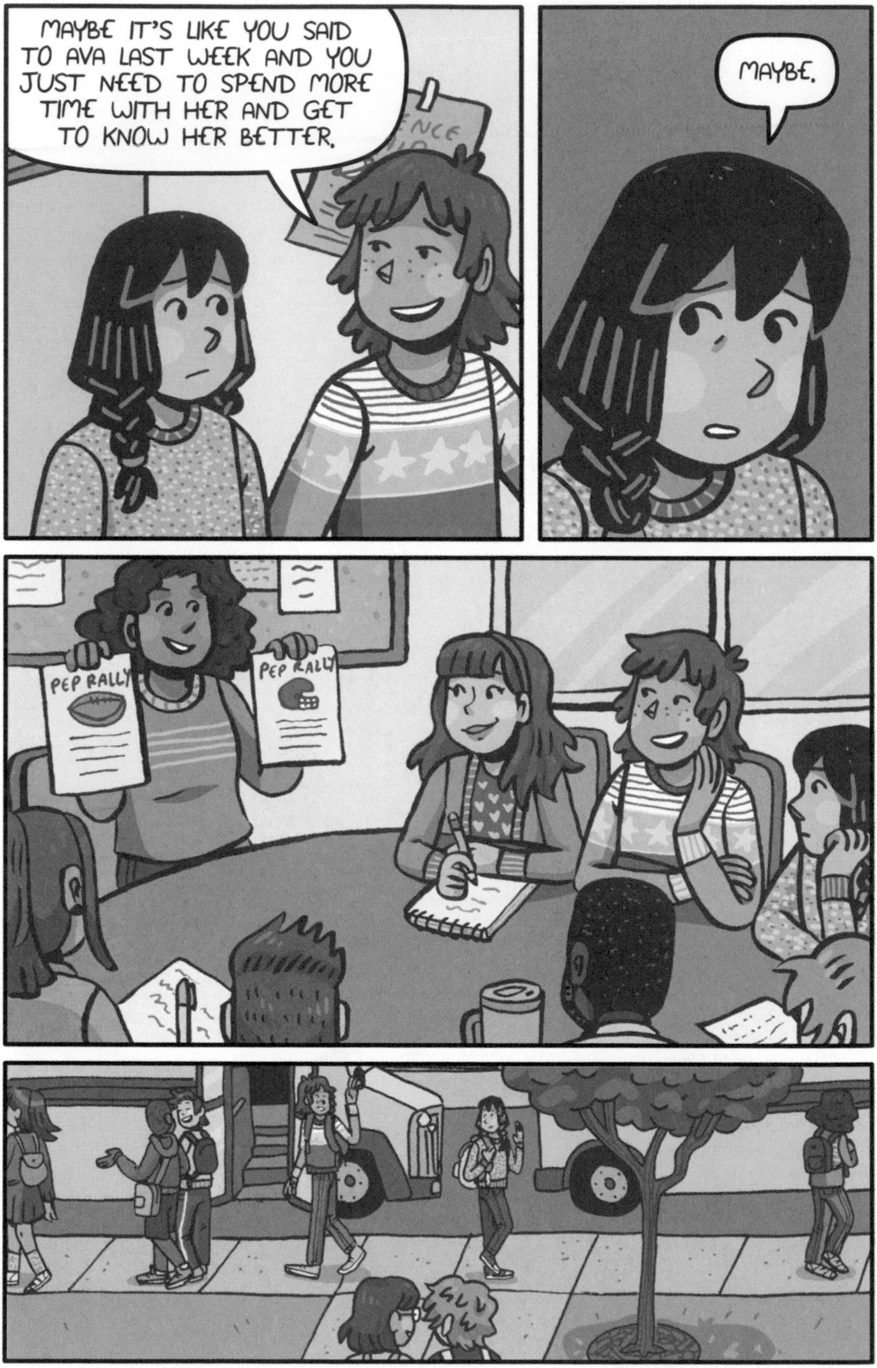
MAYBE IT'S LIKE YOU SAID TO AVA LAST WEEK AND YOU JUST NEED TO SPEND MORE TIME WITH HER AND GET TO KNOW HER BETTER.
MAYBE.
PEP RALLY
PEP RALLY

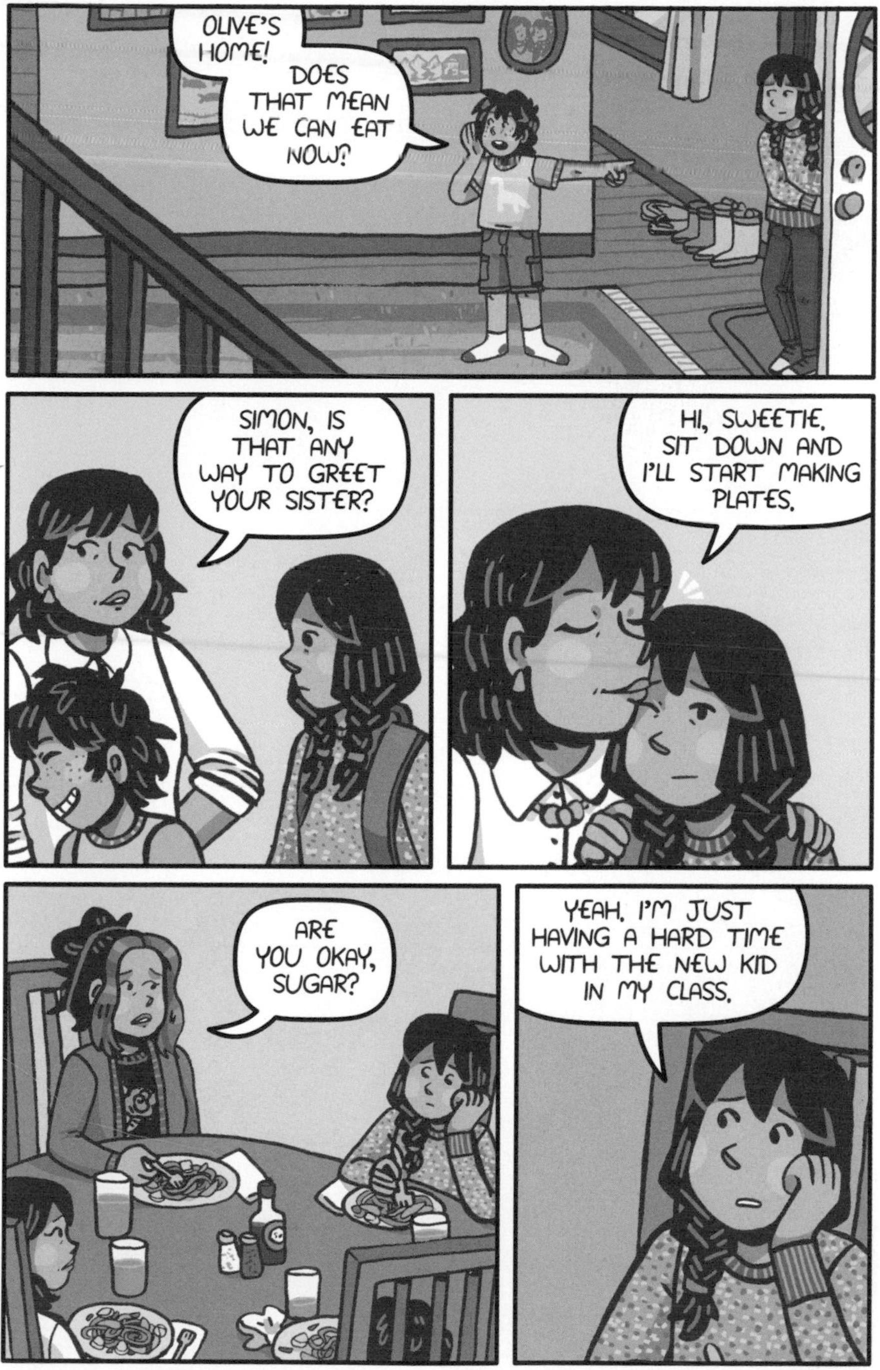
OLIVE'S HOME!
DOES THAT MEAN WE CAN EAT NOW?
SIMON, IS THAT ANY WAY TO GREET YOUR SISTER?
HI, SWEETIE. SIT DOWN AND I'LL START MAKING PLATES.
ARE YOU OKAY, SUGAR?
YEAH, I'M JUST HAVING A HARD TIME WITH THE NEW KID IN MY CLASS.

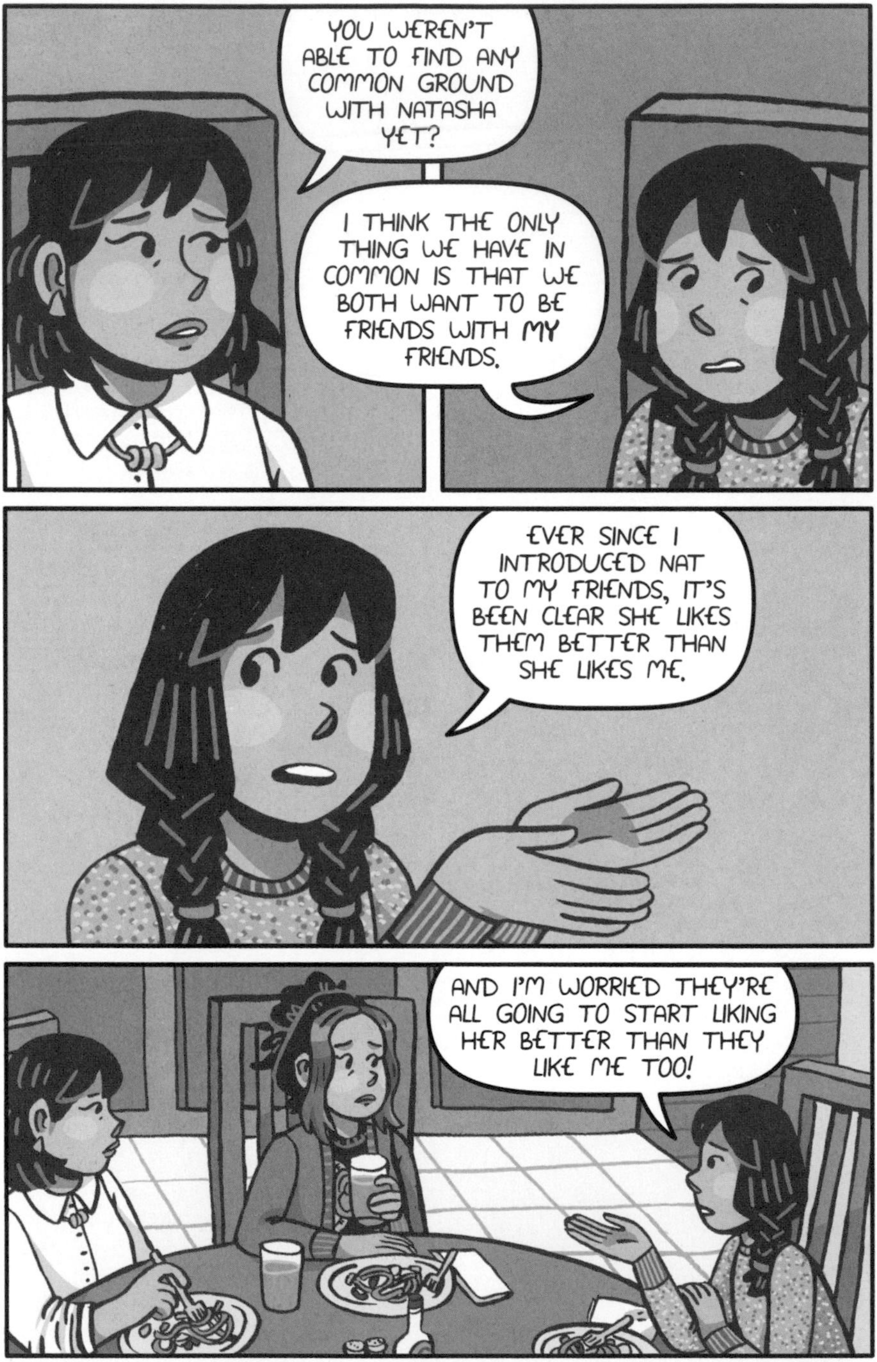
YOU WEREN'T ABLE TO FIND ANY COMMON GROUND WITH NATASHA YET?
I THINK THE ONLY THING WE HAVE IN COMMON IS THAT WE BOTH WANT TO BE FRIENDS WITH MY FRIENDS.
EVER SINCE I INTRODUCED NAT TO MY FRIENDS, IT'S BEEN CLEAR SHE LIKES THEM BETTER THAN SHE LIKES ME.
AND I'M WORRIED THEY'RE ALL GOING TO START LIKING HER BETTER THAN THEY LIKE ME TOO!

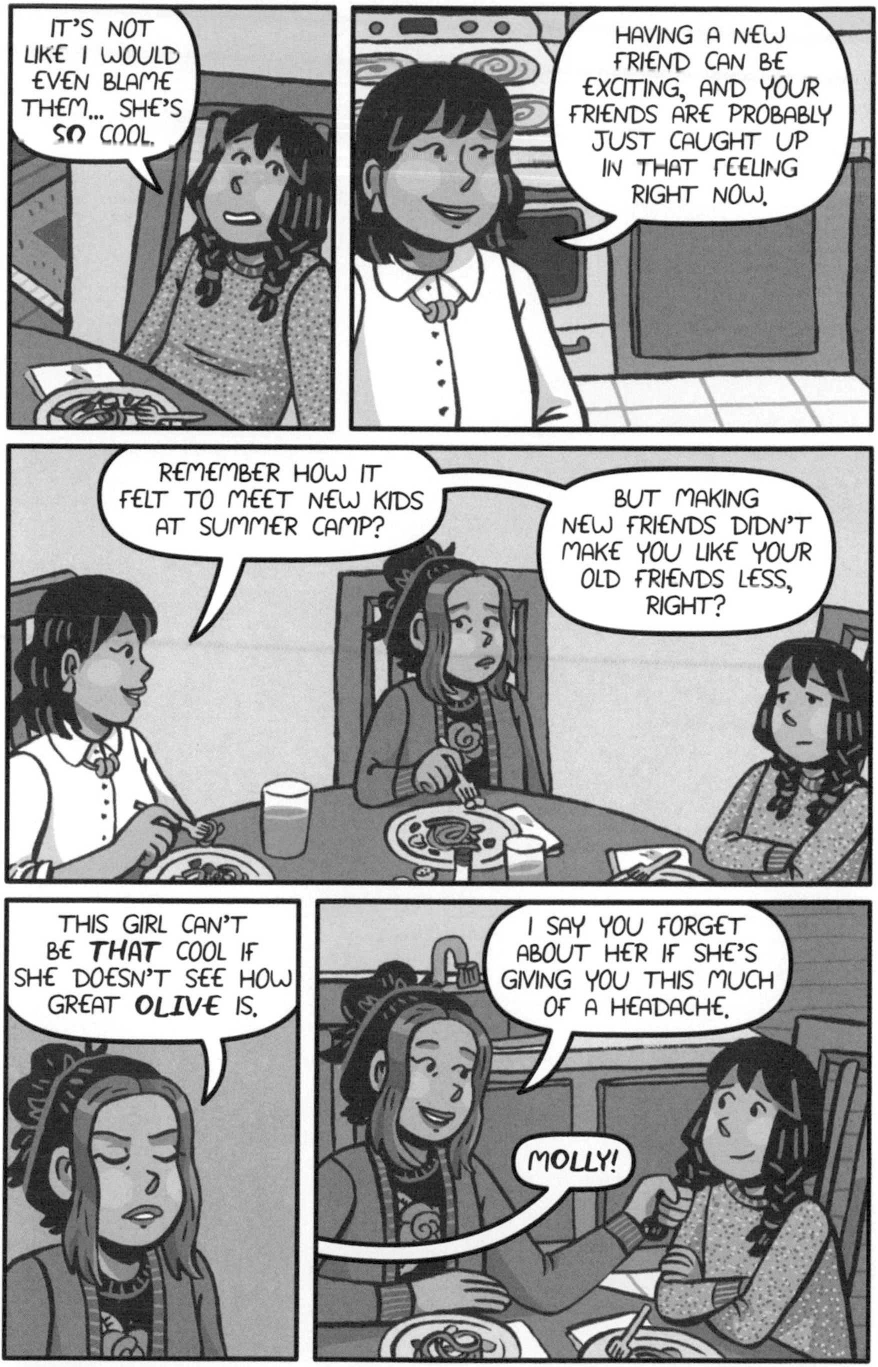
IT'S NOT LIKE I WOULD EVEN BLAME THEM... SHE'S **SO** COOL.
HAVING A NEW FRIEND CAN BE EXCITING, AND YOUR FRIENDS ARE PROBABLY JUST CAUGHT UP IN THAT FEELING RIGHT NOW.
REMEMBER HOW IT FELT TO MEET NEW KIDS AT SUMMER CAMP?
BUT MAKING NEW FRIENDS DIDN'T MAKE YOU LIKE YOUR OLD FRIENDS LESS, RIGHT?
THIS GIRL CAN'T BE **THAT** COOL IF SHE DOESN'T SEE HOW GREAT **OLIVE** IS.
I SAY YOU FORGET ABOUT HER IF SHE'S GIVING YOU THIS MUCH OF A HEADACHE.
MOLLY!

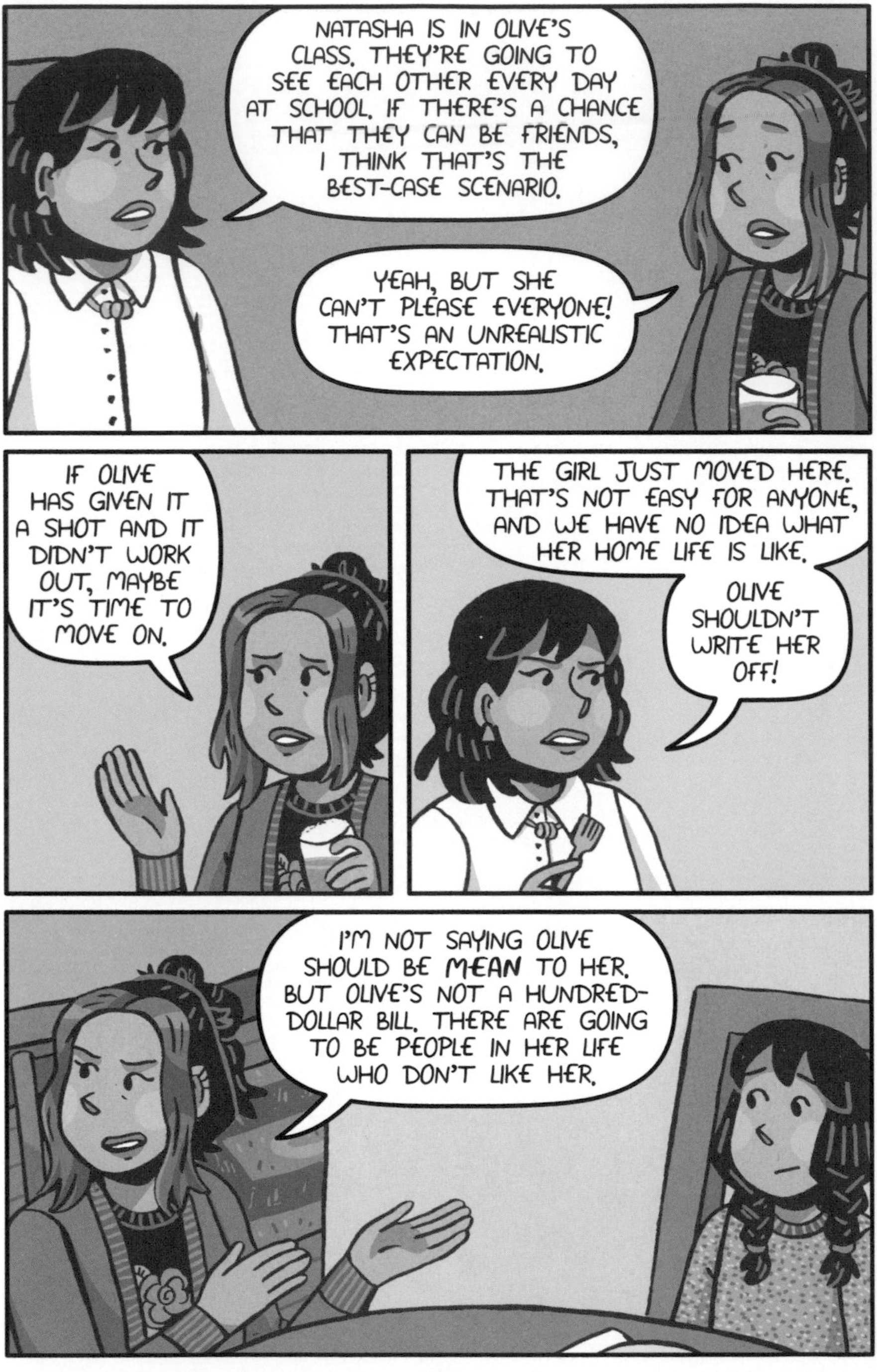
NATASHA IS IN OLIVE'S CLASS. THEY'RE GOING TO SEE EACH OTHER EVERY DAY AT SCHOOL. IF THERE'S A CHANCE THAT THEY CAN BE FRIENDS, I THINK THAT'S THE BEST-CASE SCENARIO.
YEAH, BUT SHE CAN'T PLEASE EVERYONE! THAT'S AN UNREALISTIC EXPECTATION.
IF OLIVE HAS GIVEN IT A SHOT AND IT DIDN'T WORK OUT, MAYBE IT'S TIME TO MOVE ON.
THE GIRL JUST MOVED HERE. THAT'S NOT EASY FOR ANYONE, AND WE HAVE NO IDEA WHAT HER HOME LIFE IS LIKE.
OLIVE SHOULDN'T WRITE HER OFF!
I'M NOT SAYING OLIVE SHOULD BE MEAN TO HER. BUT OLIVE'S NOT A HUNDRED-DOLLAR BILL. THERE ARE GOING TO BE PEOPLE IN HER LIFE WHO DON'T LIKE HER.

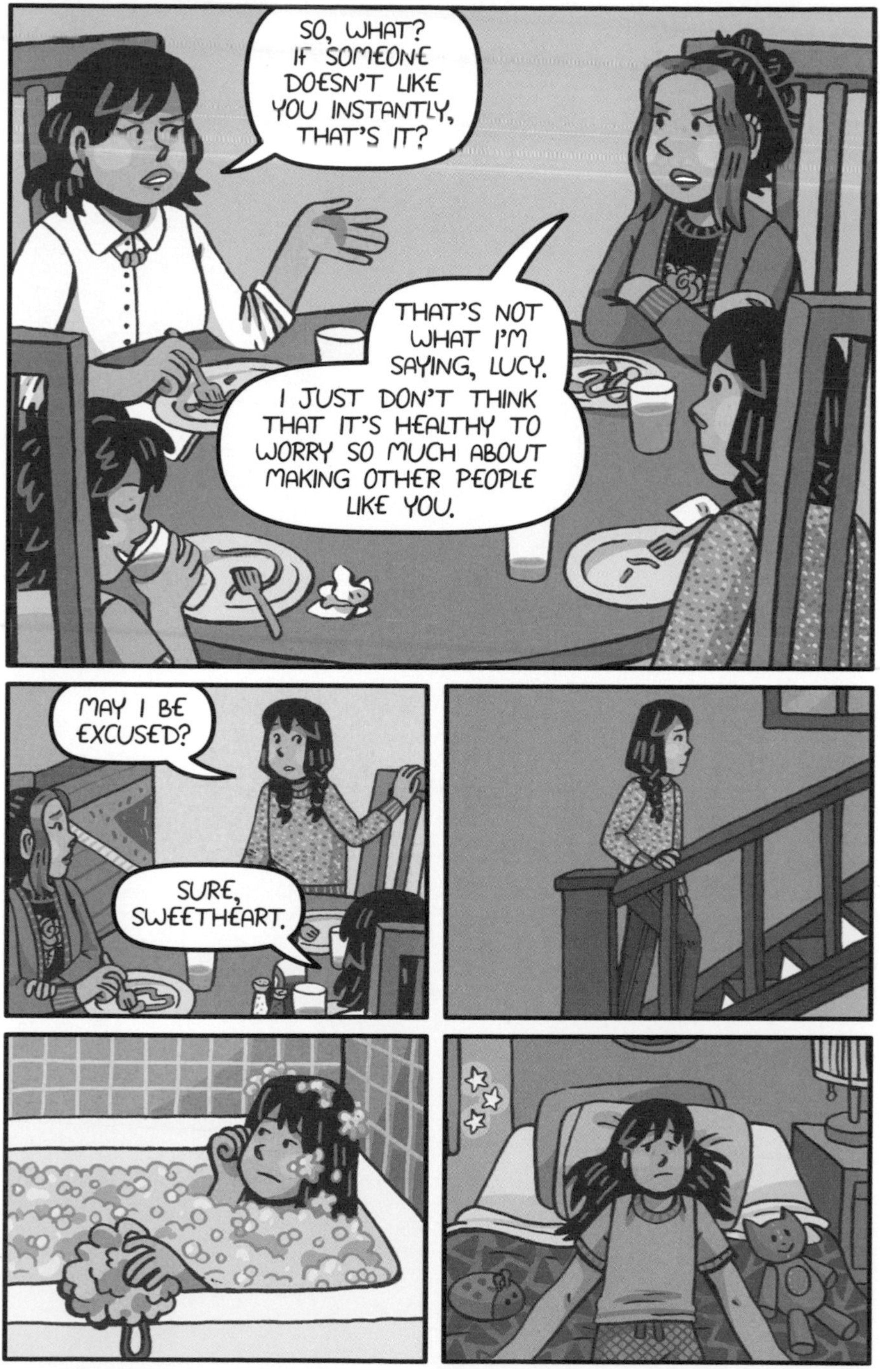
SO, WHAT? IF SOMEONE DOESN'T LIKE YOU INSTANTLY, THAT'S IT?
THAT'S NOT WHAT I'M SAYING, LUCY. I JUST DON'T THINK THAT IT'S HEALTHY TO WORRY SO MUCH ABOUT MAKING OTHER PEOPLE LIKE YOU.
MAY I BE EXCUSED?
SURE, SWEETHEART.

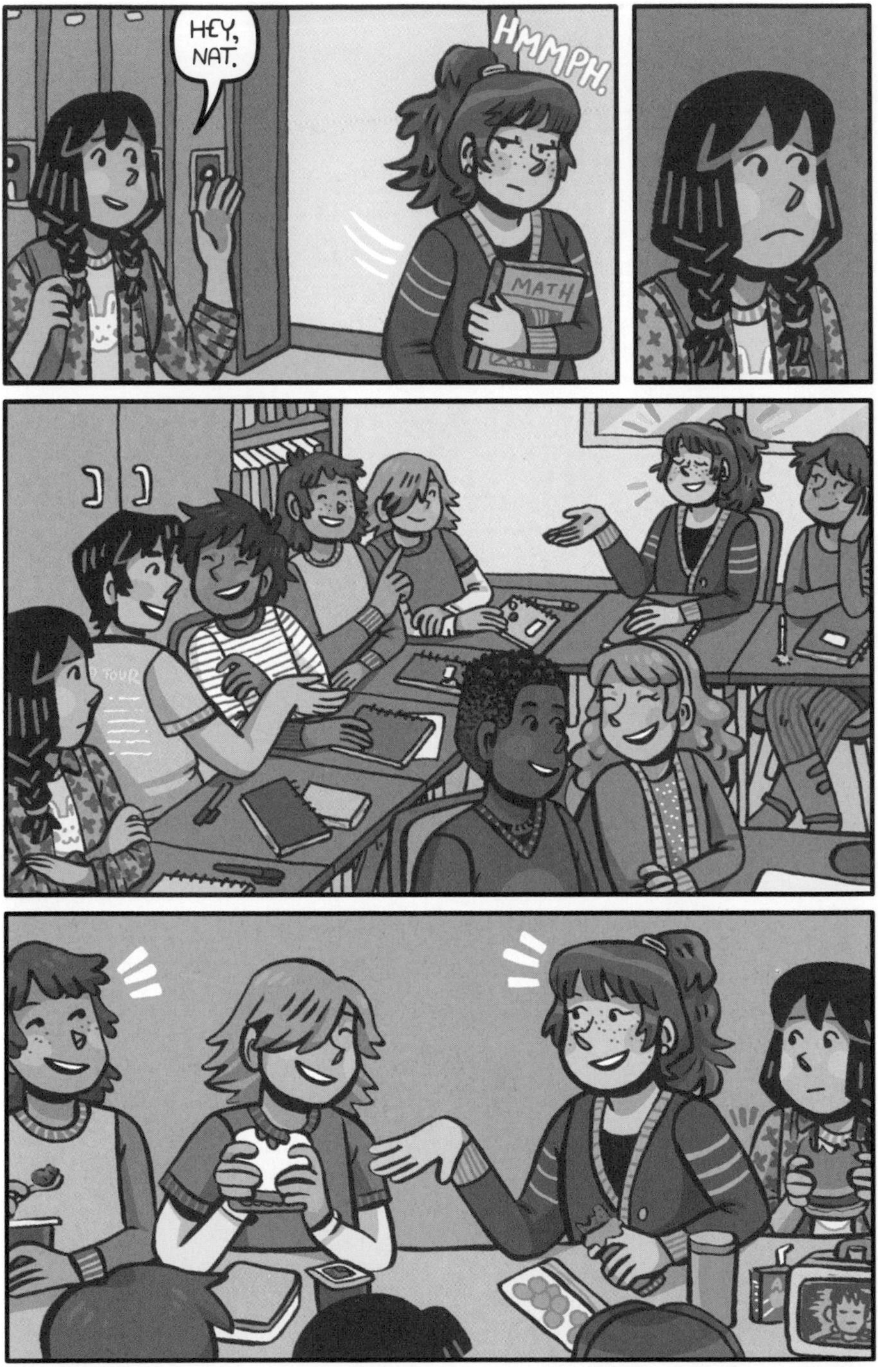
HEY, NAT.
HMMMPH.
MATH
TOUR

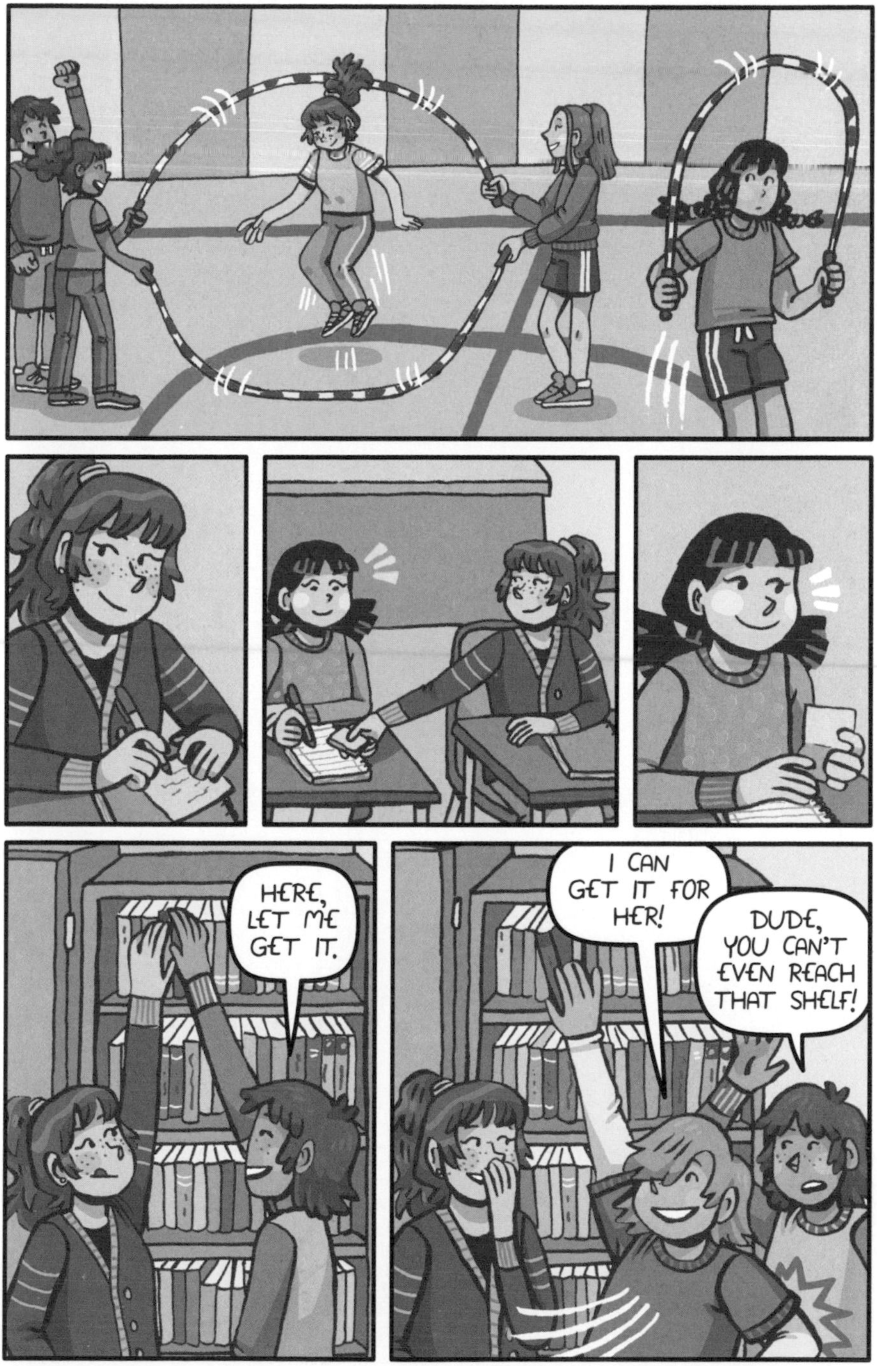
HERE, LET ME GET IT.
I CAN GET IT FOR HER!
DUDE, YOU CAN'T EVEN REACH THAT SHELF!

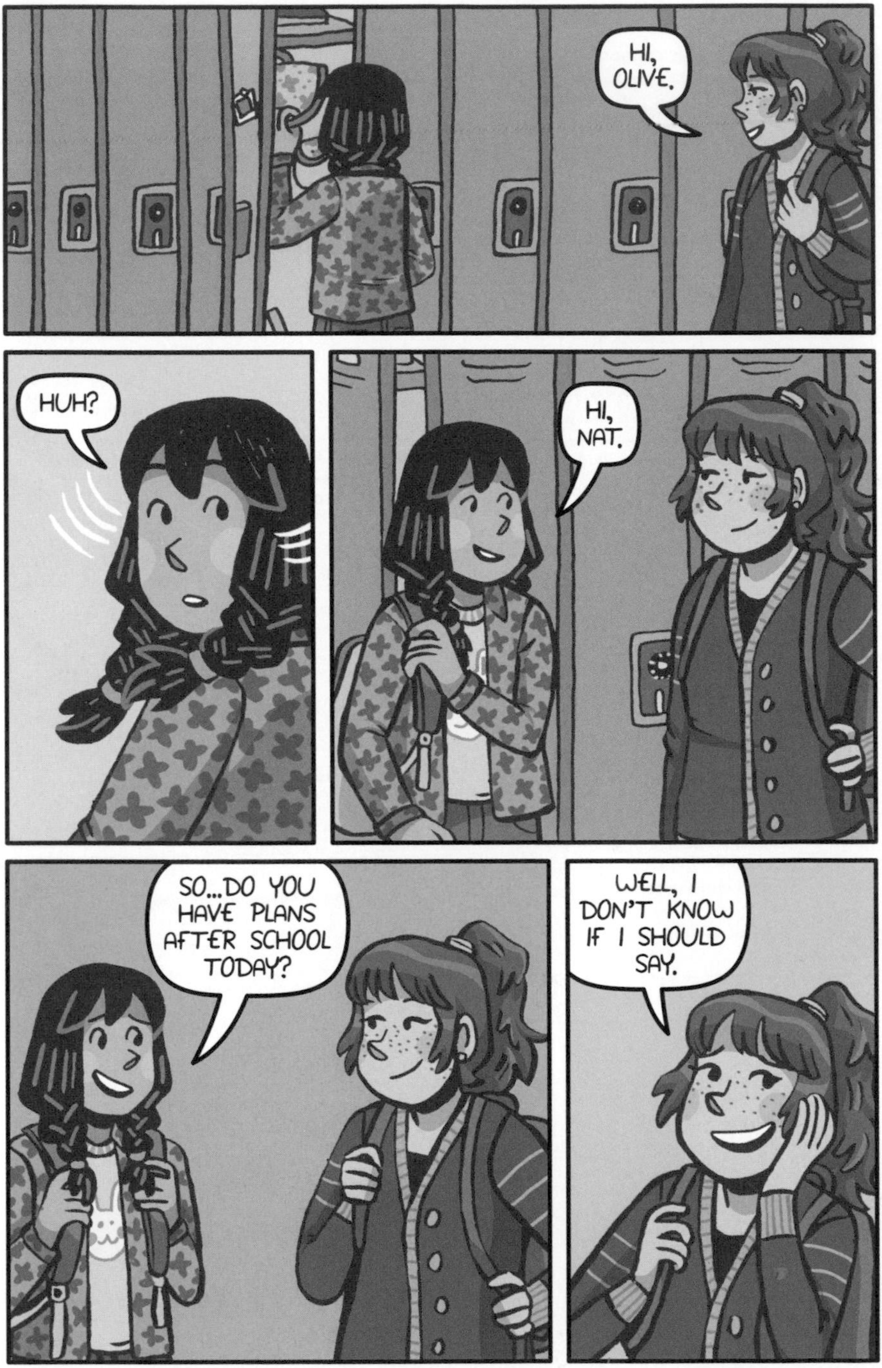
HI, OLIVE.
HUH?
HI, NAT.
SO...DO YOU HAVE PLANS AFTER SCHOOL TODAY?
WELL, I DON'T KNOW IF I SHOULD SAY.

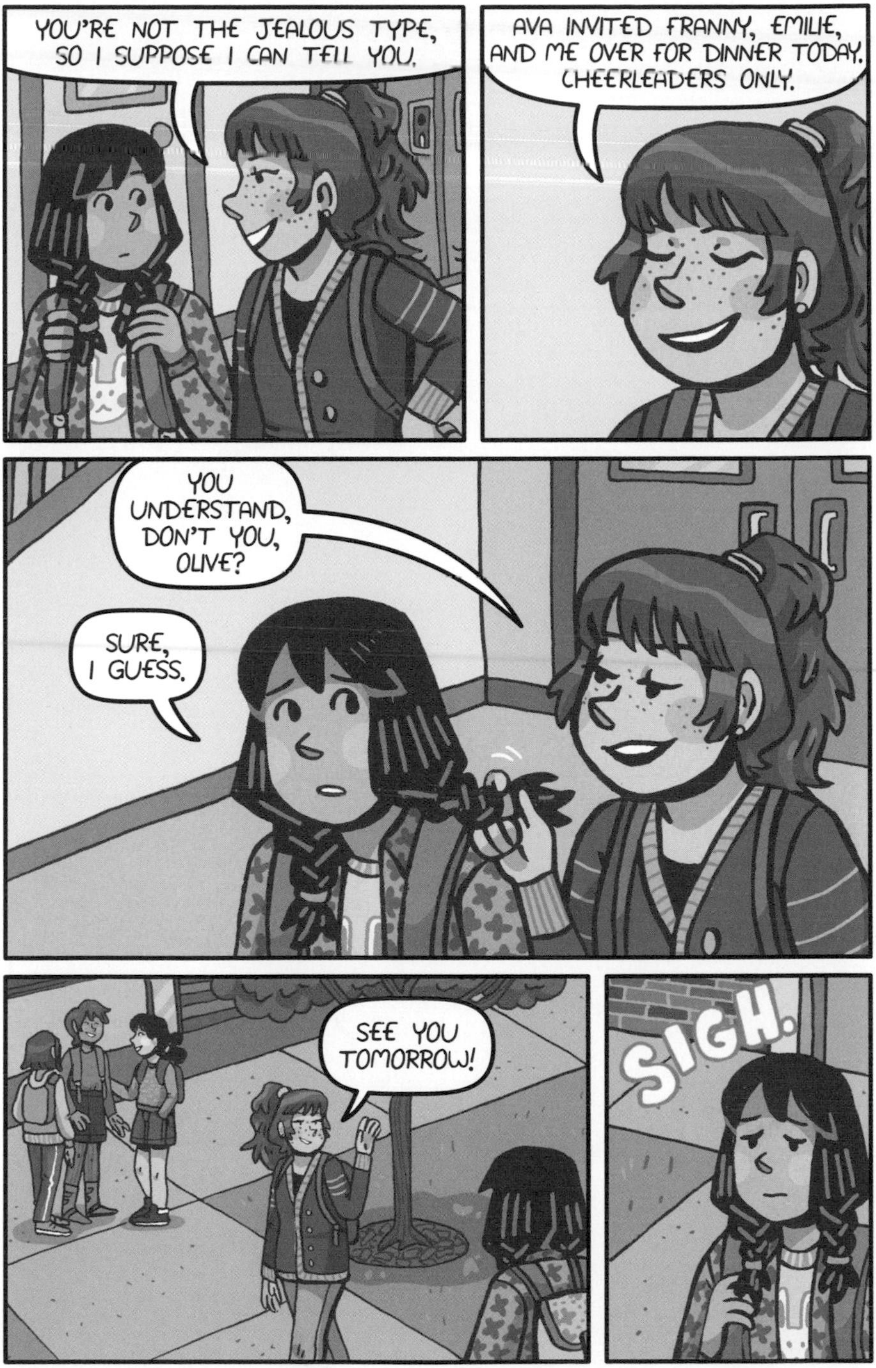
YOU'RE NOT THE JEALOUS TYPE, SO I SUPPOSE I CAN TELL YOU.
AVA INVITED FRANNY, EMILIE, AND ME OVER FOR DINNER TODAY. CHEERLEADERS ONLY.
YOU UNDERSTAND, DON'T YOU, OLIVE?
SURE, I GUESS.
SEE YOU TOMORROW!
SIGH.

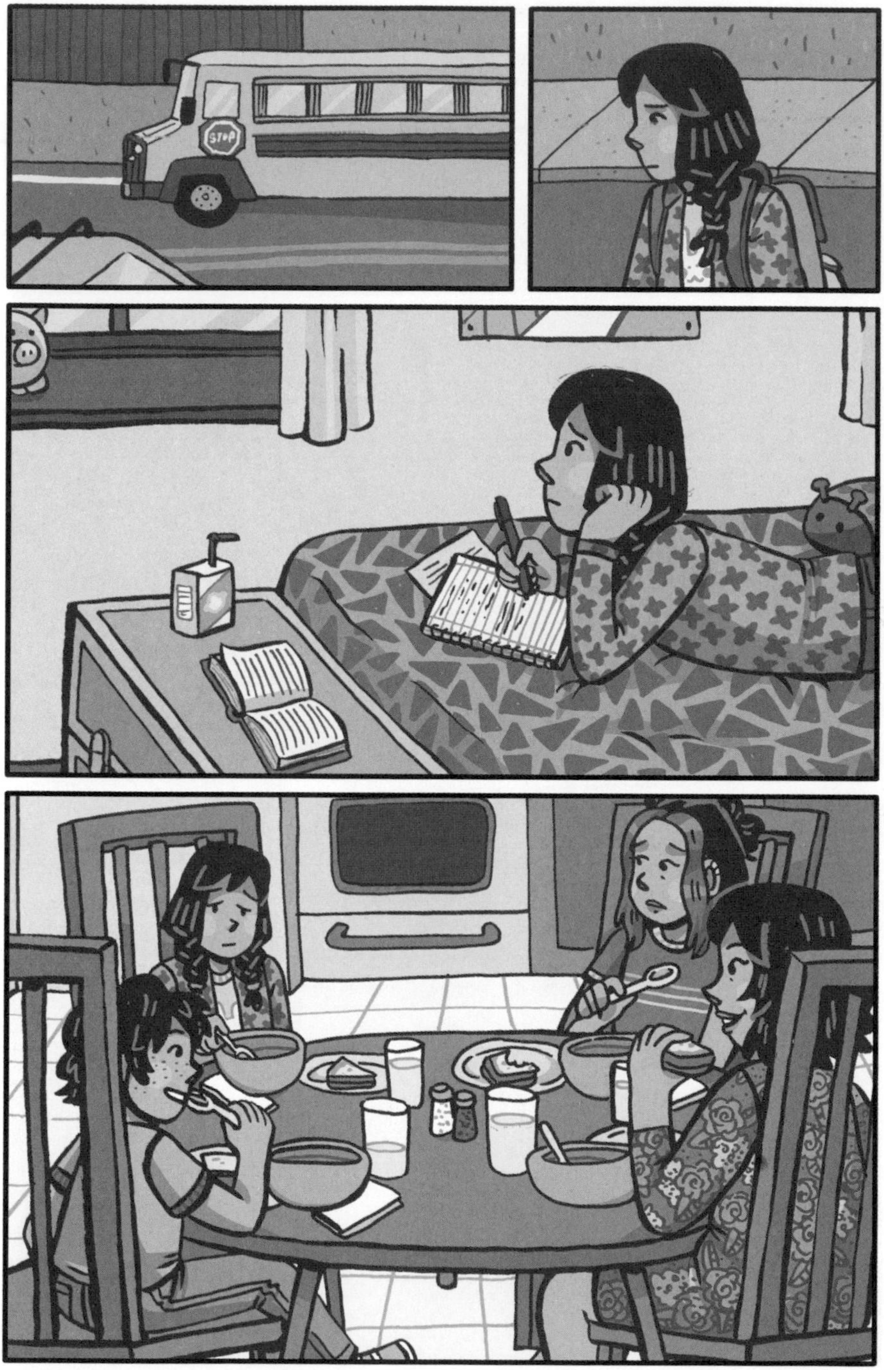
STOP

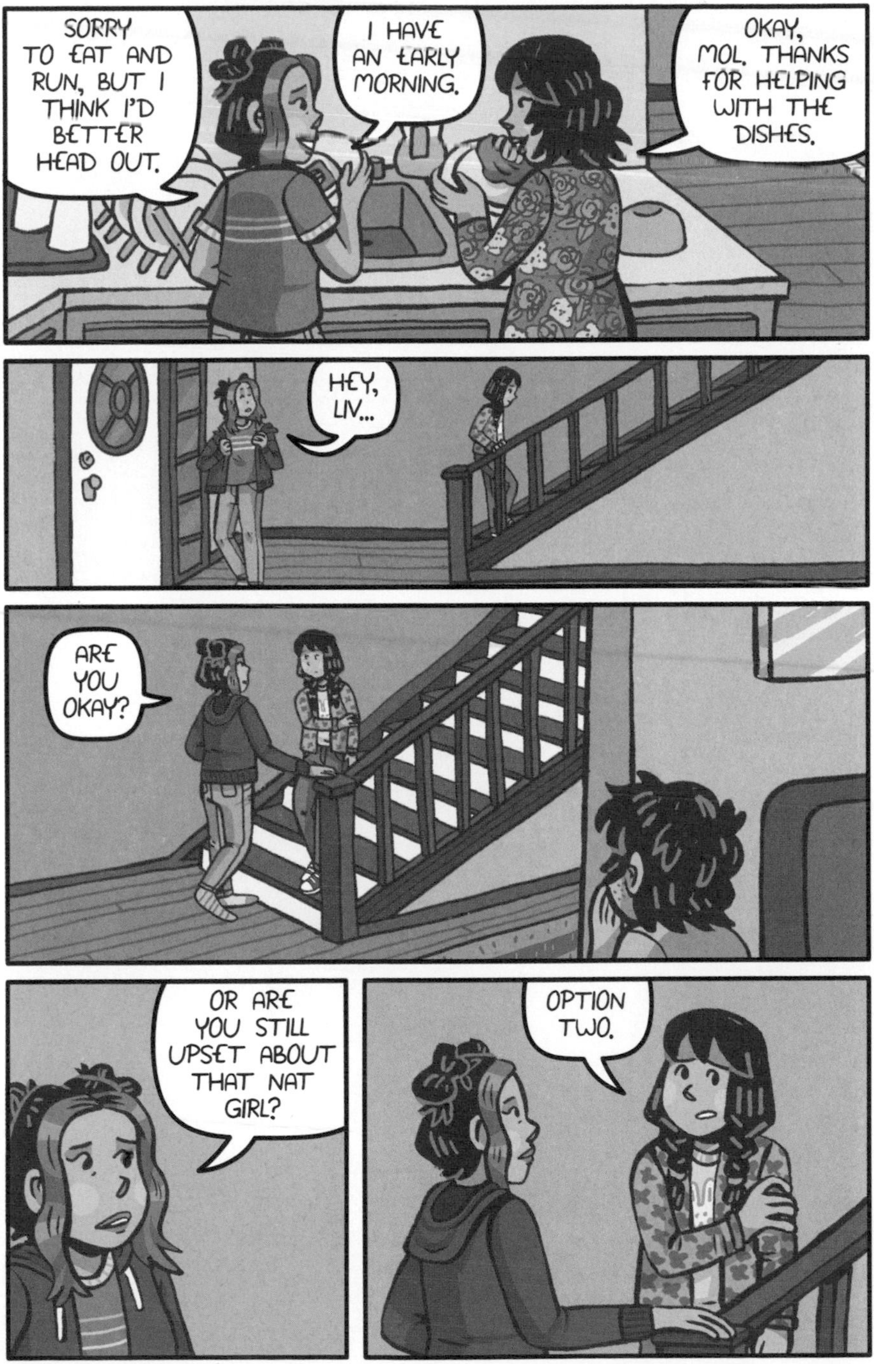
SORRY TO EAT AND RUN, BUT I THINK I'D BETTER HEAD OUT.
I HAVE AN EARLY MORNING.
OKAY, MOL. THANKS FOR HELPING WITH THE DISHES.
HEY, LIV...
ARE YOU OKAY?
OR ARE YOU STILL UPSET ABOUT THAT NAT GIRL?
OPTION TWO.

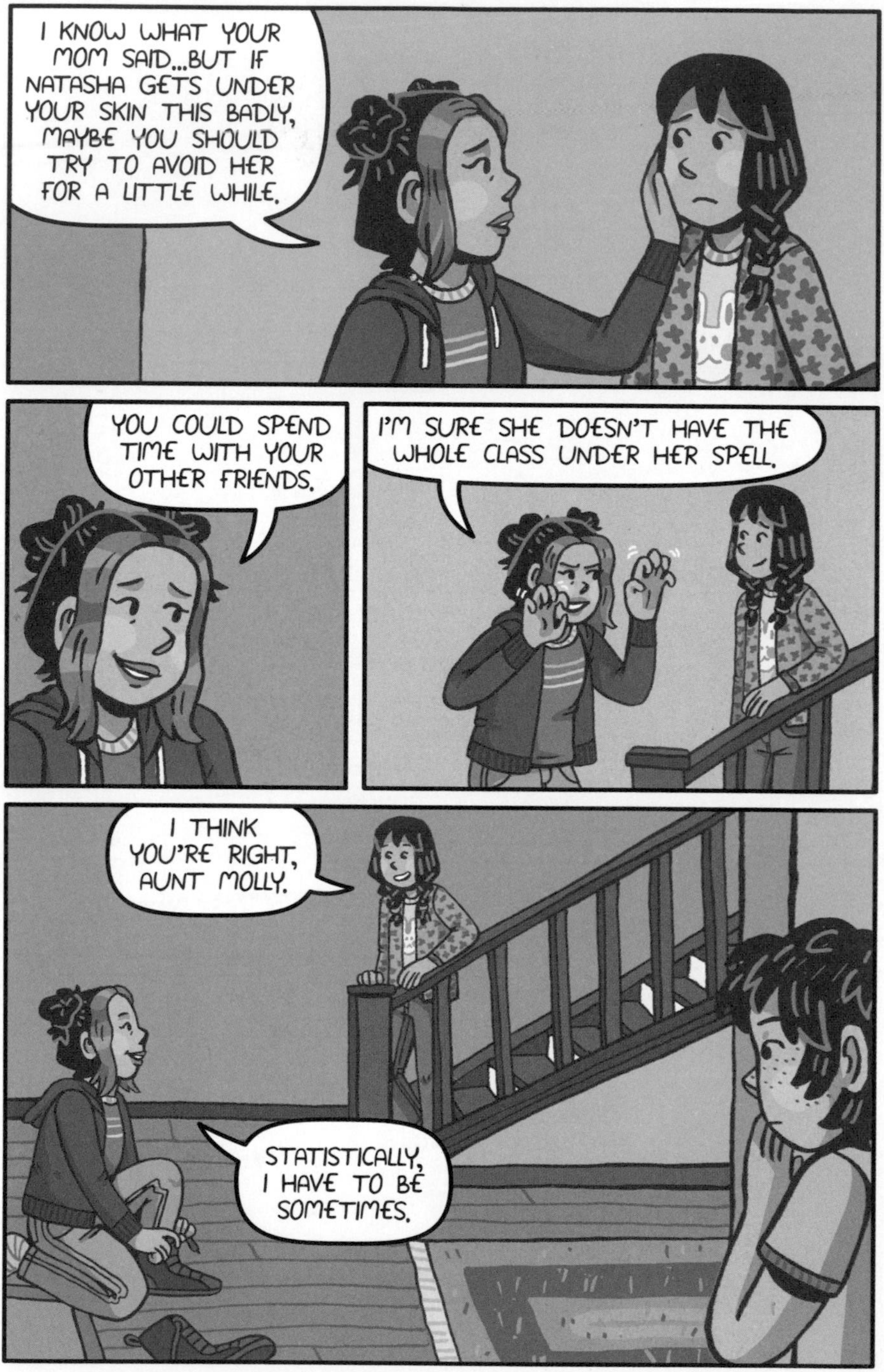
I KNOW WHAT YOUR MOM SAID...BUT IF NATASHA GETS UNDER YOUR SKIN THIS BADLY, MAYBE YOU SHOULD TRY TO AVOID HER FOR A LITTLE WHILE.
YOU COULD SPEND TIME WITH YOUR OTHER FRIENDS.
I'M SURE SHE DOESN'T HAVE THE WHOLE CLASS UNDER HER SPELL.
I THINK YOU'RE RIGHT, AUNT MOLLY.
STATISTICALLY, I HAVE TO BE SOMETIMES.

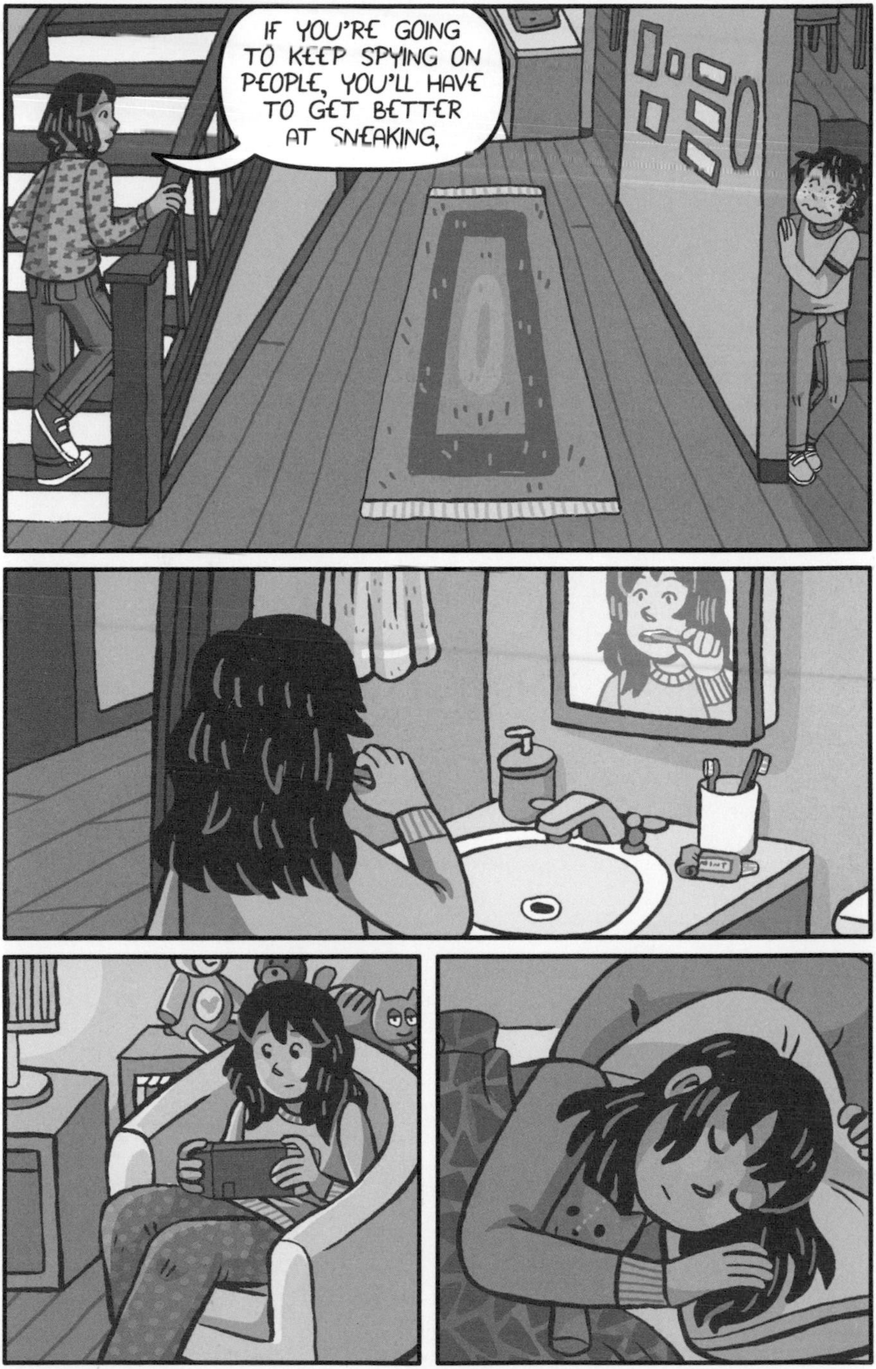
IF YOU'RE GOING TO KEEP SPYING ON PEOPLE, YOU'LL HAVE TO GET BETTER AT SNEAKING.
MINT

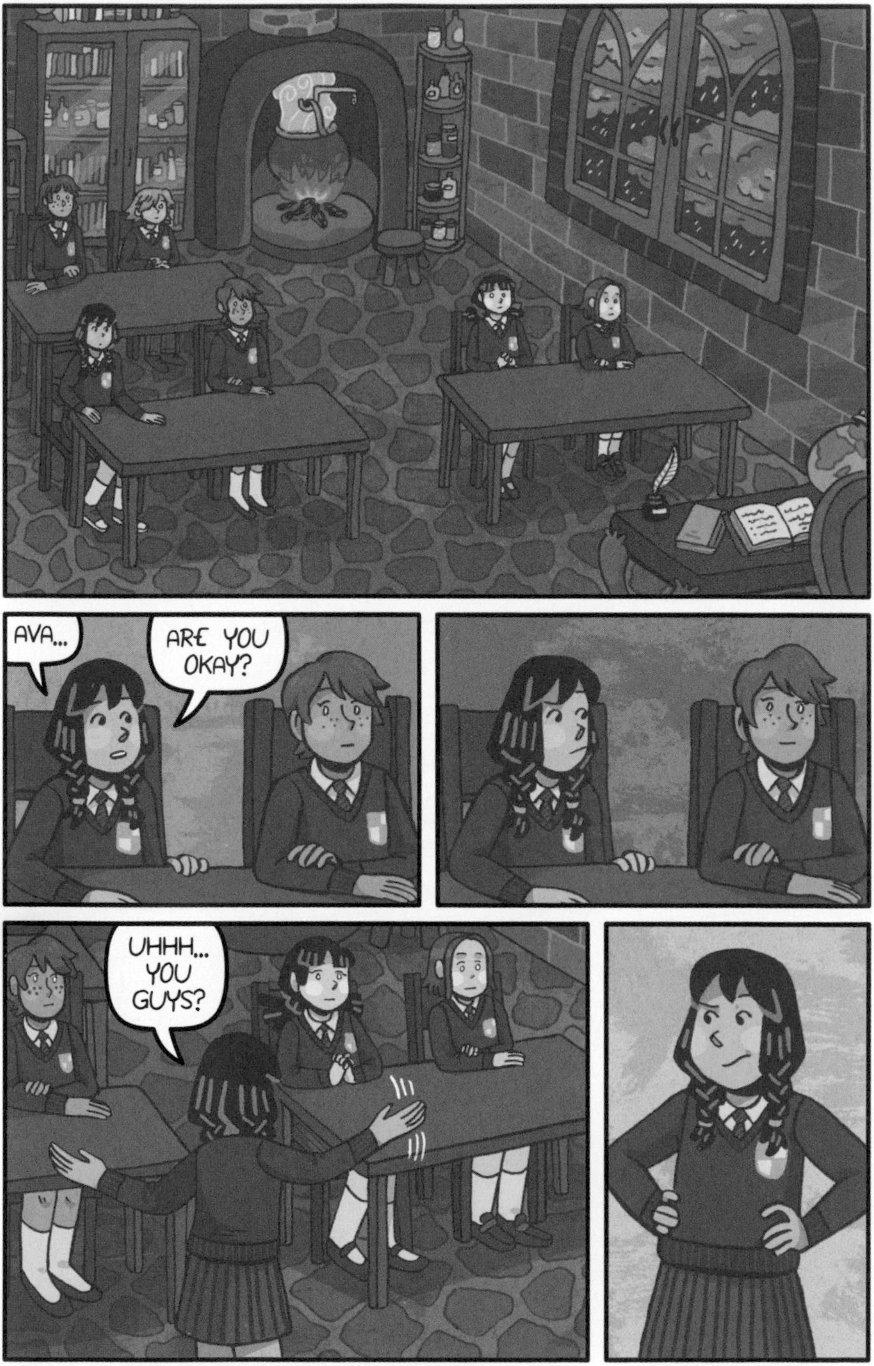
AVA...
ARE YOU OKAY?
UHHH... YOU GUYS?

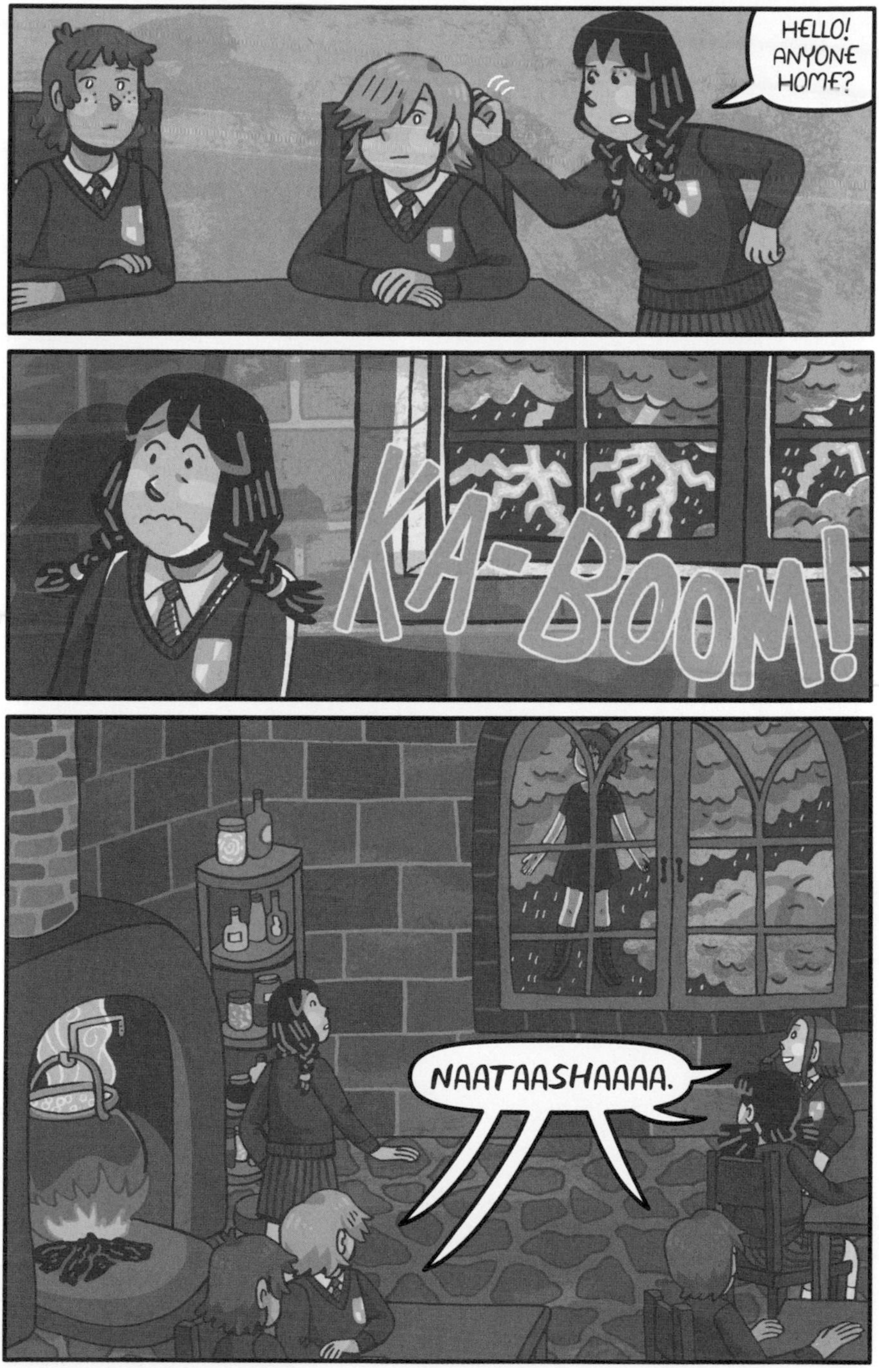
HELLO! ANYONE HOME?
KA-BOOM!
NAATAASHAAAA.

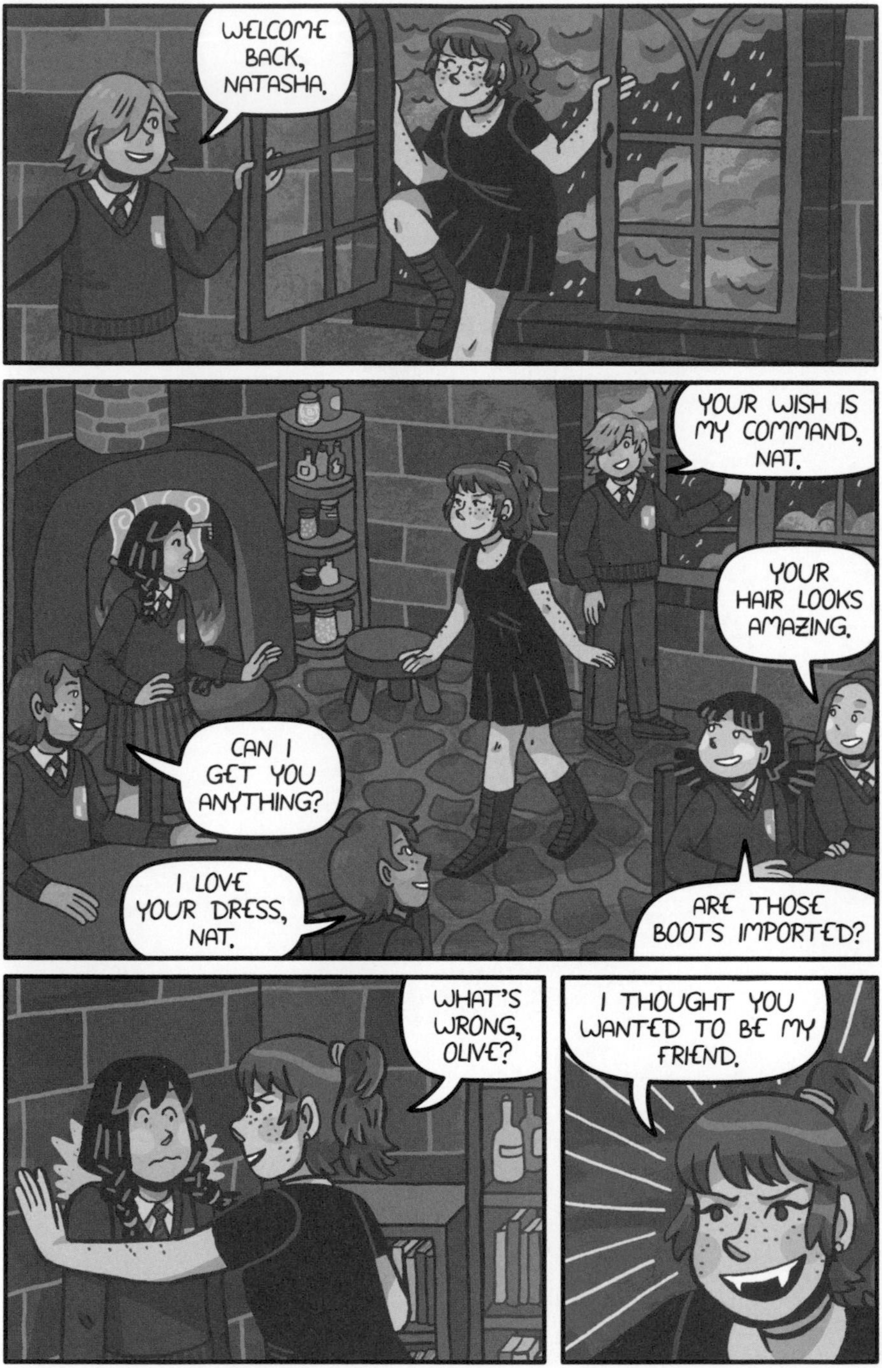
WELCOME BACK, NATASHA.
YOUR WISH IS MY COMMAND, NAT.
YOUR HAIR LOOKS AMAZING.
CAN I GET YOU ANYTHING?
I LOVE YOUR DRESS, NAT.
ARE THOSE BOOTS IMPORTED?
WHAT'S WRONG, OLIVE?
I THOUGHT YOU WANTED TO BE MY FRIEND.

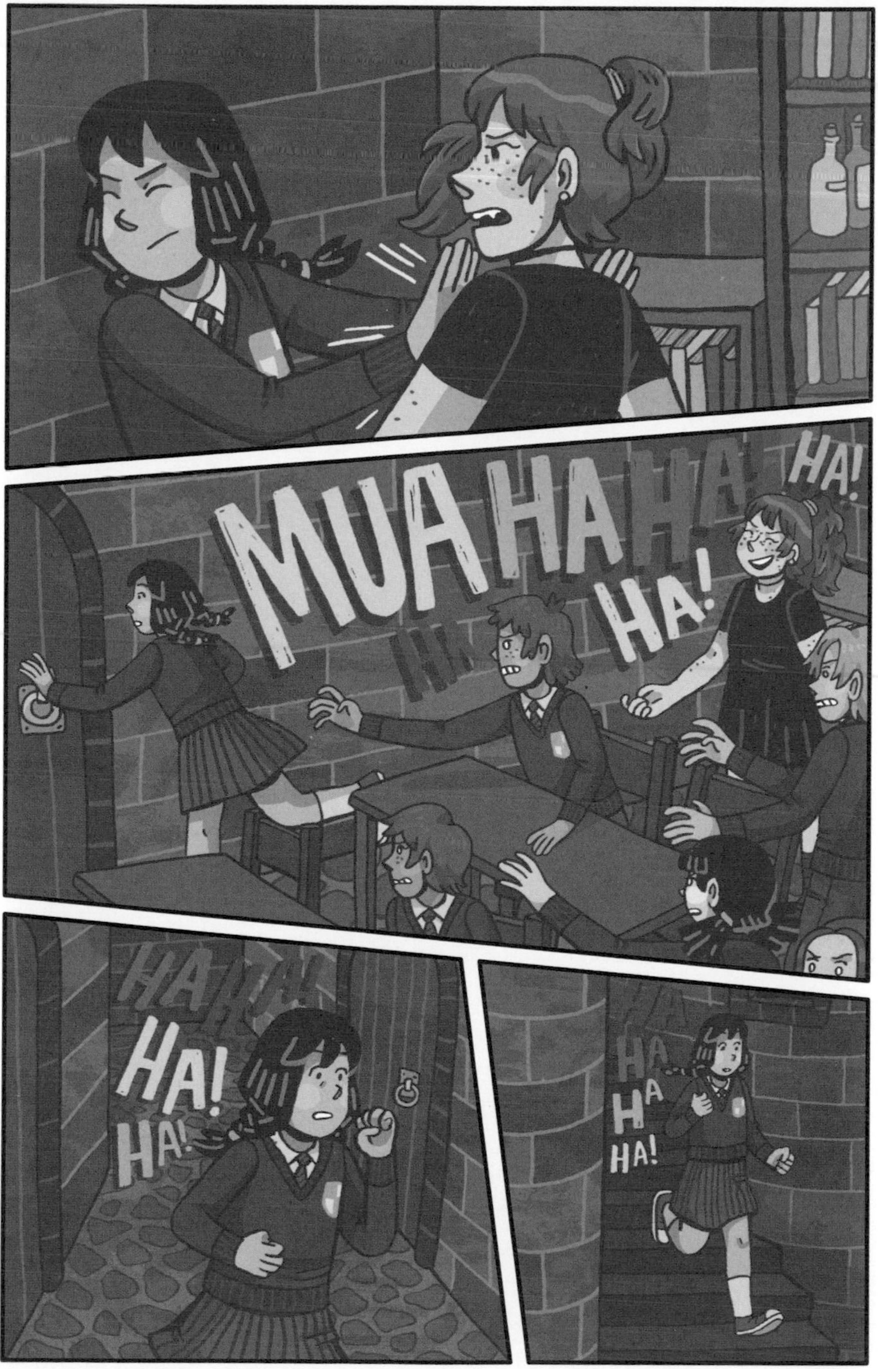
MUAHAHA!
HA!
HA!
HAHA!
HA!
HA!
HA
HA
HA!

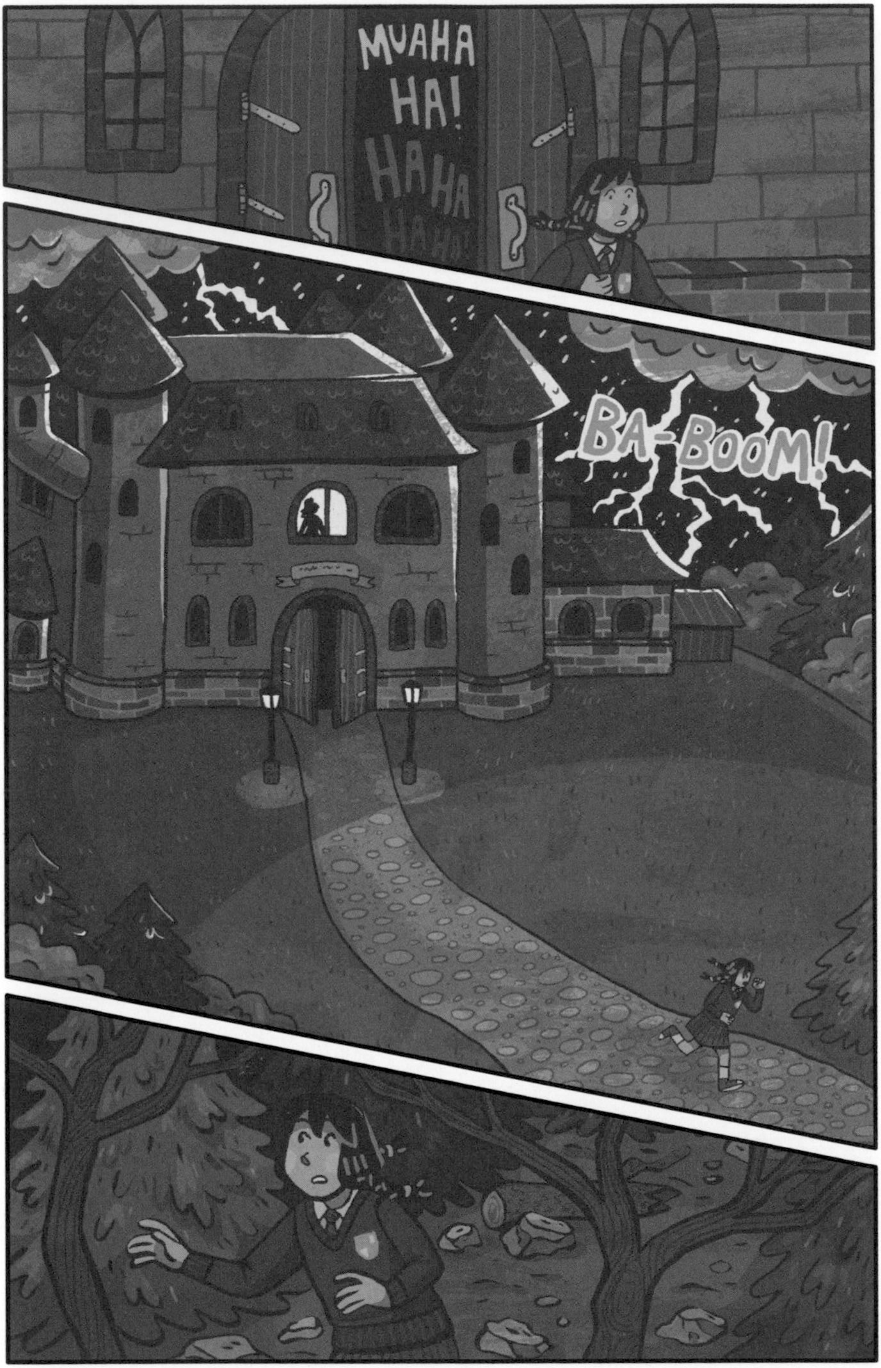
MUAHA HA! HAHAHA HAHA!
BA-BOOM!

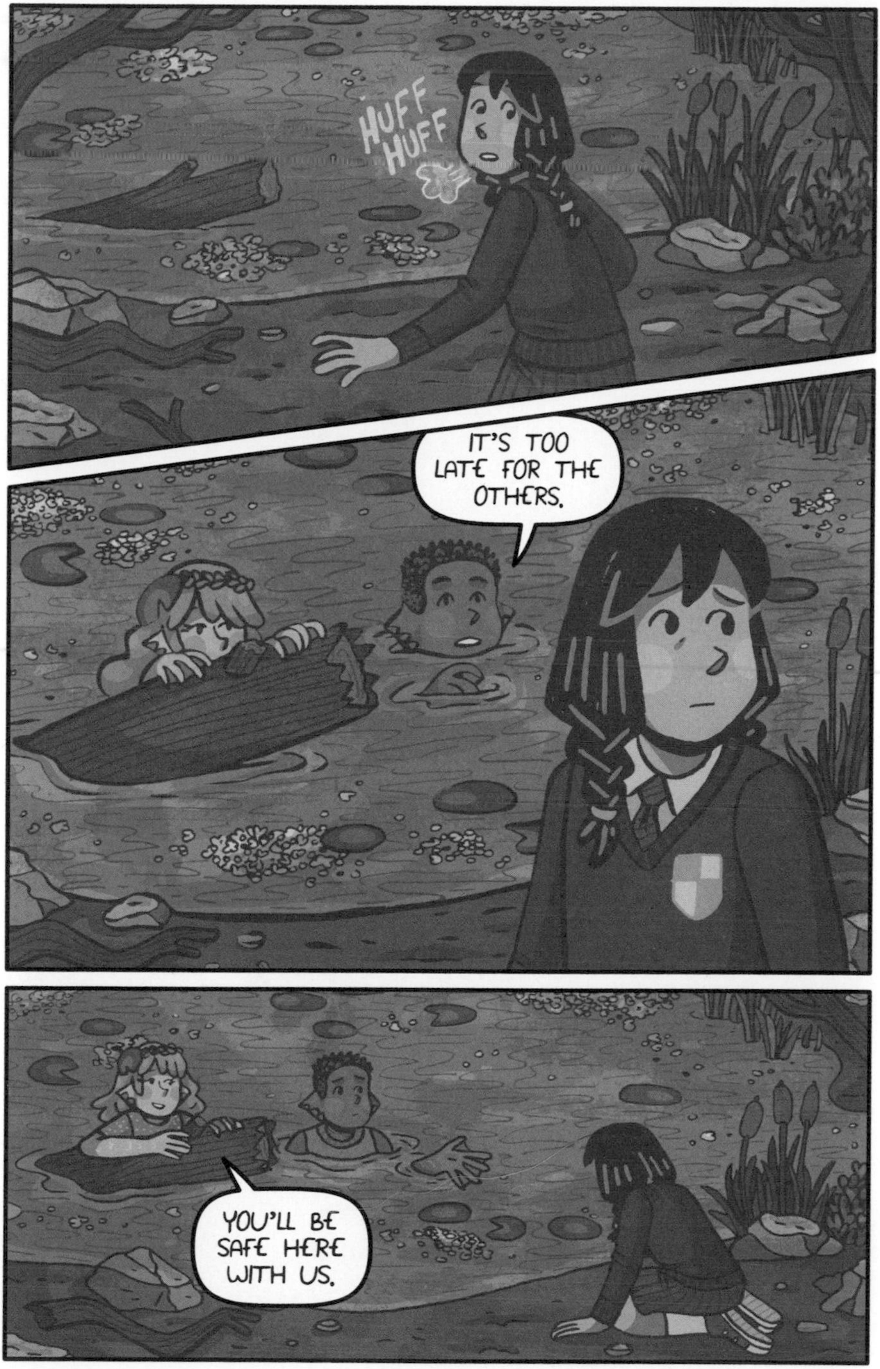
HUFF
HUFF
IT'S TOO LATE FOR THE OTHERS.
YOU'LL BE SAFE HERE WITH US.

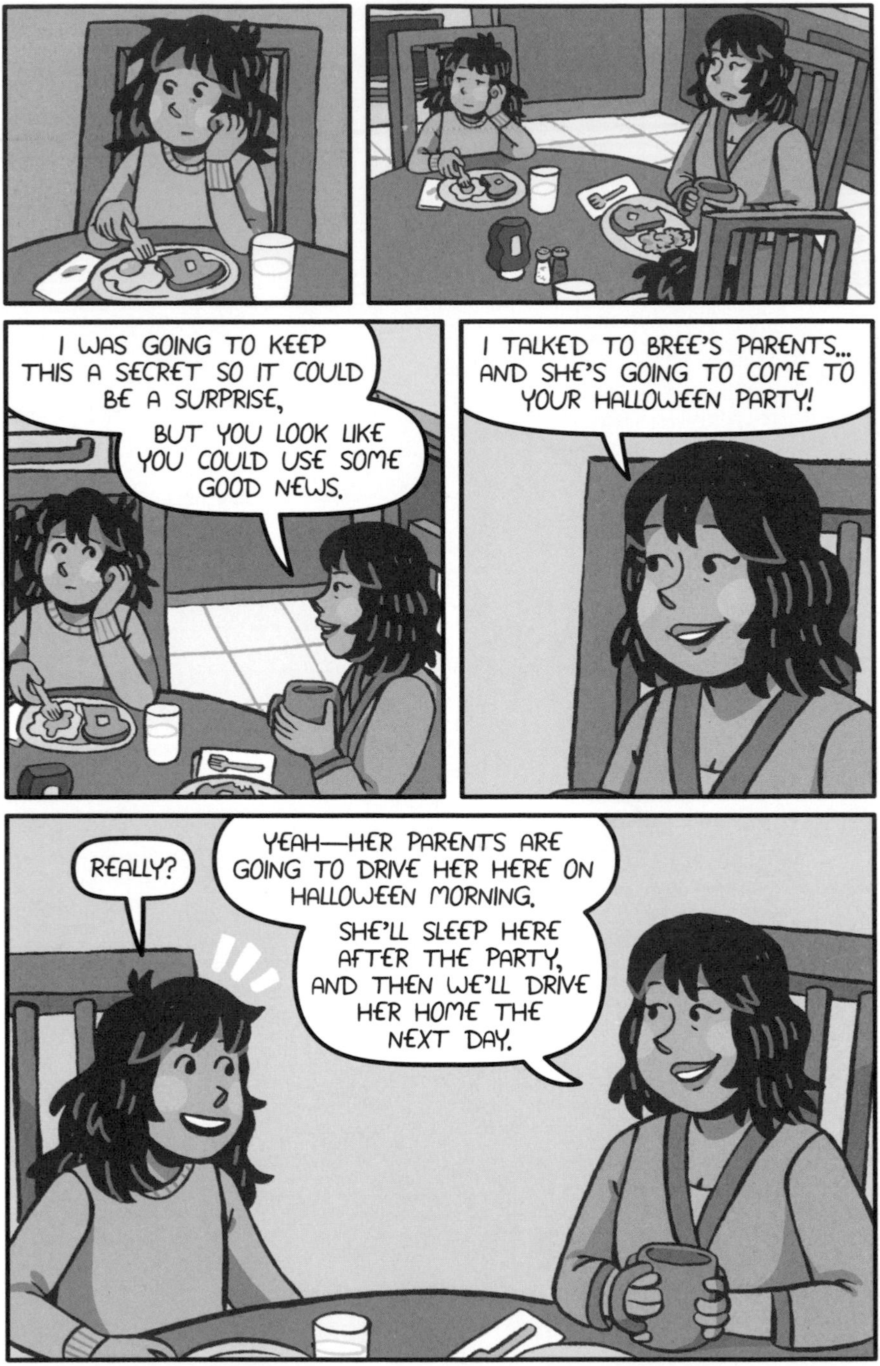
I WAS GOING TO KEEP THIS A SECRET SO IT COULD BE A SURPRISE,
BUT YOU LOOK LIKE YOU COULD USE SOME GOOD NEWS.
I TALKED TO BREE'S PARENTS... AND SHE'S GOING TO COME TO YOUR HALLOWEEN PARTY!
REALLY?
YEAH—HER PARENTS ARE GOING TO DRIVE HER HERE ON HALLOWEEN MORNING.
SHE'LL SLEEP HERE AFTER THE PARTY, AND THEN WE'LL DRIVE HER HOME THE NEXT DAY.

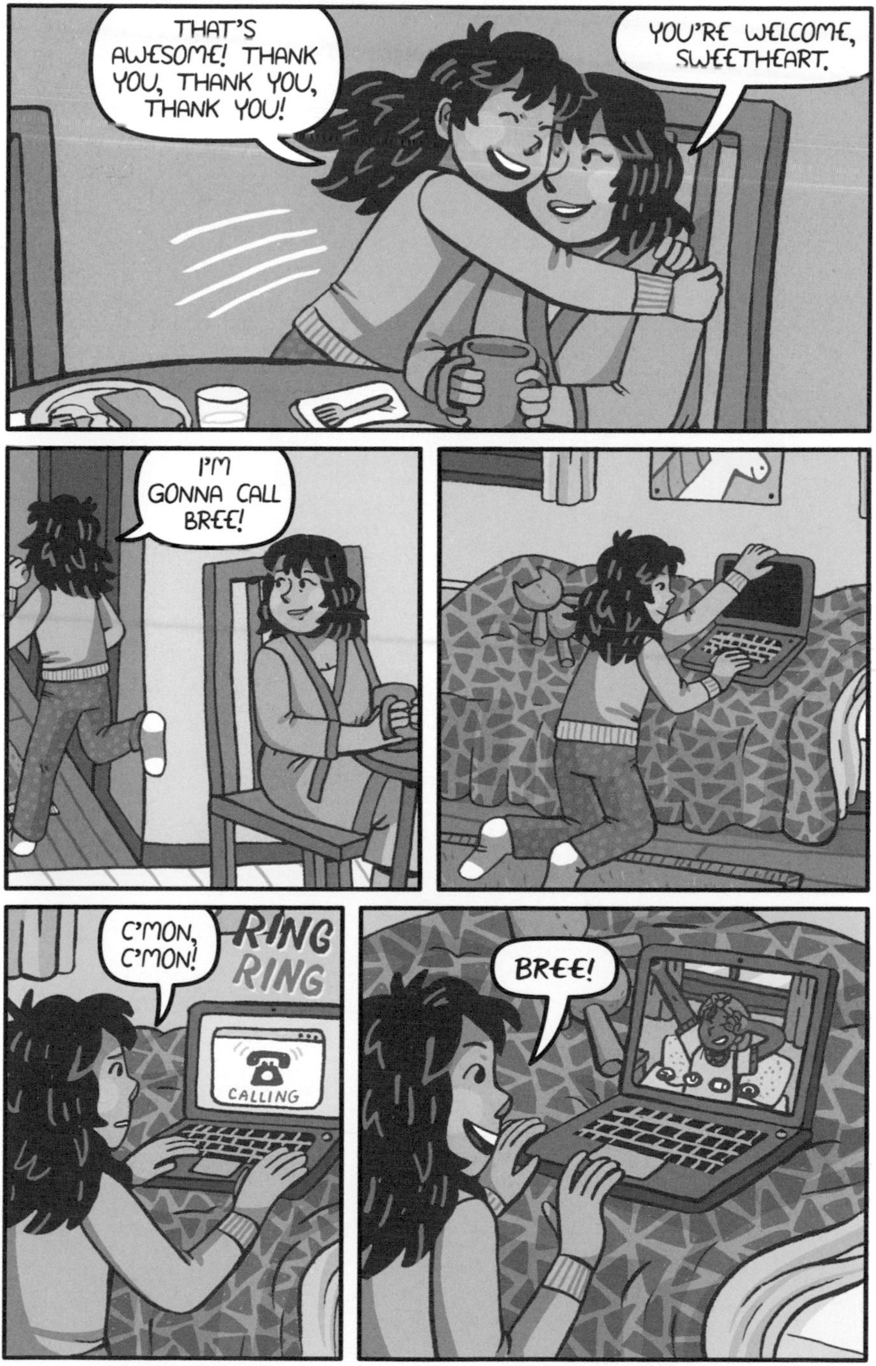
THAT'S AWESOME! THANK YOU, THANK YOU, THANK YOU!
YOU'RE WELCOME, SWEETHEART.
I'M GONNA CALL BREE!
C'MON, C'MON!
RING RING
CALLING
BREE!

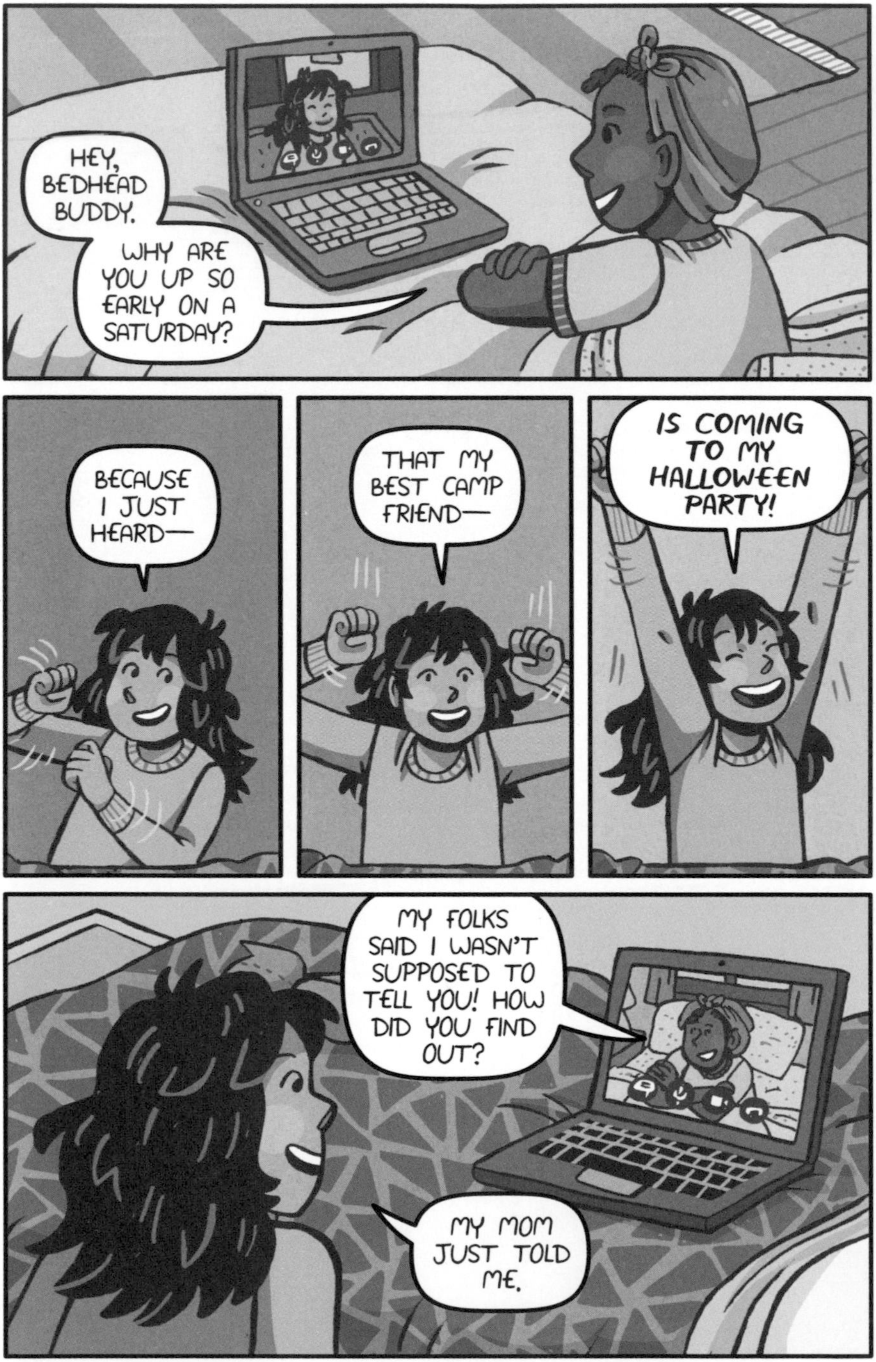
HEY, BEDHEAD BUDDY.
WHY ARE YOU UP SO EARLY ON A SATURDAY?
BECAUSE I JUST HEARD—
THAT MY BEST CAMP FRIEND—
IS COMING TO MY HALLOWEEN PARTY!
MY FOLKS SAID I WASN'T SUPPOSED TO TELL YOU! HOW DID YOU FIND OUT?
MY MOM JUST TOLD ME.

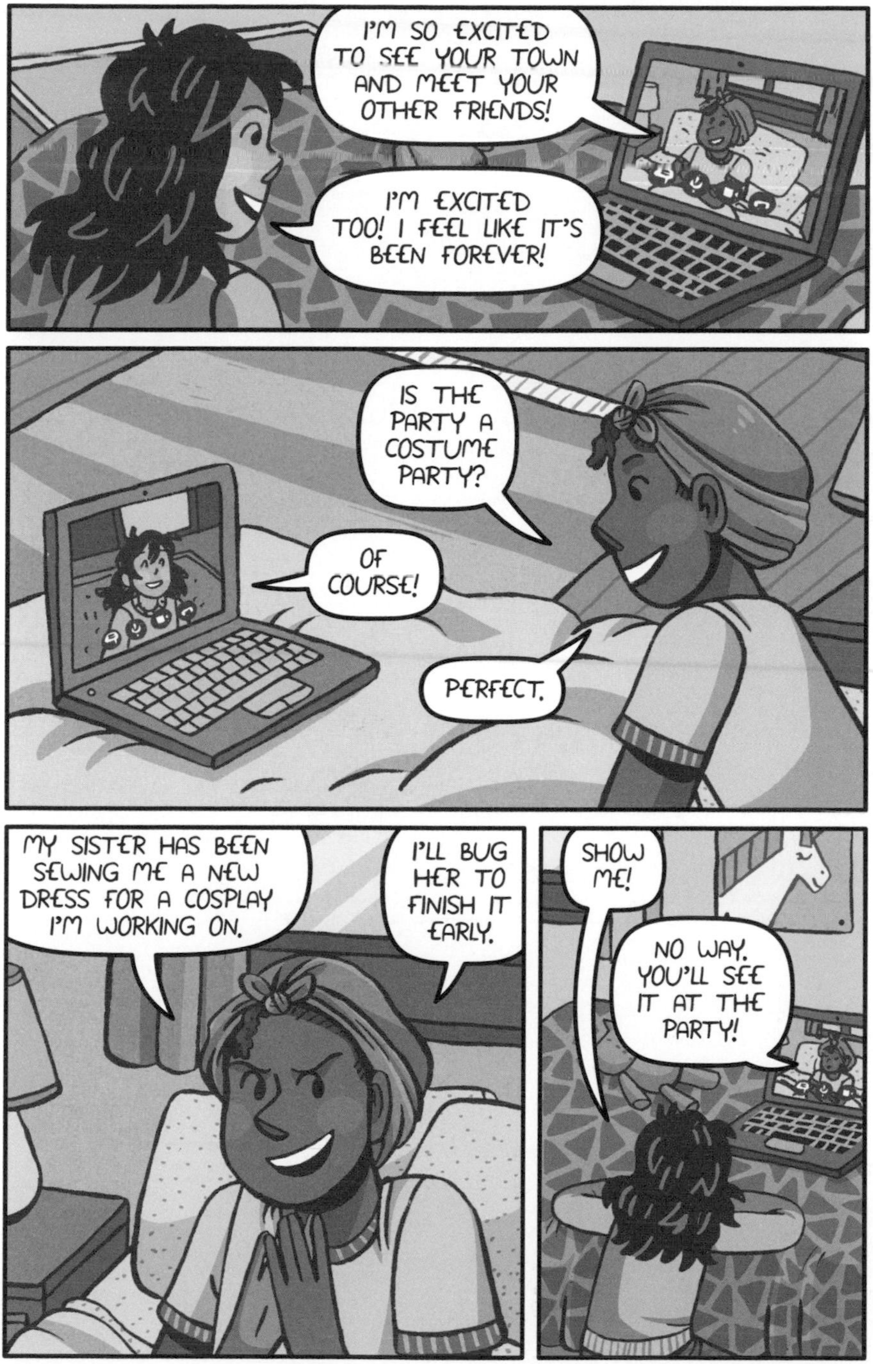
I'M SO EXCITED TO SEE YOUR TOWN AND MEET YOUR OTHER FRIENDS!
I'M EXCITED TOO! I FEEL LIKE IT'S BEEN FOREVER!
IS THE PARTY A COSTUME PARTY?
OF COURSE!
PERFECT.
MY SISTER HAS BEEN SEWING ME A NEW DRESS FOR A COSPLAY I'M WORKING ON.
I'LL BUG HER TO FINISH IT EARLY.
SHOW ME!
NO WAY. YOU'LL SEE IT AT THE PARTY!

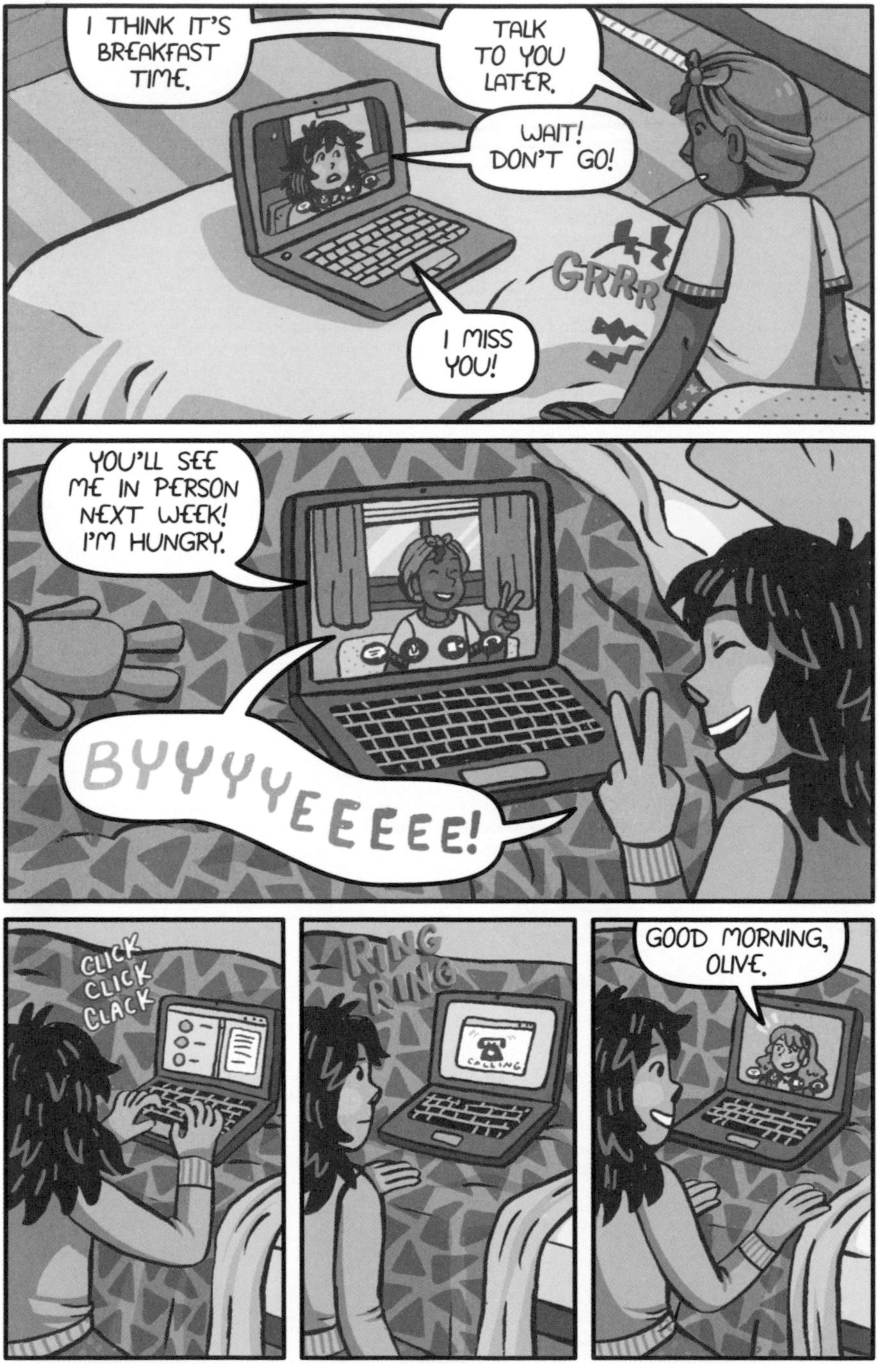
I THINK IT'S BREAKFAST TIME.
TALK TO YOU LATER.
WAIT! DON'T GO!
GRRRR
I MISS YOU!
YOU'LL SEE ME IN PERSON NEXT WEEK! I'M HUNGRY.
BYYYYEEEEE!
CLICK CLICK CLACK
RING RING
CALLING
GOOD MORNING, OLIVE.

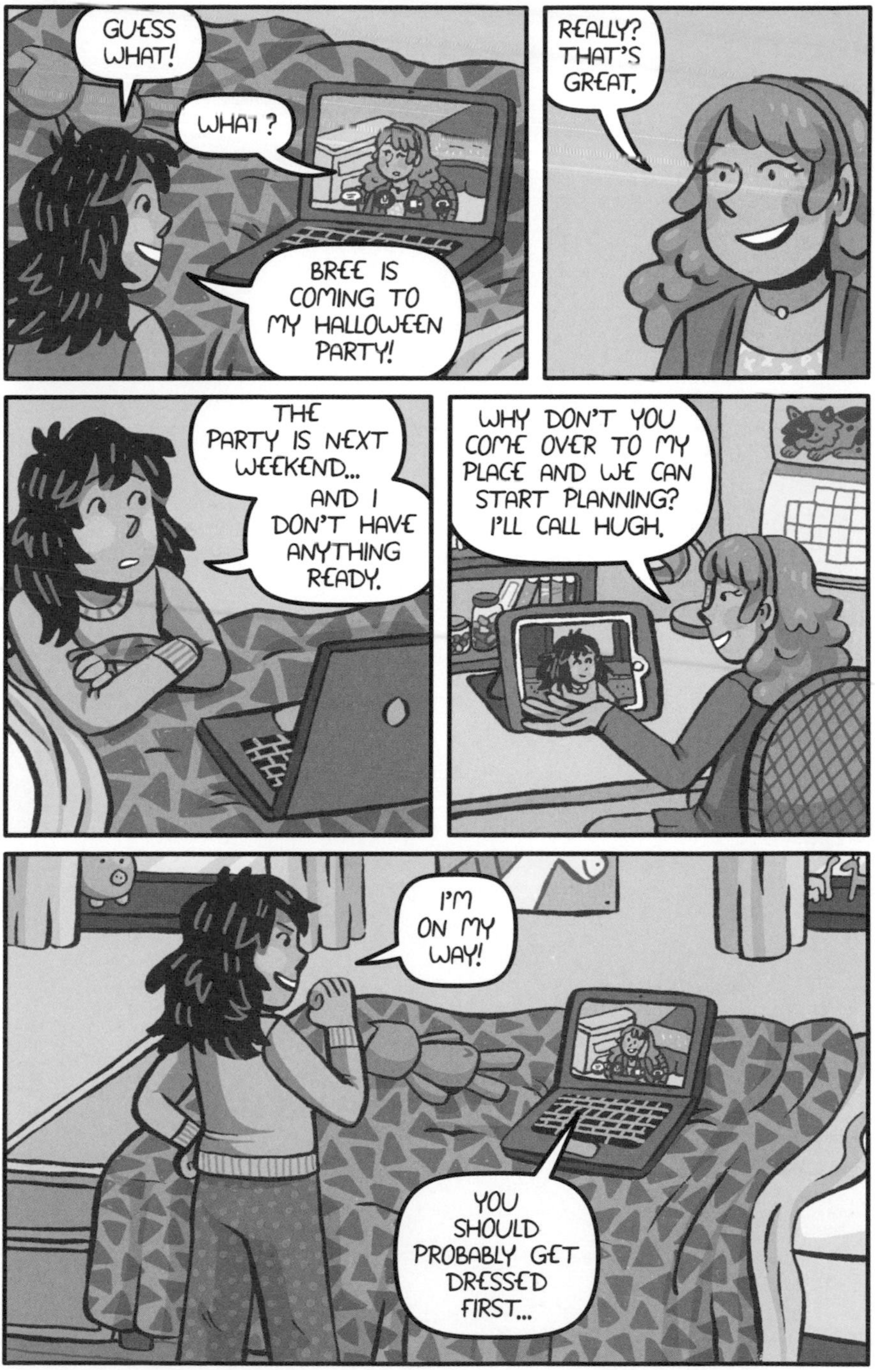
GUESS WHAT!
WHAT?
BREE IS COMING TO MY HALLOWEEN PARTY!
REALLY? THAT'S GREAT.
THE PARTY IS NEXT WEEKEND...
AND I DON'T HAVE ANYTHING READY.
WHY DON'T YOU COME OVER TO MY PLACE AND WE CAN START PLANNING? I'LL CALL HUGH.
I'M ON MY WAY!
YOU SHOULD PROBABLY GET DRESSED FIRST...

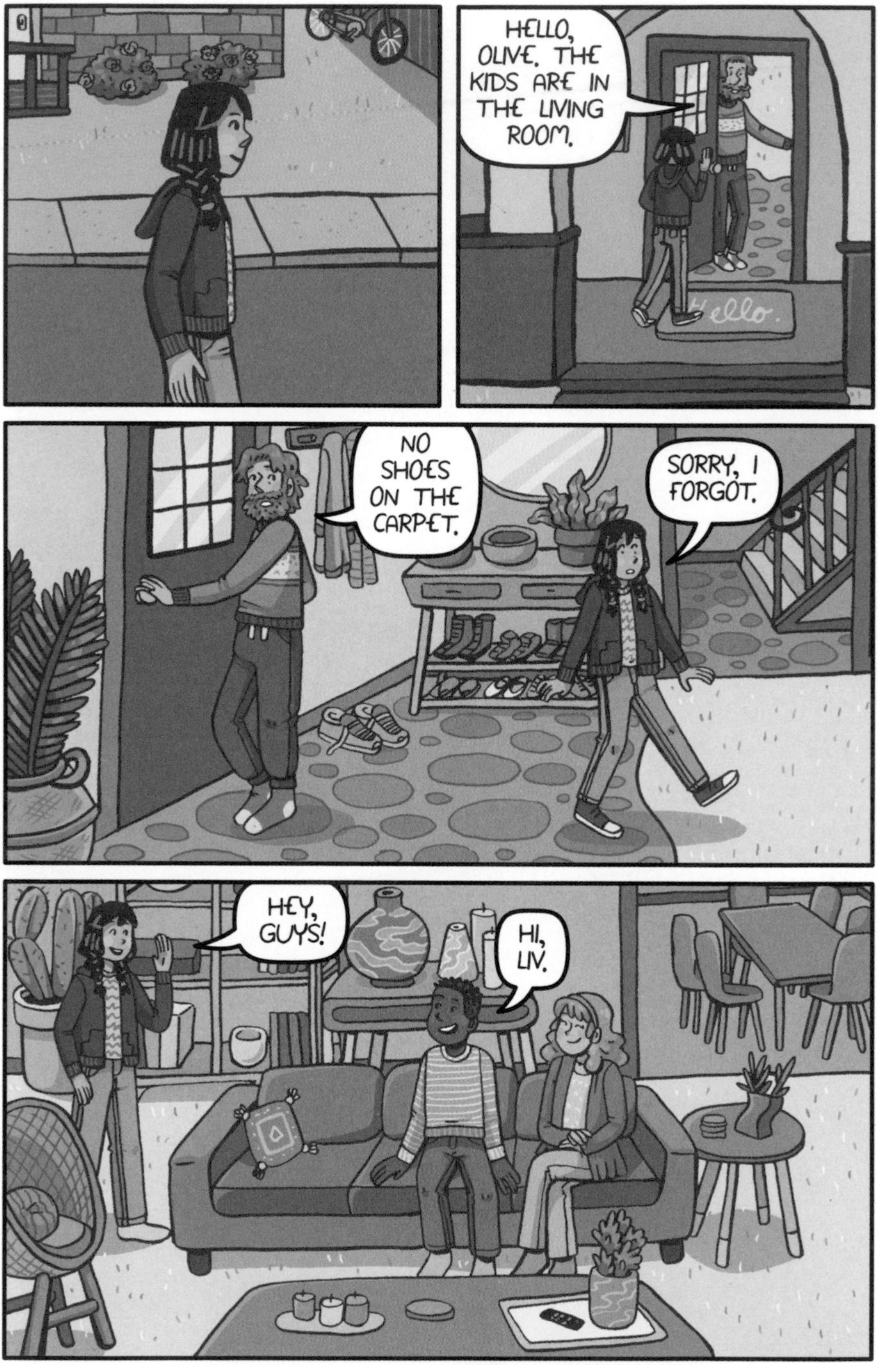
HELLO, OLIVE. THE KIDS ARE IN THE LIVING ROOM.
Hello.
NO SHOES ON THE CARPET.
SORRY, I FORGOT.
HEY, GUYS!
HI, LIV.

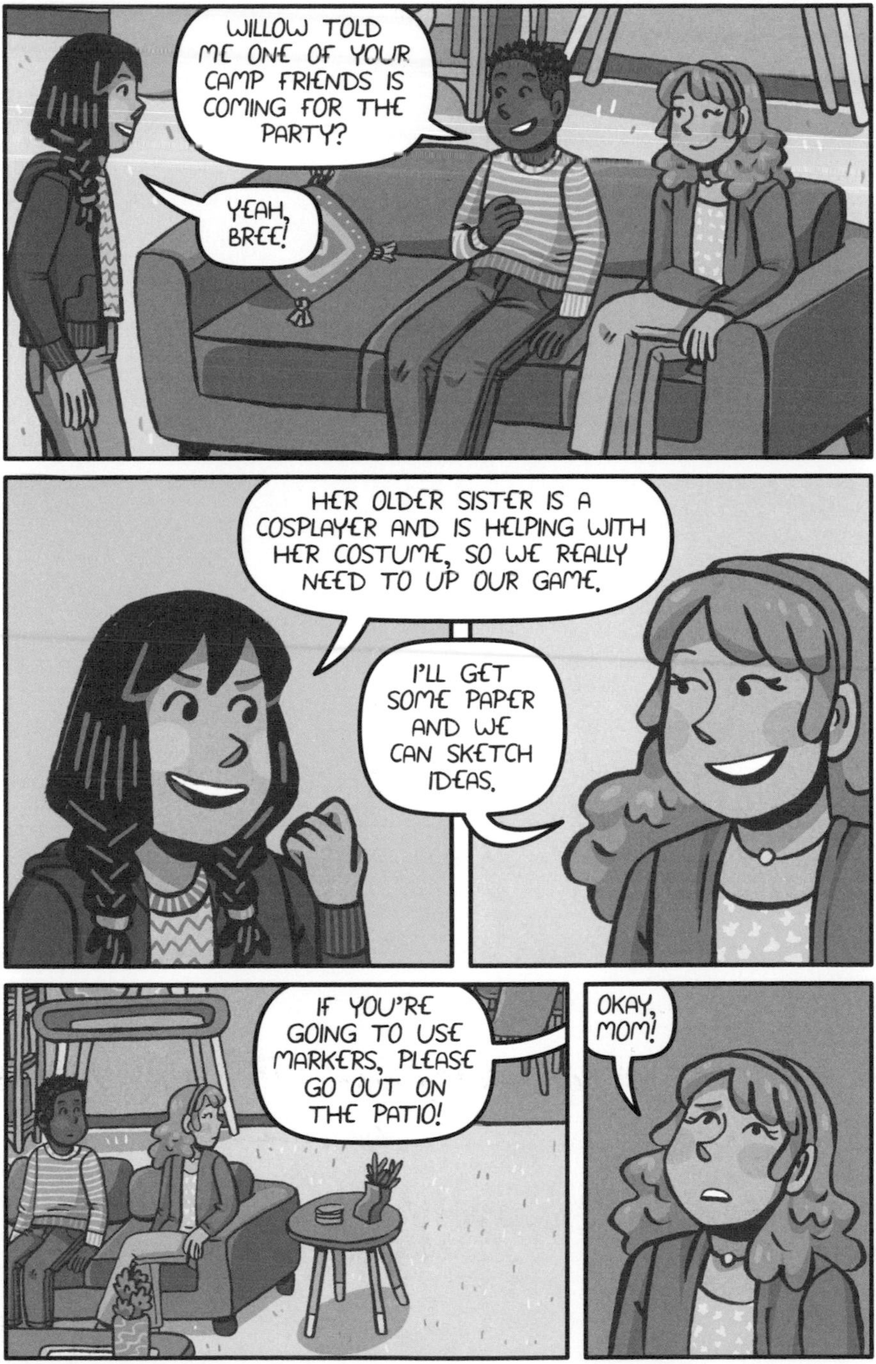
WILLOW TOLD ME ONE OF YOUR CAMP FRIENDS IS COMING FOR THE PARTY?
YEAH, BREE!
HER OLDER SISTER IS A COSPLAYER AND IS HELPING WITH HER COSTUME, SO WE REALLY NEED TO UP OUR GAME.
I'LL GET SOME PAPER AND WE CAN SKETCH IDEAS.
IF YOU'RE GOING TO USE MARKERS, PLEASE GO OUT ON THE PATIO!
OKAY, MOM!

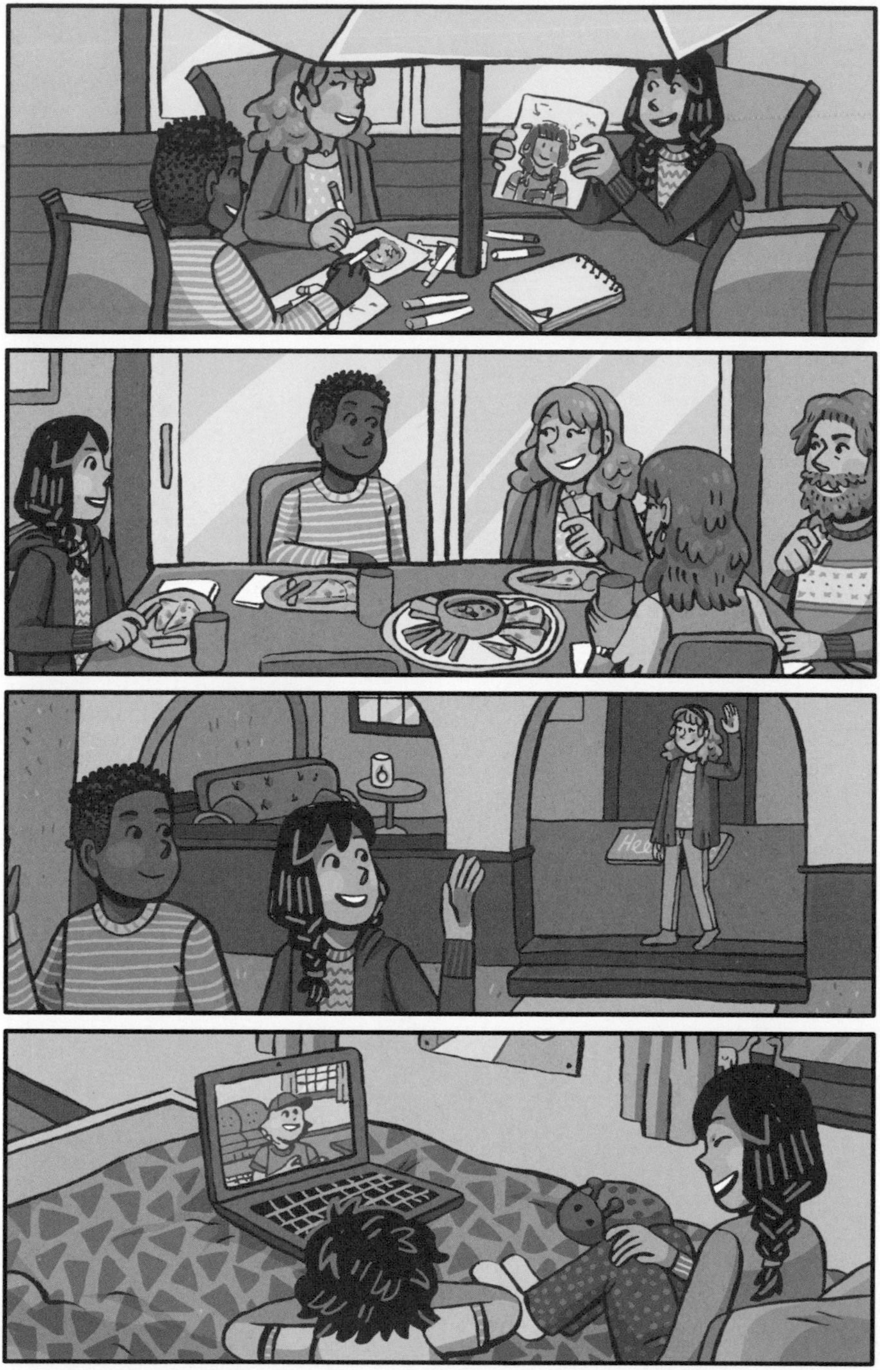

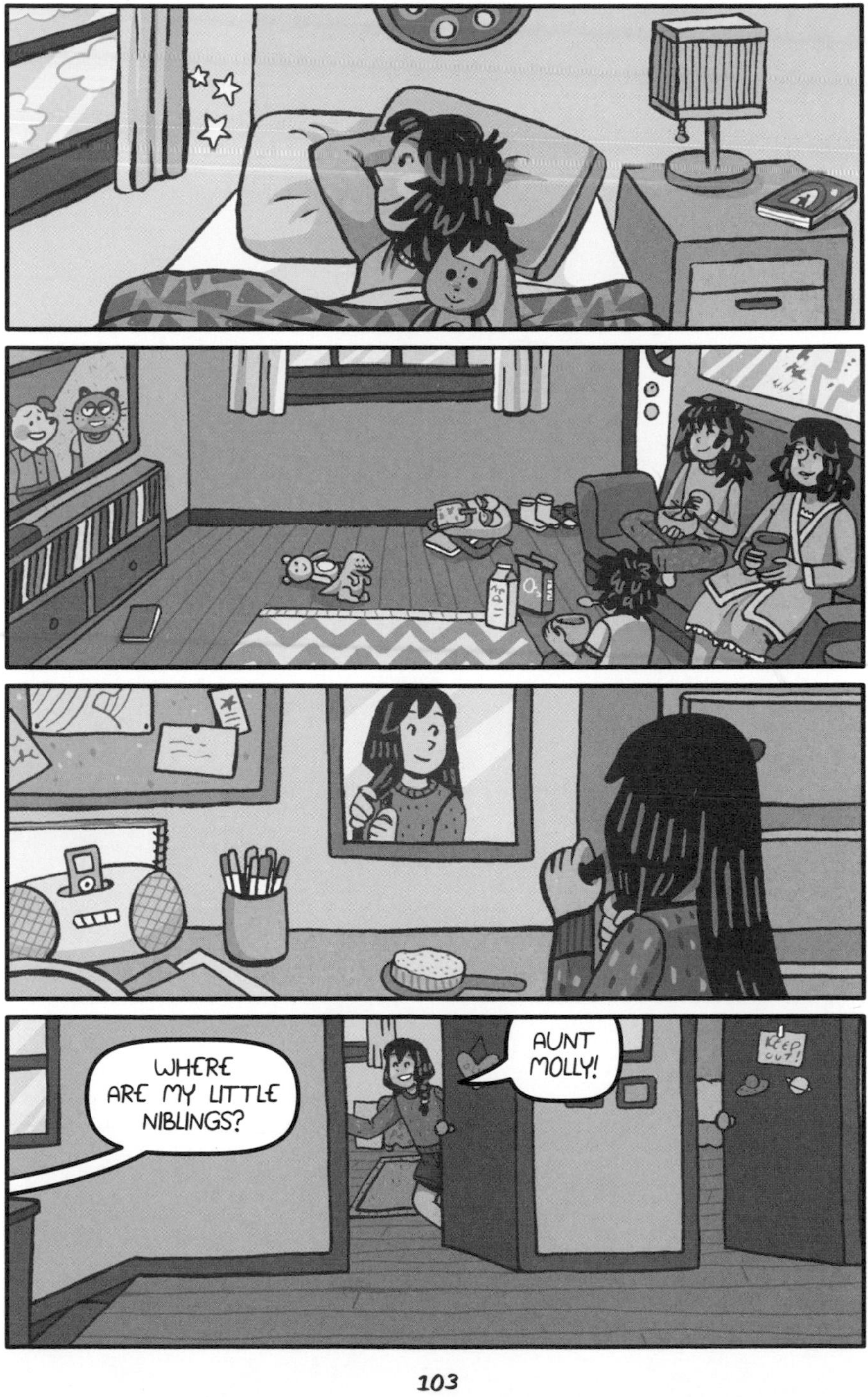
WHERE ARE MY LITTLE NIBLINGS?
AUNT MOLLY!
KEEP OUT!

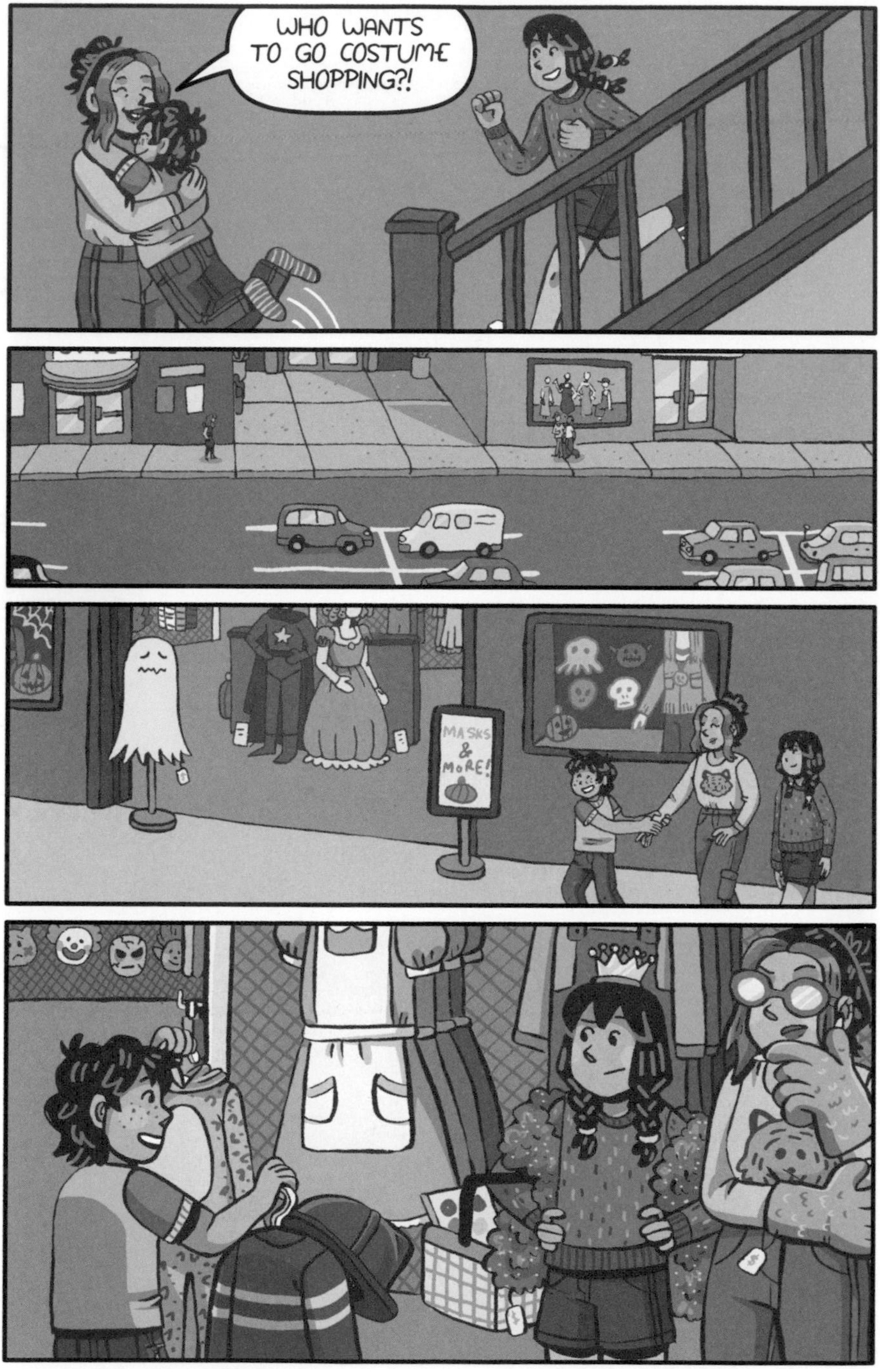
WHO WANTS TO GO COSTUME SHOPPING?!
MASKS & MORE!

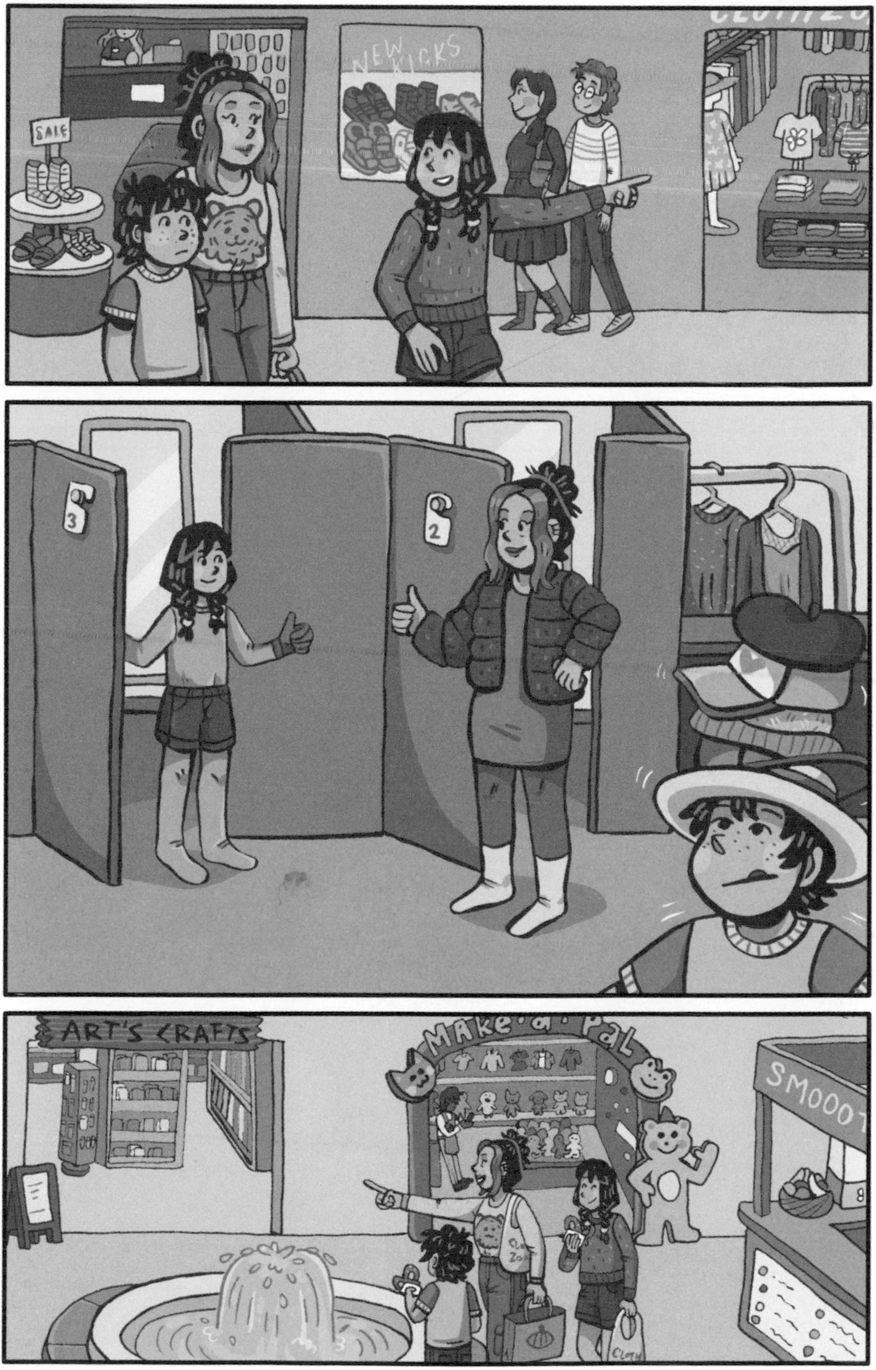
SALE
NEW KICKS
3
2
ART'S CRAFTS
MAKE·A·PAL

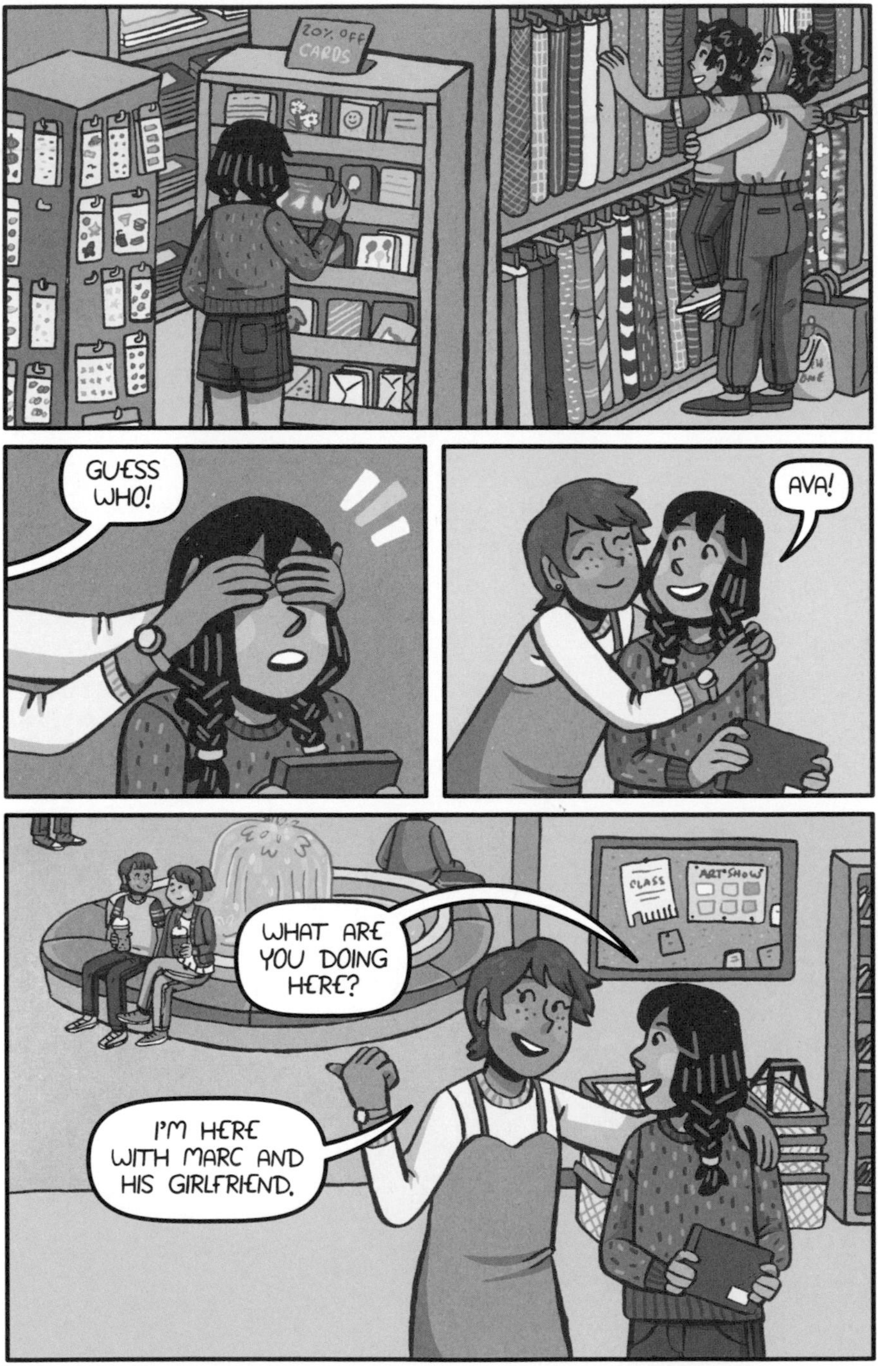
20% OFF
CARDS
GUESS WHO!
AVA!
CLASS
ART SHOW
WHAT ARE YOU DOING HERE?
I'M HERE WITH MARC AND HIS GIRLFRIEND.

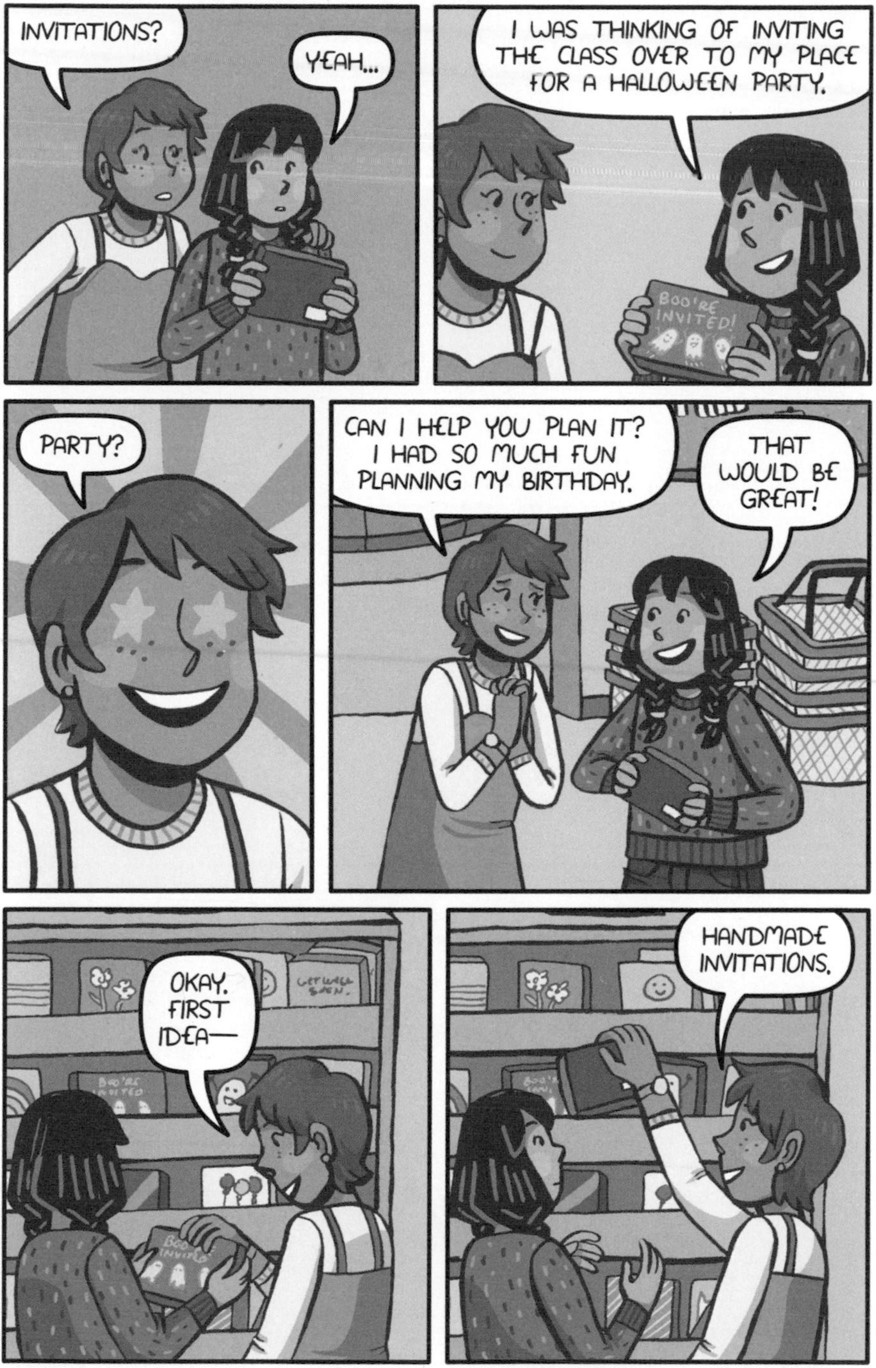
INVITATIONS?
YEAH...
I WAS THINKING OF INVITING THE CLASS OVER TO MY PLACE FOR A HALLOWEEN PARTY.
BOO'RE INVITED!
PARTY?
CAN I HELP YOU PLAN IT? I HAD SO MUCH FUN PLANNING MY BIRTHDAY.
THAT WOULD BE GREAT!
OKAY. FIRST IDEA—
HANDMADE INVITATIONS.

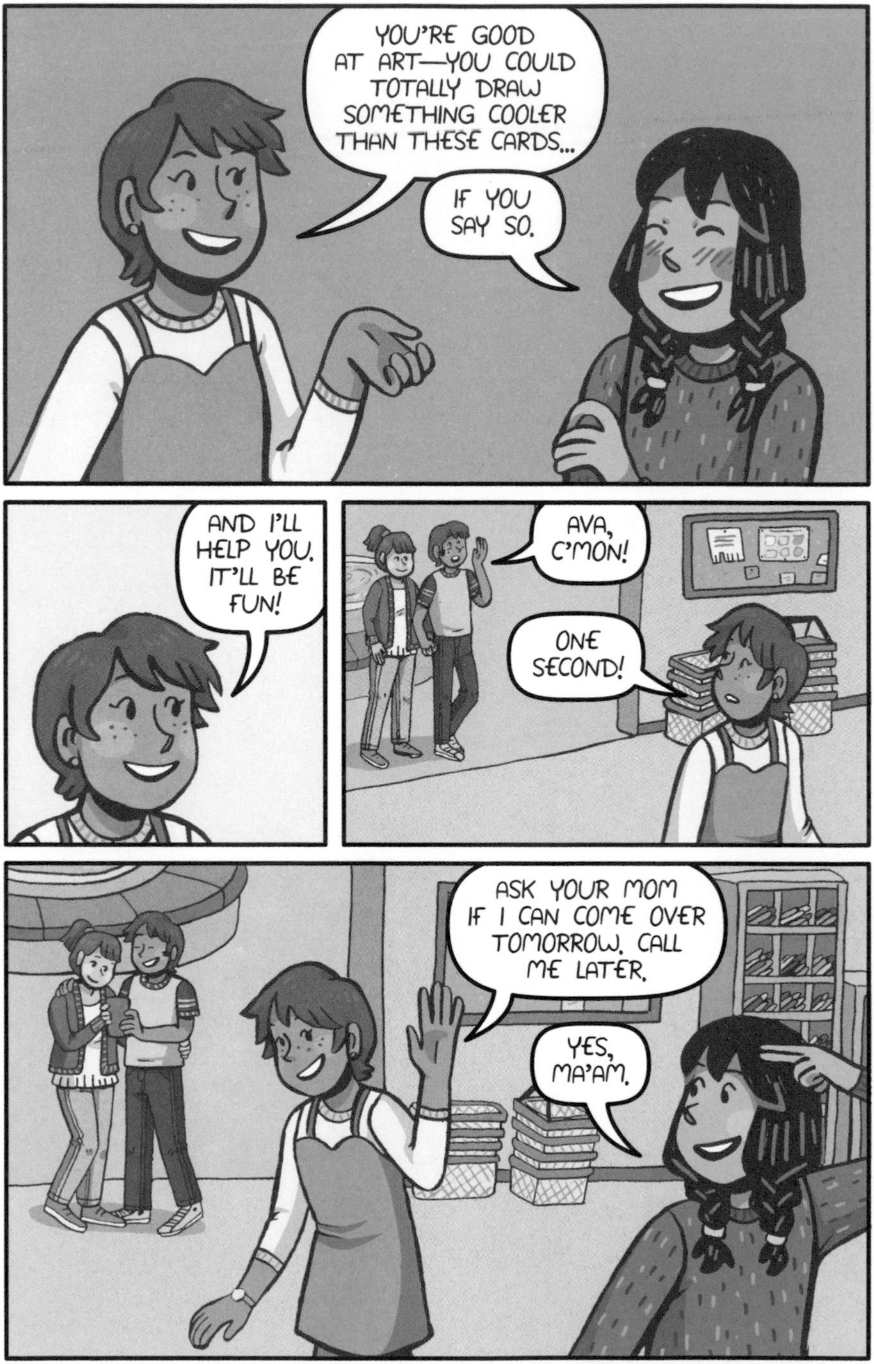
YOU'RE GOOD AT ART—YOU COULD TOTALLY DRAW SOMETHING COOLER THAN THESE CARDS...
IF YOU SAY SO.
AND I'LL HELP YOU. IT'LL BE FUN!
AVA, C'MON!
ONE SECOND!
ASK YOUR MOM IF I CAN COME OVER TOMORROW. CALL ME LATER.
YES, MA'AM.

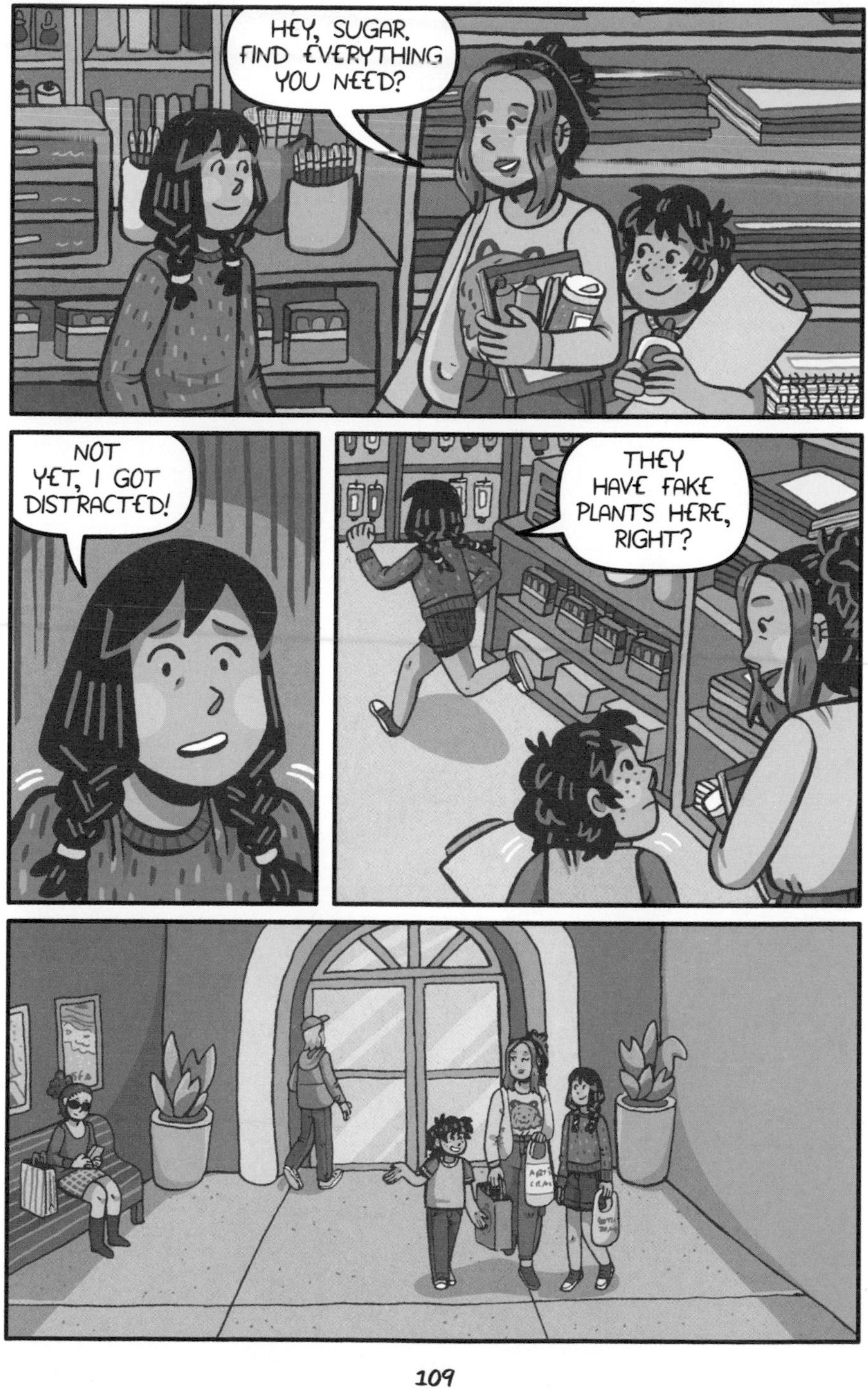
HEY, SUGAR. FIND EVERYTHING YOU NEED?
NOT YET, I GOT DISTRACTED!
THEY HAVE FAKE PLANTS HERE, RIGHT?

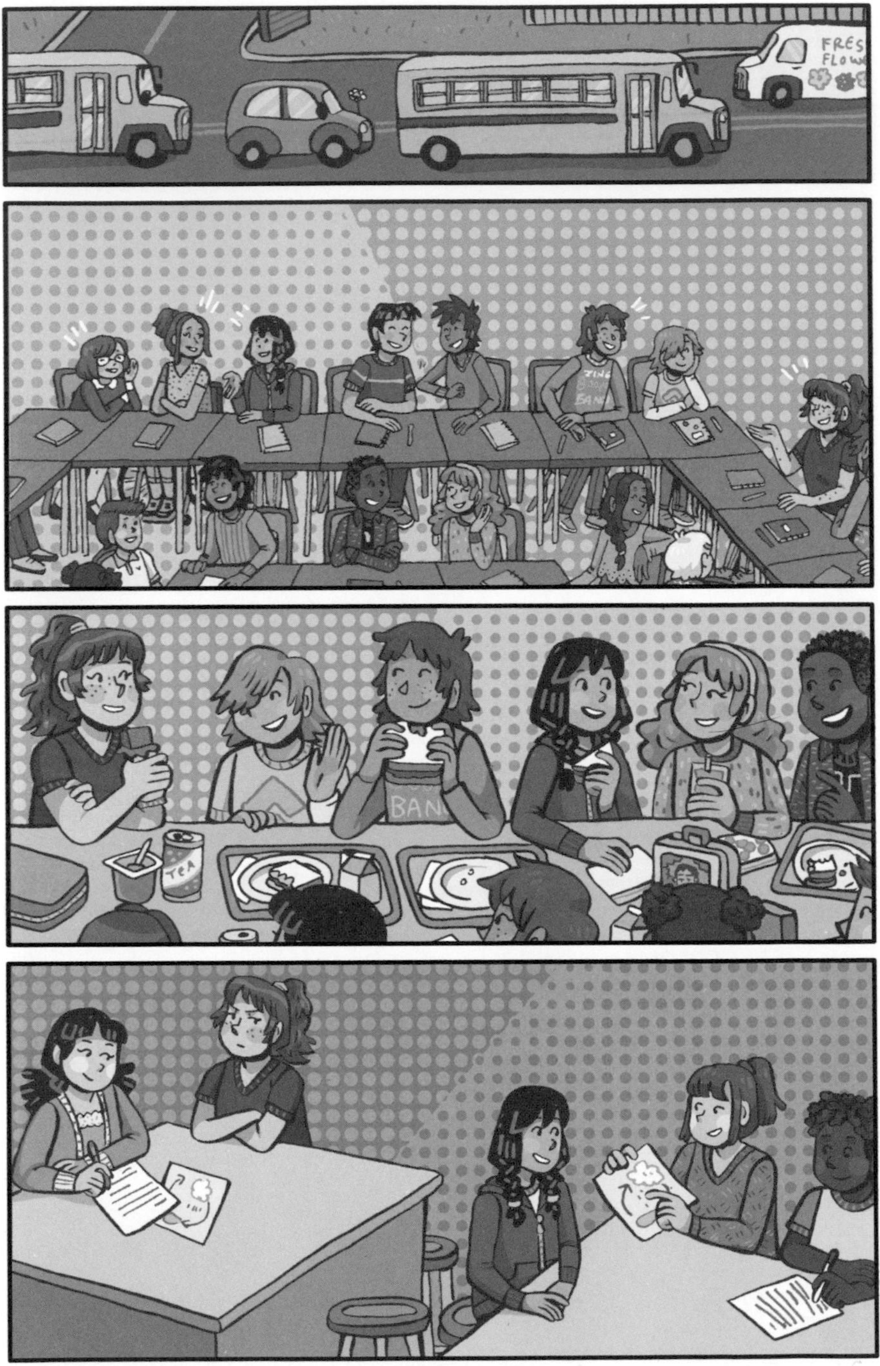
TEA

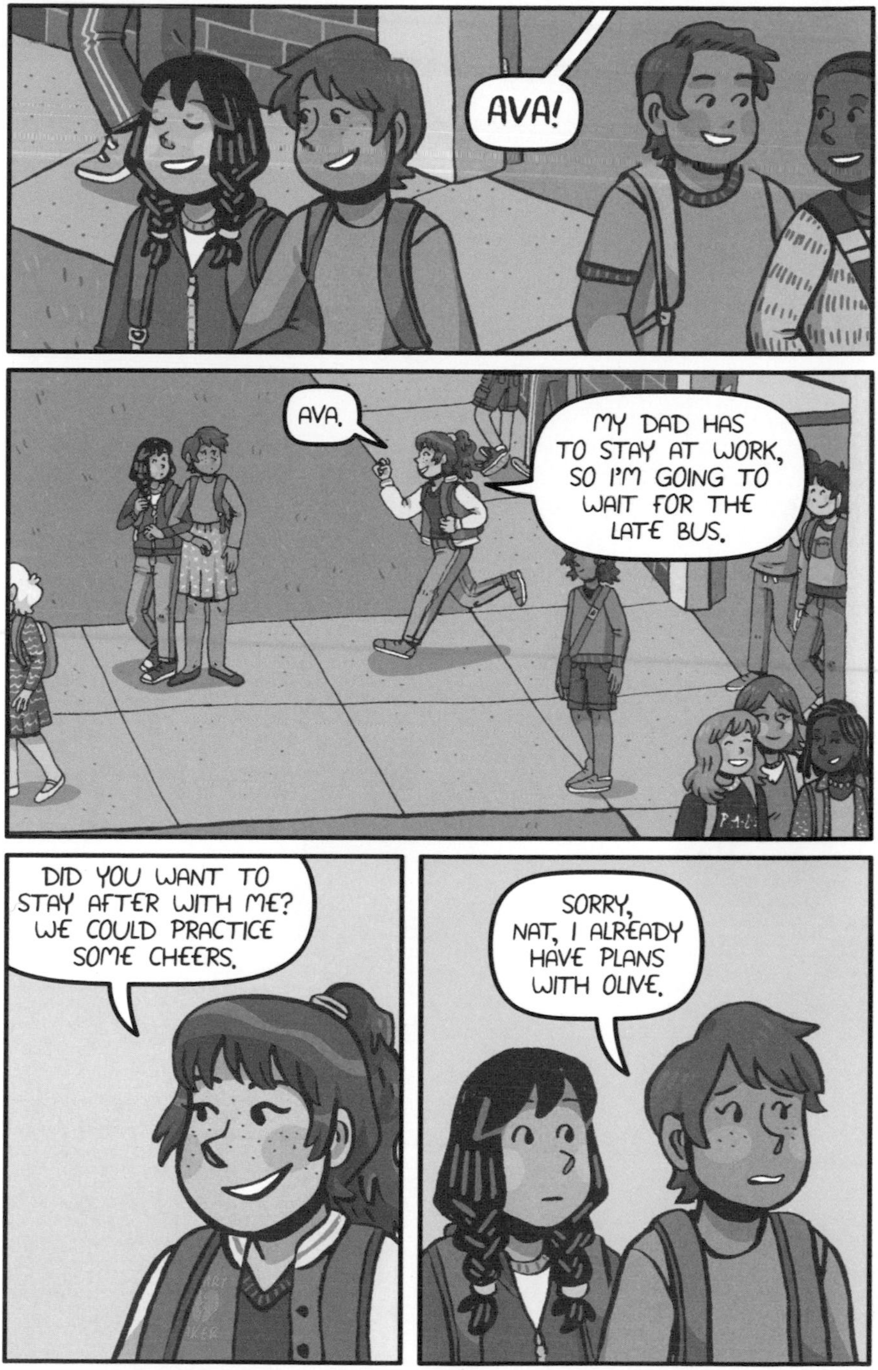
AVA!
AVA.
MY DAD HAS TO STAY AT WORK, SO I'M GOING TO WAIT FOR THE LATE BUS.
DID YOU WANT TO STAY AFTER WITH ME? WE COULD PRACTICE SOME CHEERS.
SORRY, NAT, I ALREADY HAVE PLANS WITH OLIVE.

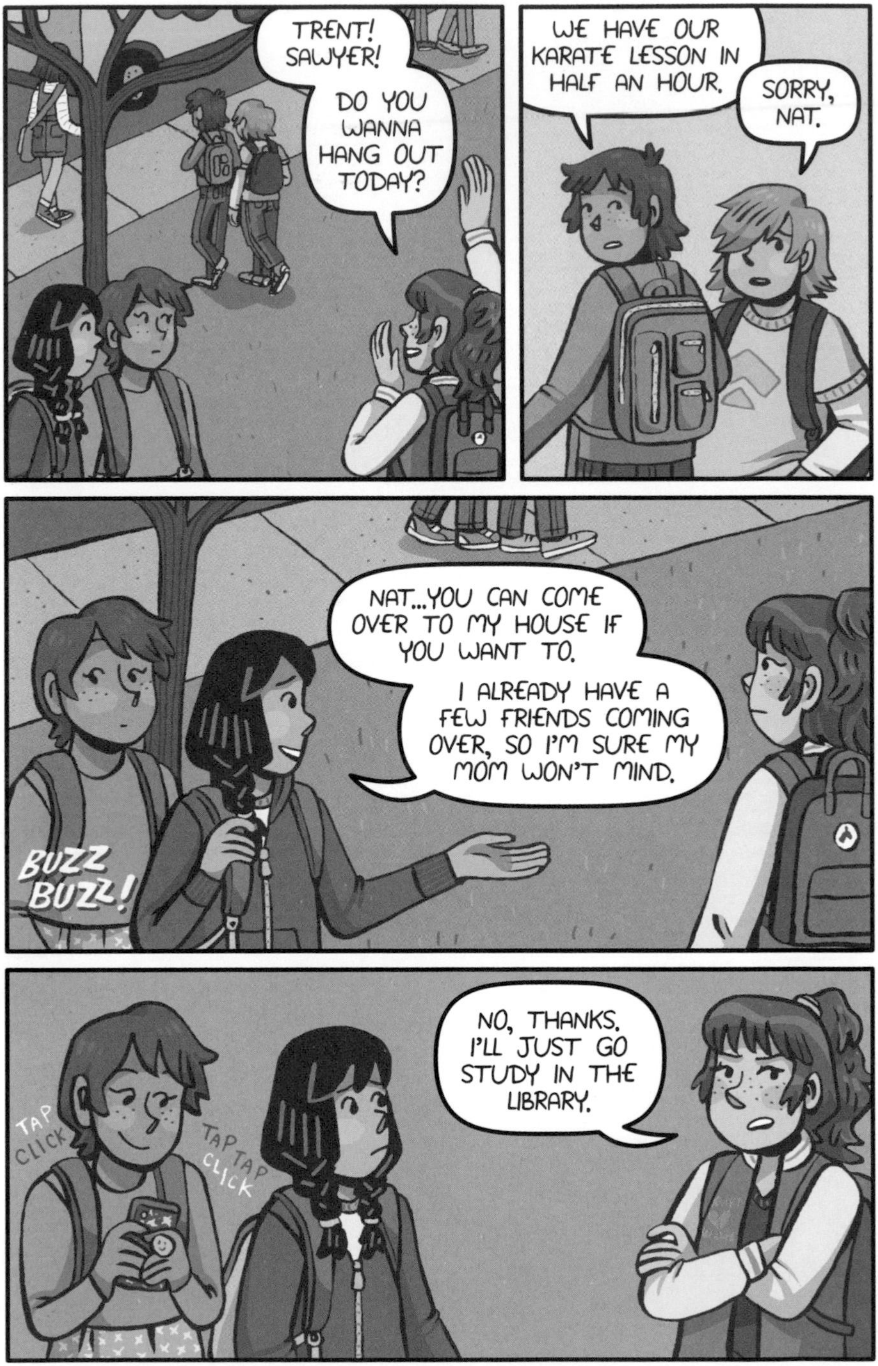

TRENT! SAWYER!
DO YOU WANNA HANG OUT TODAY?
WE HAVE OUR KARATE LESSON IN HALF AN HOUR.
SORRY, NAT.
NAT...YOU CAN COME OVER TO MY HOUSE IF YOU WANT TO.
I ALREADY HAVE A FEW FRIENDS COMING OVER, SO I'M SURE MY MOM WON'T MIND.
BUZZ BUZZ!
TAP CLICK
TAP TAP CLICK
NO, THANKS. I'LL JUST GO STUDY IN THE LIBRARY.

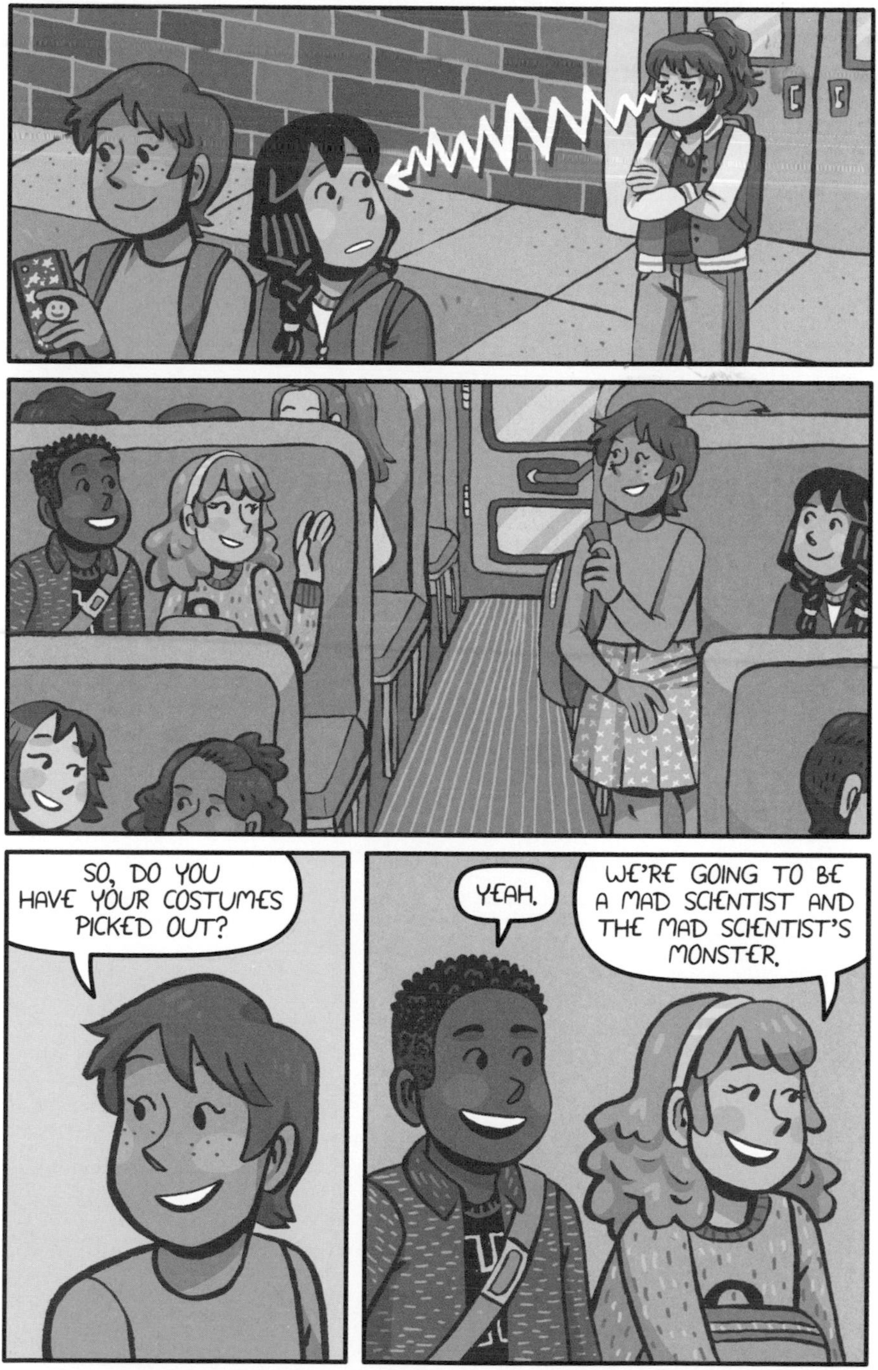
SO, DO YOU HAVE YOUR COSTUMES PICKED OUT?
YEAH.
WE'RE GOING TO BE A MAD SCIENTIST AND THE MAD SCIENTIST'S MONSTER.

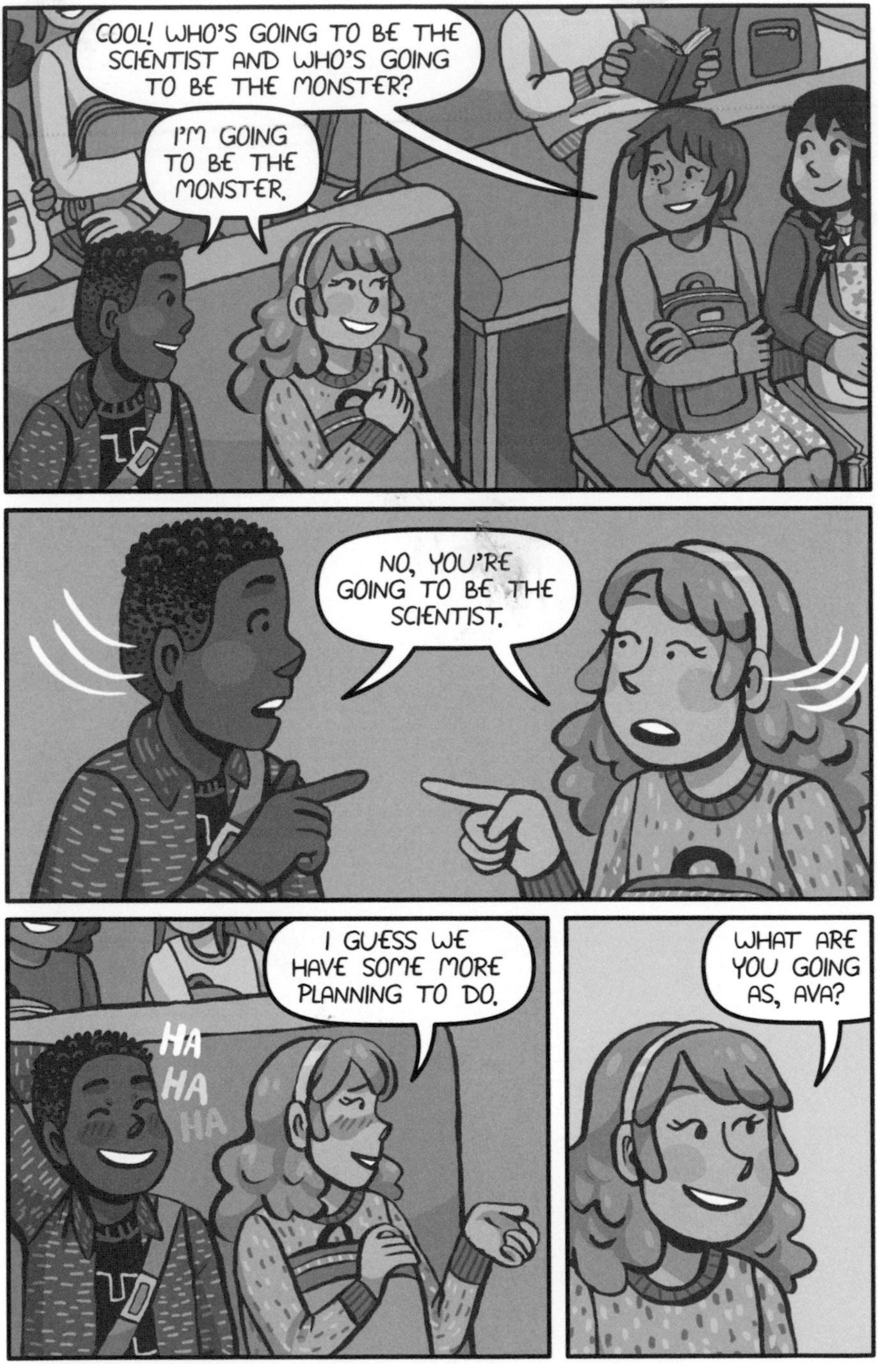
COOL! WHO'S GOING TO BE THE SCIENTIST AND WHO'S GOING TO BE THE MONSTER?
I'M GOING TO BE THE MONSTER.
NO, YOU'RE GOING TO BE THE SCIENTIST.
I GUESS WE HAVE SOME MORE PLANNING TO DO.
HA HA HA
WHAT ARE YOU GOING AS, AVA?

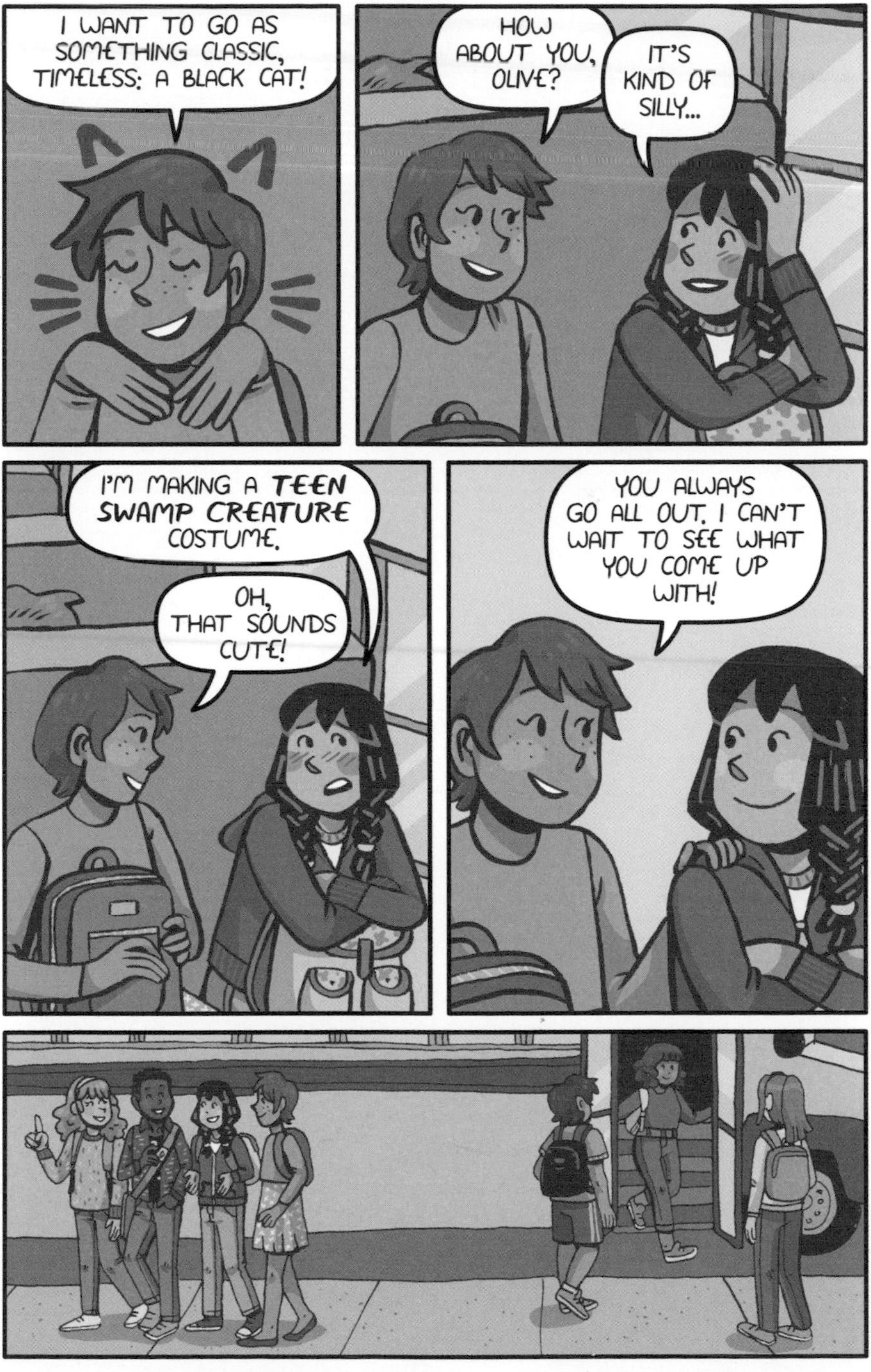
I WANT TO GO AS SOMETHING CLASSIC, TIMELESS: A BLACK CAT!
HOW ABOUT YOU, OLIVE?
IT'S KIND OF SILLY...
I'M MAKING A **TEEN SWAMP CREATURE** COSTUME.
OH, THAT SOUNDS CUTE!
YOU ALWAYS GO ALL OUT. I CAN'T WAIT TO SEE WHAT YOU COME UP WITH!

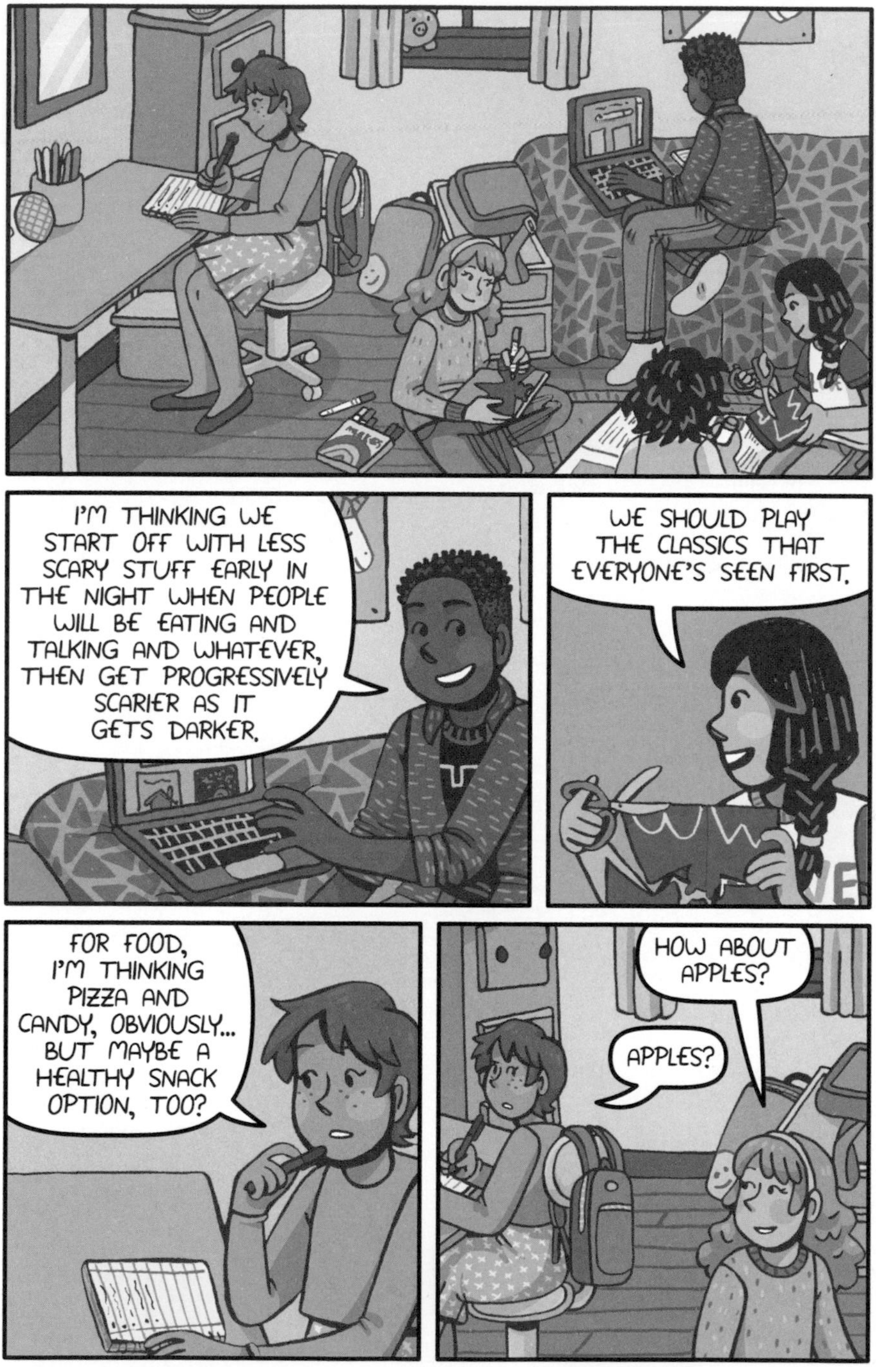
I'M THINKING WE START OFF WITH LESS SCARY STUFF EARLY IN THE NIGHT WHEN PEOPLE WILL BE EATING AND TALKING AND WHATEVER, THEN GET PROGRESSIVELY SCARIER AS IT GETS DARKER.
WE SHOULD PLAY THE CLASSICS THAT EVERYONE'S SEEN FIRST.
FOR FOOD, I'M THINKING PIZZA AND CANDY, OBVIOUSLY... BUT MAYBE A HEALTHY SNACK OPTION, TOO?
HOW ABOUT APPLES?
APPLES?

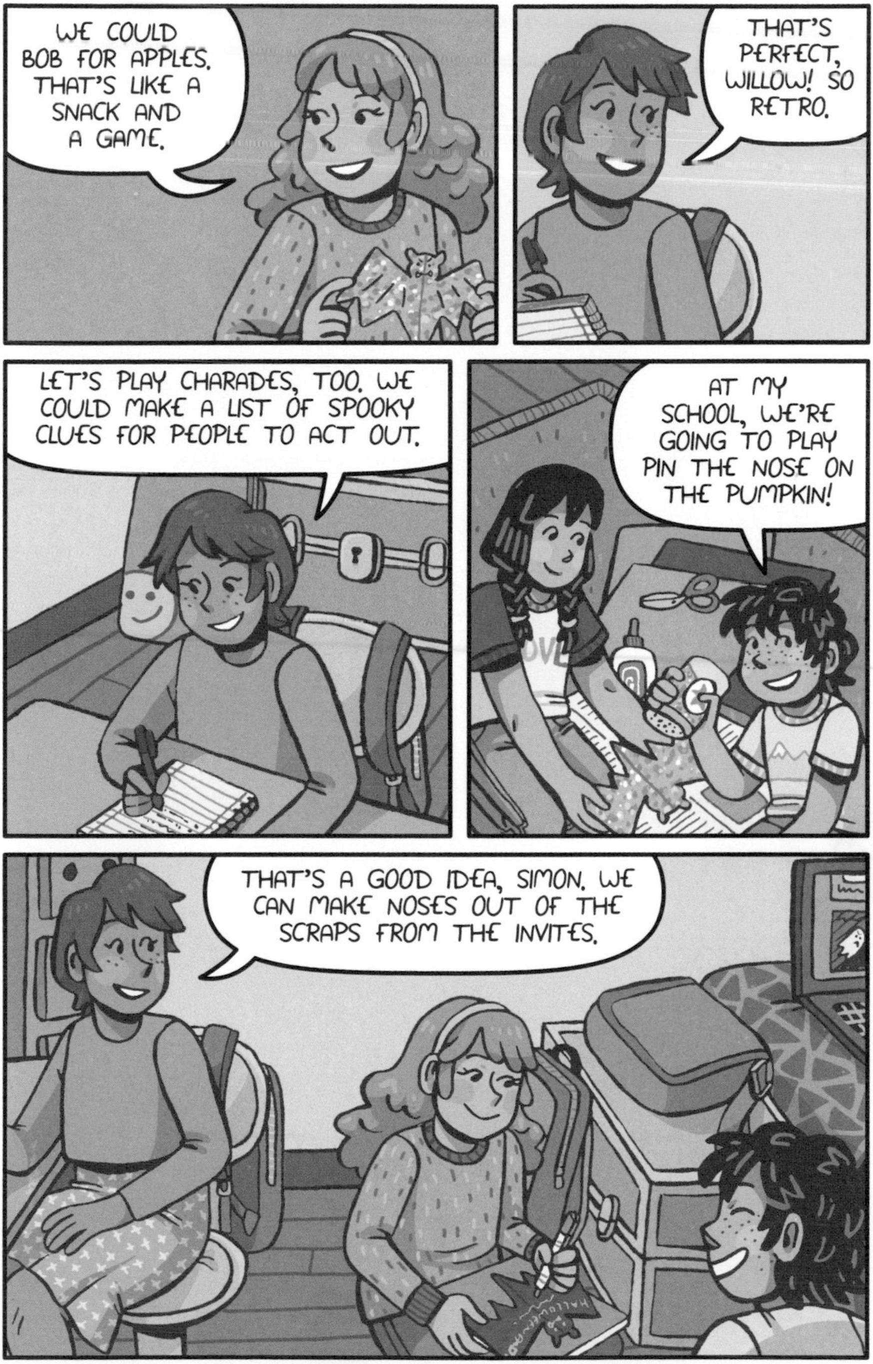
WE COULD BOB FOR APPLES. THAT'S LIKE A SNACK AND A GAME.
THAT'S PERFECT, WILLOW! SO RETRO.
LET'S PLAY CHARADES, TOO. WE COULD MAKE A LIST OF SPOOKY CLUES FOR PEOPLE TO ACT OUT.
AT MY SCHOOL, WE'RE GOING TO PLAY PIN THE NOSE ON THE PUMPKIN!
THAT'S A GOOD IDEA, SIMON. WE CAN MAKE NOSES OUT OF THE SCRAPS FROM THE INVITES.

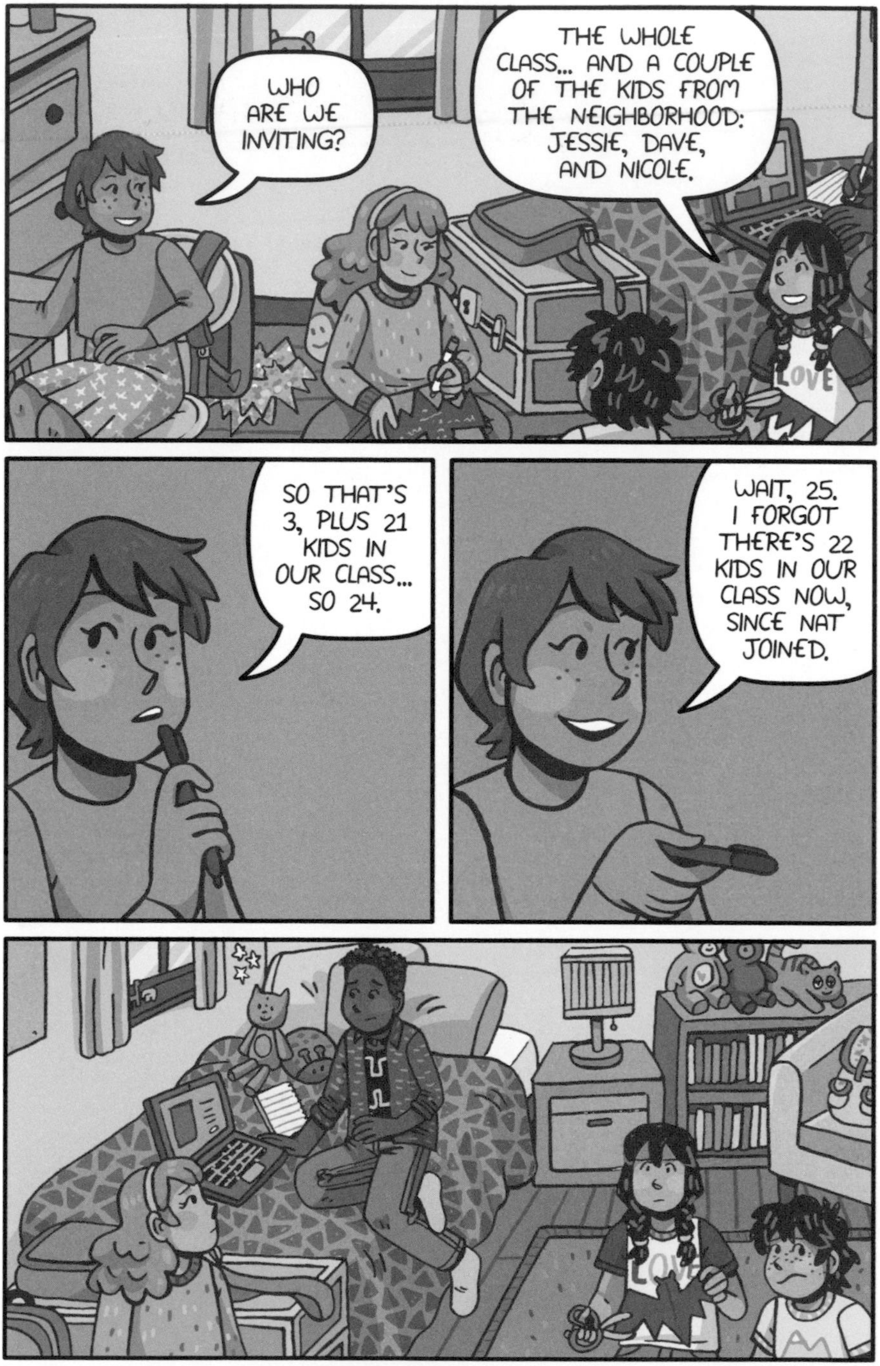
WHO ARE WE INVITING?
THE WHOLE CLASS... AND A COUPLE OF THE KIDS FROM THE NEIGHBORHOOD: JESSIE, DAVE, AND NICOLE.
LOVE
SO THAT'S 3, PLUS 21 KIDS IN OUR CLASS... SO 24.
WAIT, 25. I FORGOT THERE'S 22 KIDS IN OUR CLASS NOW, SINCE NAT JOINED.
LOVE

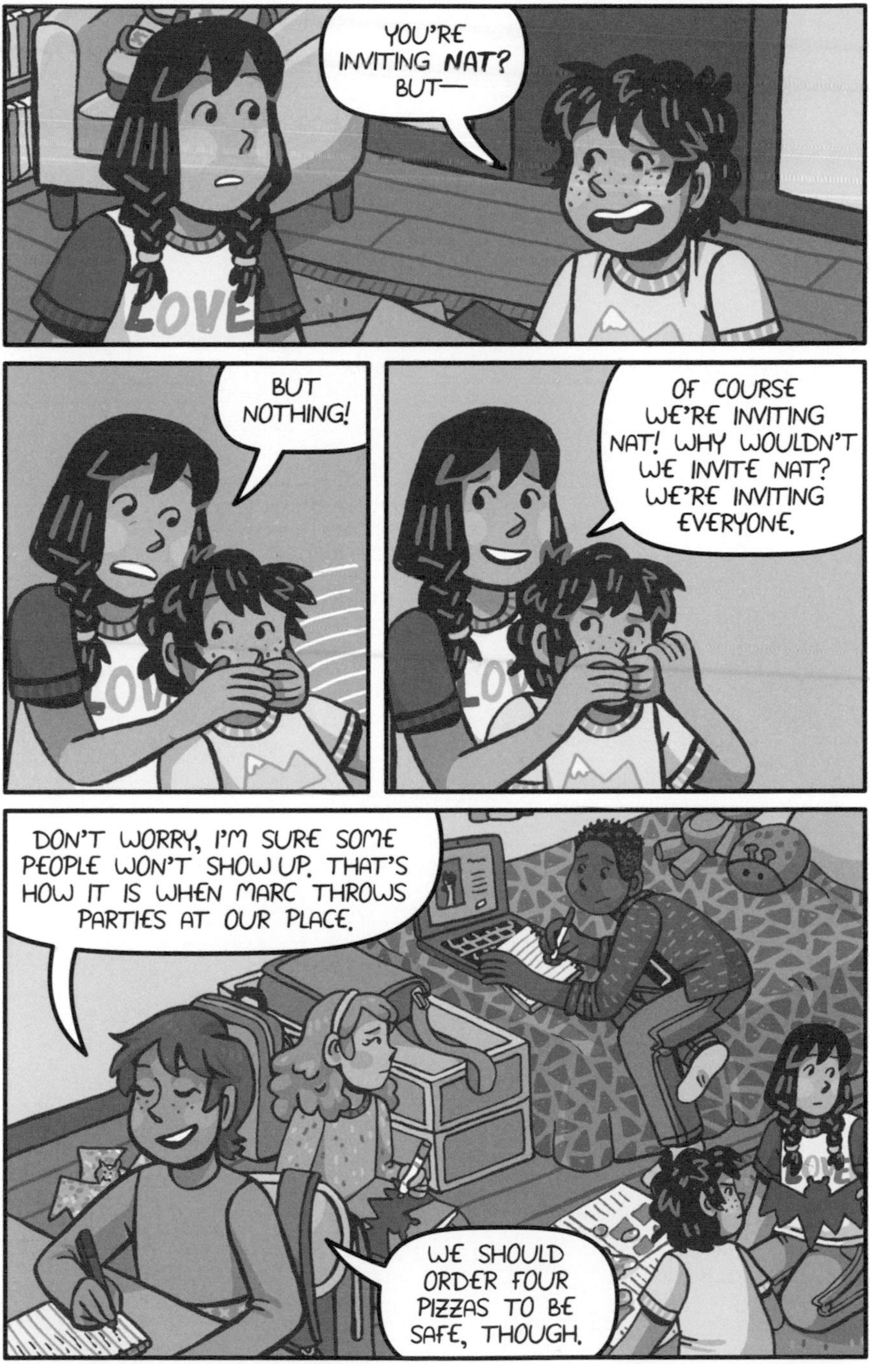
YOU'RE INVITING NAT? BUT—
BUT NOTHING!
OF COURSE WE'RE INVITING NAT! WHY WOULDN'T WE INVITE NAT? WE'RE INVITING EVERYONE.
DON'T WORRY, I'M SURE SOME PEOPLE WON'T SHOW UP. THAT'S HOW IT IS WHEN MARC THROWS PARTIES AT OUR PLACE.
WE SHOULD ORDER FOUR PIZZAS TO BE SAFE, THOUGH.

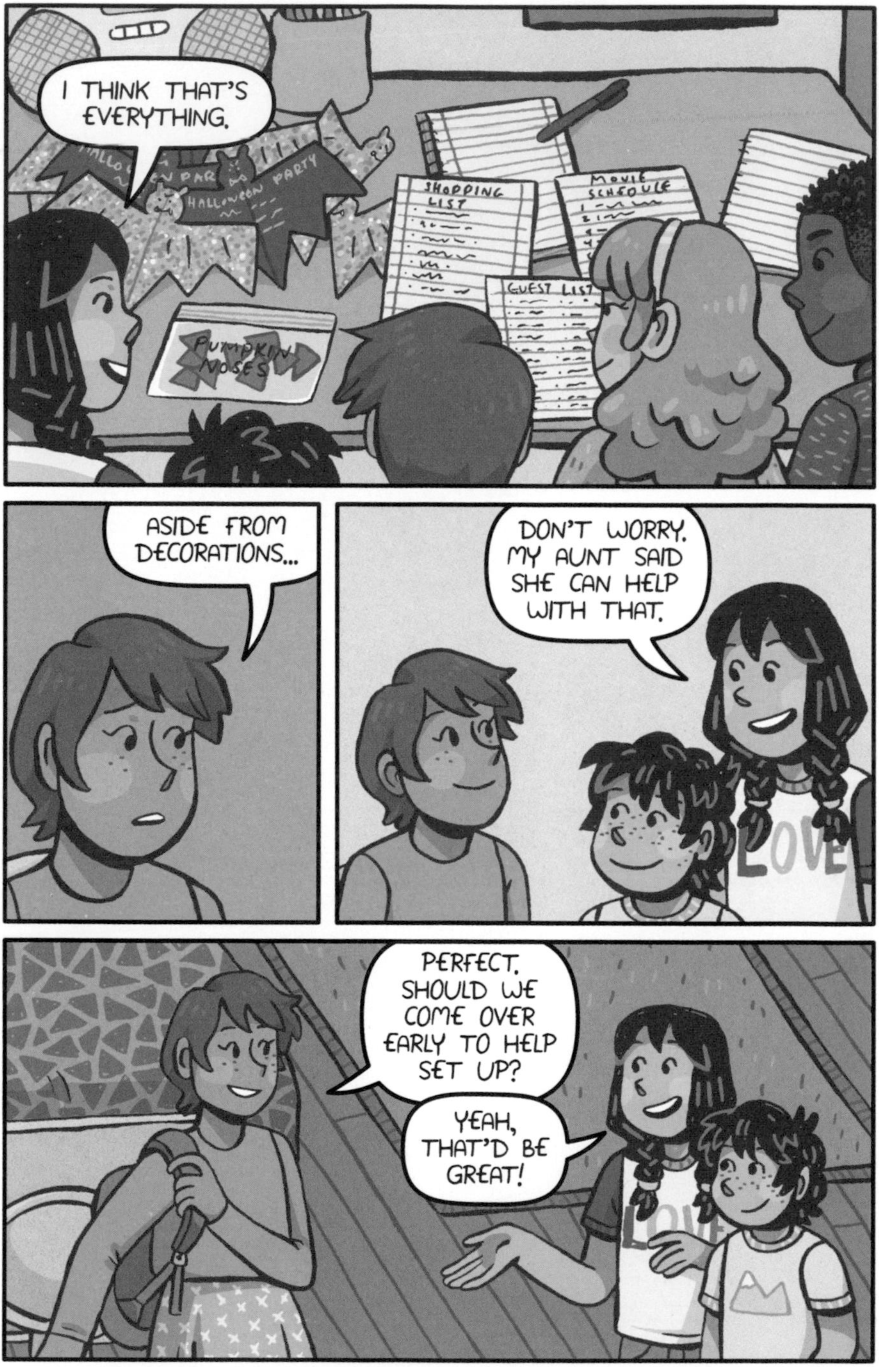
I THINK THAT'S EVERYTHING.
HALLOWEEN PARTY
SHOPPING LIST
MOVIE SCHEDULE
GUEST LIST
PUMPKIN NOSES
ASIDE FROM DECORATIONS...
DON'T WORRY. MY AUNT SAID SHE CAN HELP WITH THAT.
LOVE
PERFECT. SHOULD WE COME OVER EARLY TO HELP SET UP?
YEAH, THAT'D BE GREAT!
LOVE

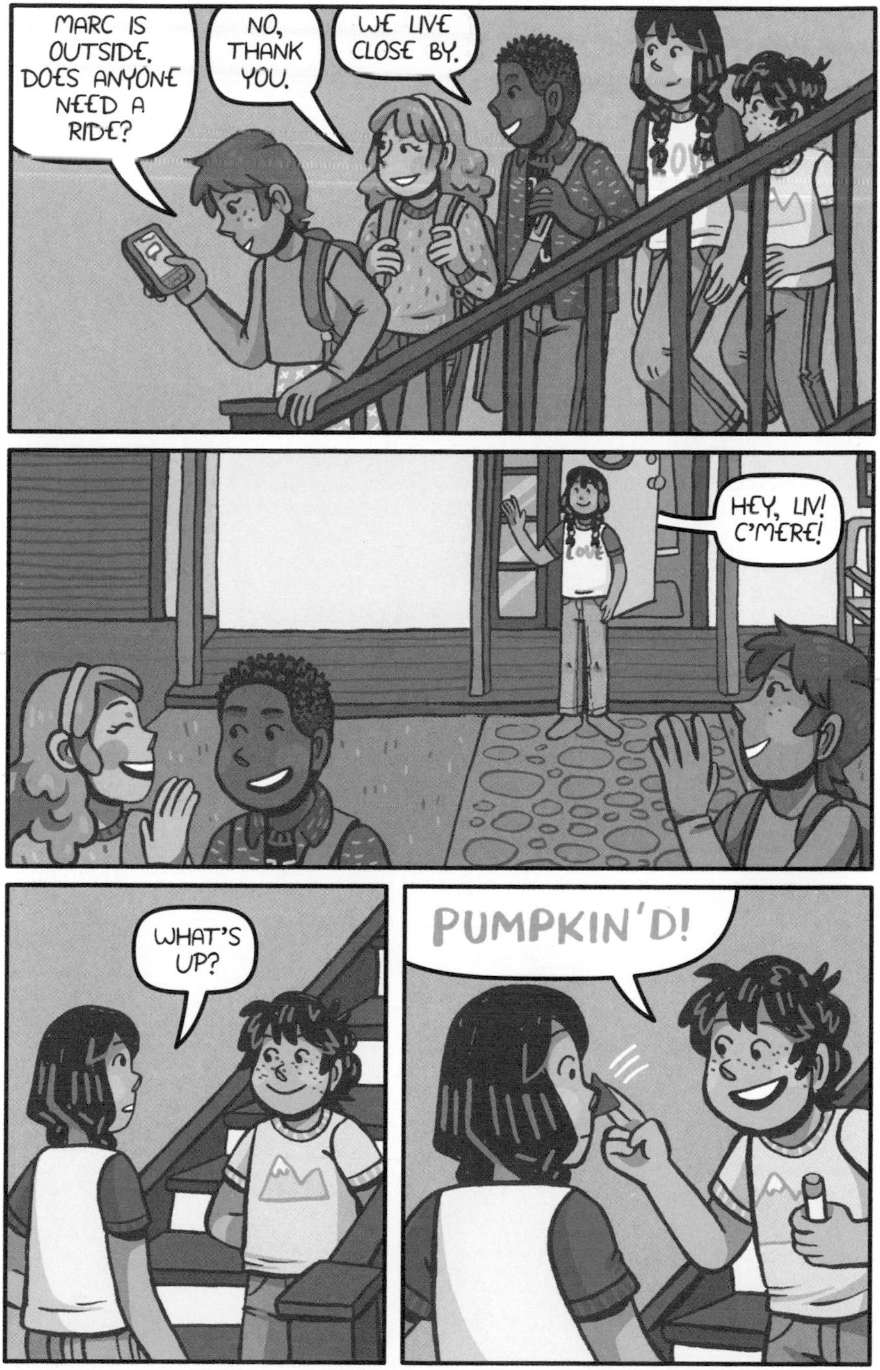
MARC IS OUTSIDE. DOES ANYONE NEED A RIDE?
NO, THANK YOU.
WE LIVE CLOSE BY.
HEY, LIV! C'MERE!
WHAT'S UP?
PUMPKIN'D!

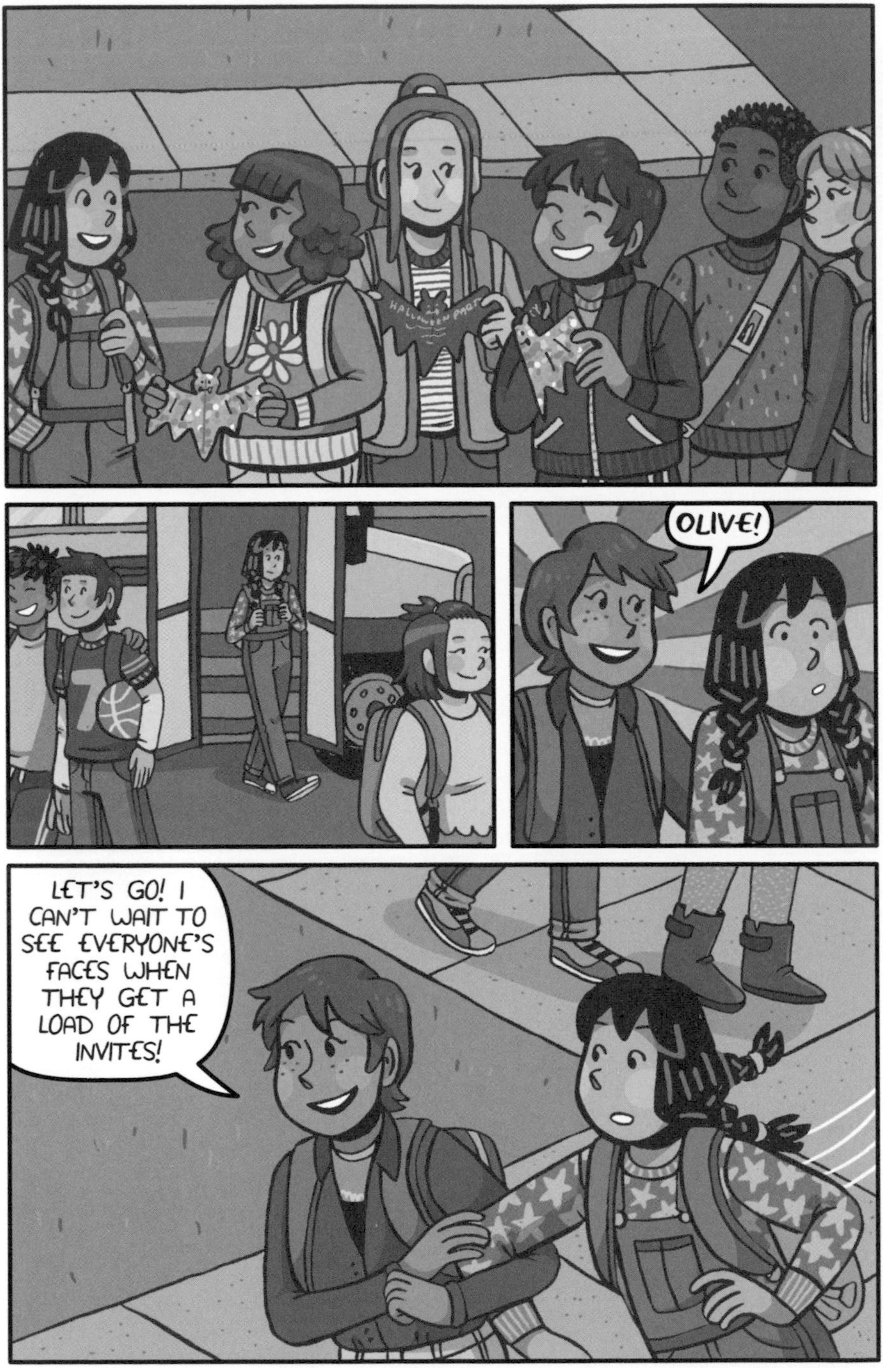
HALLOWEEN PARTY
OLIVE!
LET'S GO! I CAN'T WAIT TO SEE EVERYONE'S FACES WHEN THEY GET A LOAD OF THE INVITES!

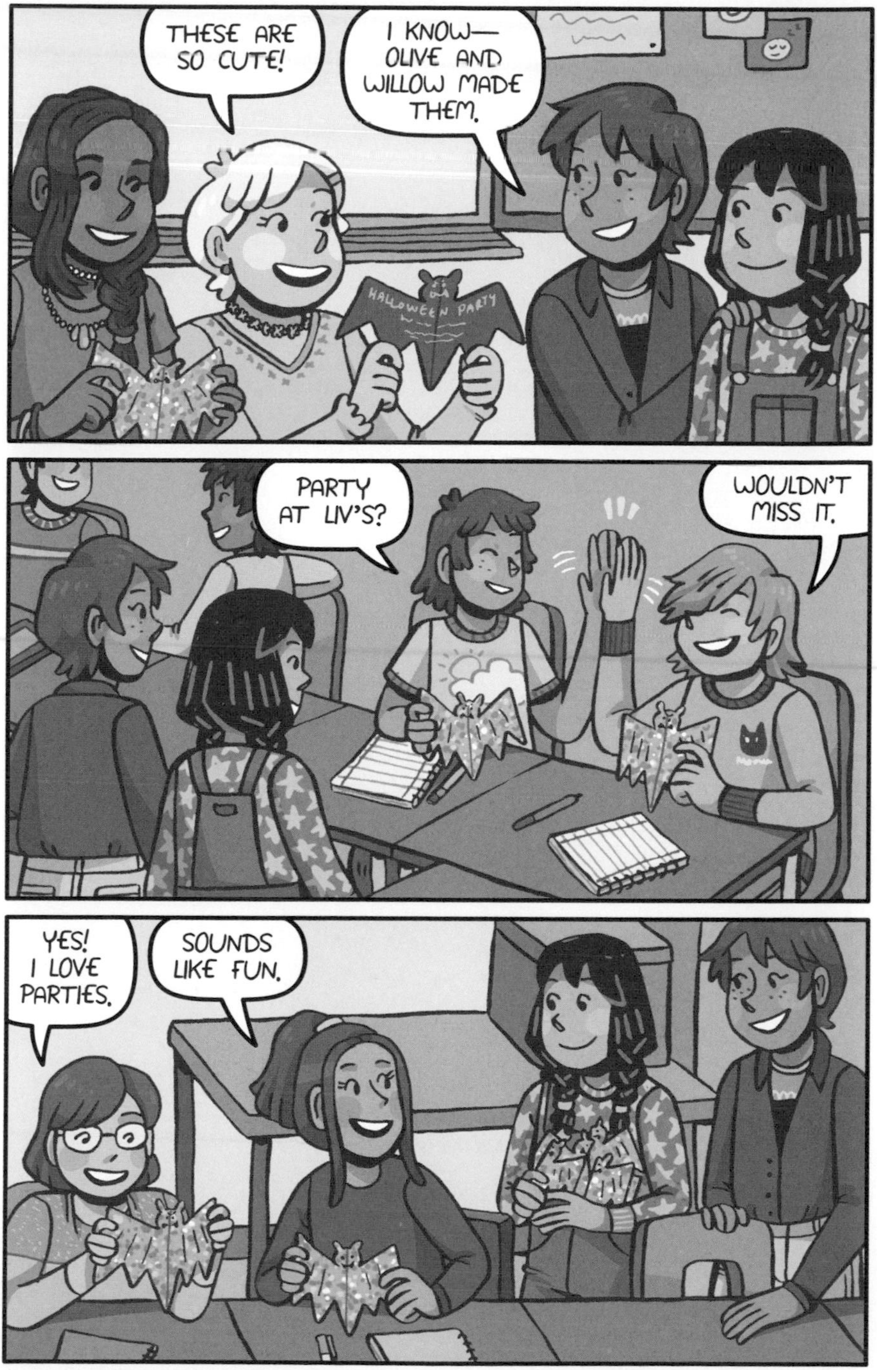
THESE ARE SO CUTE!
I KNOW— OLIVE AND WILLOW MADE THEM.
HALLOWEEN PARTY
PARTY AT LIV'S?
WOULDN'T MISS IT.
YES! I LOVE PARTIES.
SOUNDS LIKE FUN.

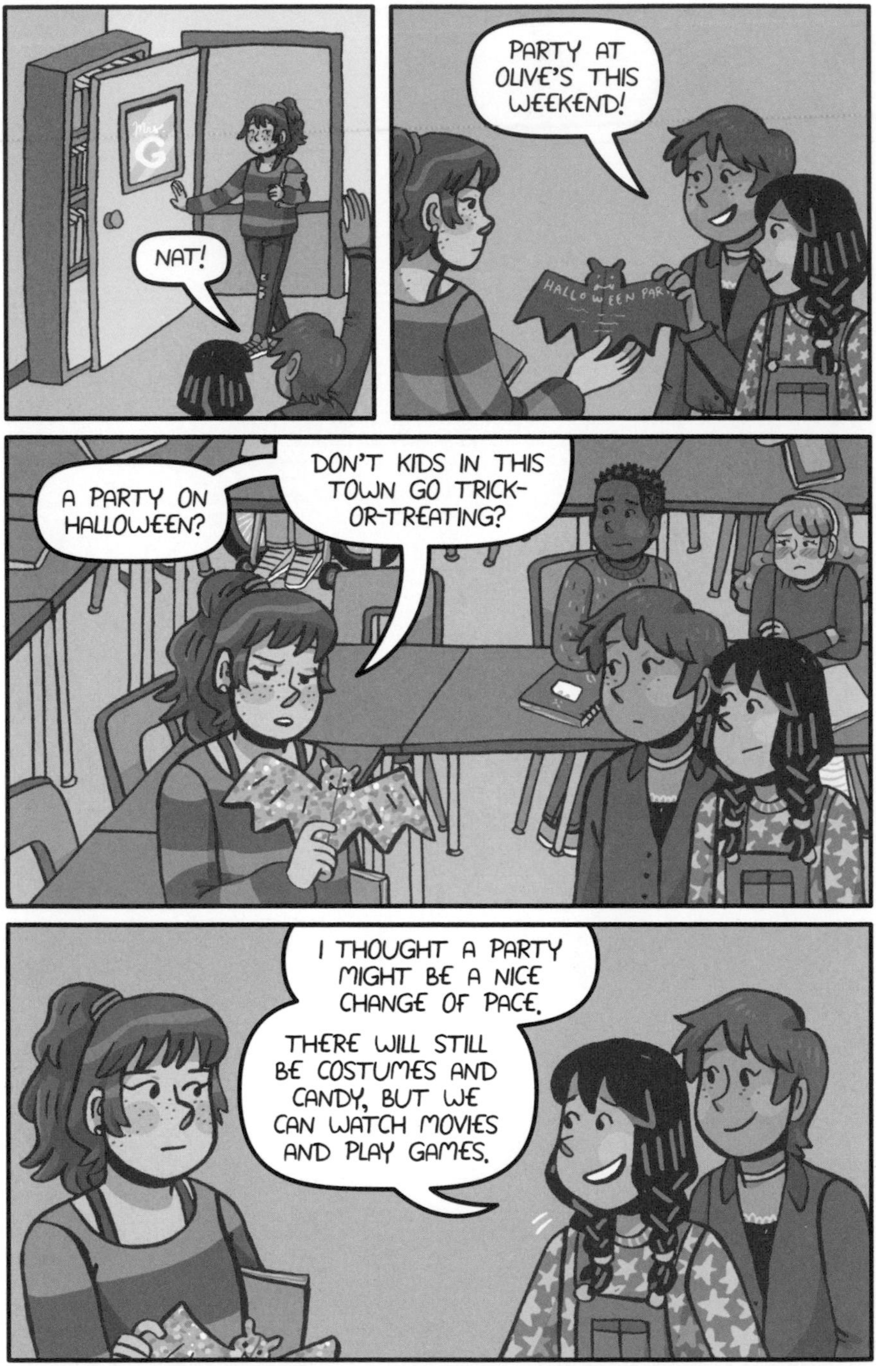
NAT!
PARTY AT OLIVE'S THIS WEEKEND!
HALLOWEEN PAR
A PARTY ON HALLOWEEN?
DON'T KIDS IN THIS TOWN GO TRICK-OR-TREATING?
I THOUGHT A PARTY MIGHT BE A NICE CHANGE OF PACE.
THERE WILL STILL BE COSTUMES AND CANDY, BUT WE CAN WATCH MOVIES AND PLAY GAMES.

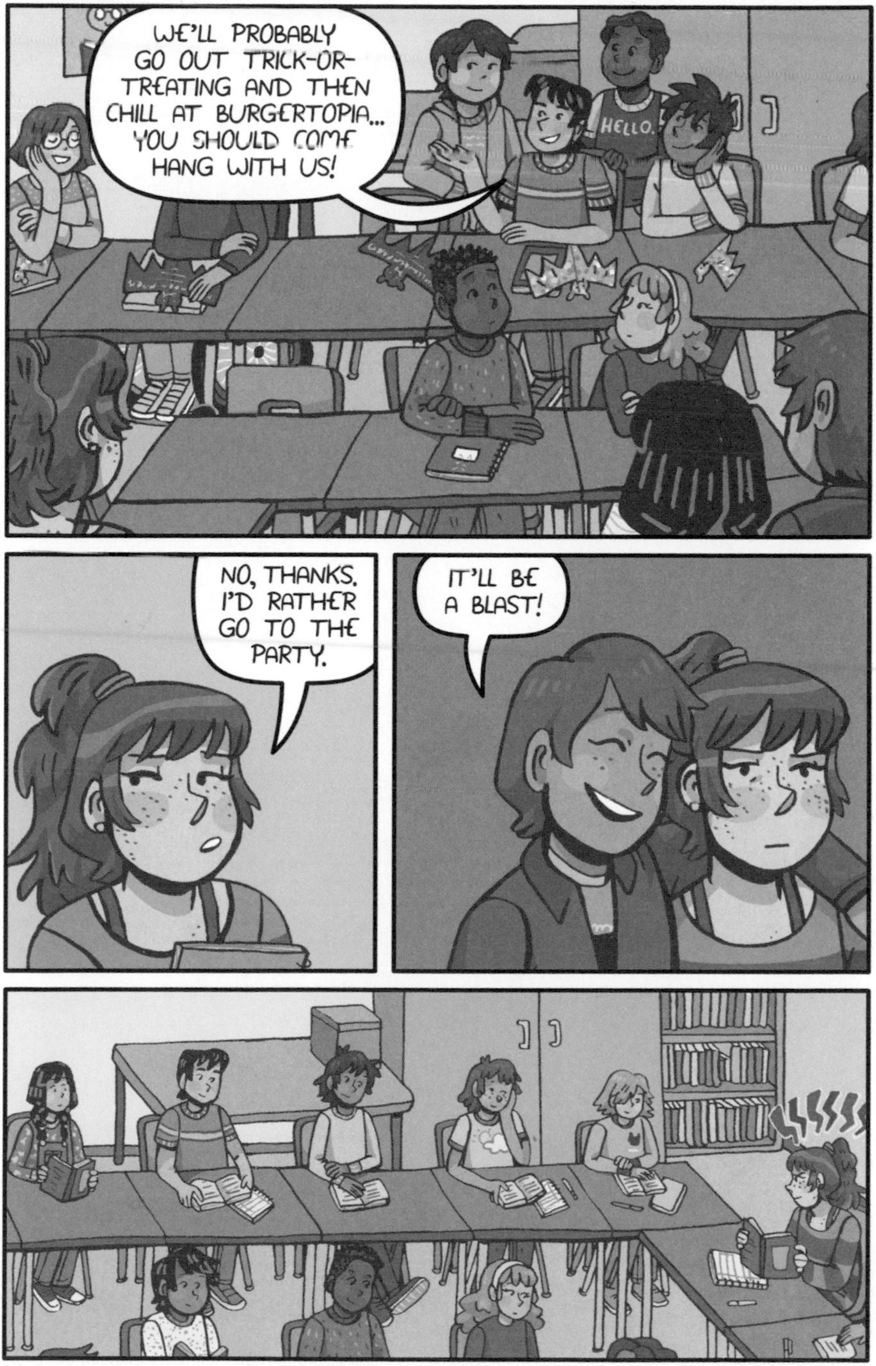
WE'LL PROBABLY GO OUT TRICK-OR-TREATING AND THEN CHILL AT BURGERTOPIA... YOU SHOULD COME HANG WITH US!
HELLO.
NO, THANKS. I'D RATHER GO TO THE PARTY.
IT'LL BE A BLAST!

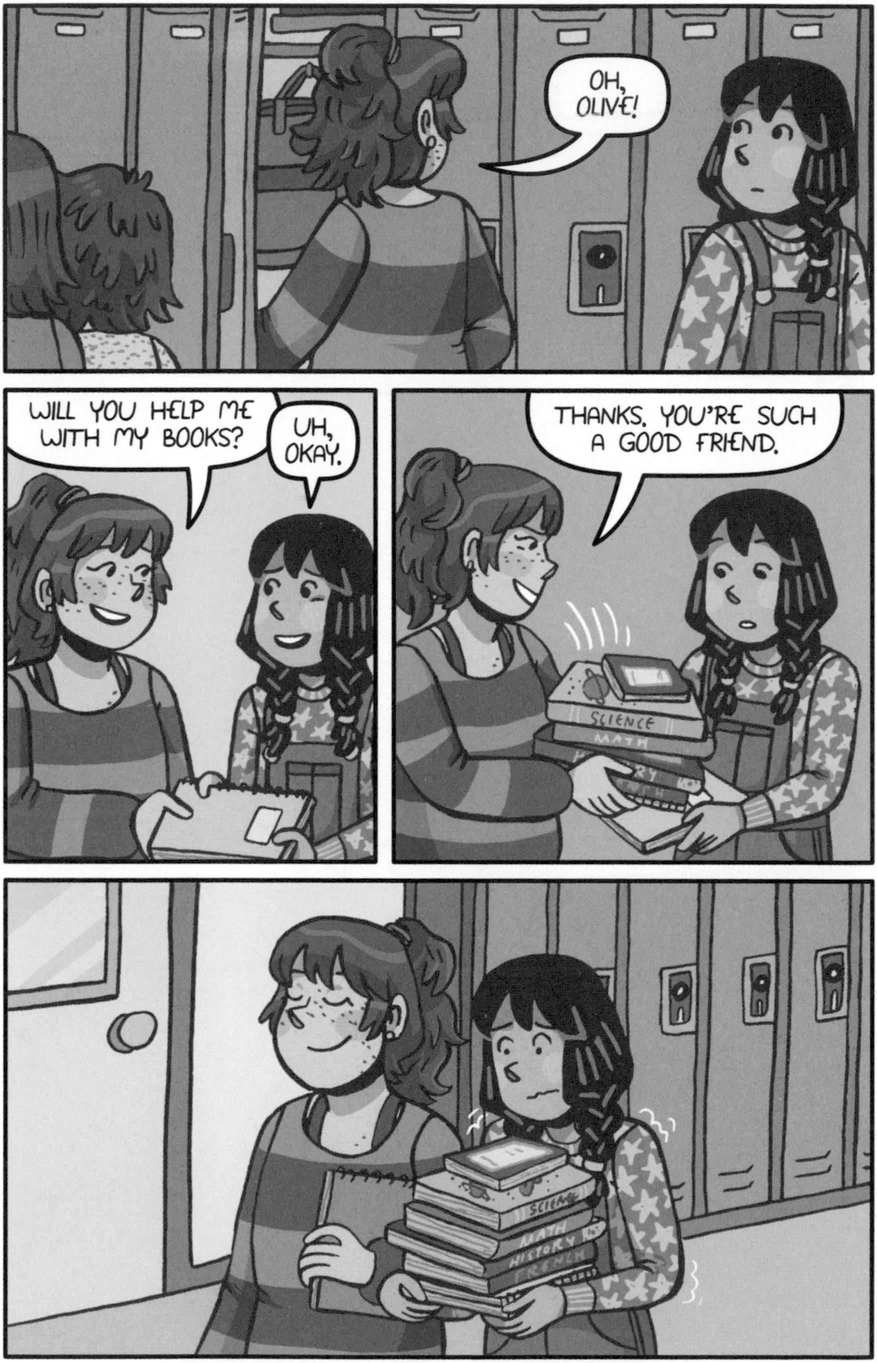
OH, OLIVE!
WILL YOU HELP ME WITH MY BOOKS?
UH, OKAY.
THANKS. YOU'RE SUCH A GOOD FRIEND.
SCIENCE
MATH
MATH
HISTORY
FRENCH

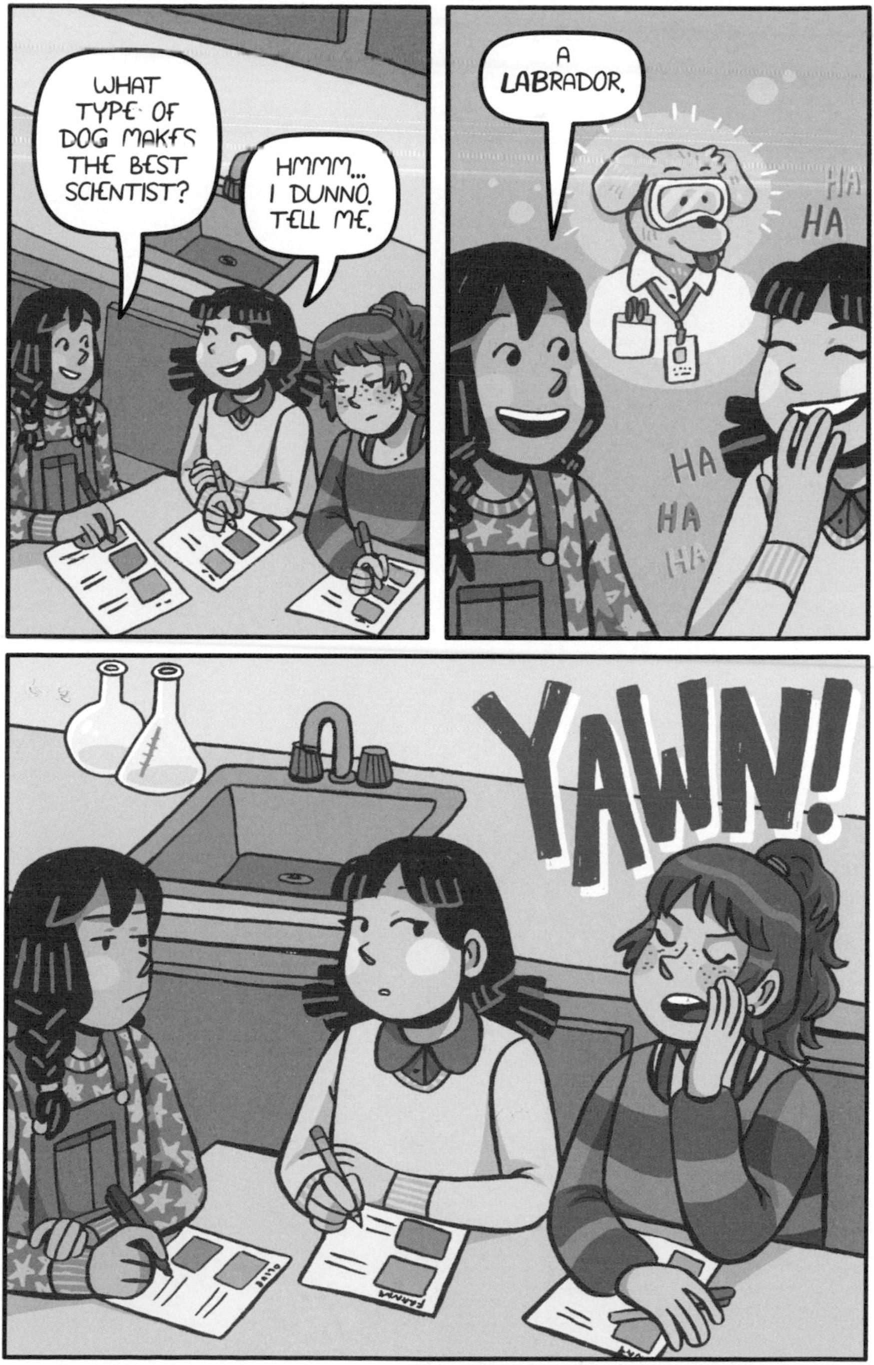
WHAT TYPE OF DOG MAKES THE BEST SCIENTIST?
HMMM... I DUNNO. TELL ME.
A LABRADOR.
HA HA
HA HA HA
YAWN!

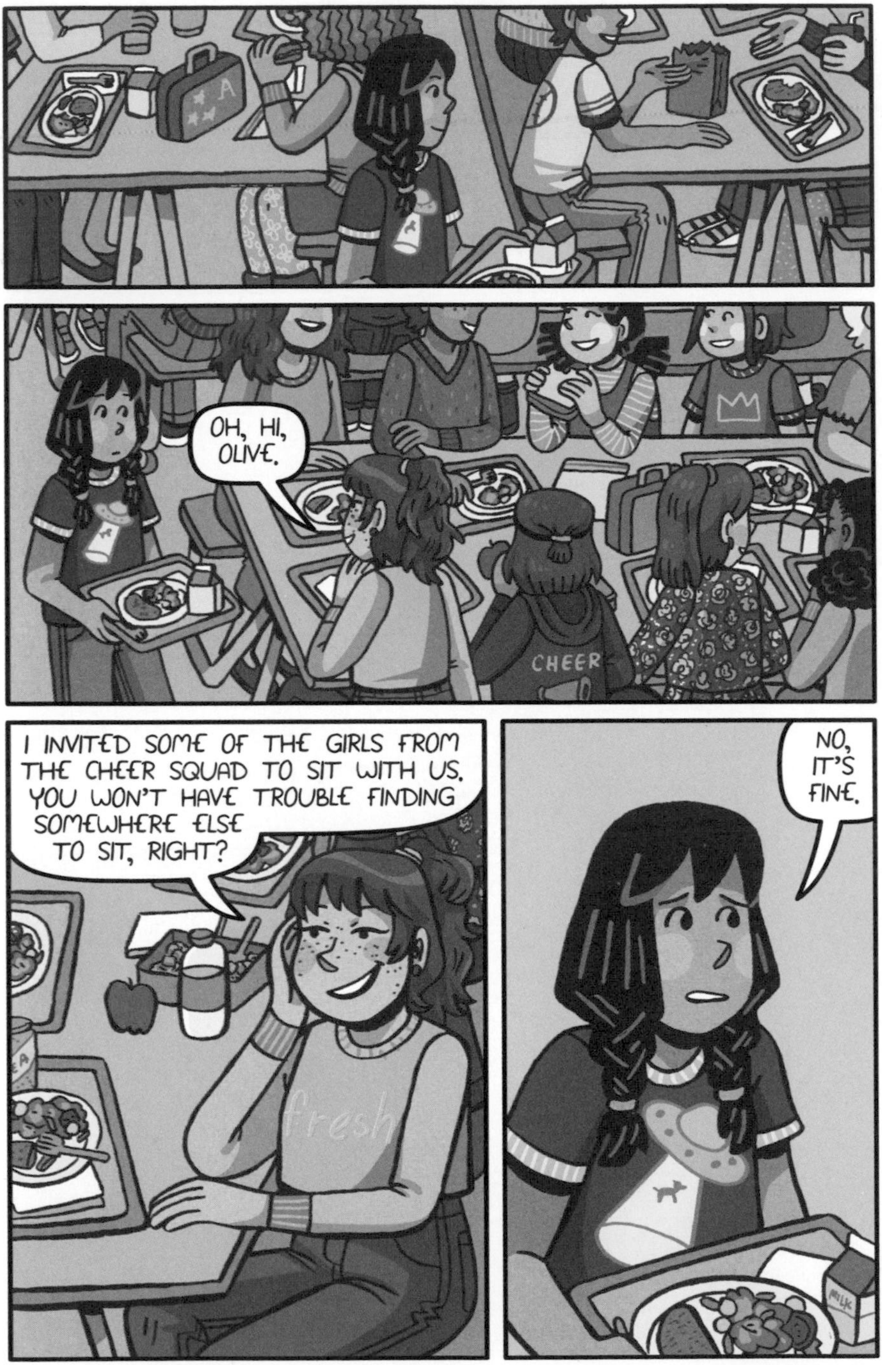
OH, HI, OLIVE.
CHEER
I INVITED SOME OF THE GIRLS FROM THE CHEER SQUAD TO SIT WITH US. YOU WON'T HAVE TROUBLE FINDING SOMEWHERE ELSE TO SIT, RIGHT?
fresh
NO, IT'S FINE.
MILK

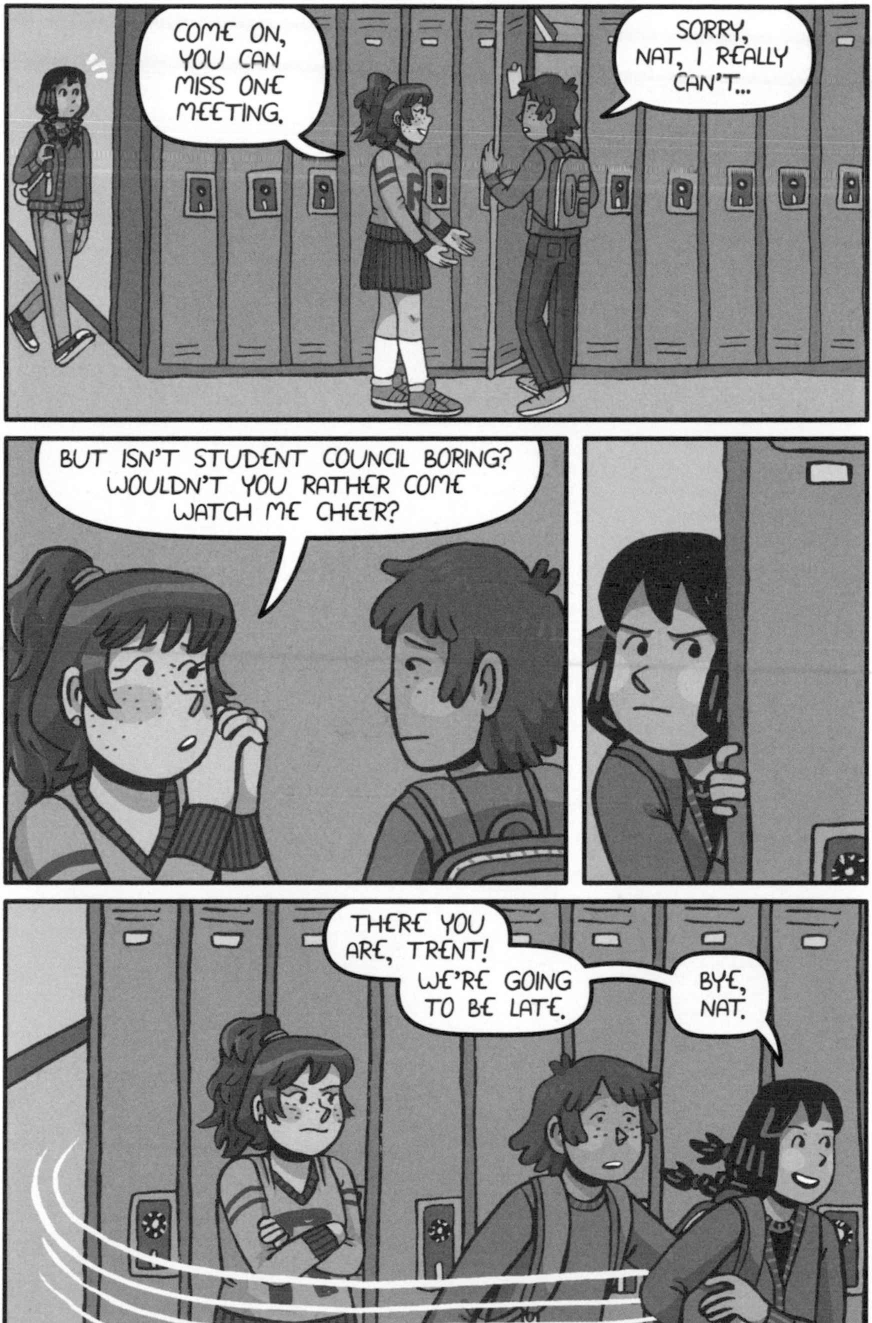
COME ON, YOU CAN MISS ONE MEETING.
SORRY, NAT, I REALLY CAN'T...
BUT ISN'T STUDENT COUNCIL BORING? WOULDN'T YOU RATHER COME WATCH ME CHEER?
THERE YOU ARE, TRENT!
WE'RE GOING TO BE LATE.
BYE, NAT.

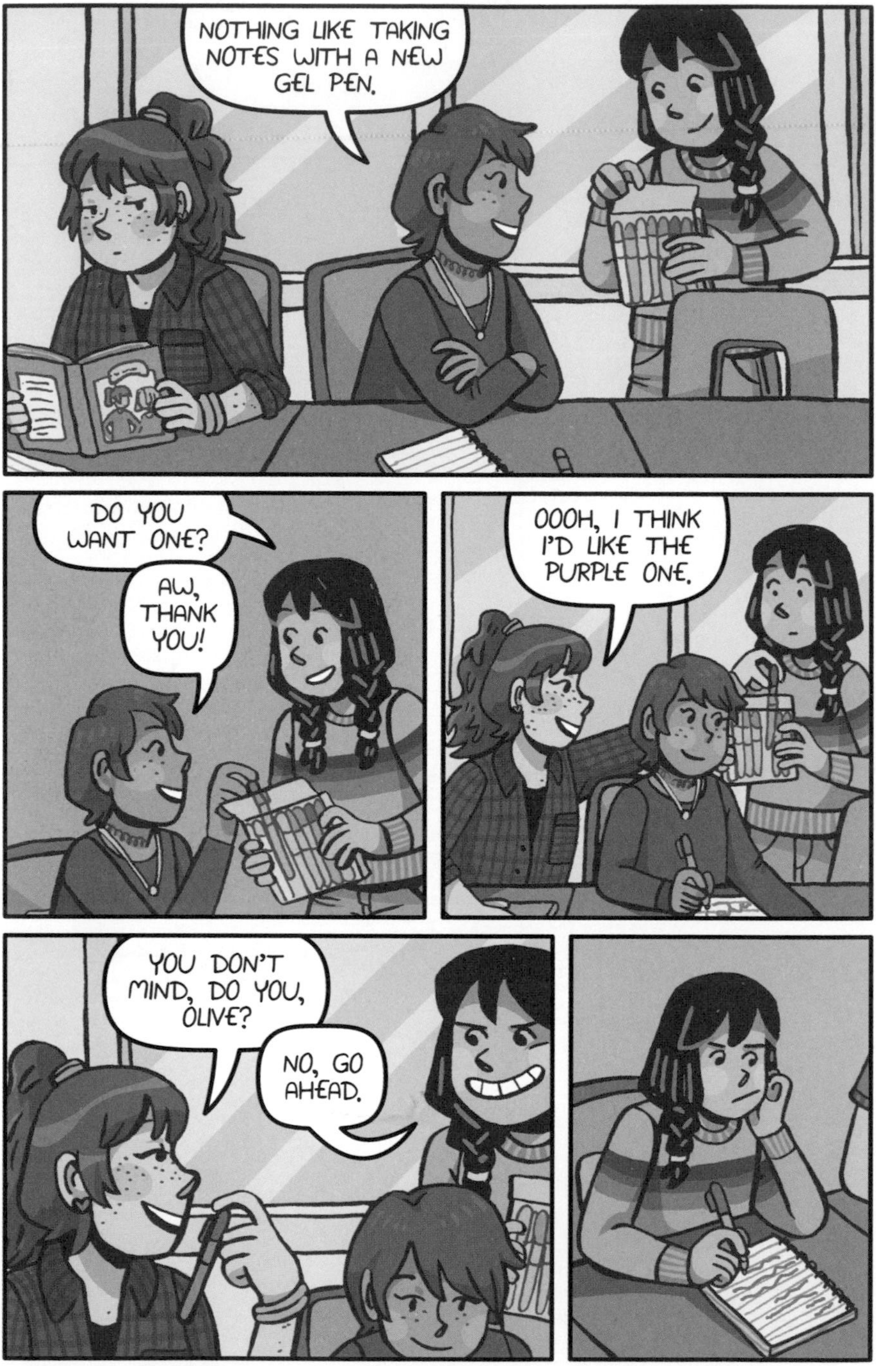
NOTHING LIKE TAKING NOTES WITH A NEW GEL PEN.
DO YOU WANT ONE?
AW, THANK YOU!
OOOH, I THINK I'D LIKE THE PURPLE ONE.
YOU DON'T MIND, DO YOU, OLIVE?
NO, GO AHEAD.

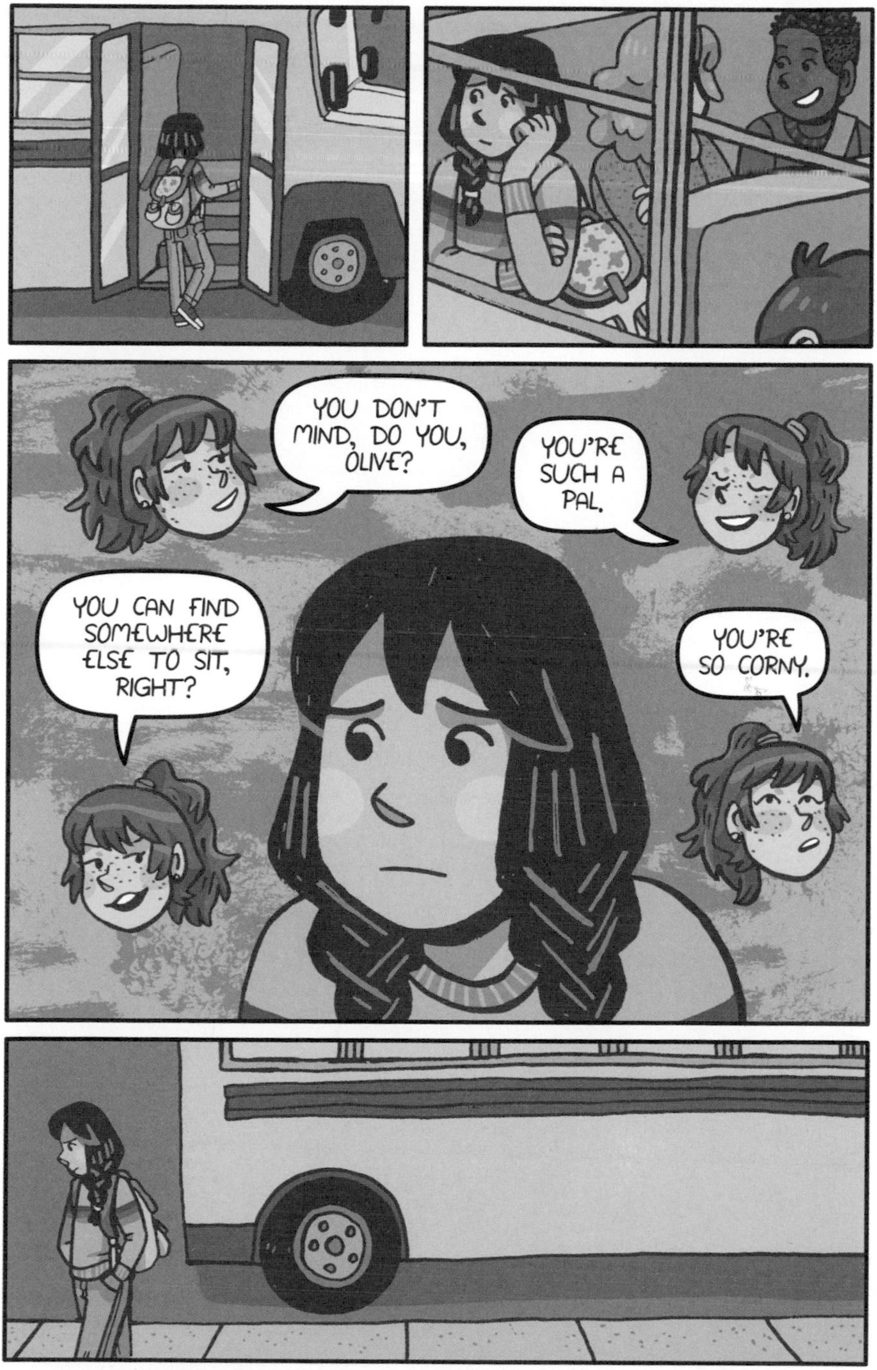
YOU DON'T MIND, DO YOU, OLIVE?
YOU'RE SUCH A PAL.
YOU CAN FIND SOMEWHERE ELSE TO SIT, RIGHT?
YOU'RE SO CORNY.

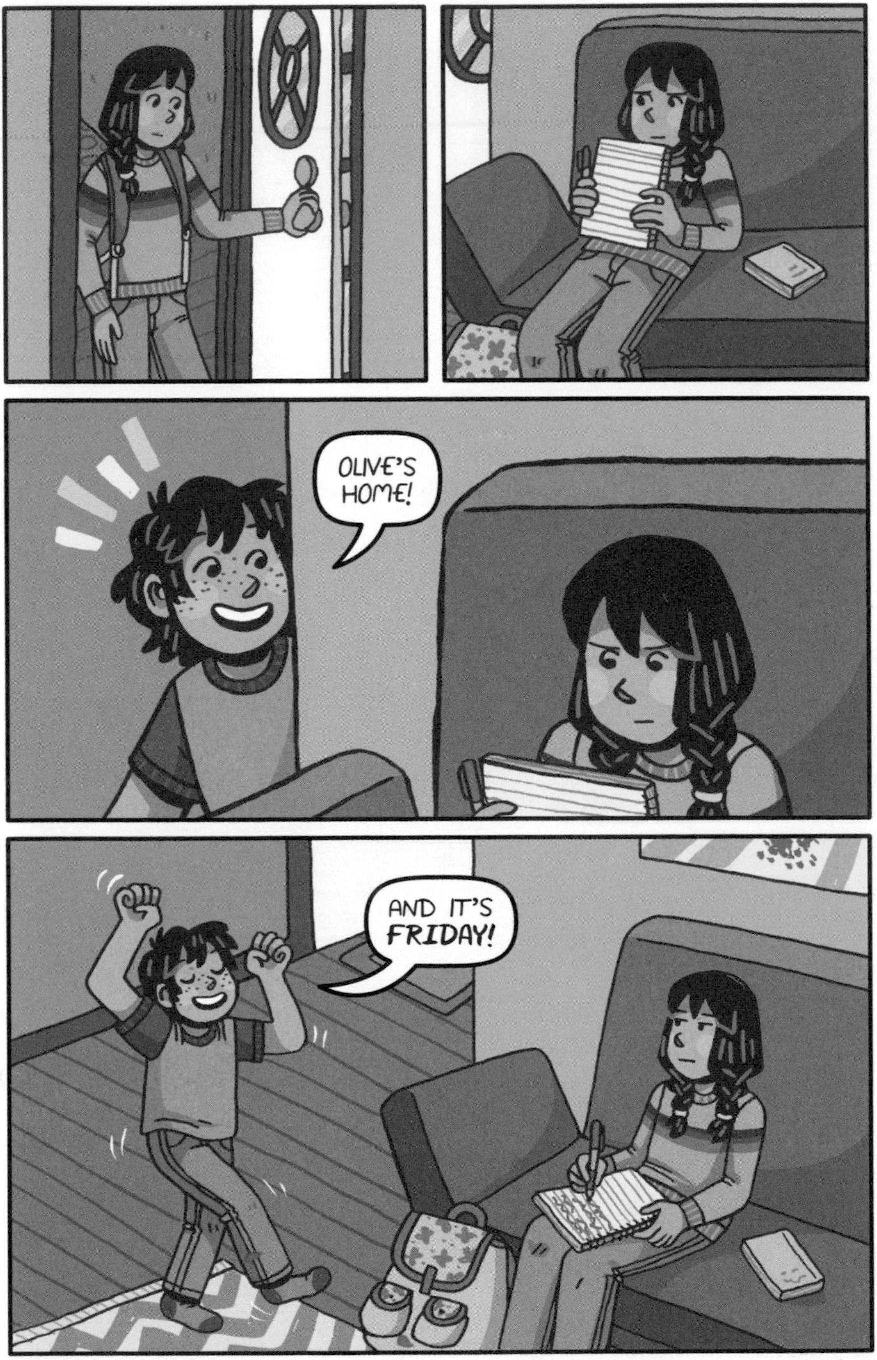
OLIVE'S HOME!
AND IT'S FRIDAY!

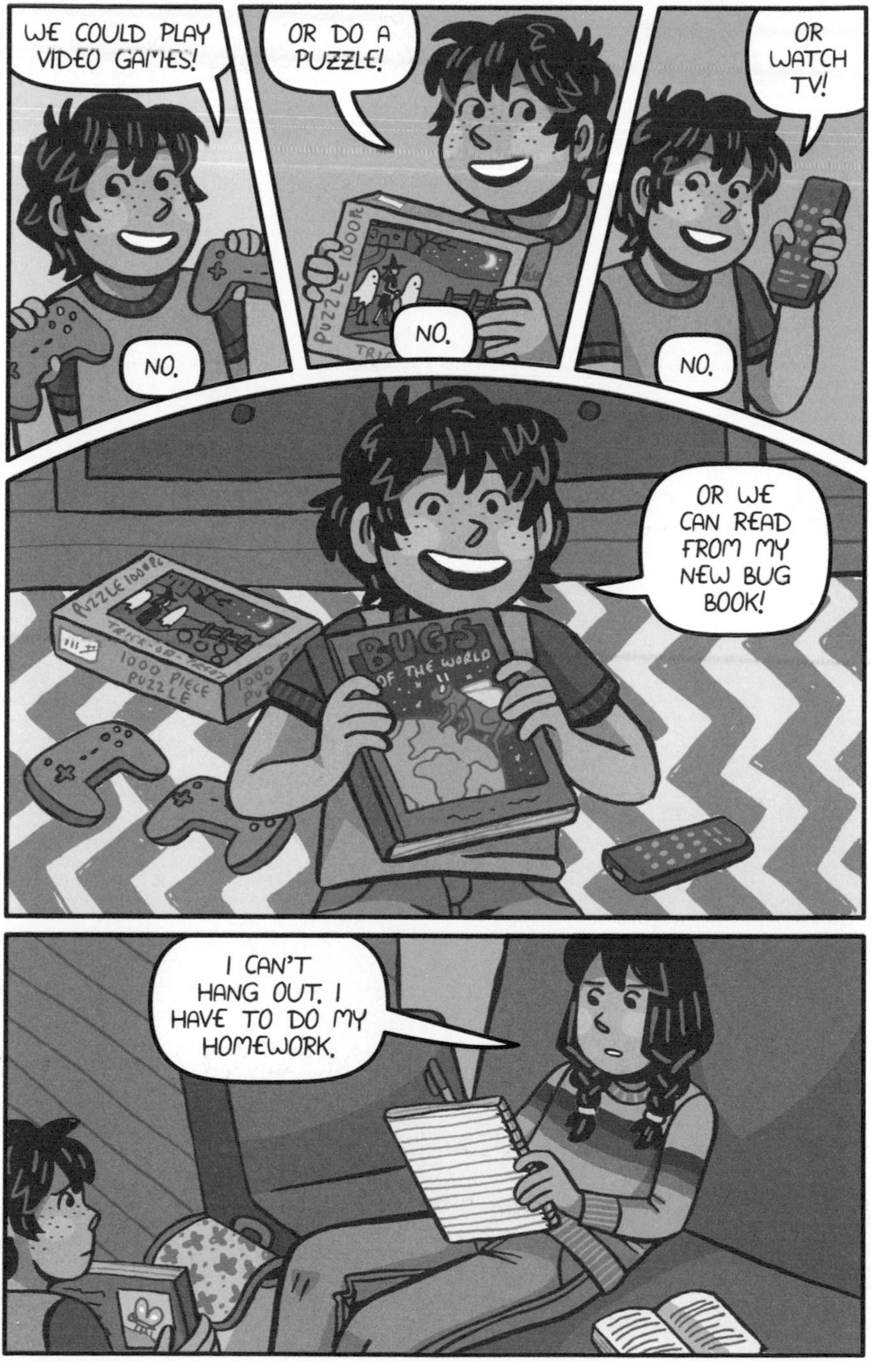
WE COULD PLAY VIDEO GAMES!
NO.
OR DO A PUZZLE!
PUZZLE 1000PC
NO.
OR WATCH TV!
NO.
OR WE CAN READ FROM MY NEW BUG BOOK!
PUZZLE 1000PC
TRICK-OR-TREAT
1000 PIECE PUZZLE
BUGS OF THE WORLD
I CAN'T HANG OUT. I HAVE TO DO MY HOMEWORK.

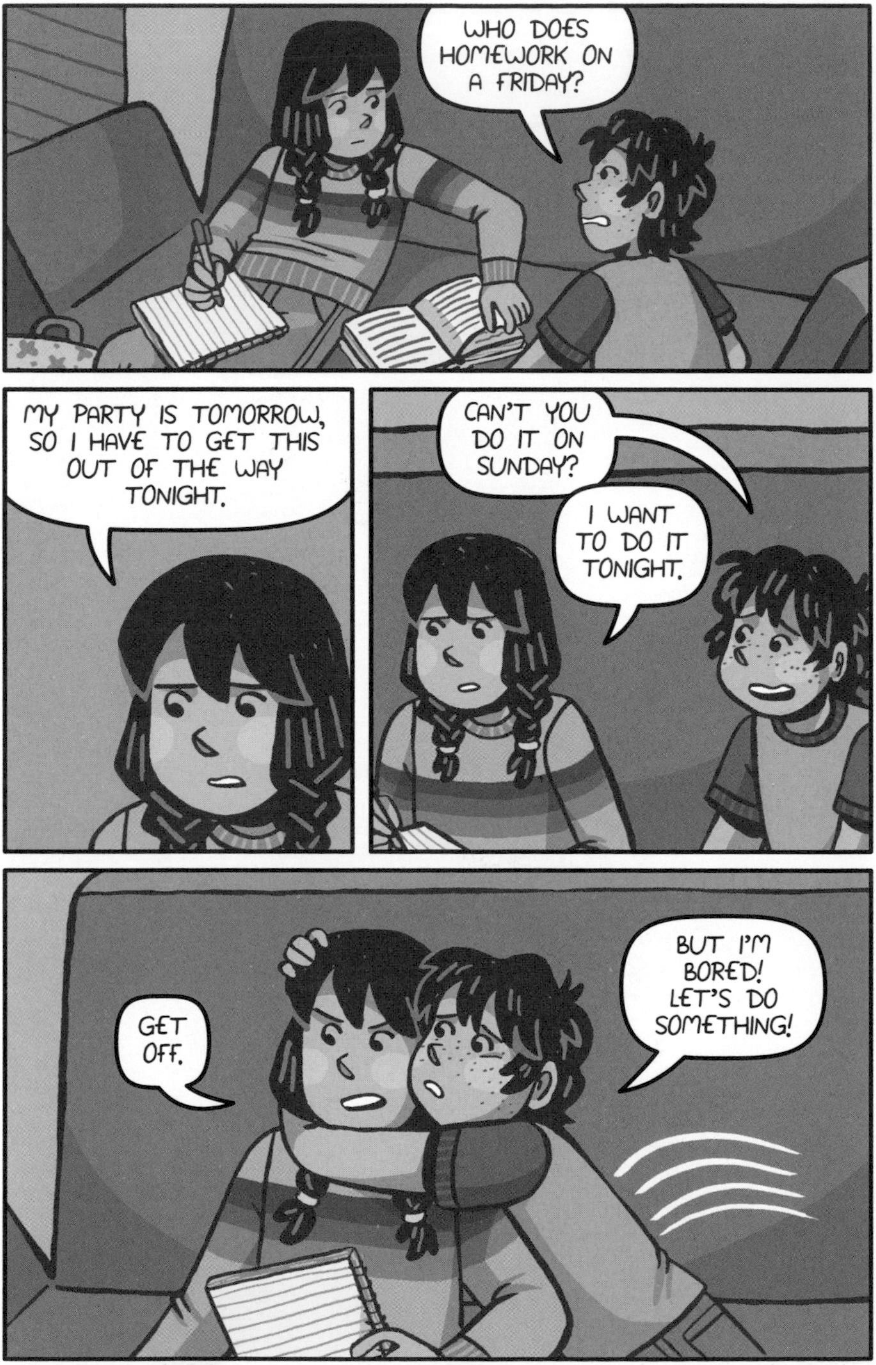
WHO DOES HOMEWORK ON A FRIDAY?
MY PARTY IS TOMORROW, SO I HAVE TO GET THIS OUT OF THE WAY TONIGHT.
CAN'T YOU DO IT ON SUNDAY?
I WANT TO DO IT TONIGHT.
BUT I'M BORED! LET'S DO SOMETHING!
GET OFF.

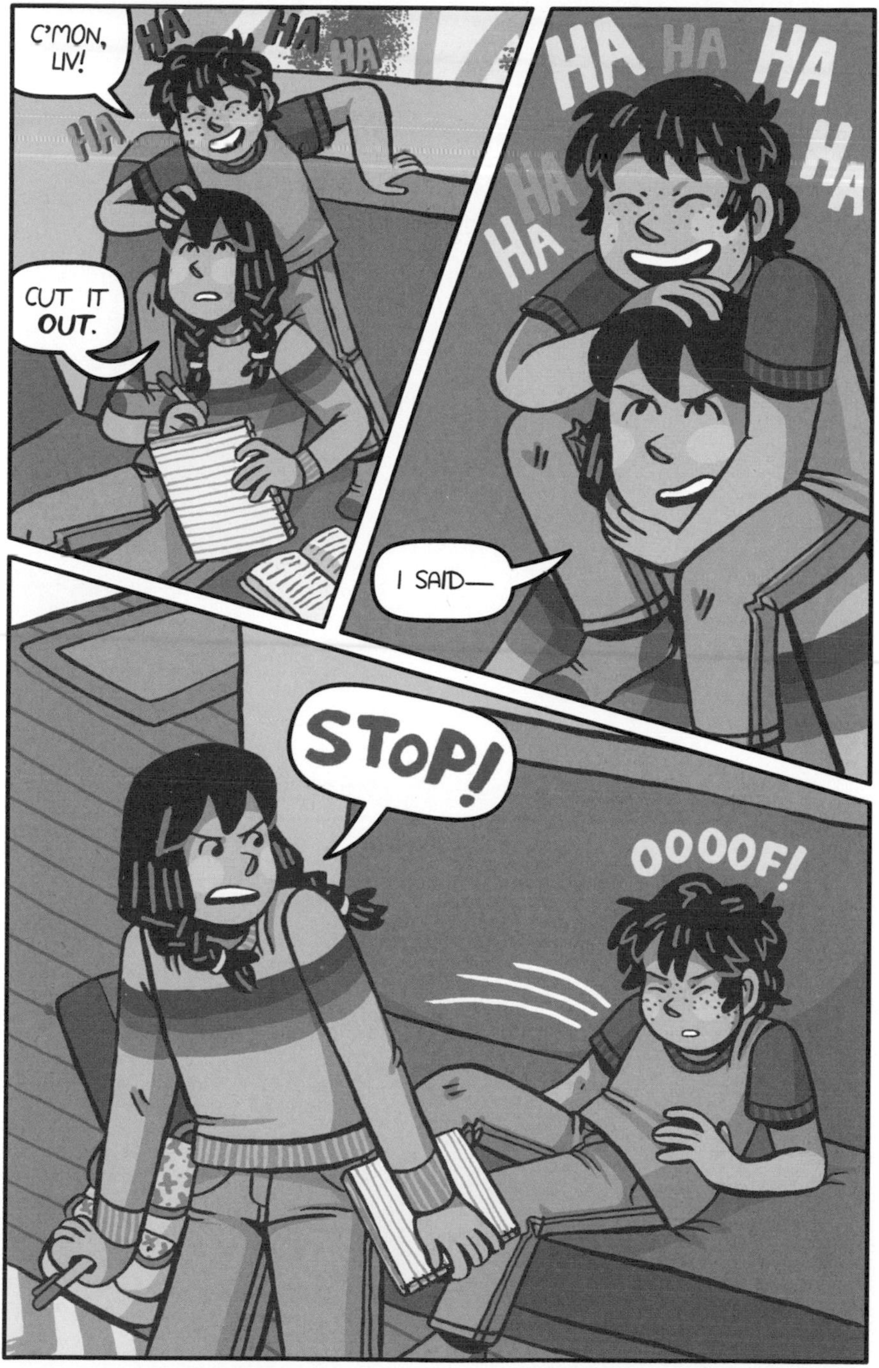
C'MON, LIV!
HA HA HA HA
CUT IT OUT.
HA HA HA HA HA HA HA HA HA
I SAID—
STOP!
OOOOF!

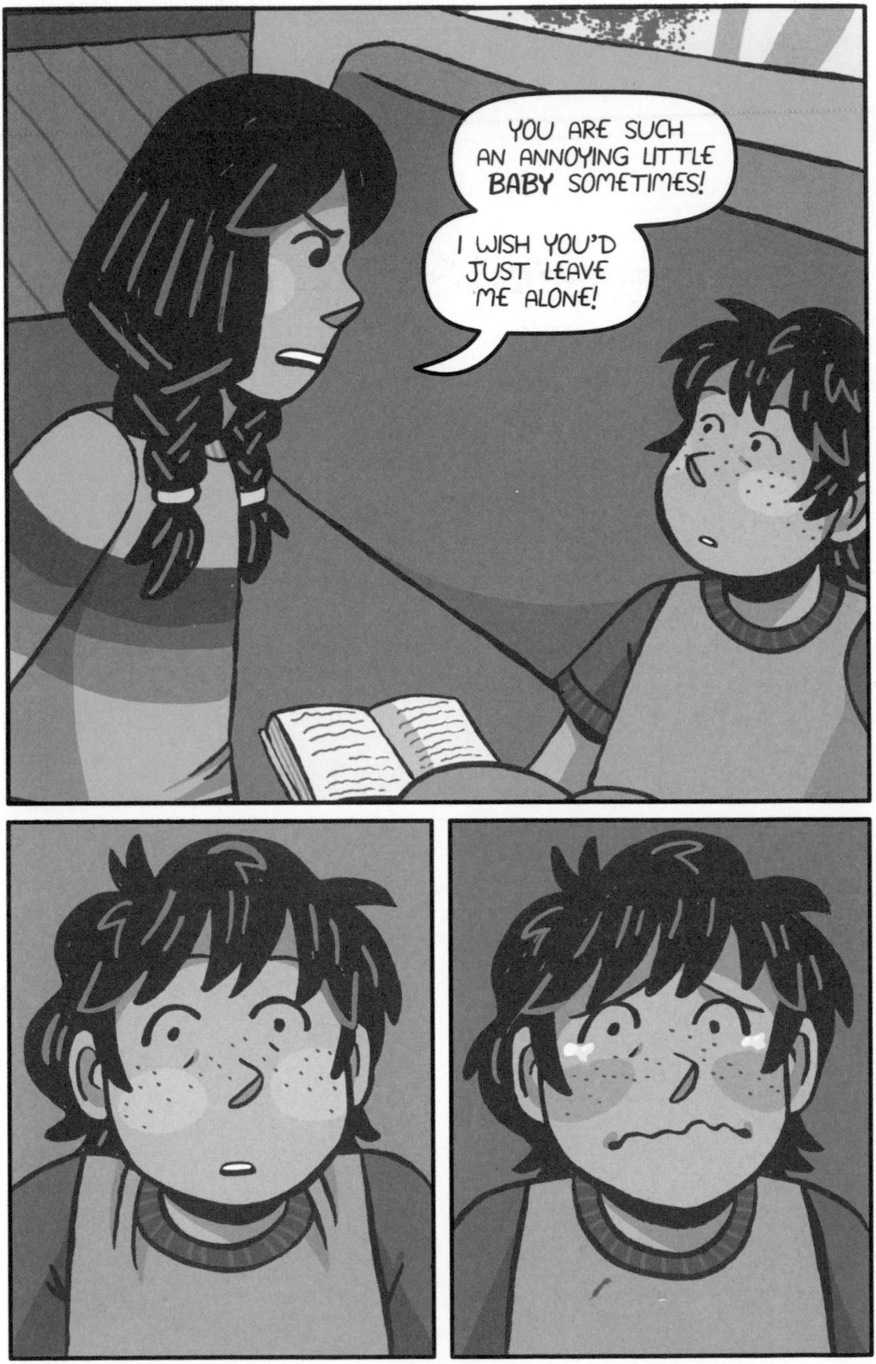
YOU ARE SUCH AN ANNOYING LITTLE BABY SOMETIMES!
I WISH YOU'D JUST LEAVE ME ALONE!

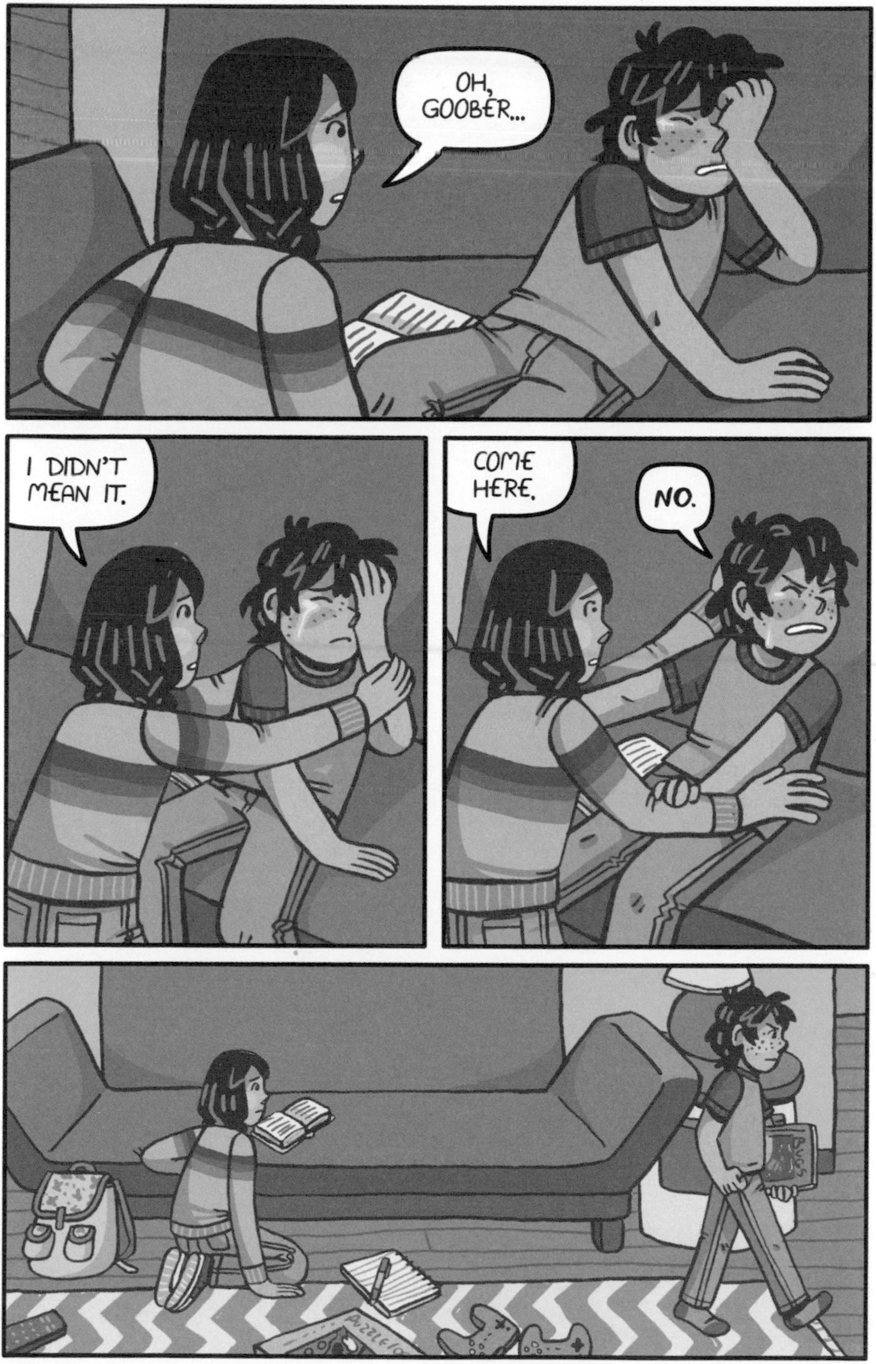
OH, GOOBER...
I DIDN'T MEAN IT.
COME HERE.
NO.

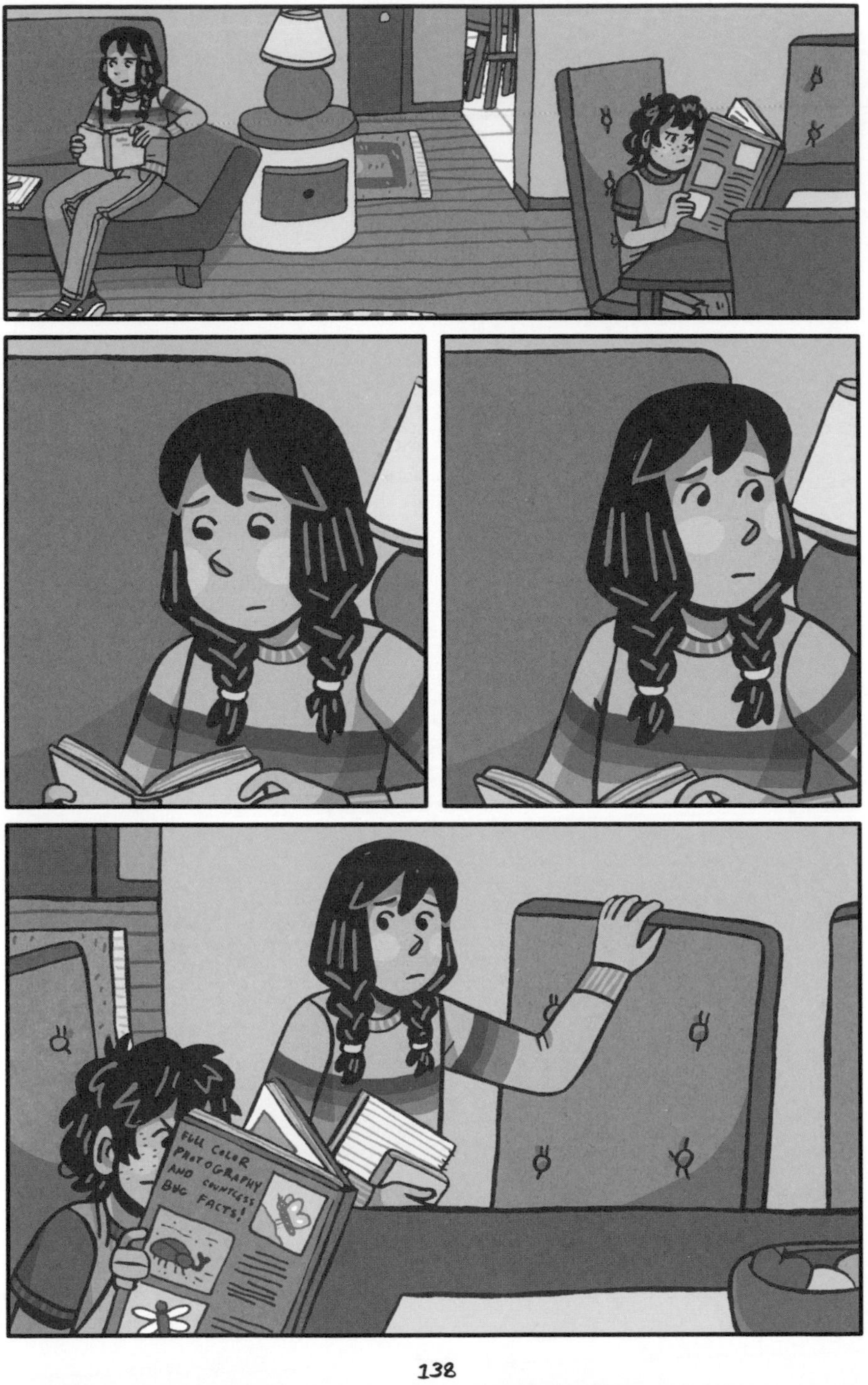
FULL COLOR PHOTOGRAPHY AND COUNTLESS BUG FACTS!

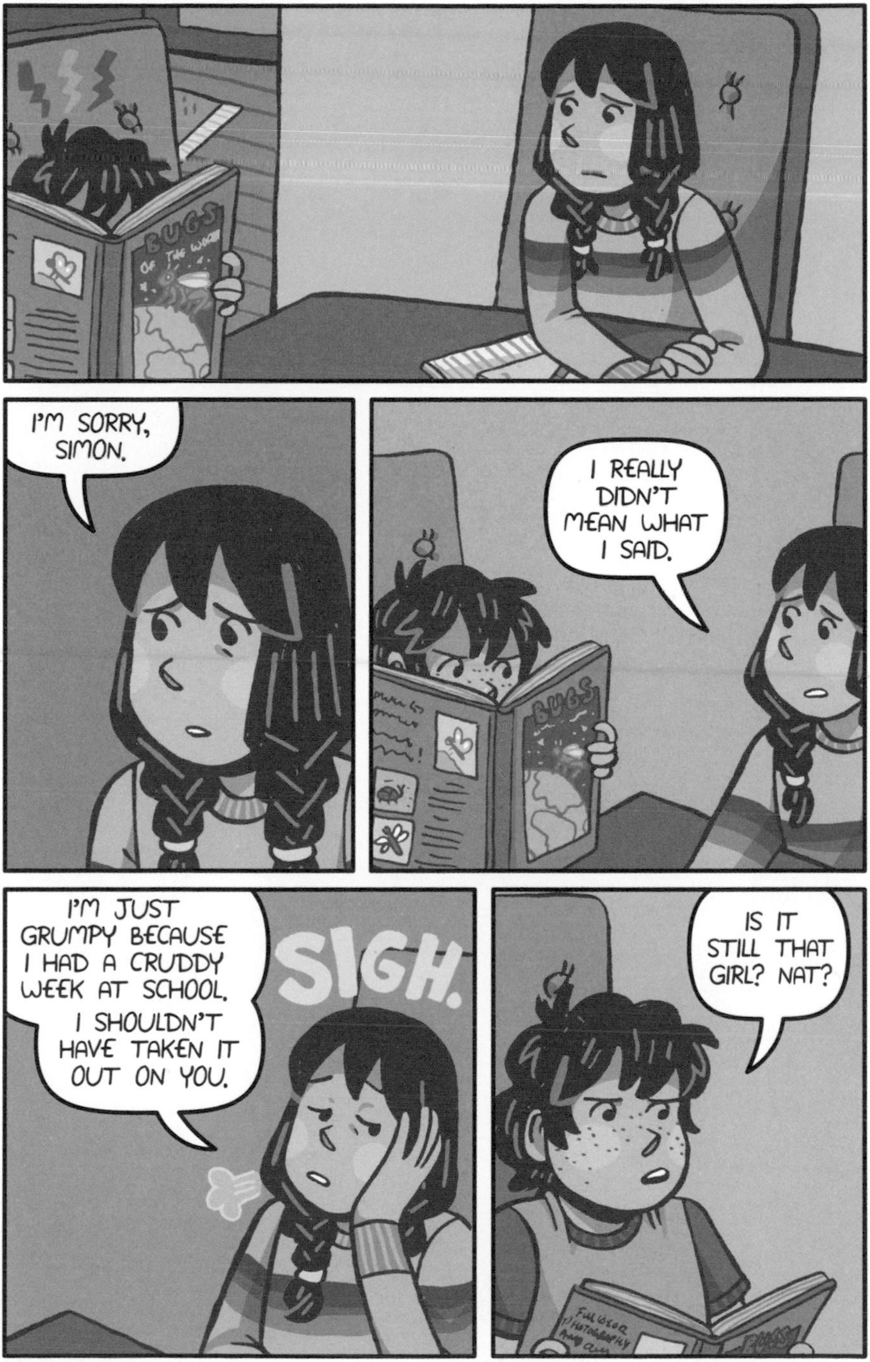
BUGS OF THE WORLD
I'M SORRY, SIMON.
I REALLY DIDN'T MEAN WHAT I SAID.
BUGS
I'M JUST GRUMPY BECAUSE I HAD A CRUDDY WEEK AT SCHOOL.
I SHOULDN'T HAVE TAKEN IT OUT ON YOU.
SIGH.
IS IT STILL THAT GIRL? NAT?

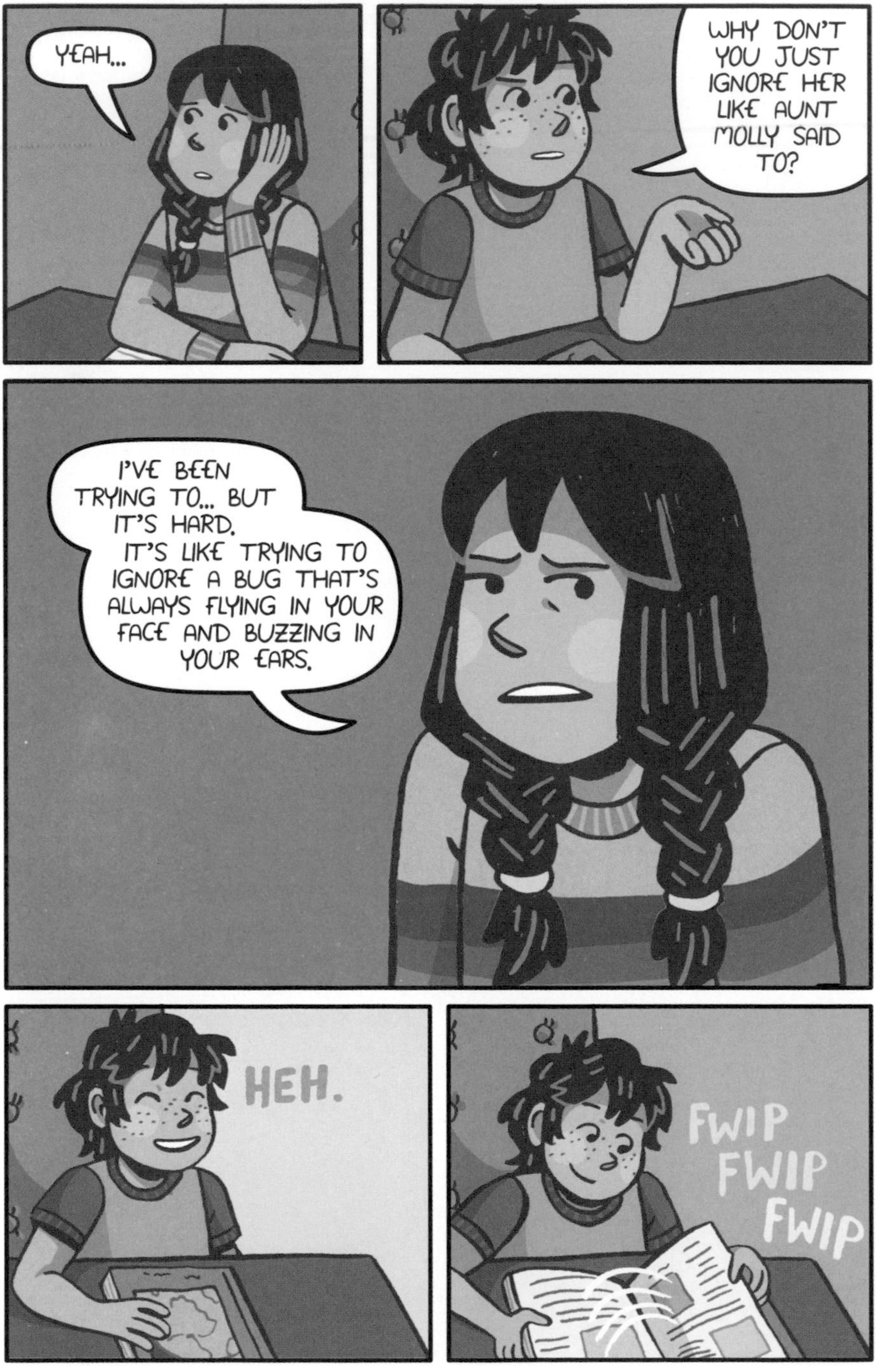
YEAH...
WHY DON'T YOU JUST IGNORE HER LIKE AUNT MOLLY SAID TO?
I'VE BEEN TRYING TO... BUT IT'S HARD. IT'S LIKE TRYING TO IGNORE A BUG THAT'S ALWAYS FLYING IN YOUR FACE AND BUZZING IN YOUR EARS.
HEH.
FWIP FWIP FWIP

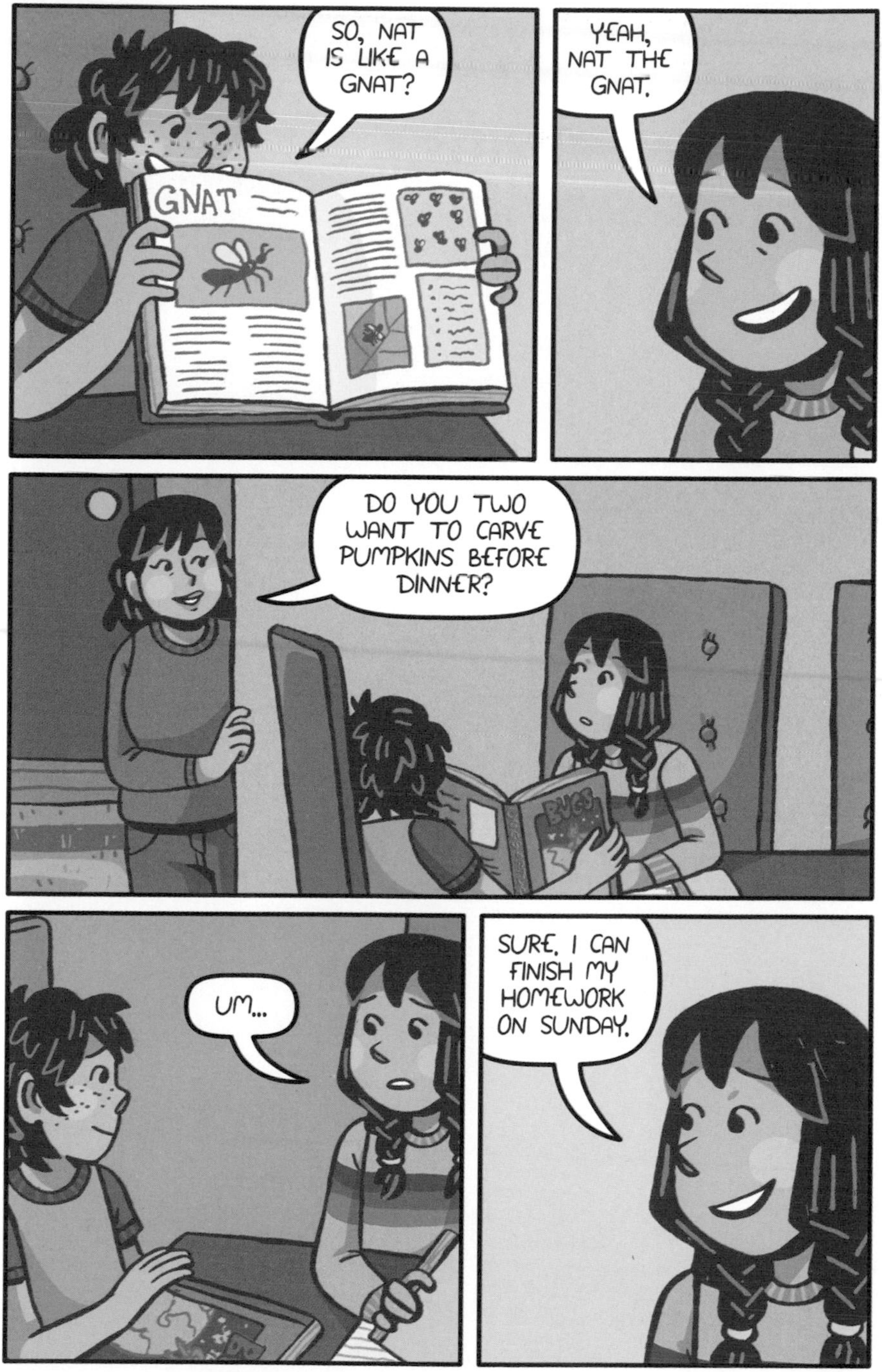
SO, NAT IS LIKE A GNAT?
GNAT
YEAH, NAT THE GNAT.
DO YOU TWO WANT TO CARVE PUMPKINS BEFORE DINNER?
BUGS
UM...
SURE. I CAN FINISH MY HOMEWORK ON SUNDAY.

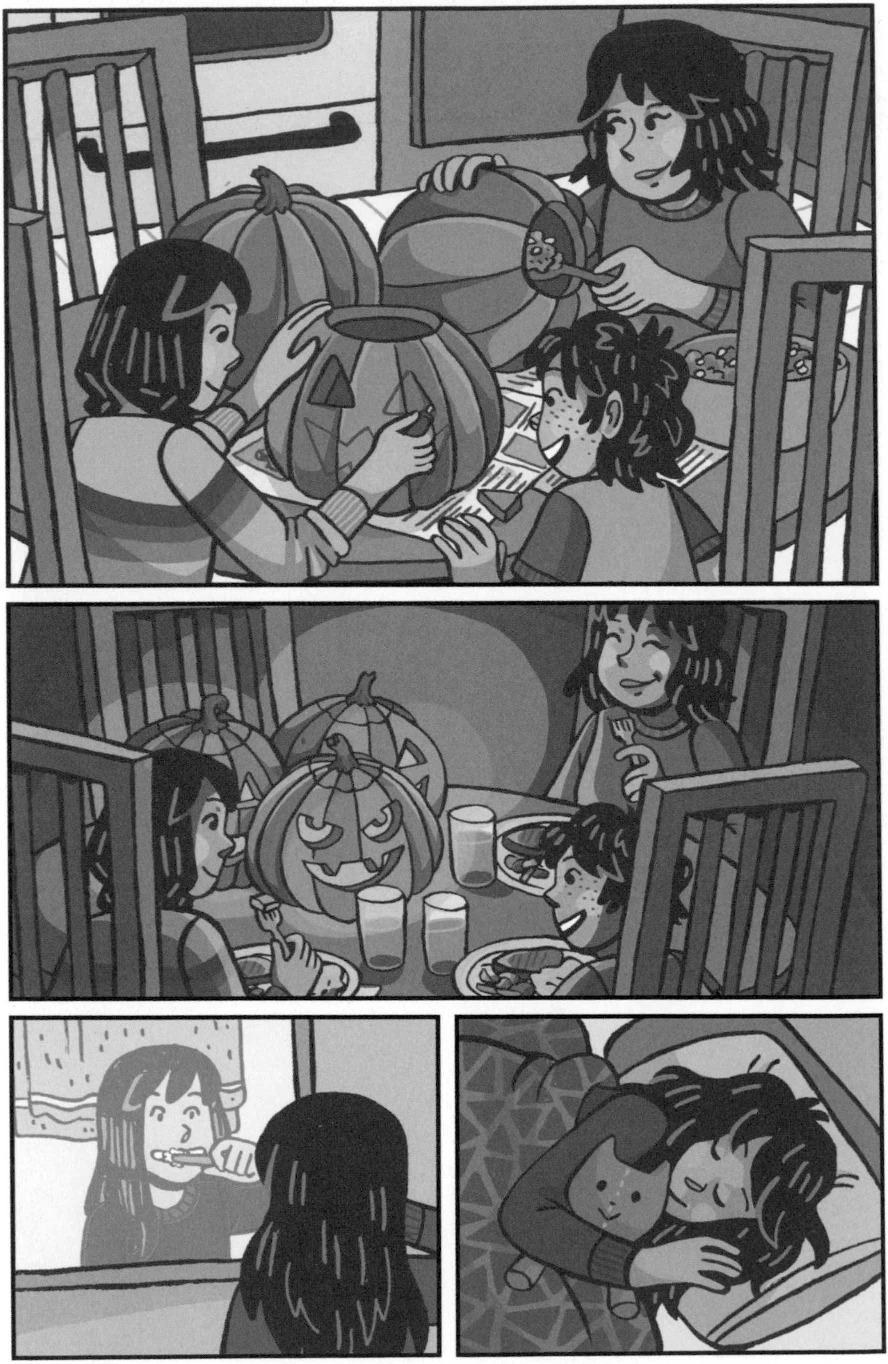

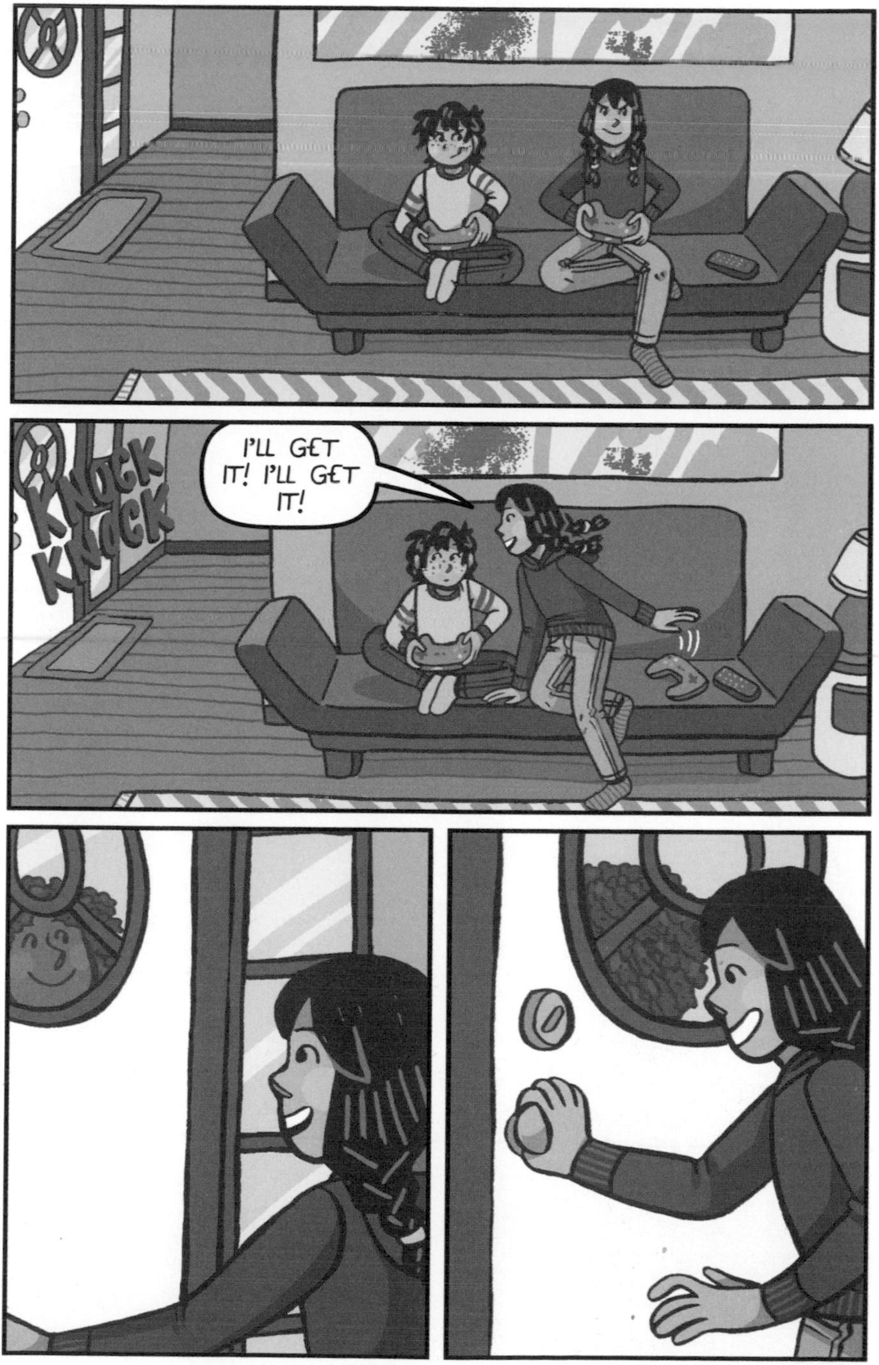
KNOCK KNOCK
I'LL GET IT! I'LL GET IT!

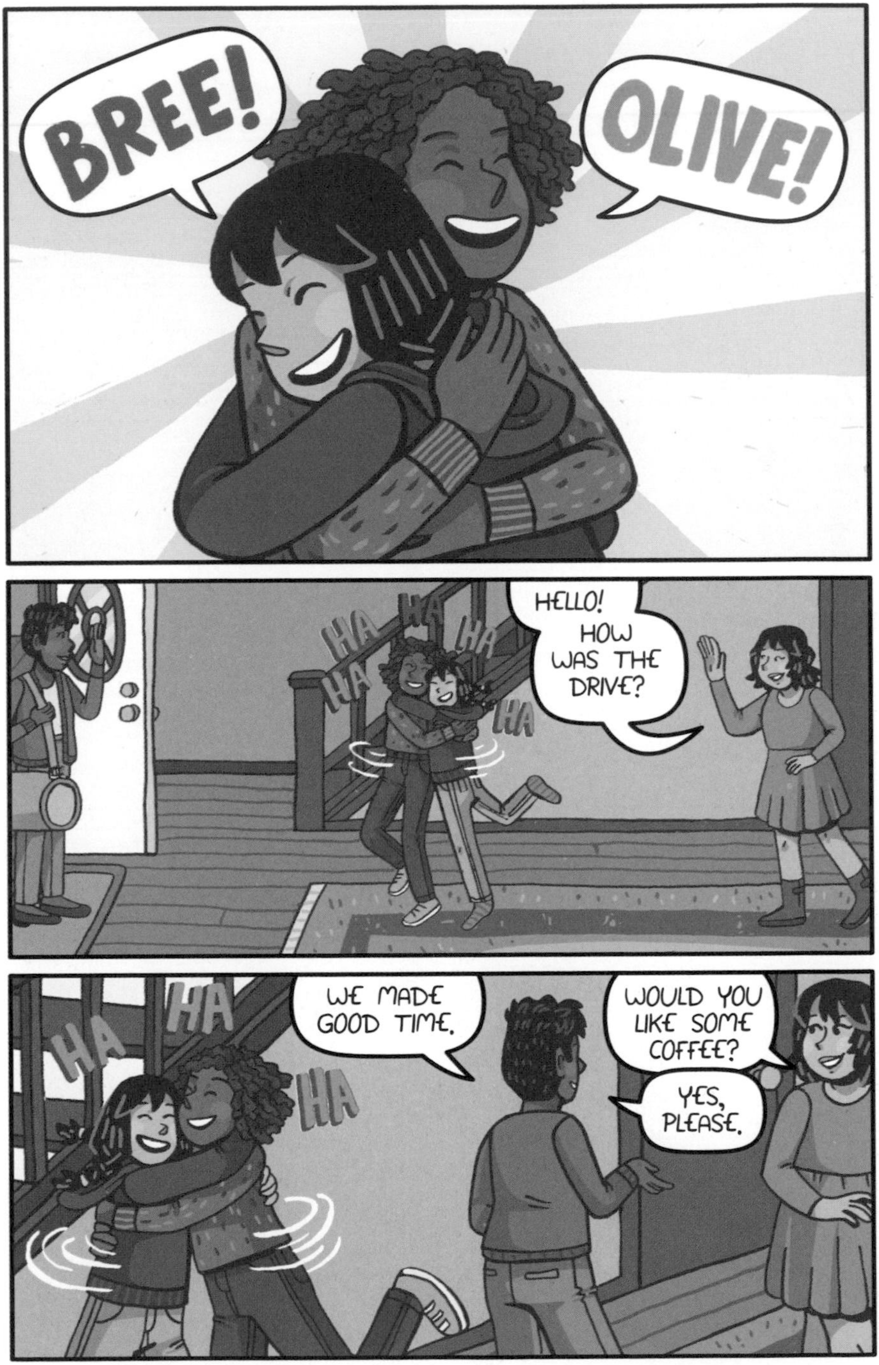
BREE!
OLIVE!
HA HA HA HA HA
HELLO! HOW WAS THE DRIVE?
HA HA HA
WE MADE GOOD TIME.
WOULD YOU LIKE SOME COFFEE?
YES, PLEASE.

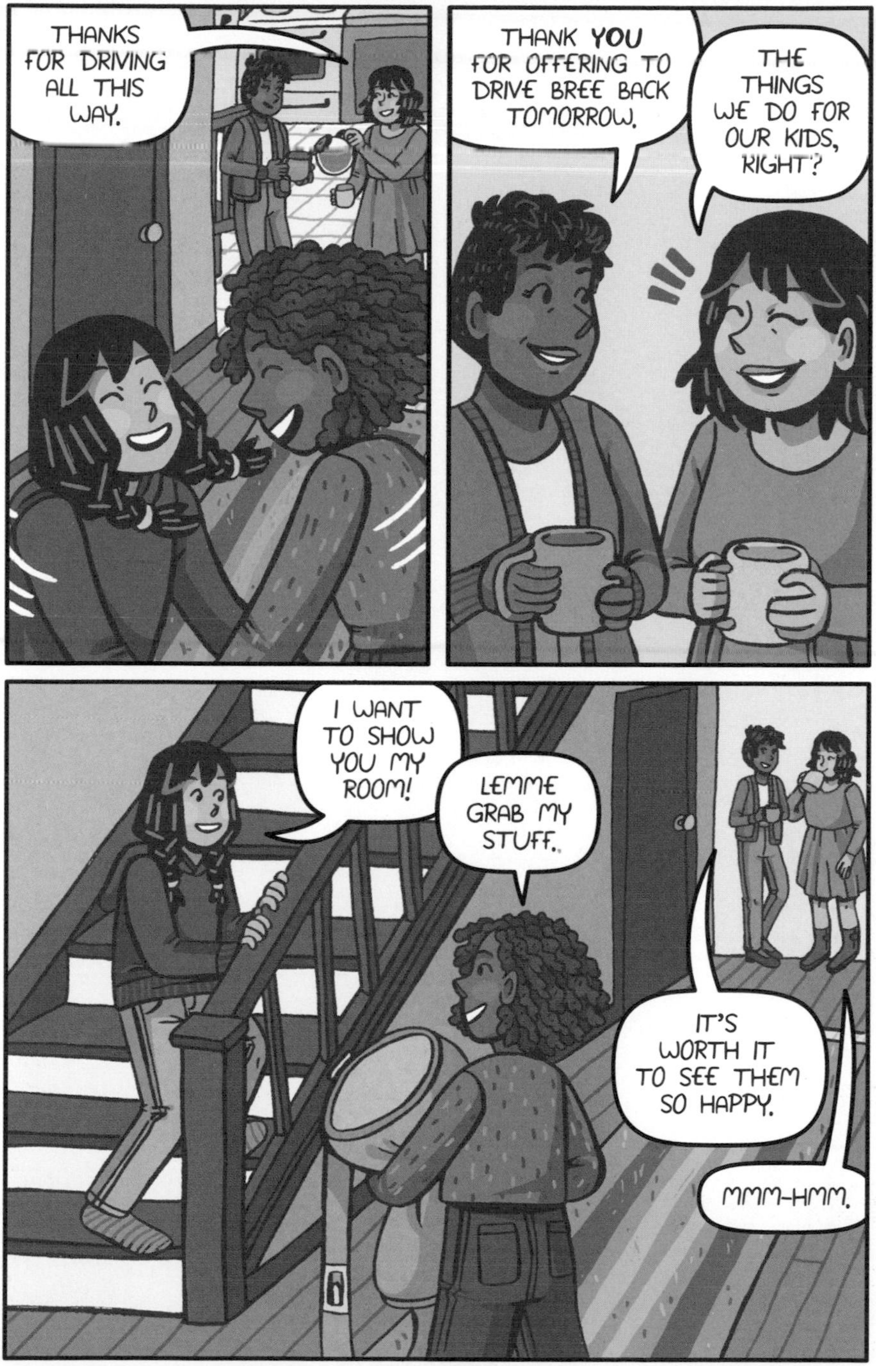
THANKS FOR DRIVING ALL THIS WAY.
THANK YOU FOR OFFERING TO DRIVE BREE BACK TOMORROW.
THE THINGS WE DO FOR OUR KIDS, RIGHT?
I WANT TO SHOW YOU MY ROOM!
LEMME GRAB MY STUFF.
IT'S WORTH IT TO SEE THEM SO HAPPY.
MMM-HMM.

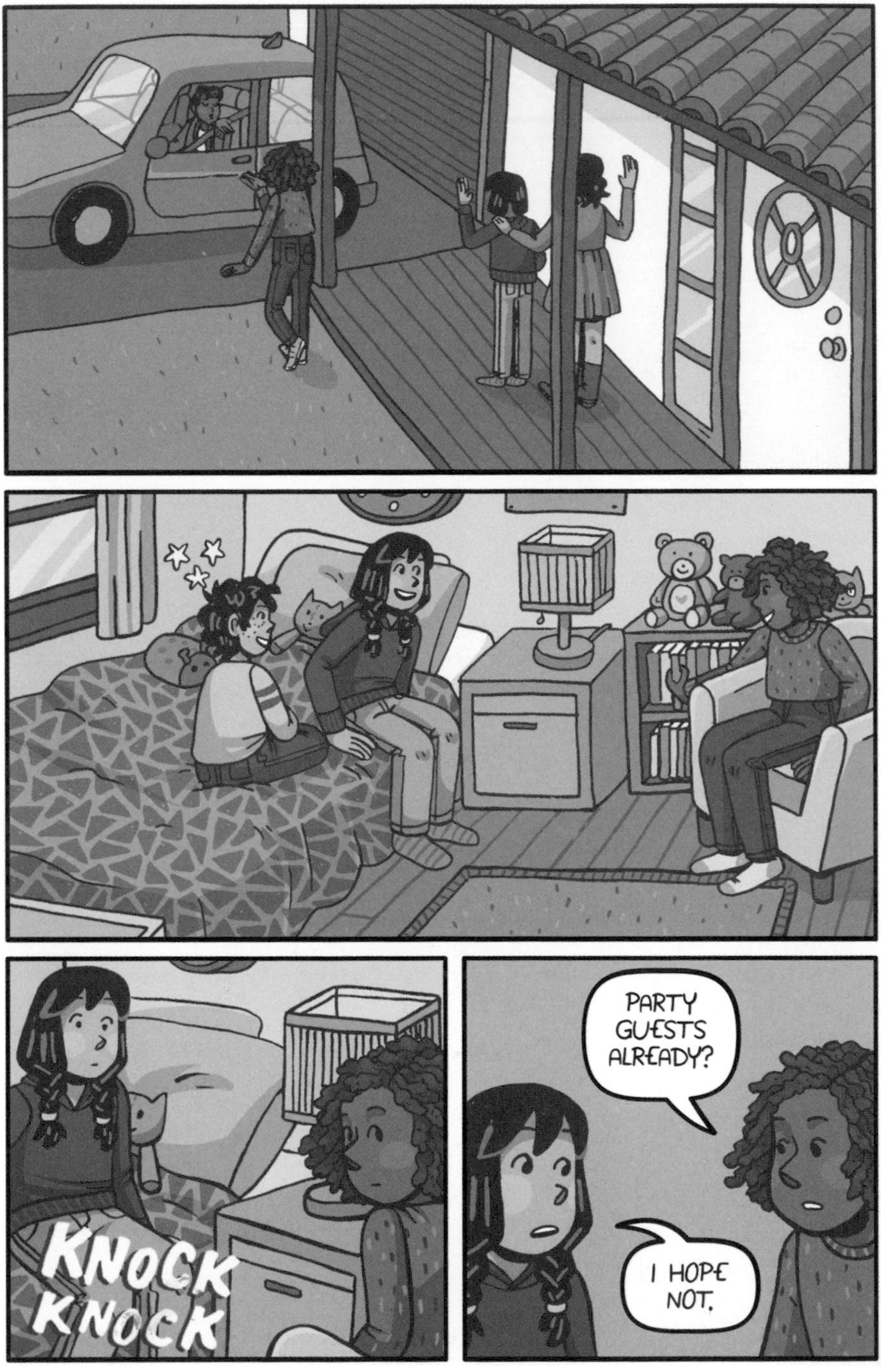
KNOCK
KNOCK
PARTY GUESTS ALREADY?
I HOPE NOT.

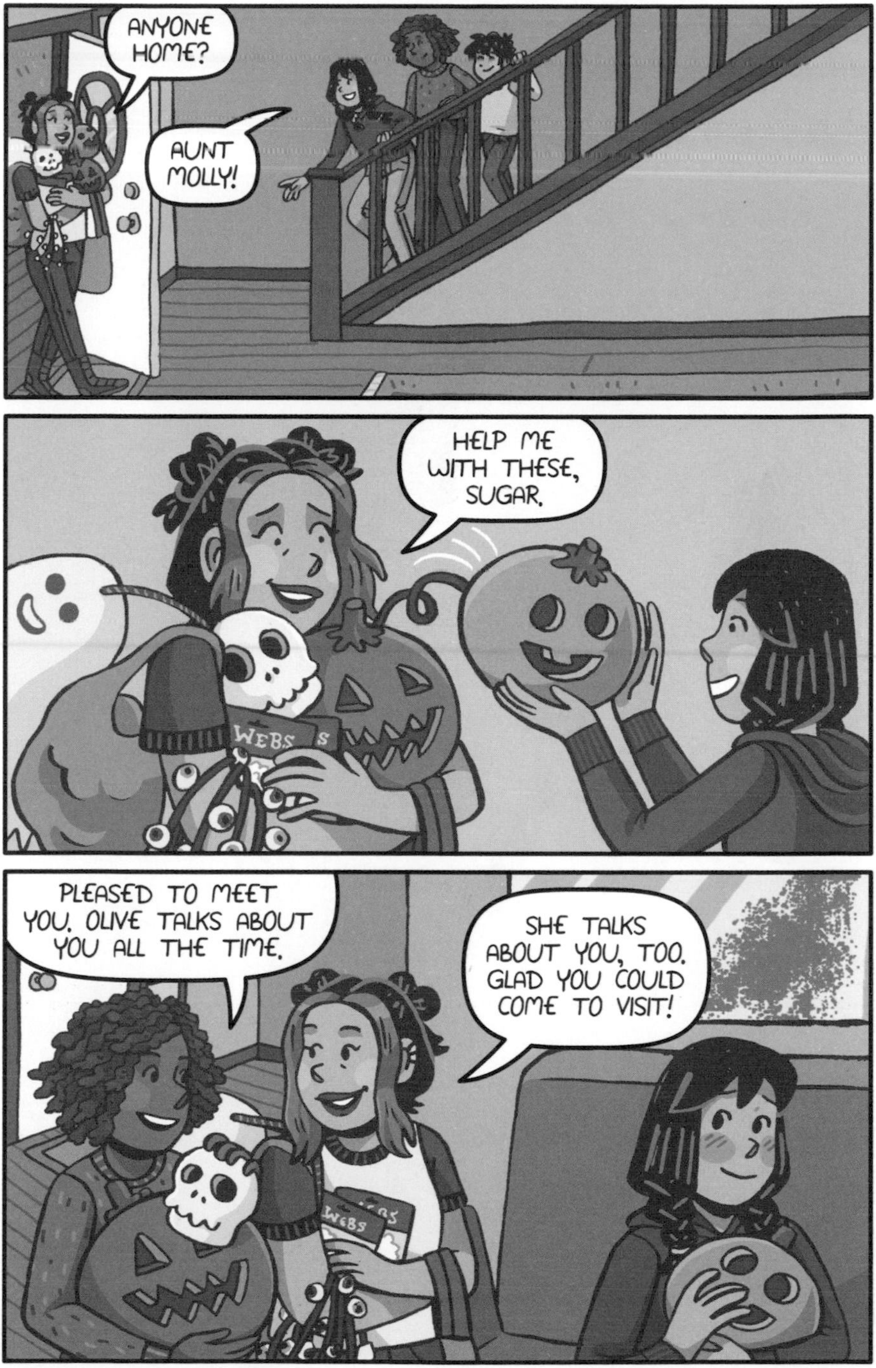
ANYONE HOME?
AUNT MOLLY!
HELP ME WITH THESE, SUGAR.
WEBS
PLEASED TO MEET YOU. OLIVE TALKS ABOUT YOU ALL THE TIME.
SHE TALKS ABOUT YOU, TOO. GLAD YOU COULD COME TO VISIT!

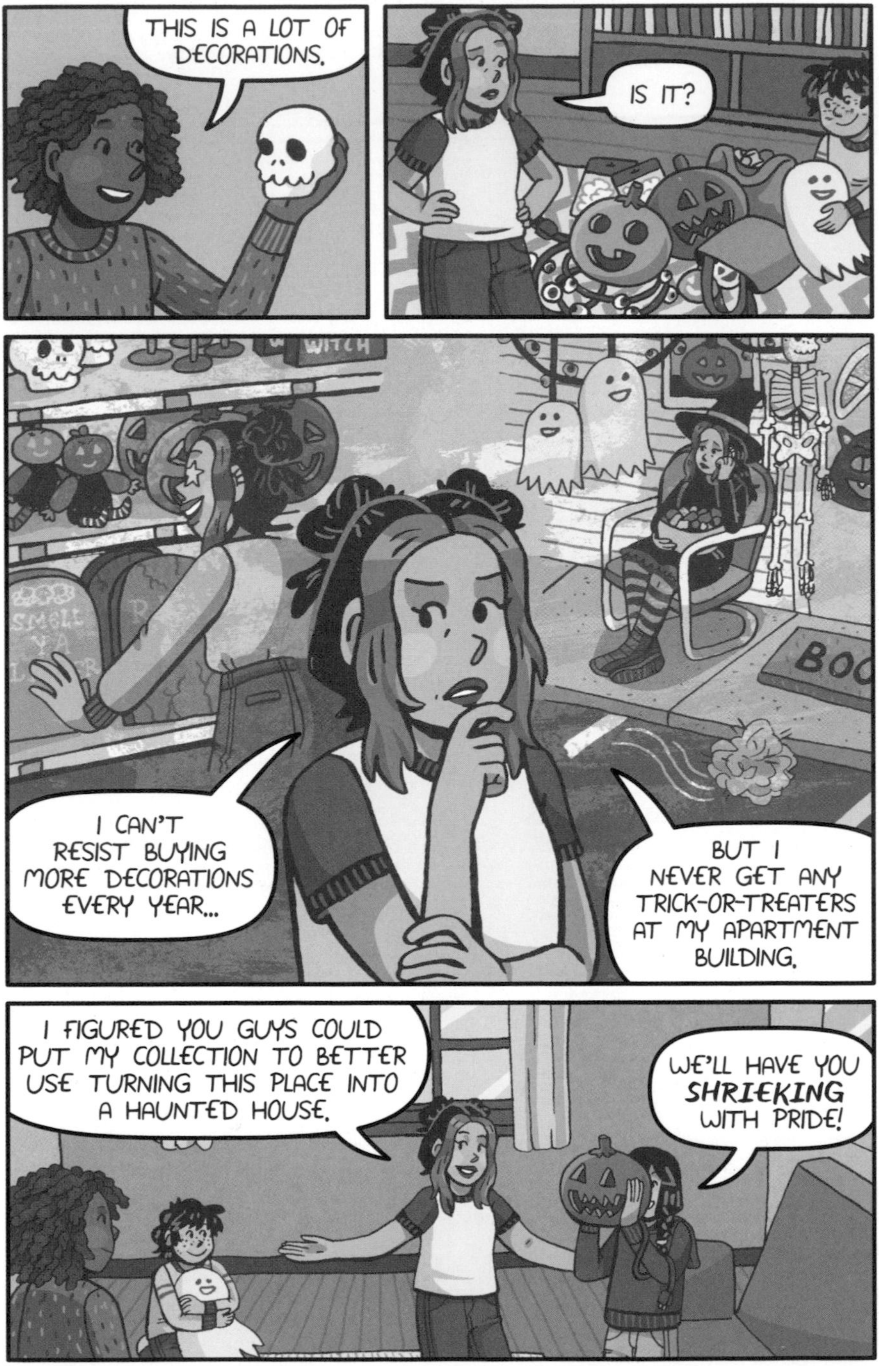
THIS IS A LOT OF DECORATIONS.
IS IT?
WITCH
SMELL YA L... R
BOO
I CAN'T RESIST BUYING MORE DECORATIONS EVERY YEAR...
BUT I NEVER GET ANY TRICK-OR-TREATERS AT MY APARTMENT BUILDING.
I FIGURED YOU GUYS COULD PUT MY COLLECTION TO BETTER USE TURNING THIS PLACE INTO A HAUNTED HOUSE.
WE'LL HAVE YOU **SHRIEKING** WITH PRIDE!

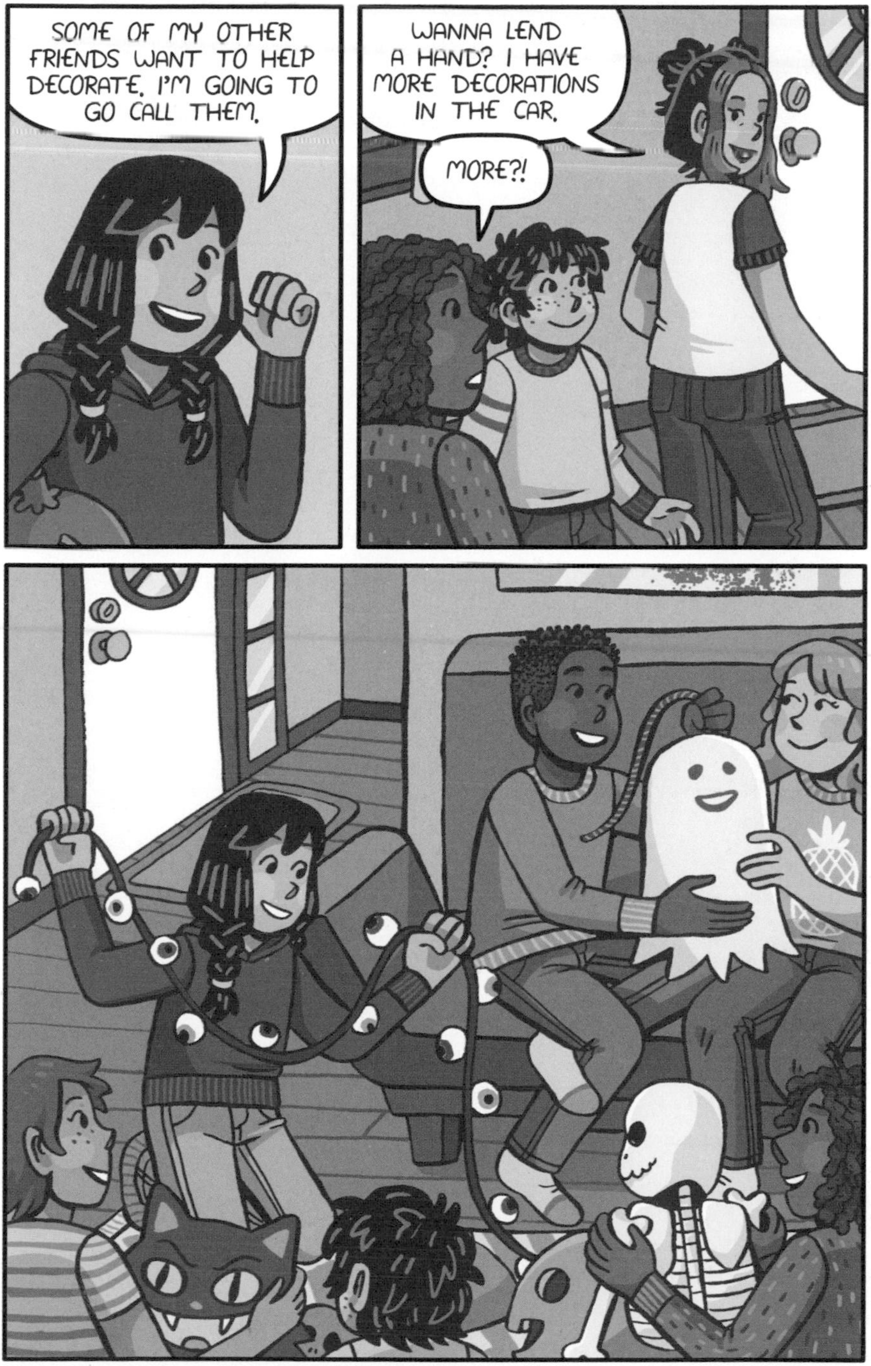
SOME OF MY OTHER FRIENDS WANT TO HELP DECORATE. I'M GOING TO GO CALL THEM.
WANNA LEND A HAND? I HAVE MORE DECORATIONS IN THE CAR.
MORE?!

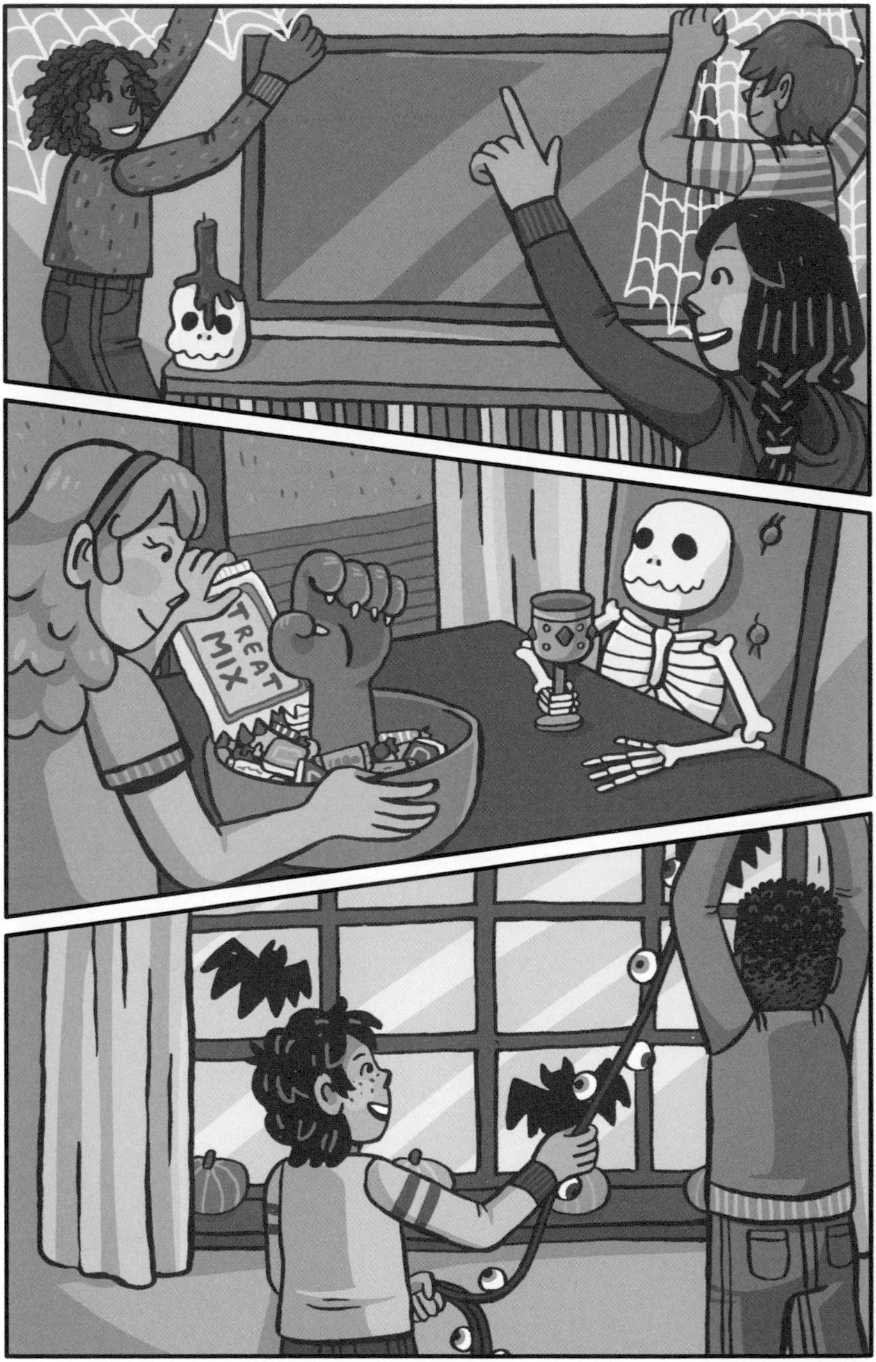
TREAT MIX

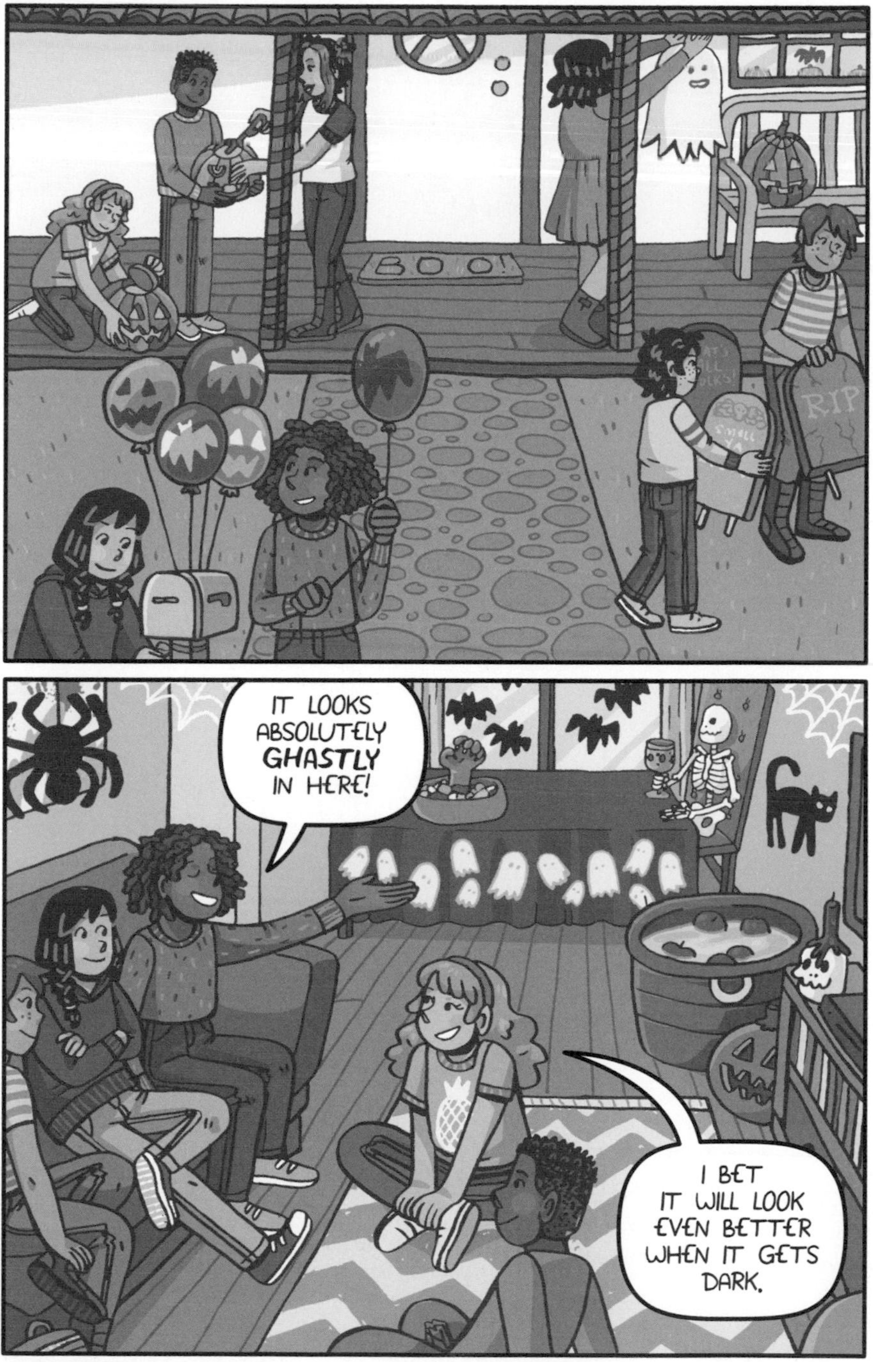
BOO!
RIP
IT LOOKS ABSOLUTELY **GHASTLY** IN HERE!
I BET IT WILL LOOK EVEN BETTER WHEN IT GETS DARK.

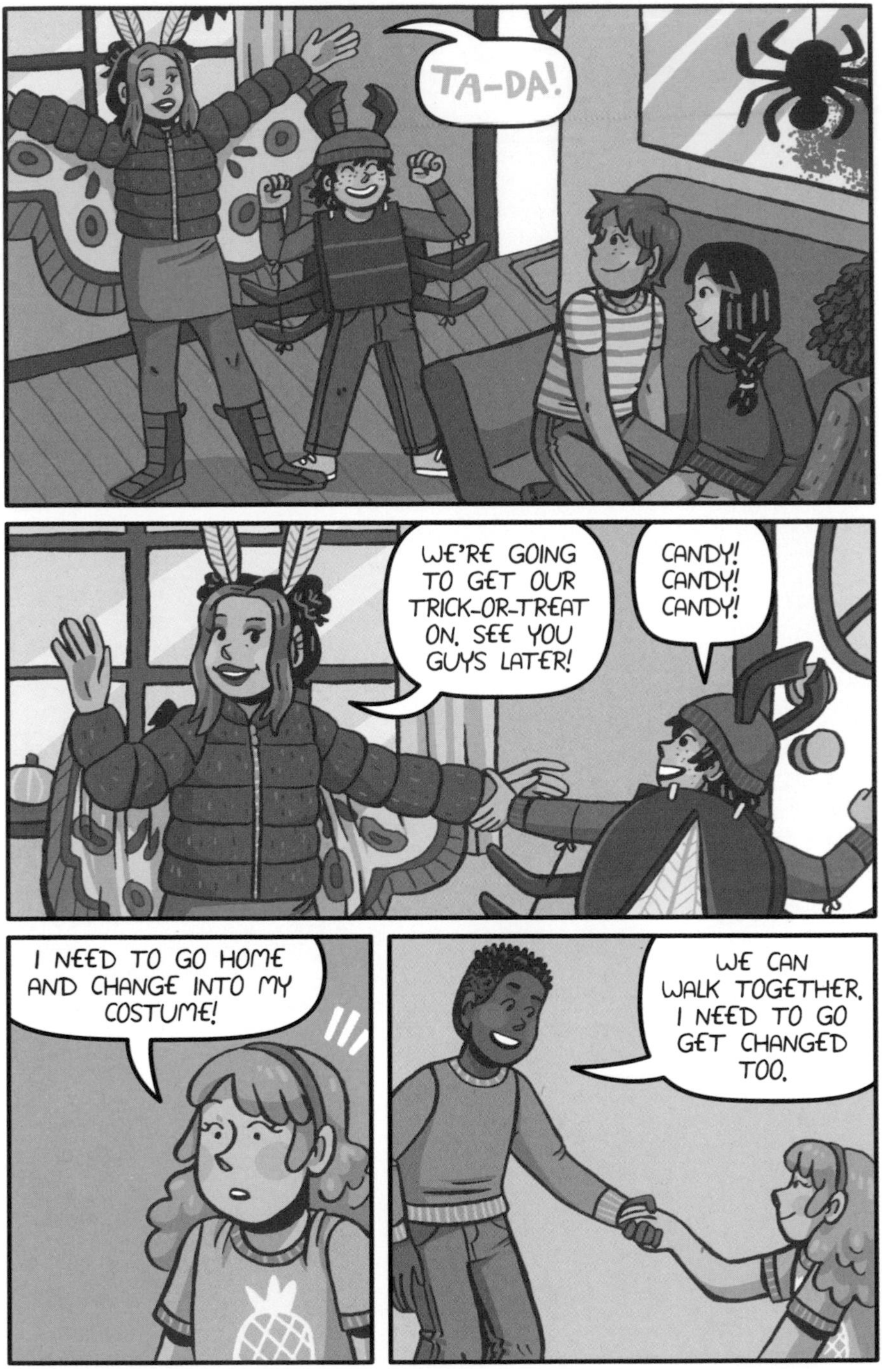
TA-DA!
WE'RE GOING TO GET OUR TRICK-OR-TREAT ON. SEE YOU GUYS LATER!
CANDY! CANDY! CANDY!
I NEED TO GO HOME AND CHANGE INTO MY COSTUME!
WE CAN WALK TOGETHER. I NEED TO GO GET CHANGED TOO.

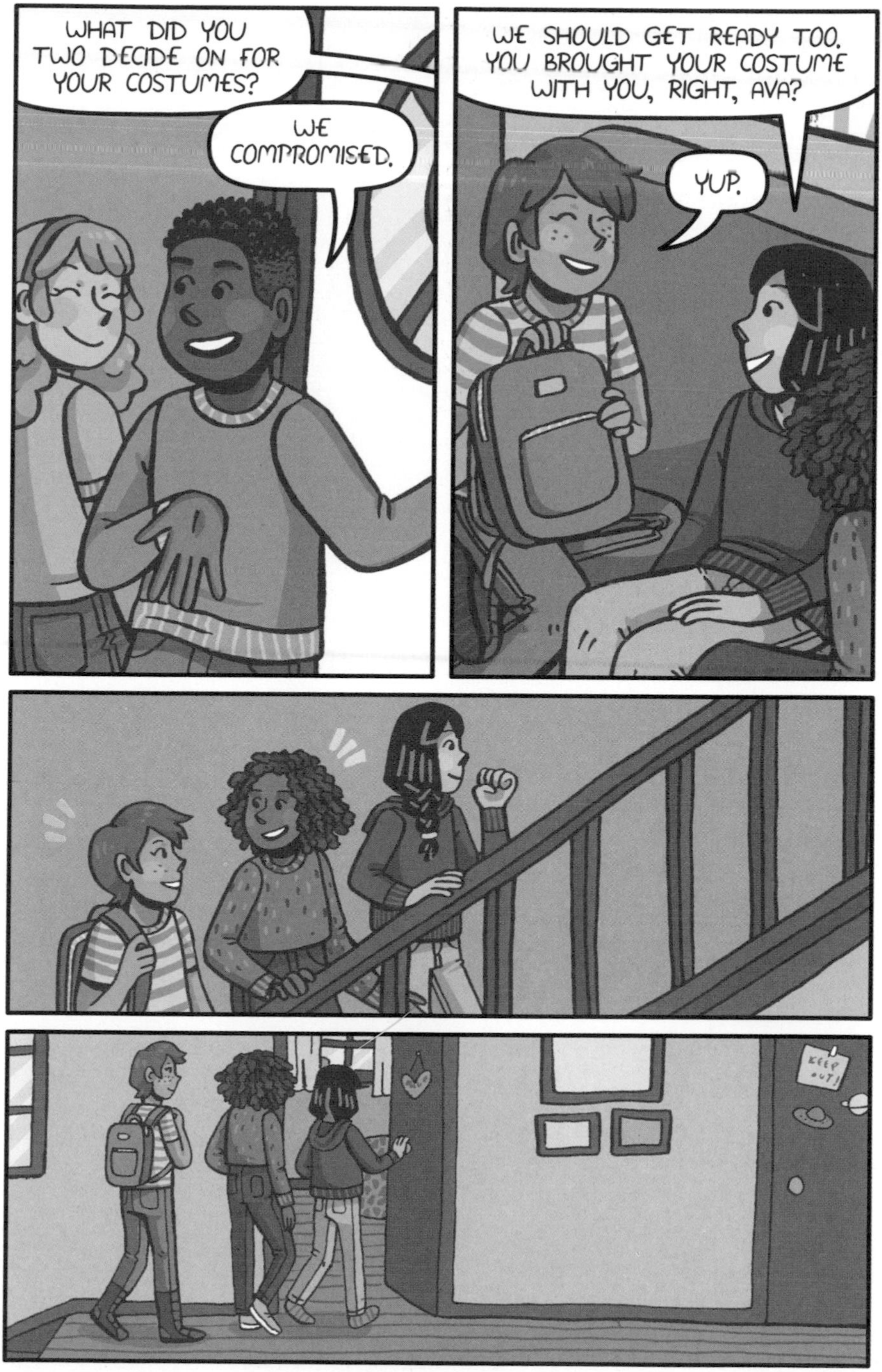
WHAT DID YOU TWO DECIDE ON FOR YOUR COSTUMES?
WE COMPROMISED.
WE SHOULD GET READY TOO. YOU BROUGHT YOUR COSTUME WITH YOU, RIGHT, AVA?
YUP.
KEEP OUT!

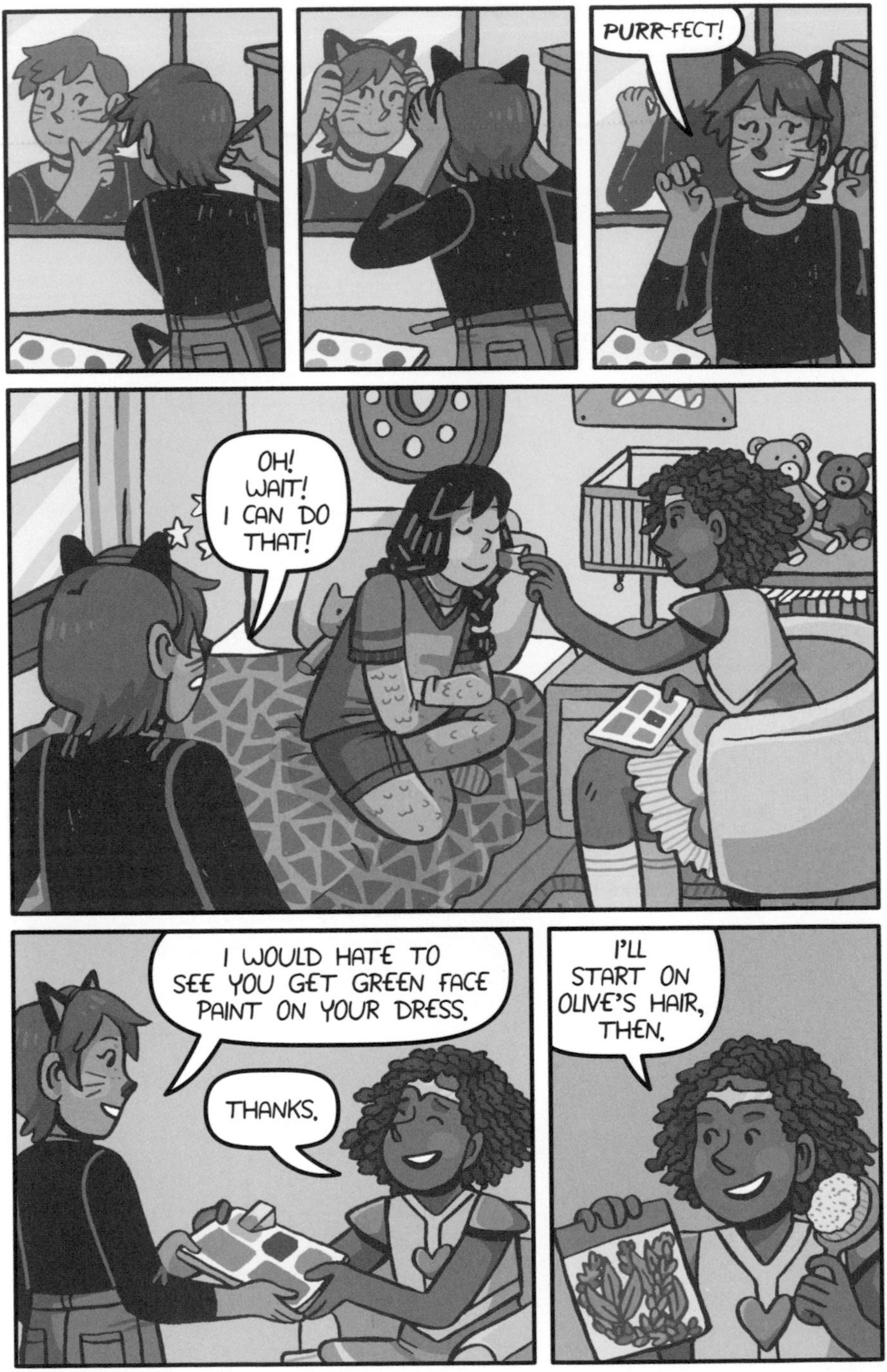
PURR-FECT!
OH! WAIT! I CAN DO THAT!
I WOULD HATE TO SEE YOU GET GREEN FACE PAINT ON YOUR DRESS.
THANKS.
I'LL START ON OLIVE'S HAIR, THEN.

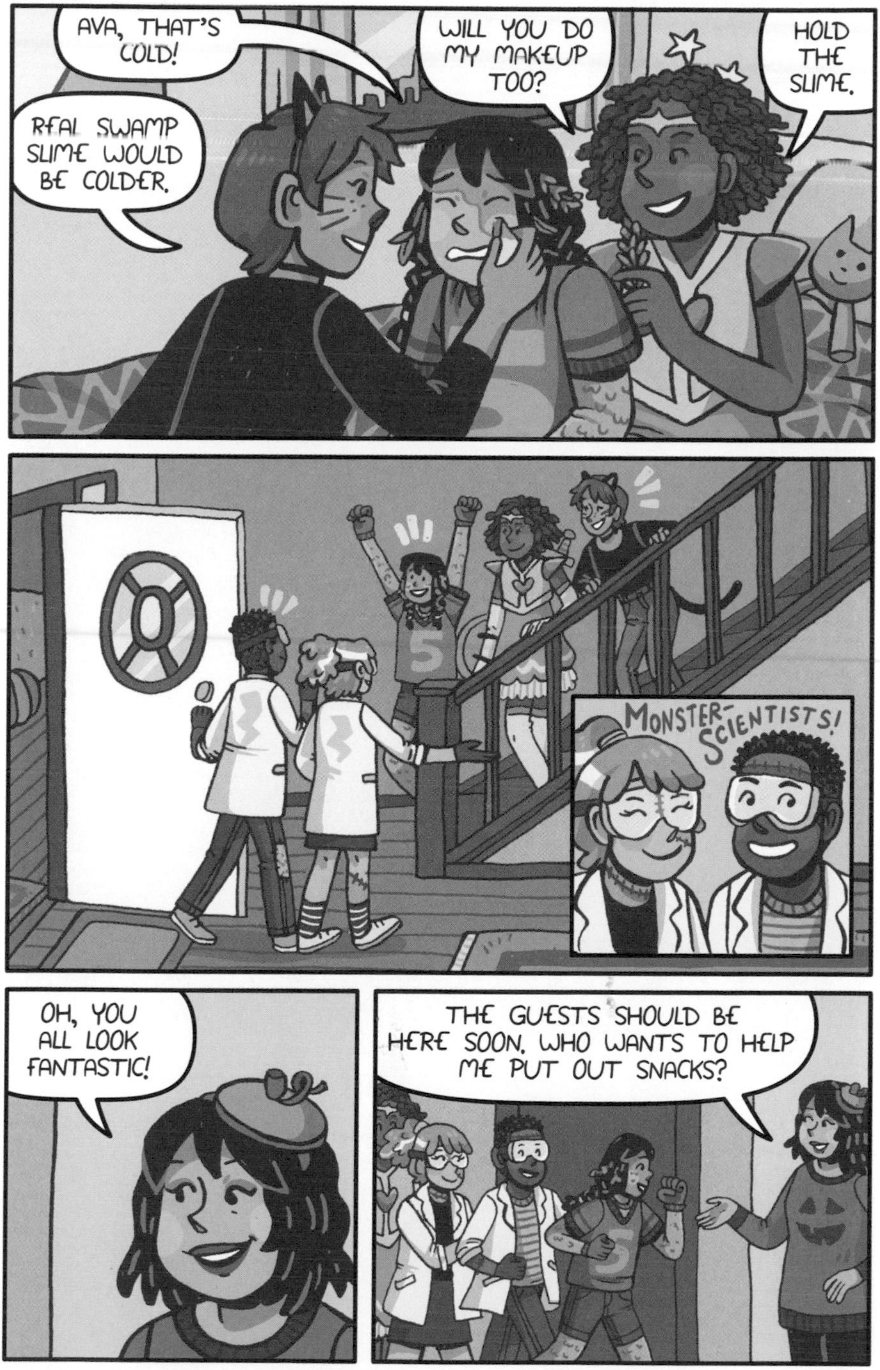
AVA, THAT'S COLD!
REAL SWAMP SLIME WOULD BE COLDER.
WILL YOU DO MY MAKEUP TOO?
HOLD THE SLIME.
MONSTER-SCIENTISTS!
OH, YOU ALL LOOK FANTASTIC!
THE GUESTS SHOULD BE HERE SOON. WHO WANTS TO HELP ME PUT OUT SNACKS?

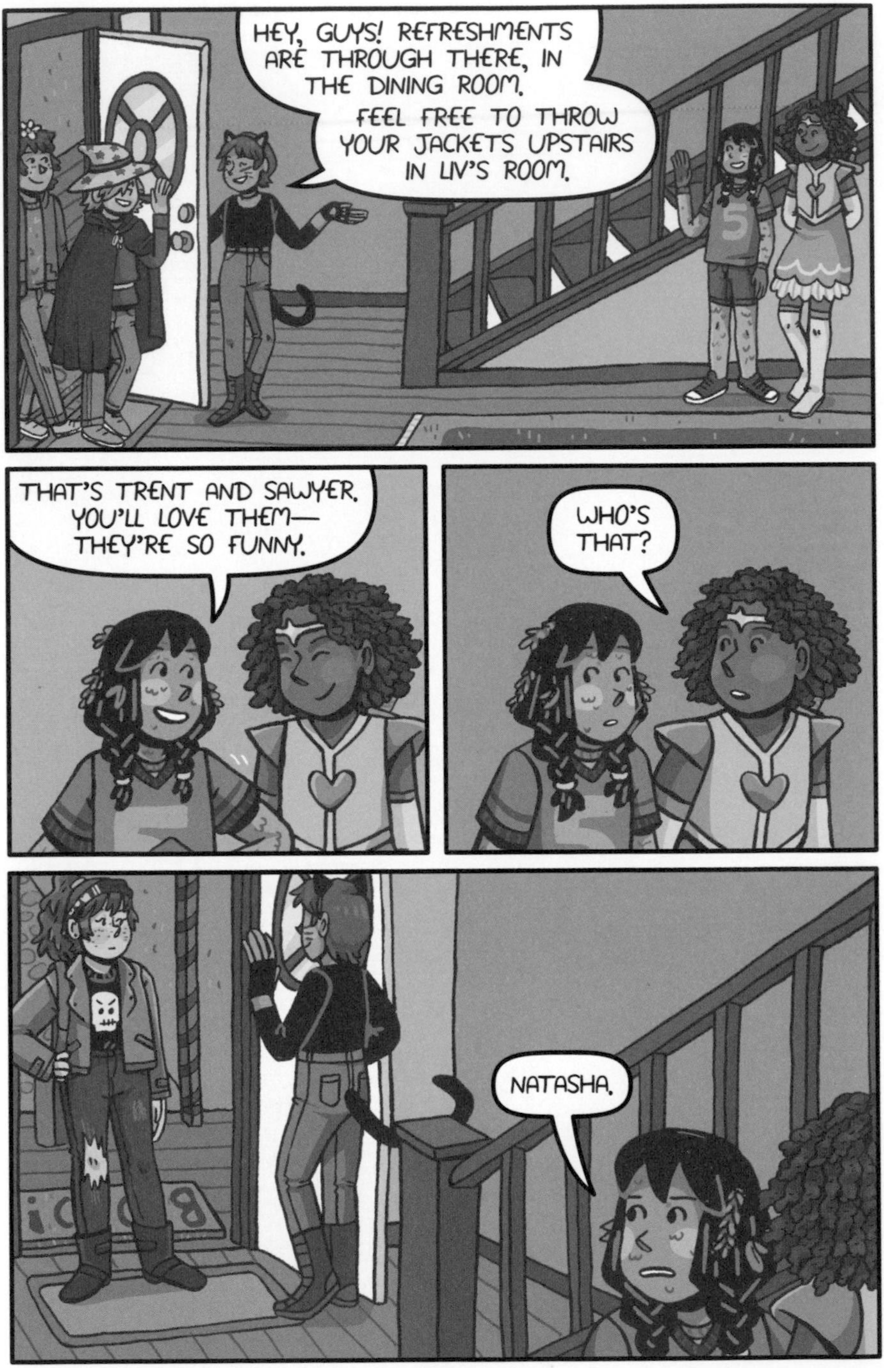
HEY, GUYS! REFRESHMENTS ARE THROUGH THERE, IN THE DINING ROOM.
FEEL FREE TO THROW YOUR JACKETS UPSTAIRS IN LIV'S ROOM.
THAT'S TRENT AND SAWYER. YOU'LL LOVE THEM— THEY'RE SO FUNNY.
WHO'S THAT?
NATASHA.

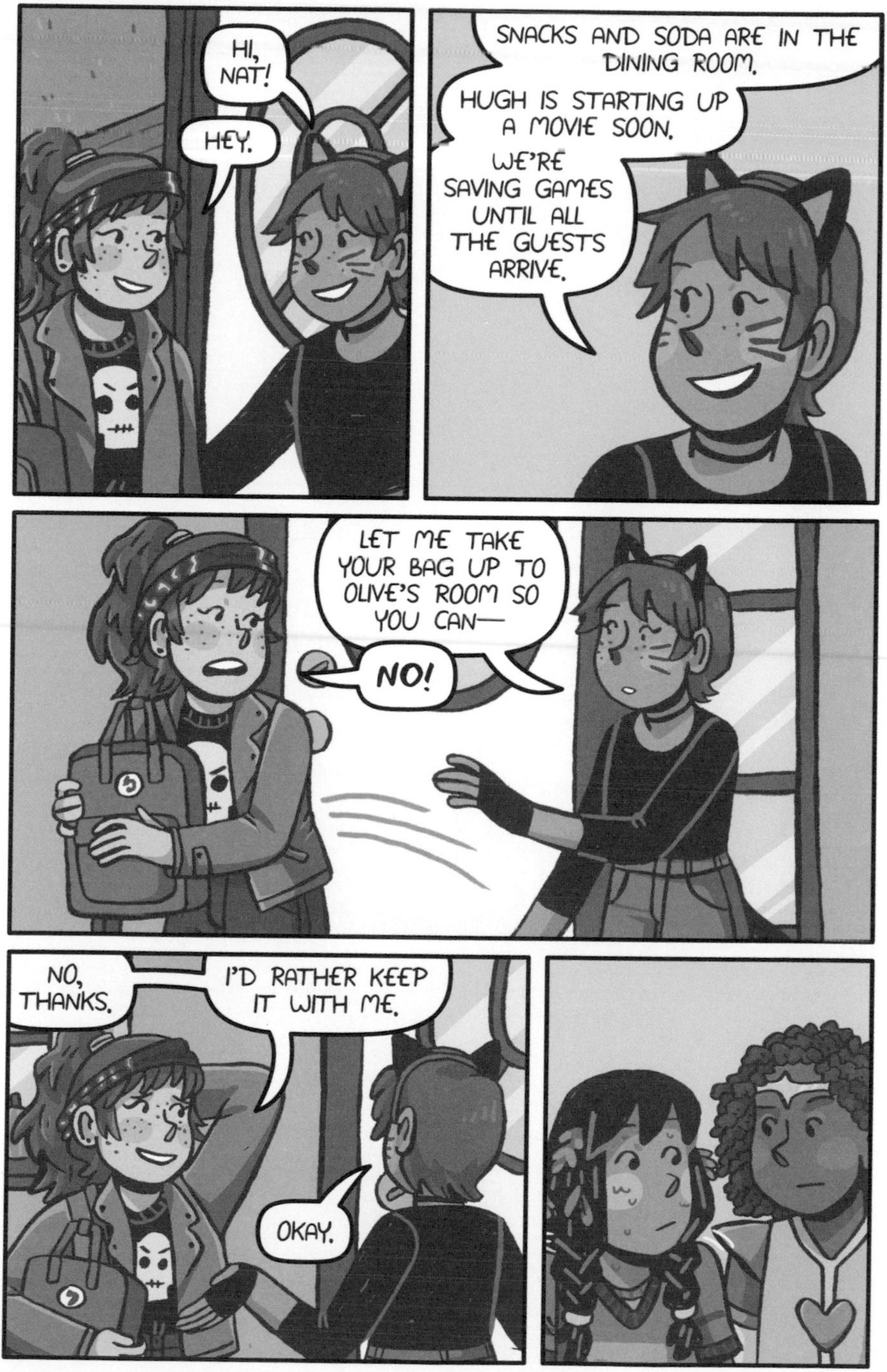
HI, NAT!
HEY.
SNACKS AND SODA ARE IN THE DINING ROOM.
HUGH IS STARTING UP A MOVIE SOON.
WE'RE SAVING GAMES UNTIL ALL THE GUESTS ARRIVE.
LET ME TAKE YOUR BAG UP TO OLIVE'S ROOM SO YOU CAN—
NO!
NO, THANKS.
I'D RATHER KEEP IT WITH ME.
OKAY.

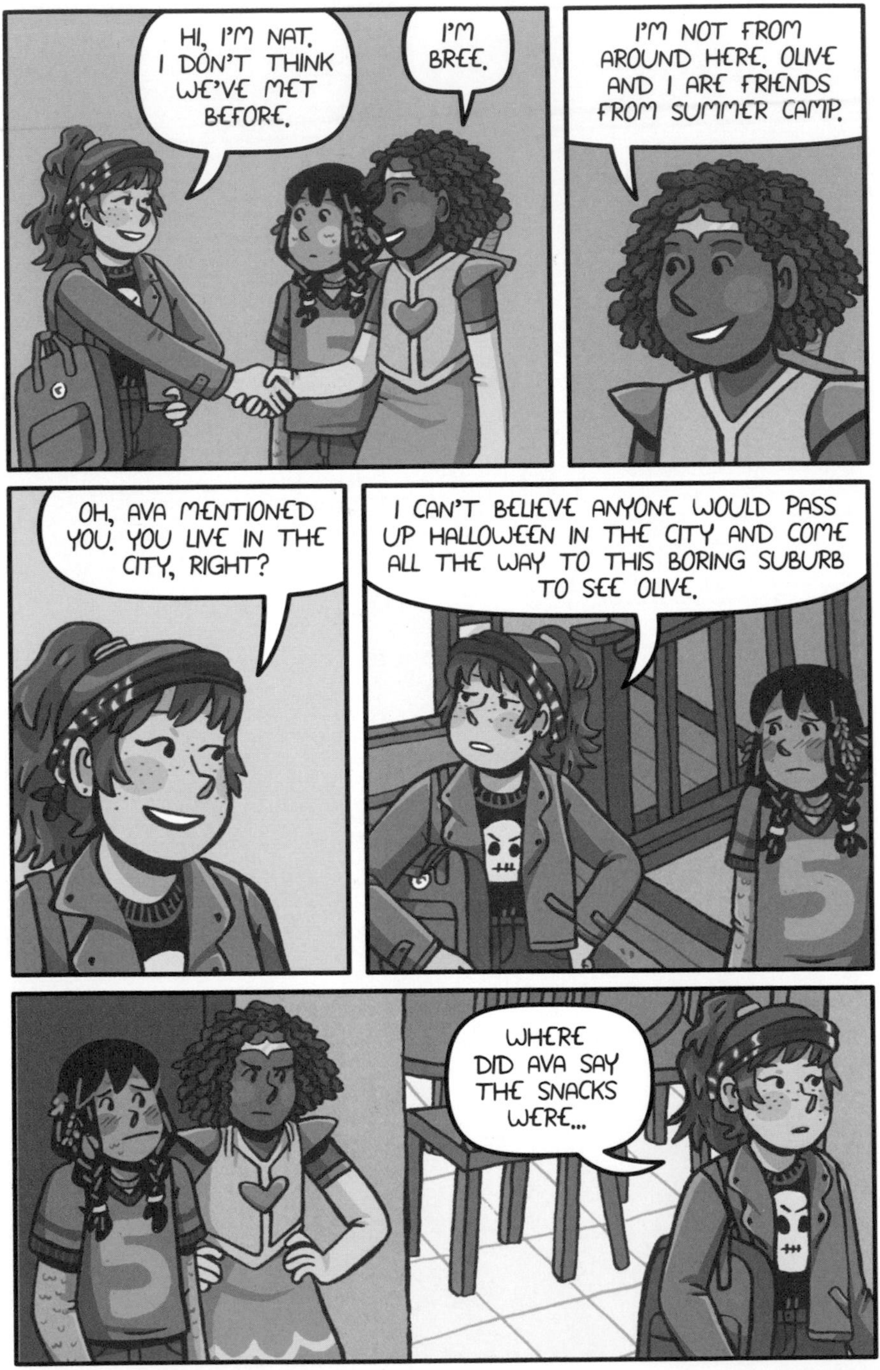
HI, I'M NAT. I DON'T THINK WE'VE MET BEFORE.
I'M BREE.
I'M NOT FROM AROUND HERE. OLIVE AND I ARE FRIENDS FROM SUMMER CAMP.
OH, AVA MENTIONED YOU. YOU LIVE IN THE CITY, RIGHT?
I CAN'T BELIEVE ANYONE WOULD PASS UP HALLOWEEN IN THE CITY AND COME ALL THE WAY TO THIS BORING SUBURB TO SEE OLIVE.
WHERE DID AVA SAY THE SNACKS WERE...

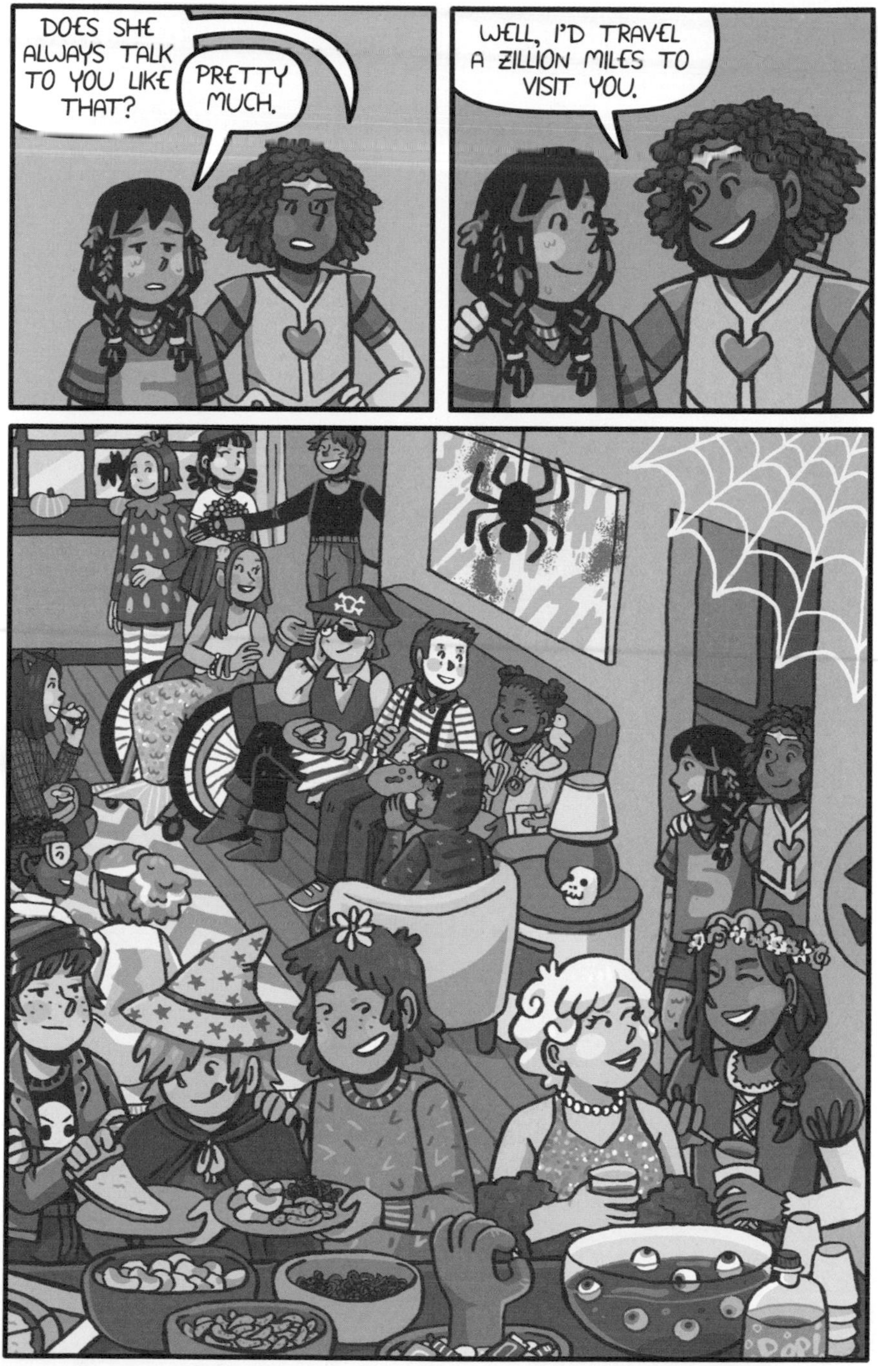
DOES SHE ALWAYS TALK TO YOU LIKE THAT?
PRETTY MUCH.
WELL, I'D TRAVEL A ZILLION MILES TO VISIT YOU.
POP!

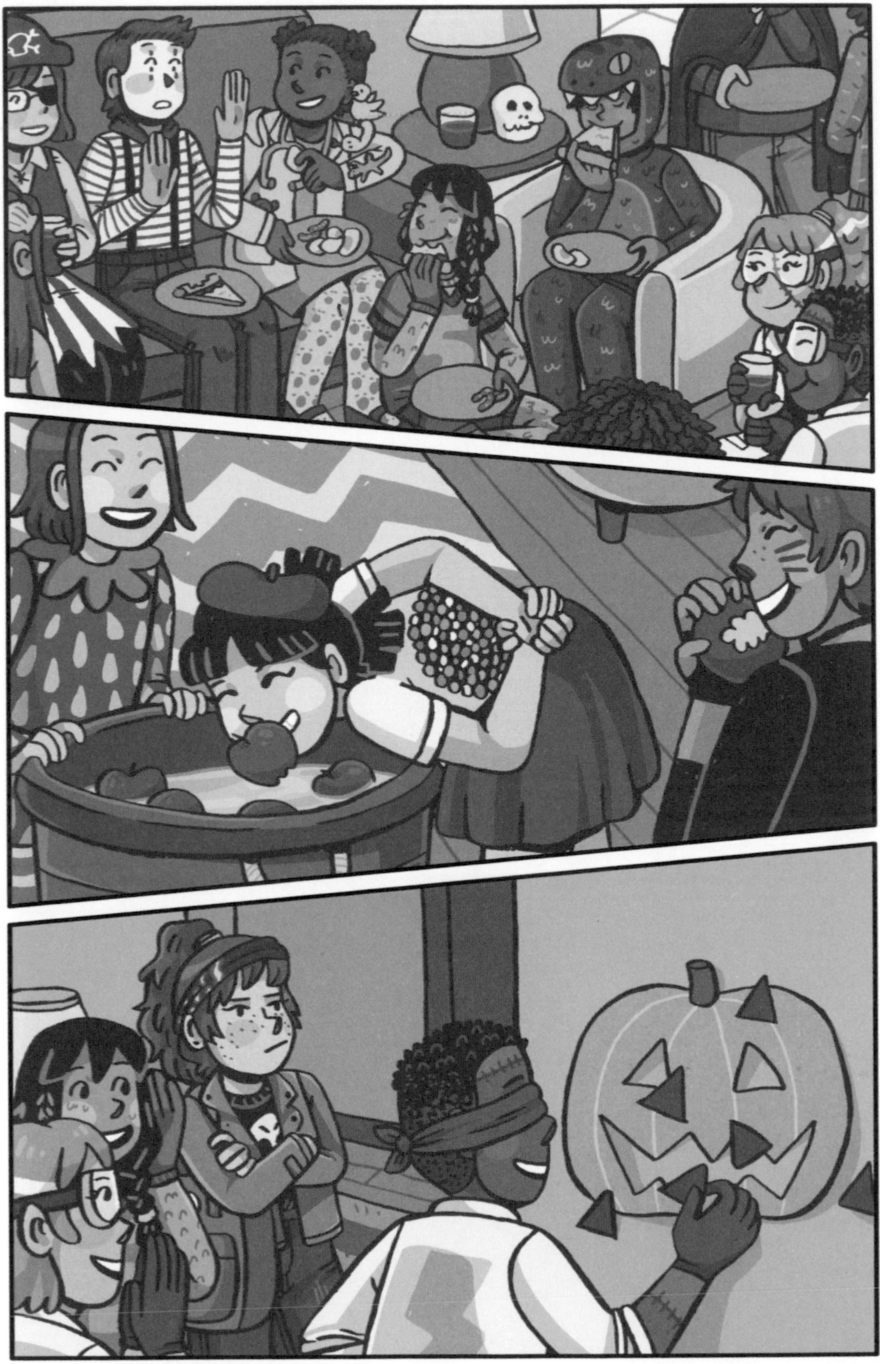

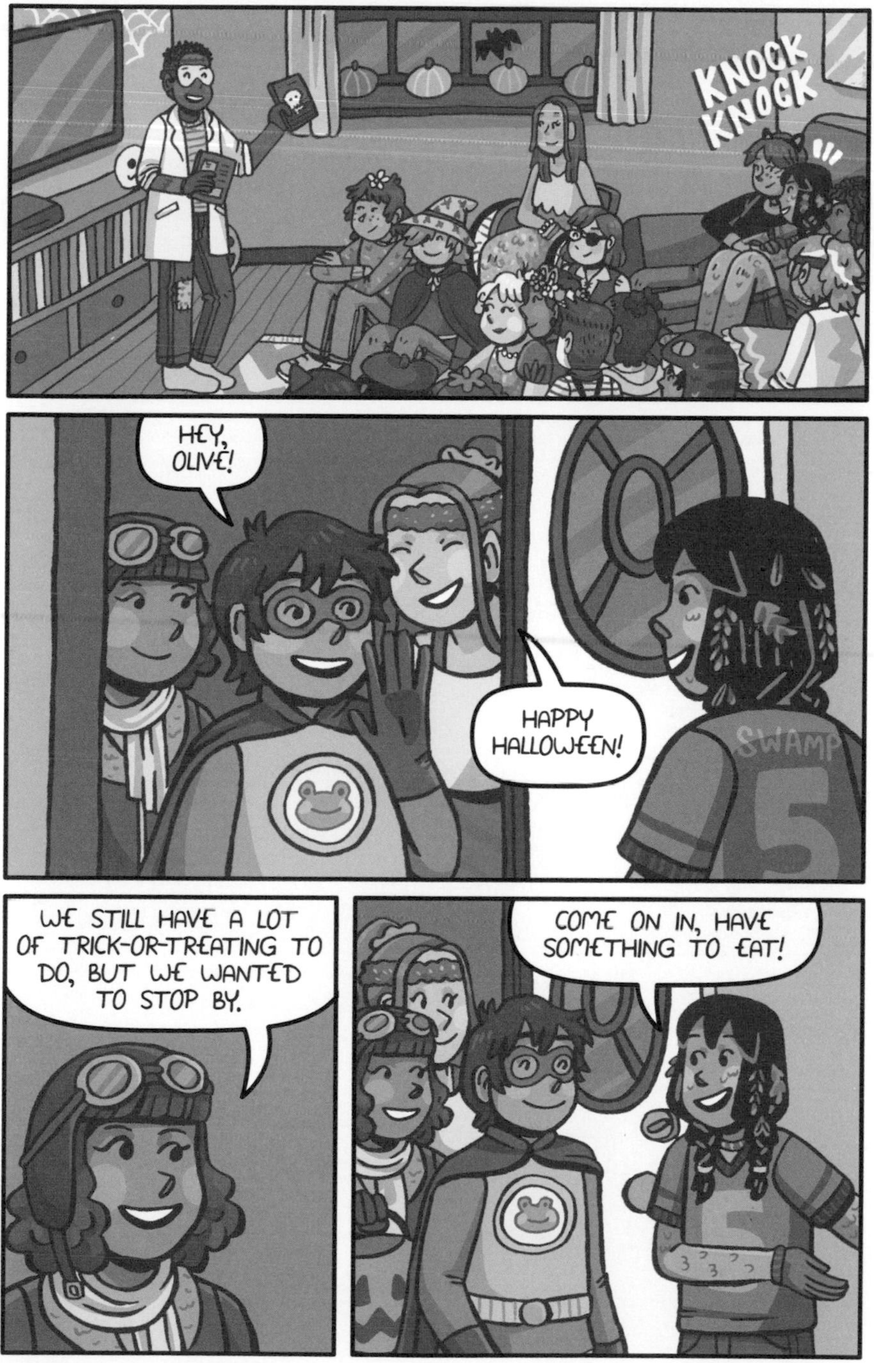
KNOCK KNOCK
HEY, OLIVE!
HAPPY HALLOWEEN!
SWAMP 5
WE STILL HAVE A LOT OF TRICK-OR-TREATING TO DO, BUT WE WANTED TO STOP BY.
COME ON IN, HAVE SOMETHING TO EAT!

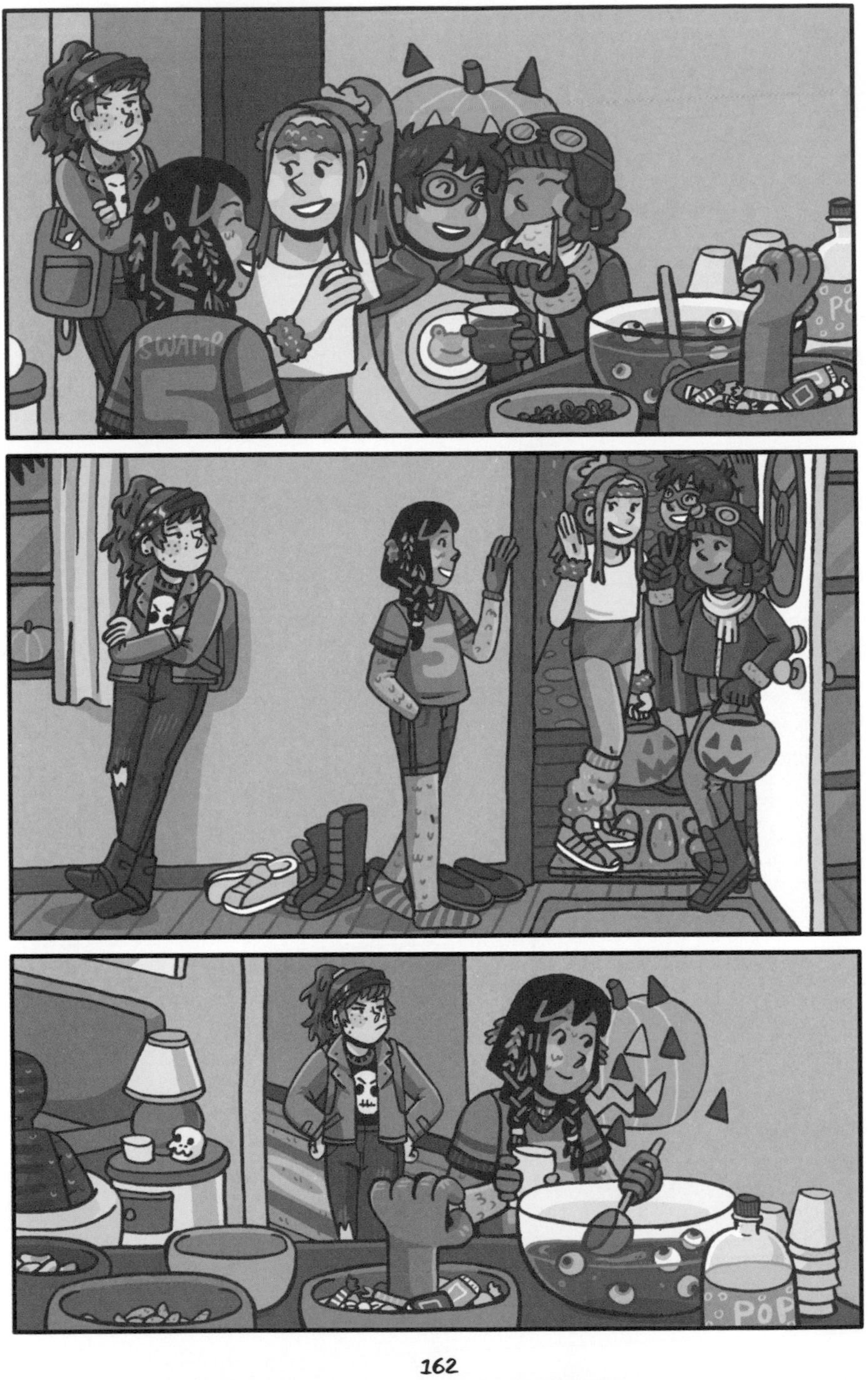
SWAMP
5
POP

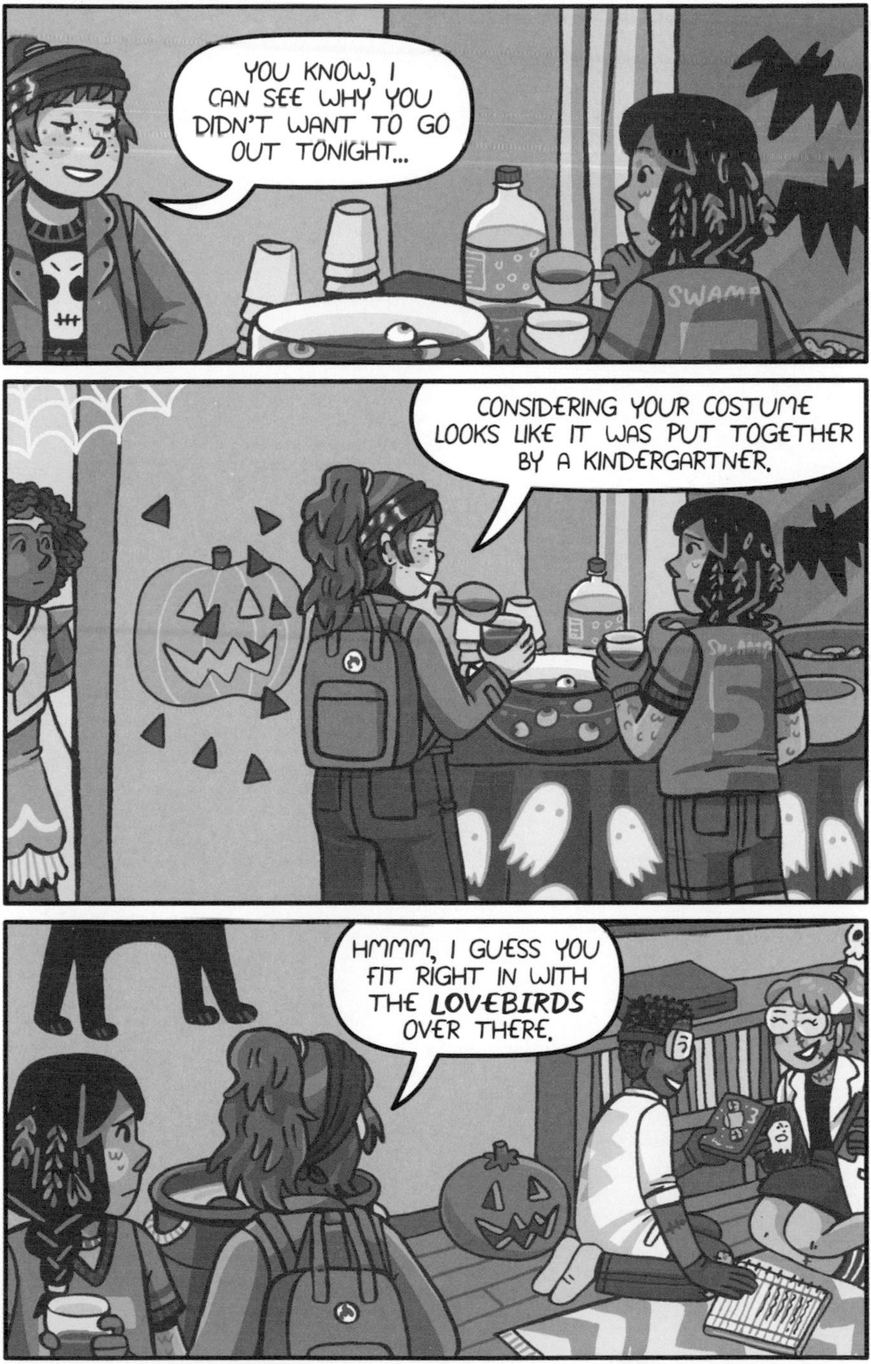

YOU KNOW, I CAN SEE WHY YOU DIDN'T WANT TO GO OUT TONIGHT...
SWAMP
CONSIDERING YOUR COSTUME LOOKS LIKE IT WAS PUT TOGETHER BY A KINDERGARTNER.
SWAMP
5
HMMM, I GUESS YOU FIT RIGHT IN WITH THE **LOVEBIRDS** OVER THERE.

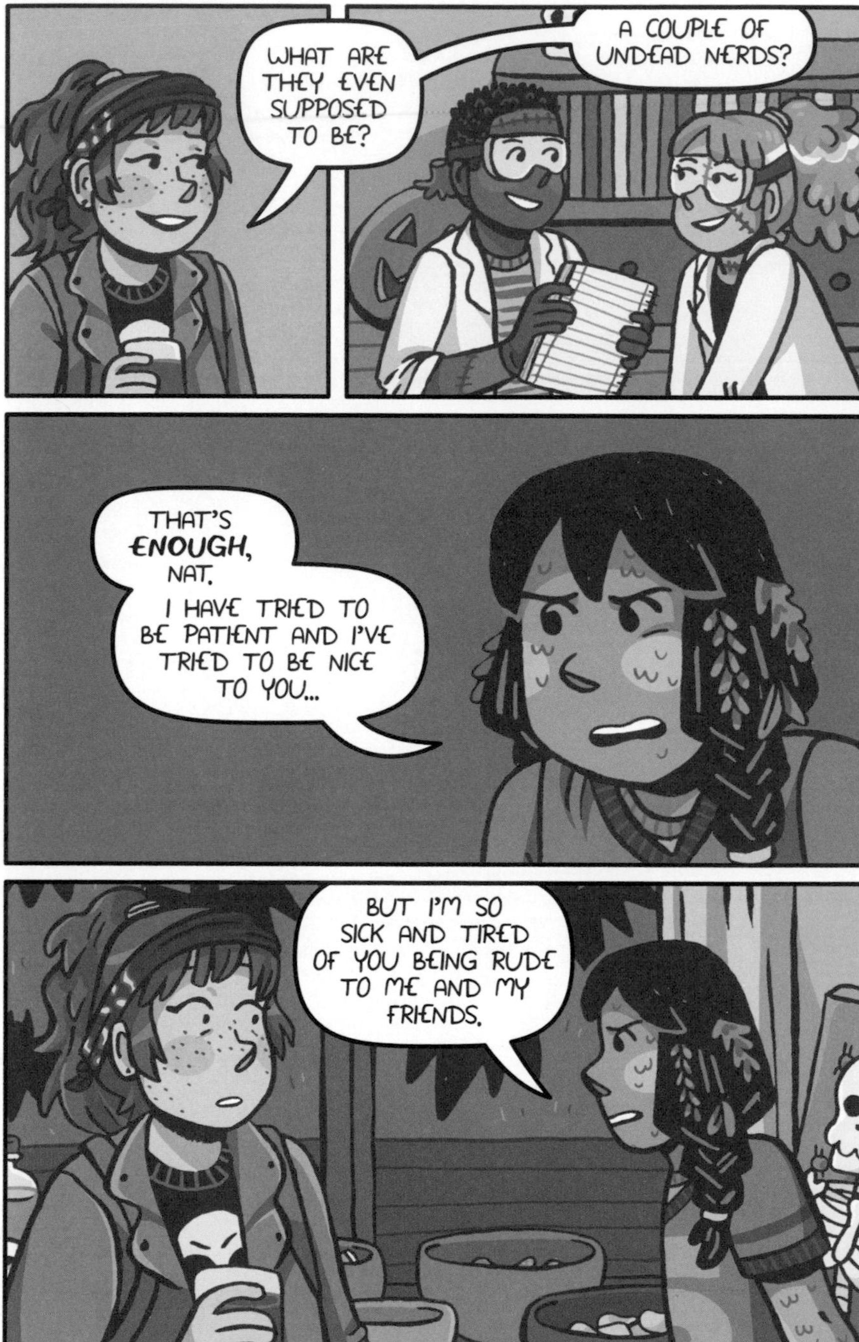
WHAT ARE THEY EVEN SUPPOSED TO BE?
A COUPLE OF UNDEAD NERDS?
THAT'S **ENOUGH,** NAT.
I HAVE TRIED TO BE PATIENT AND I'VE TRIED TO BE NICE TO YOU...
BUT I'M SO SICK AND TIRED OF YOU BEING RUDE TO ME AND MY FRIENDS.

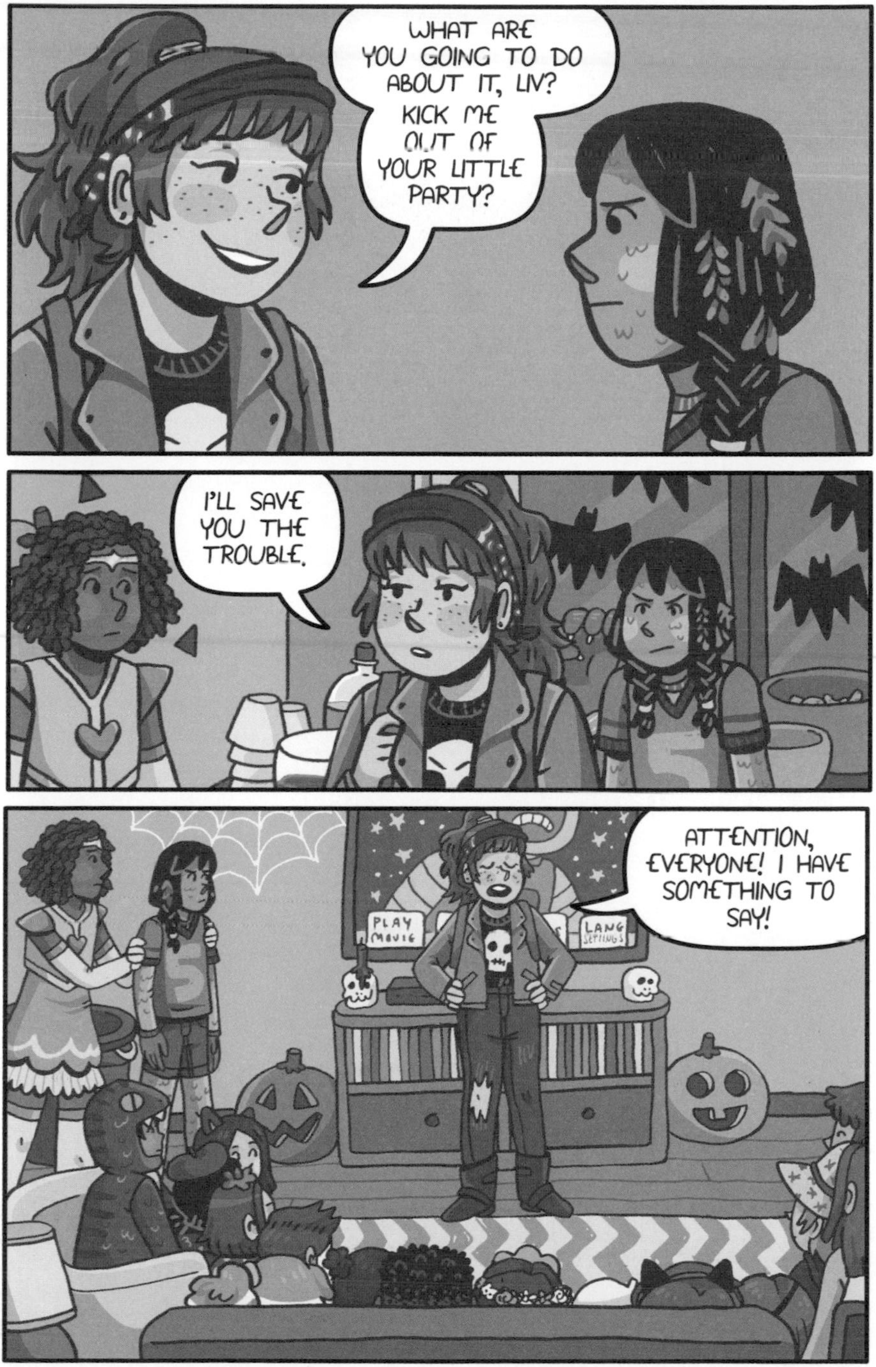
WHAT ARE YOU GOING TO DO ABOUT IT, LIV? KICK ME OUT OF YOUR LITTLE PARTY?
I'LL SAVE YOU THE TROUBLE.
PLAY MOVIE
LANG SETTINGS
ATTENTION, EVERYONE! I HAVE SOMETHING TO SAY!

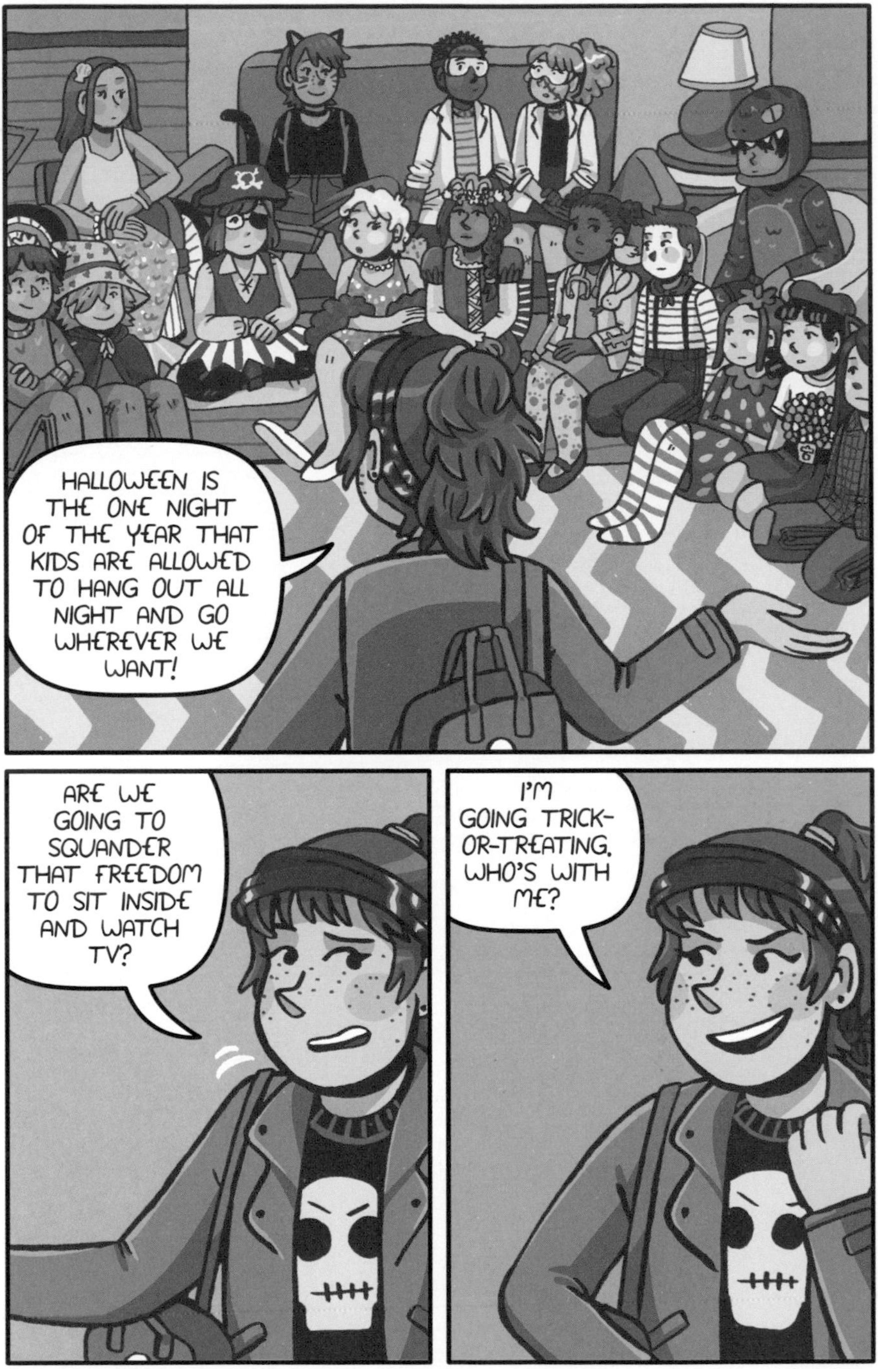
HALLOWEEN IS THE ONE NIGHT OF THE YEAR THAT KIDS ARE ALLOWED TO HANG OUT ALL NIGHT AND GO WHEREVER WE WANT!
ARE WE GOING TO SQUANDER THAT FREEDOM TO SIT INSIDE AND WATCH TV?
I'M GOING TRICK-OR-TREATING. WHO'S WITH ME?

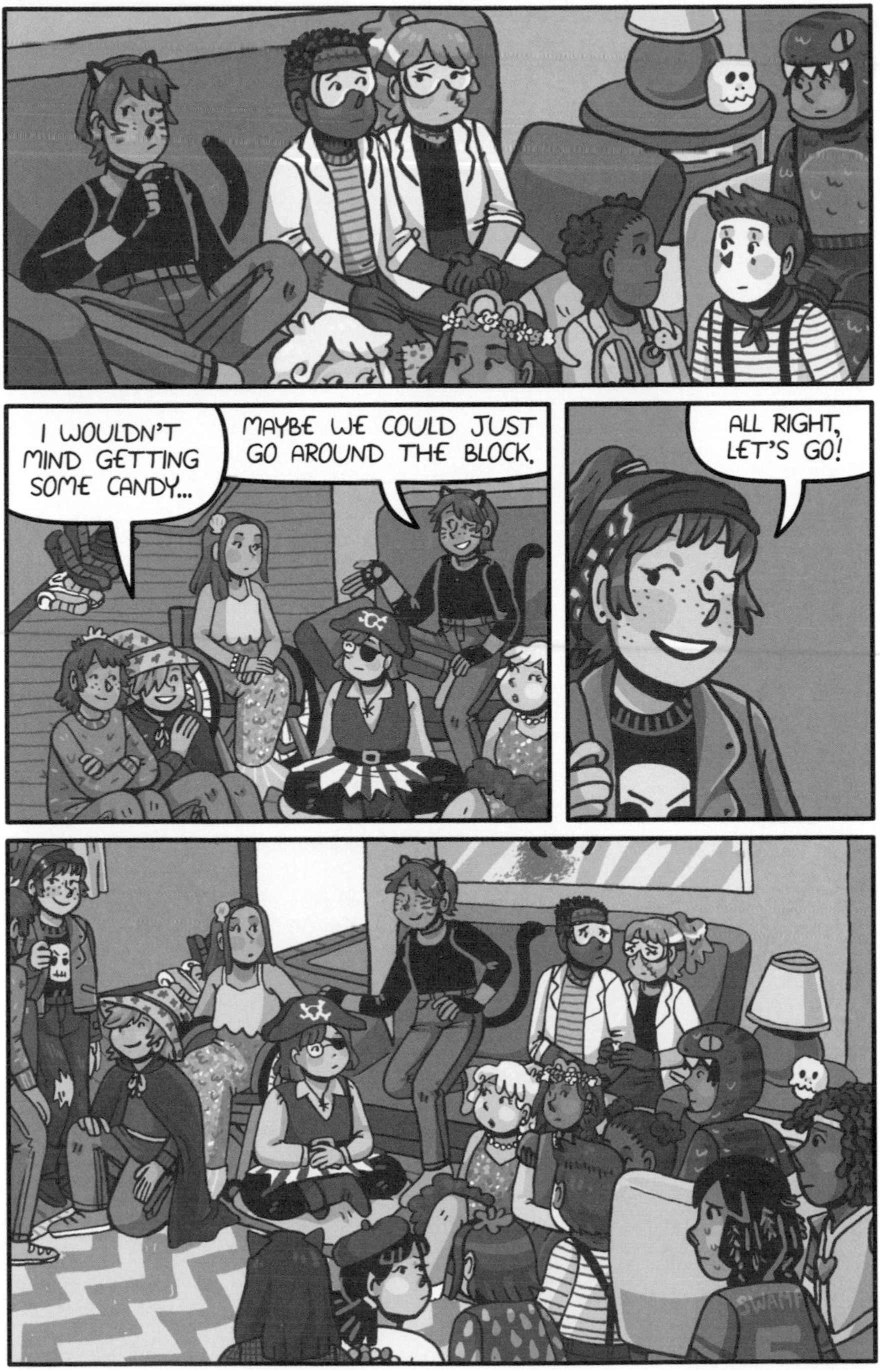
I WOULDN'T MIND GETTING SOME CANDY...
MAYBE WE COULD JUST GO AROUND THE BLOCK.
ALL RIGHT, LET'S GO!
SWAMP

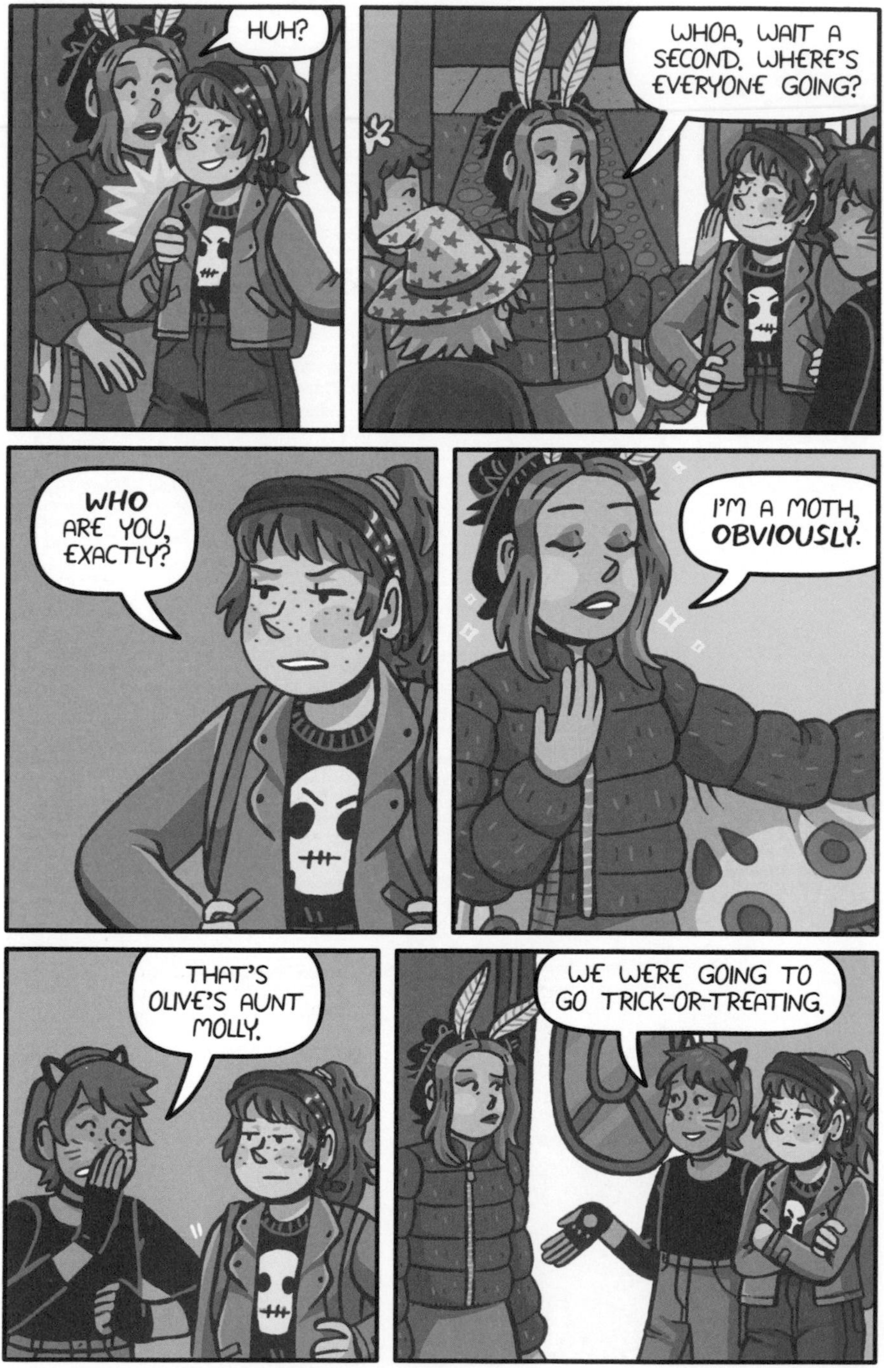
HUH?
WHOA, WAIT A SECOND. WHERE'S EVERYONE GOING?
WHO ARE YOU, EXACTLY?
I'M A MOTH, **OBVIOUSLY.**
THAT'S OLIVE'S AUNT MOLLY.
WE WERE GOING TO GO TRICK-OR-TREATING.

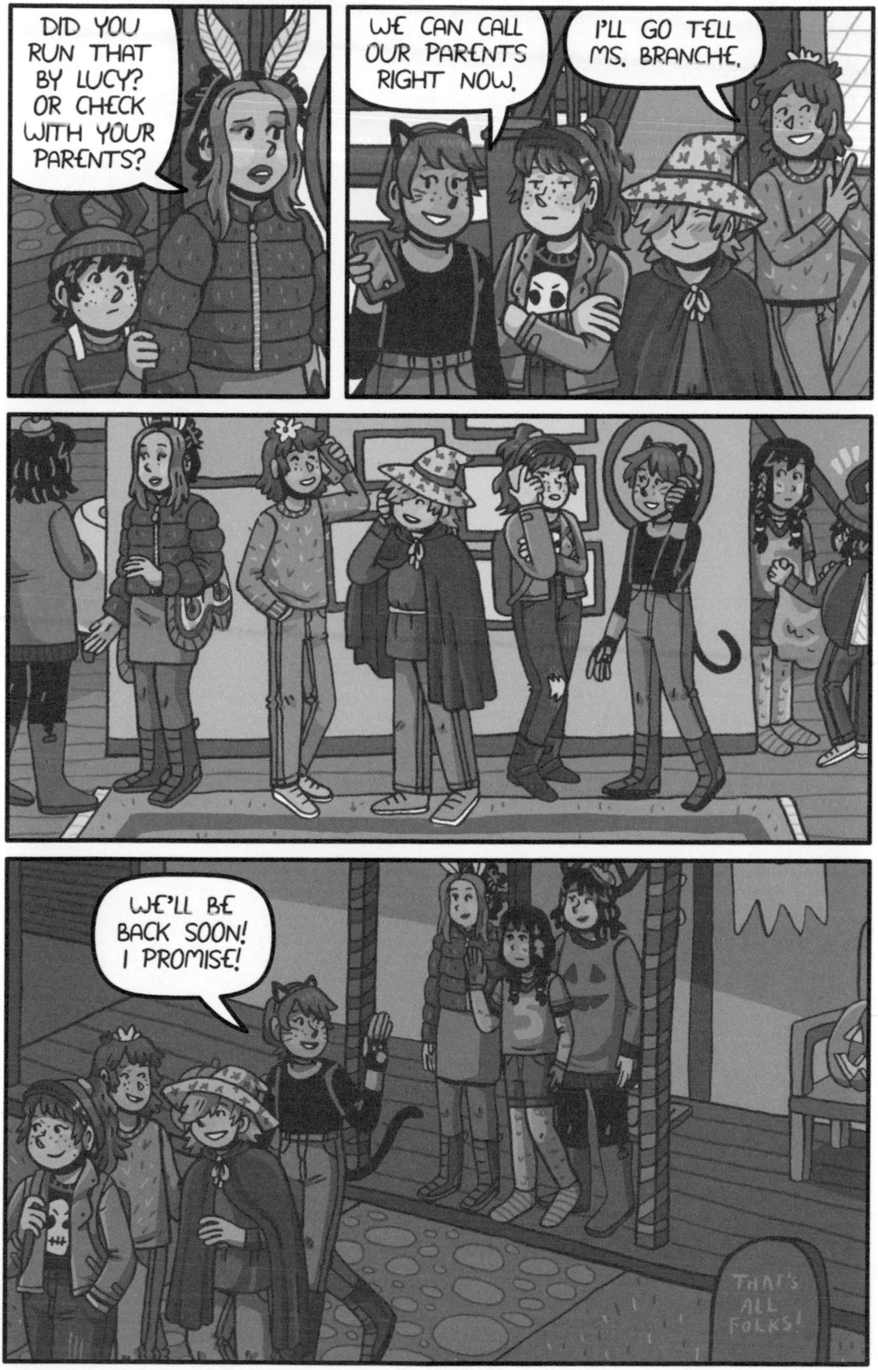

DID YOU RUN THAT BY LUCY? OR CHECK WITH YOUR PARENTS?
WE CAN CALL OUR PARENTS RIGHT NOW.
I'LL GO TELL MS. BRANCHE.
WE'LL BE BACK SOON! I PROMISE!
THAT'S ALL FOLKS!

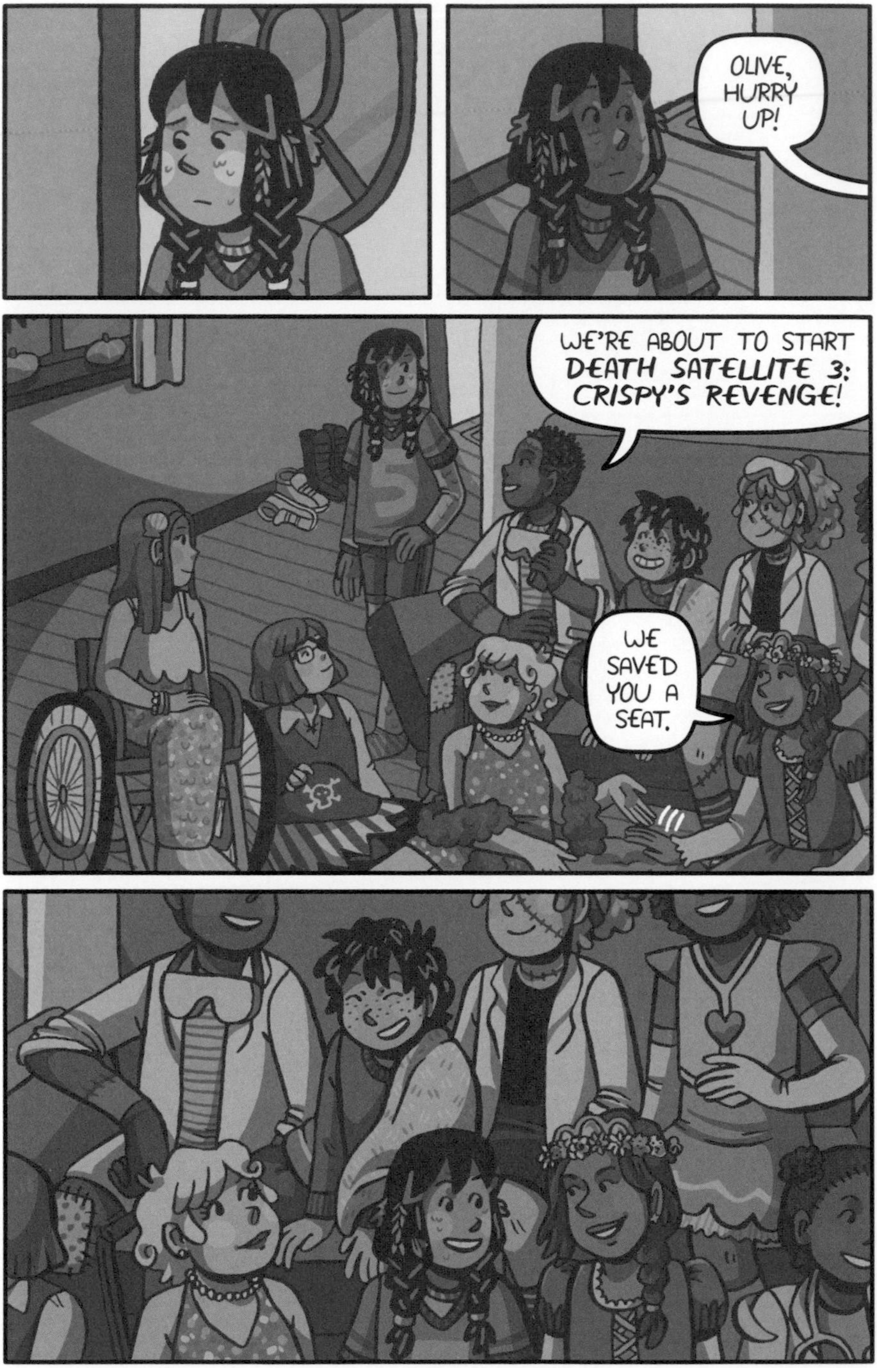
OLIVE, HURRY UP!
WE'RE ABOUT TO START **DEATH SATELLITE 3: CRISPY'S REVENGE!**
WE SAVED YOU A SEAT.

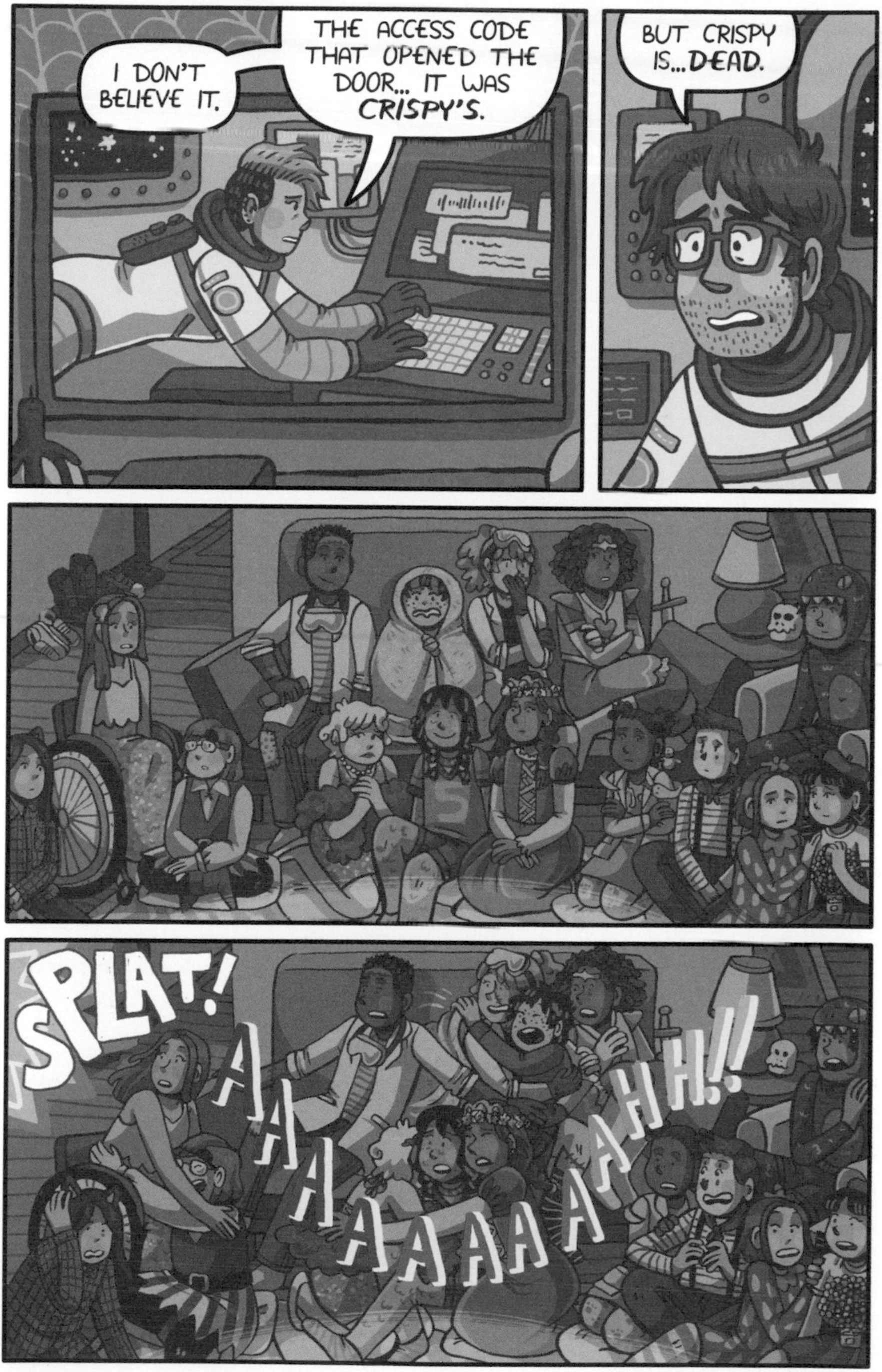
I DON'T BELIEVE IT.
THE ACCESS CODE THAT OPENED THE DOOR... IT WAS CRISPY'S.
BUT CRISPY IS... DEAD.
SPLAT!
AAAAAAAAAAAAHH!!

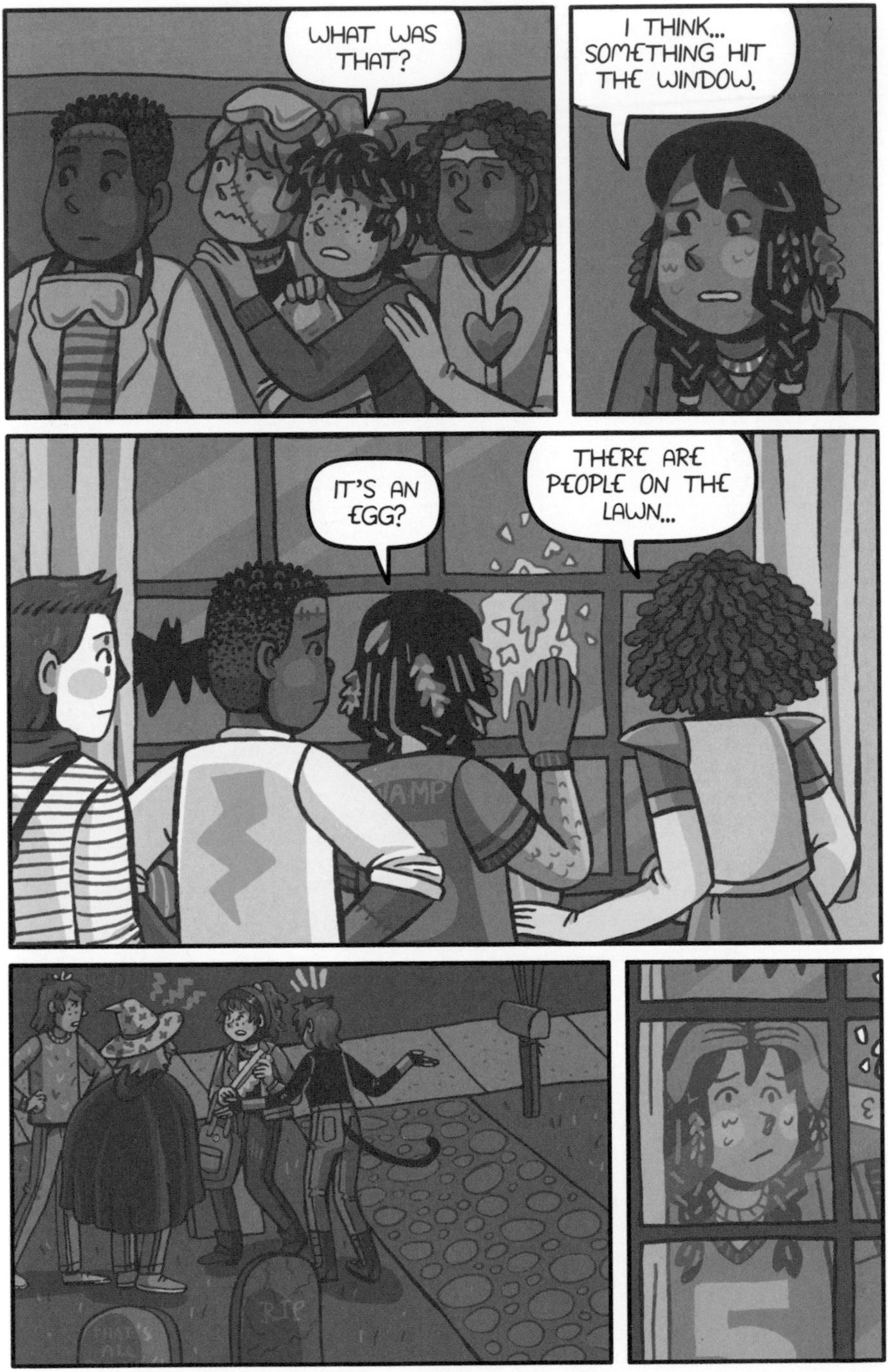
WHAT WAS THAT?
I THINK... SOMETHING HIT THE WINDOW.
IT'S AN EGG?
THERE ARE PEOPLE ON THE LAWN...

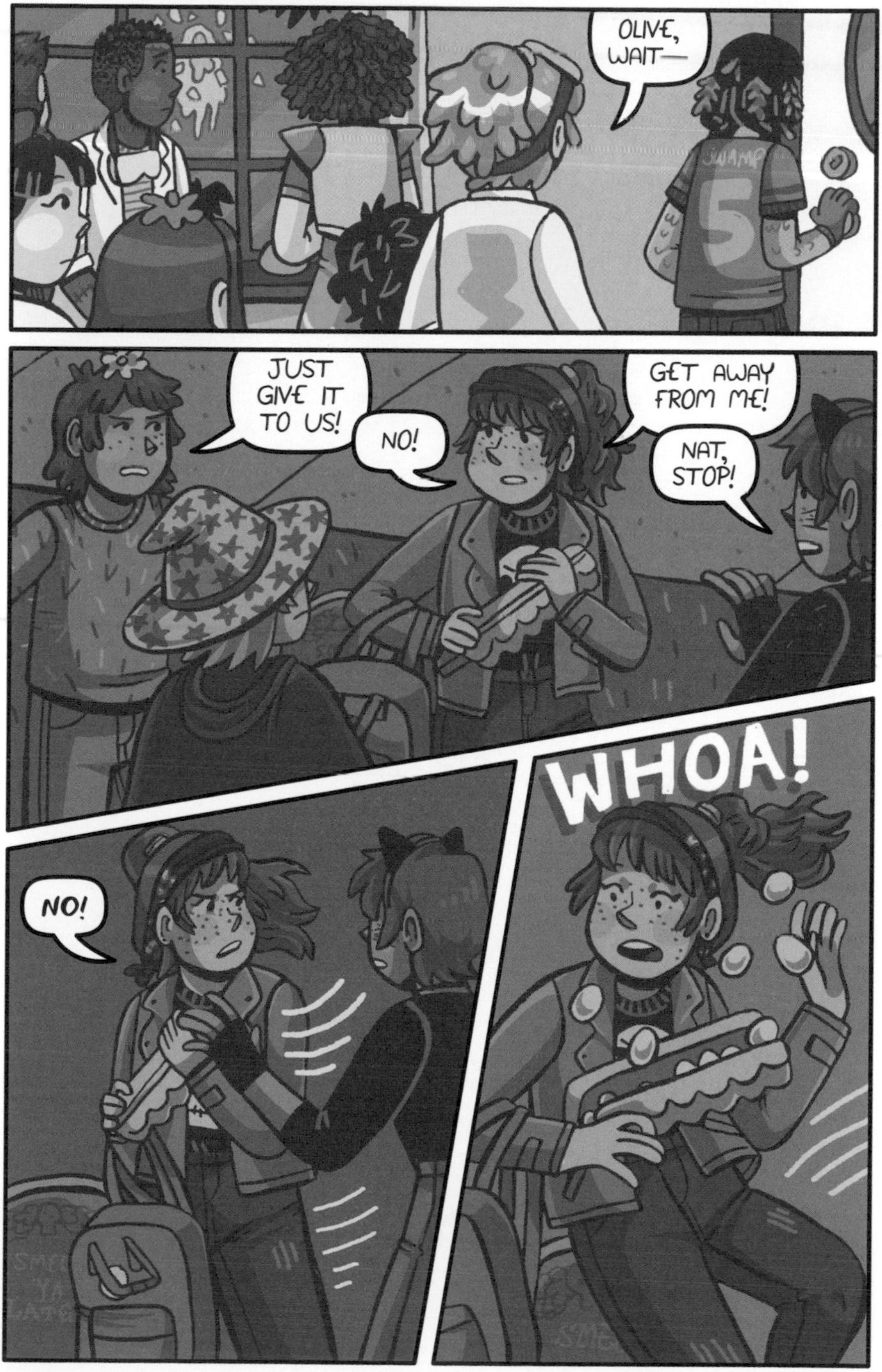
OLIVE, WAIT—
SWAMP 5
JUST GIVE IT TO US!
NO!
GET AWAY FROM ME!
NAT, STOP!
NO!
WHOA!

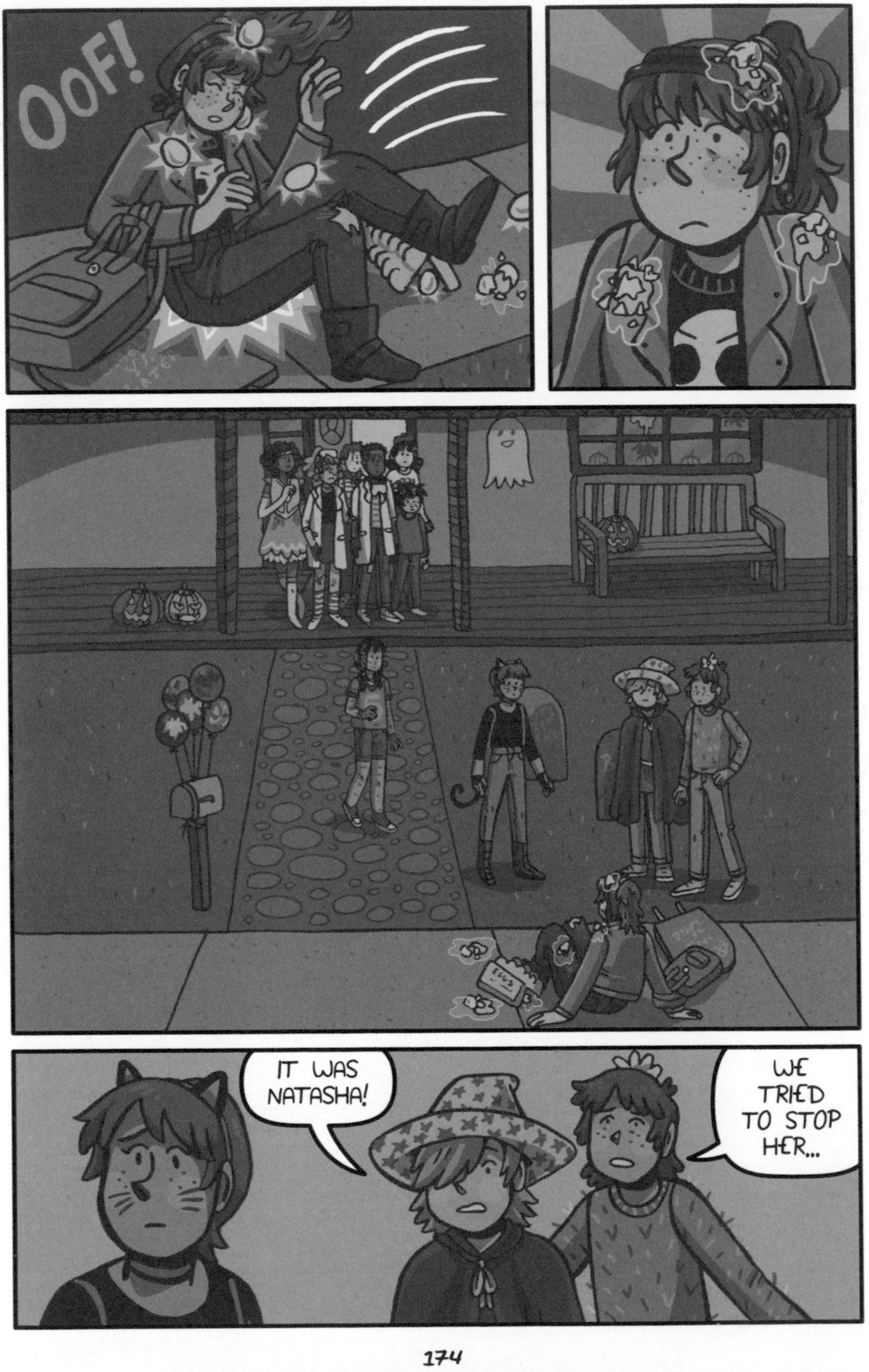
OOF!
IT WAS NATASHA!
WE TRIED TO STOP HER...

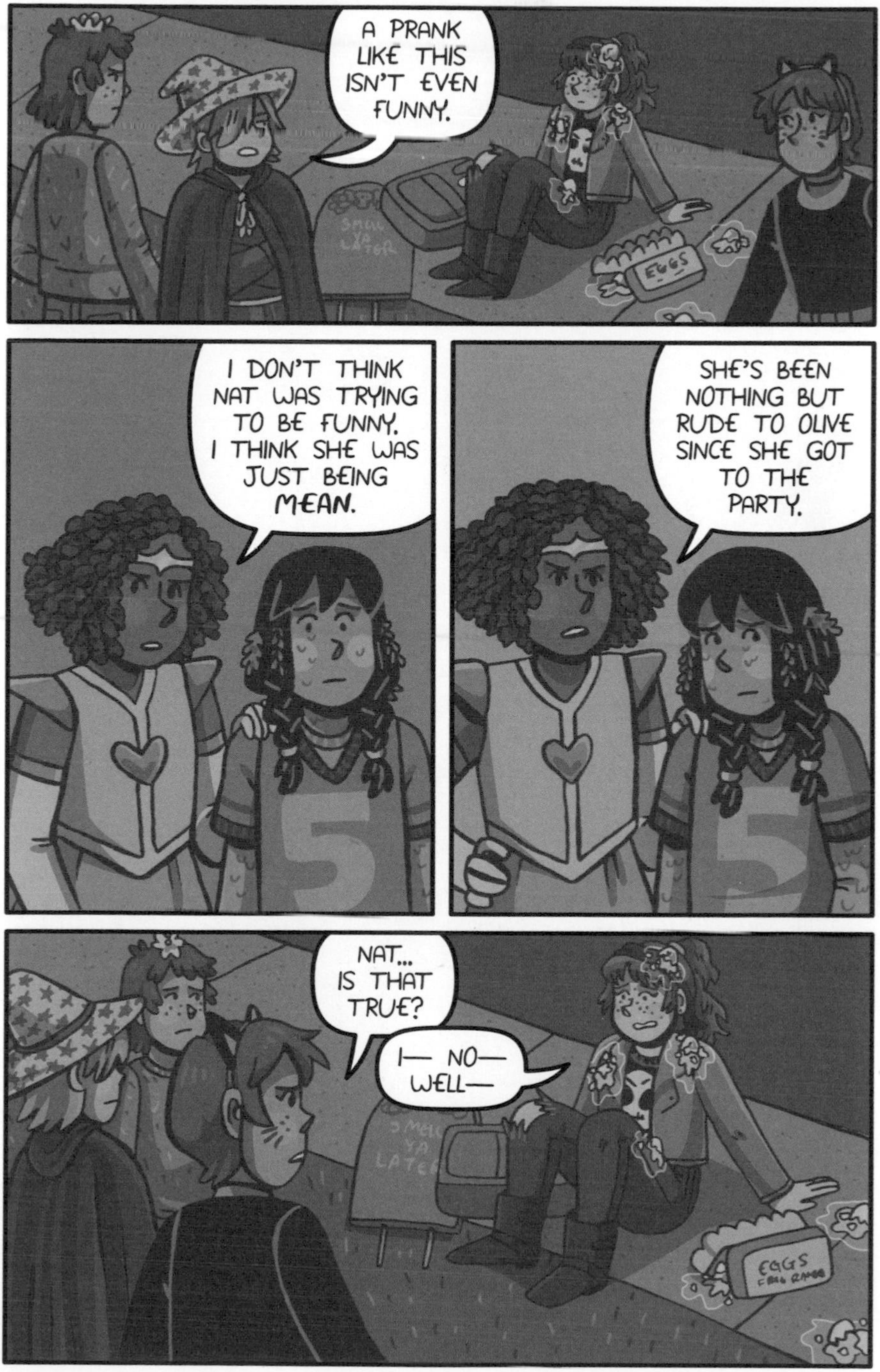
A PRANK LIKE THIS ISN'T EVEN FUNNY.
I DON'T THINK NAT WAS TRYING TO BE FUNNY. I THINK SHE WAS JUST BEING MEAN.
SHE'S BEEN NOTHING BUT RUDE TO OLIVE SINCE SHE GOT TO THE PARTY.
NAT... IS THAT TRUE?
I— NO— WELL—
EGGS

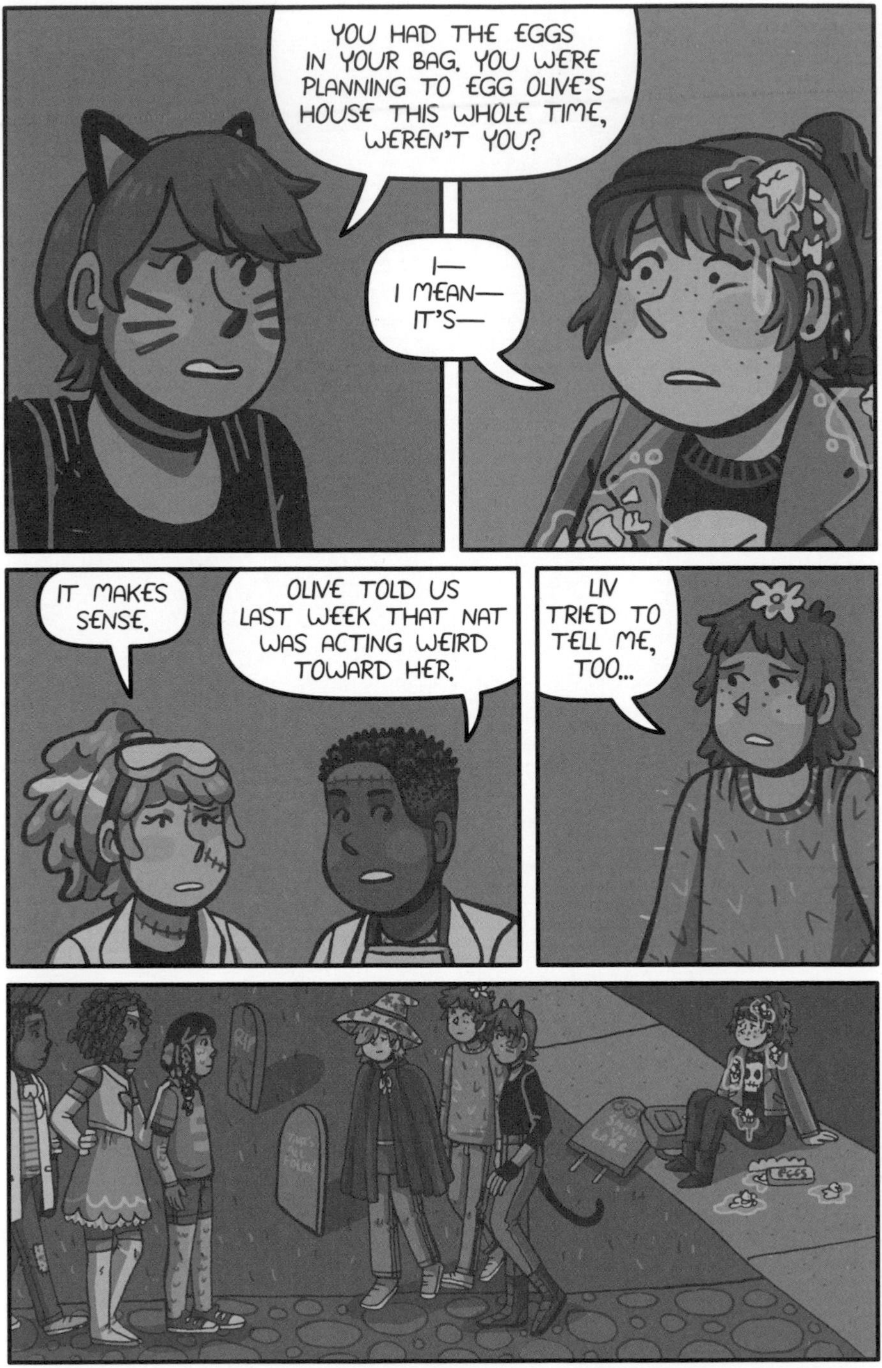
YOU HAD THE EGGS IN YOUR BAG. YOU WERE PLANNING TO EGG OLIVE'S HOUSE THIS WHOLE TIME, WEREN'T YOU?
I— I MEAN— IT'S—
IT MAKES SENSE.
OLIVE TOLD US LAST WEEK THAT NAT WAS ACTING WEIRD TOWARD HER.
LIV TRIED TO TELL ME, TOO...

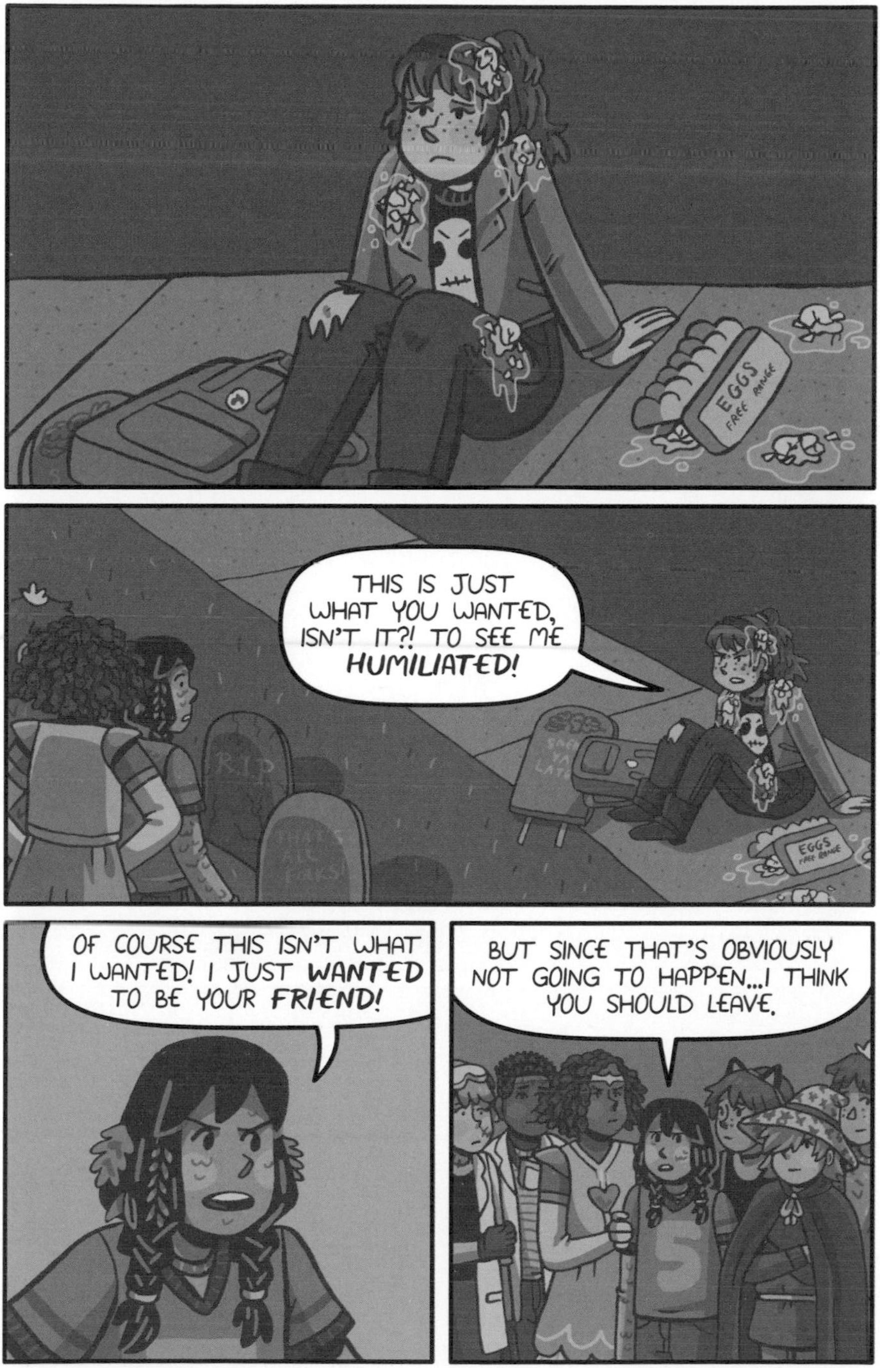
EGGS
FREE RANGE
THIS IS JUST WHAT YOU WANTED, ISN'T IT?! TO SEE ME **HUMILIATED!**
R.I.P
OF COURSE THIS ISN'T WHAT I WANTED! I JUST **WANTED** TO BE YOUR **FRIEND!**
BUT SINCE THAT'S OBVIOUSLY NOT GOING TO HAPPEN...I THINK YOU SHOULD LEAVE.

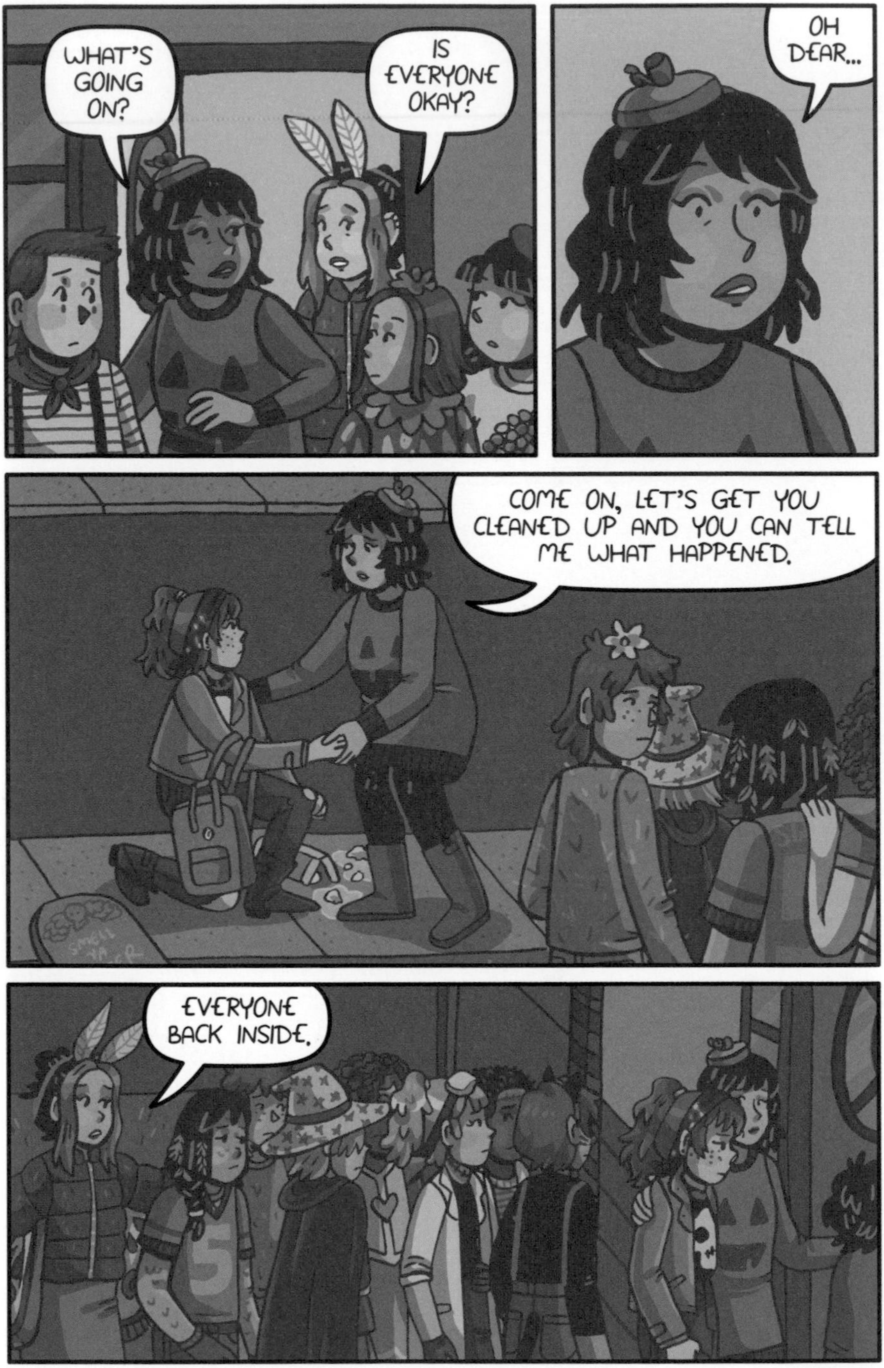
WHAT'S GOING ON?
IS EVERYONE OKAY?
OH DEAR...
COME ON, LET'S GET YOU CLEANED UP AND YOU CAN TELL ME WHAT HAPPENED.
EVERYONE BACK INSIDE.

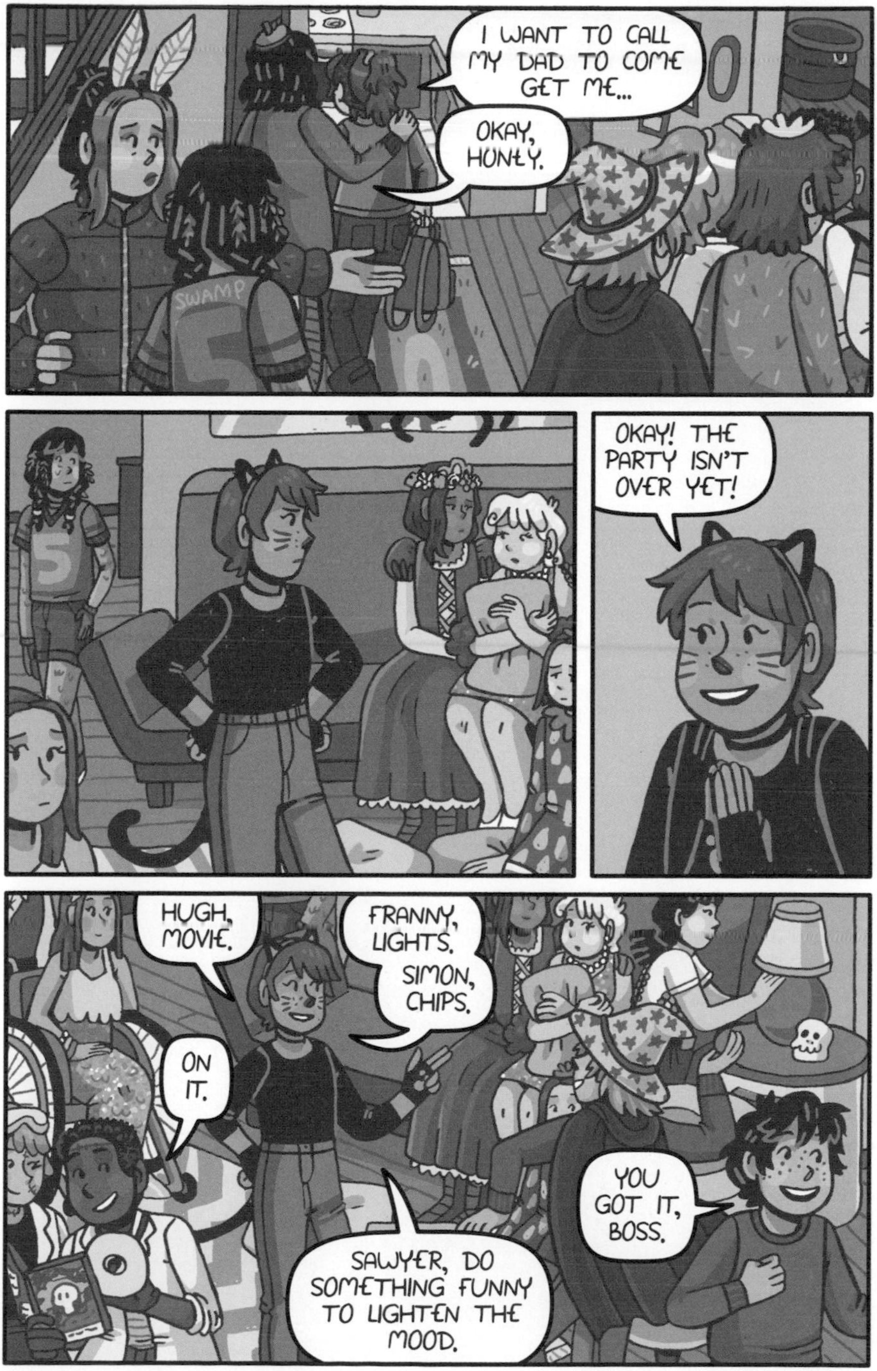
I WANT TO CALL MY DAD TO COME GET ME...
OKAY, HONEY.
SWAMP
OKAY! THE PARTY ISN'T OVER YET!
HUGH, MOVIE.
FRANNY, LIGHTS.
SIMON, CHIPS.
ON IT.
YOU GOT IT, BOSS.
SAWYER, DO SOMETHING FUNNY TO LIGHTEN THE MOOD.

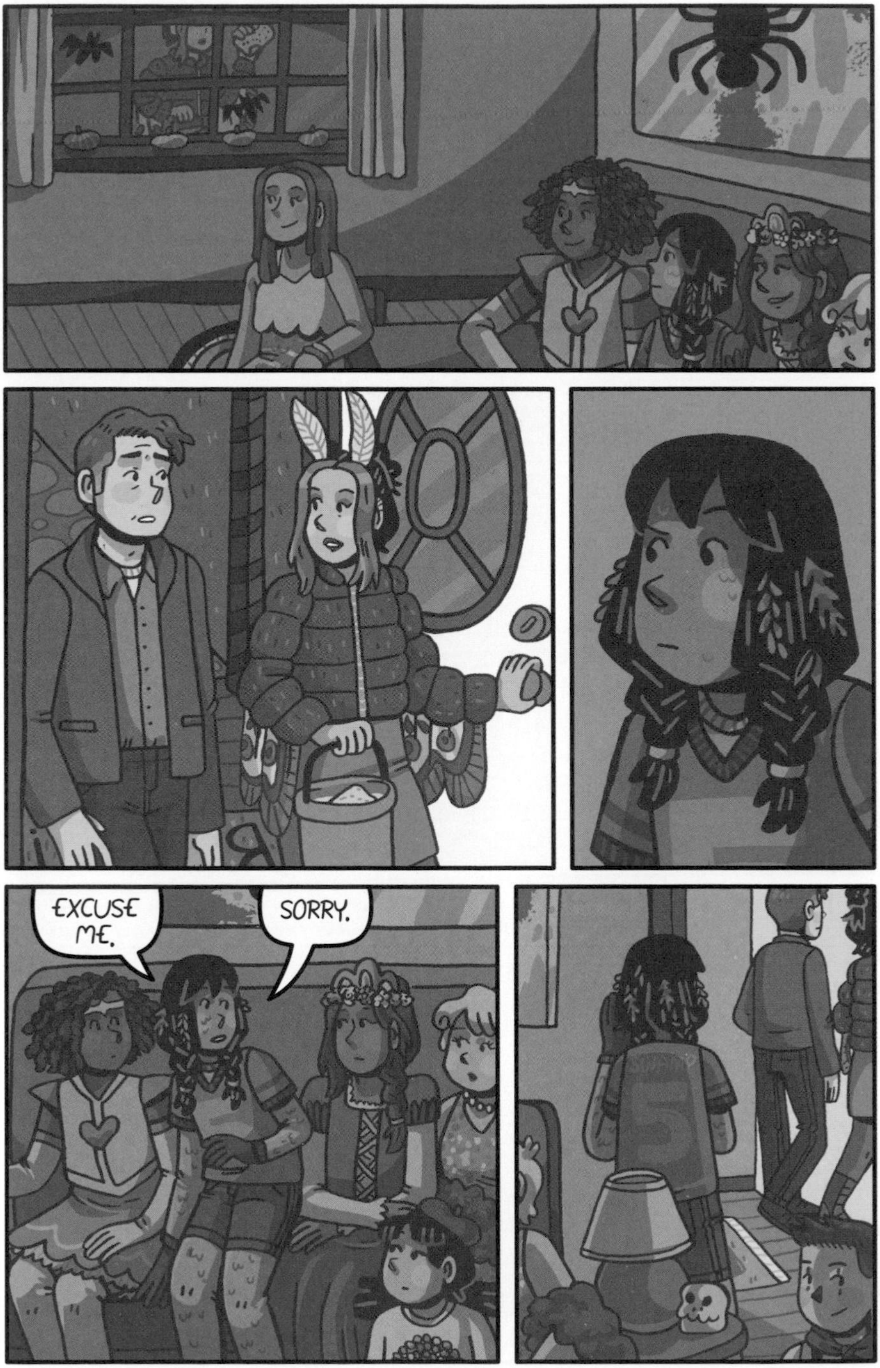
EXCUSE ME.
SORRY.

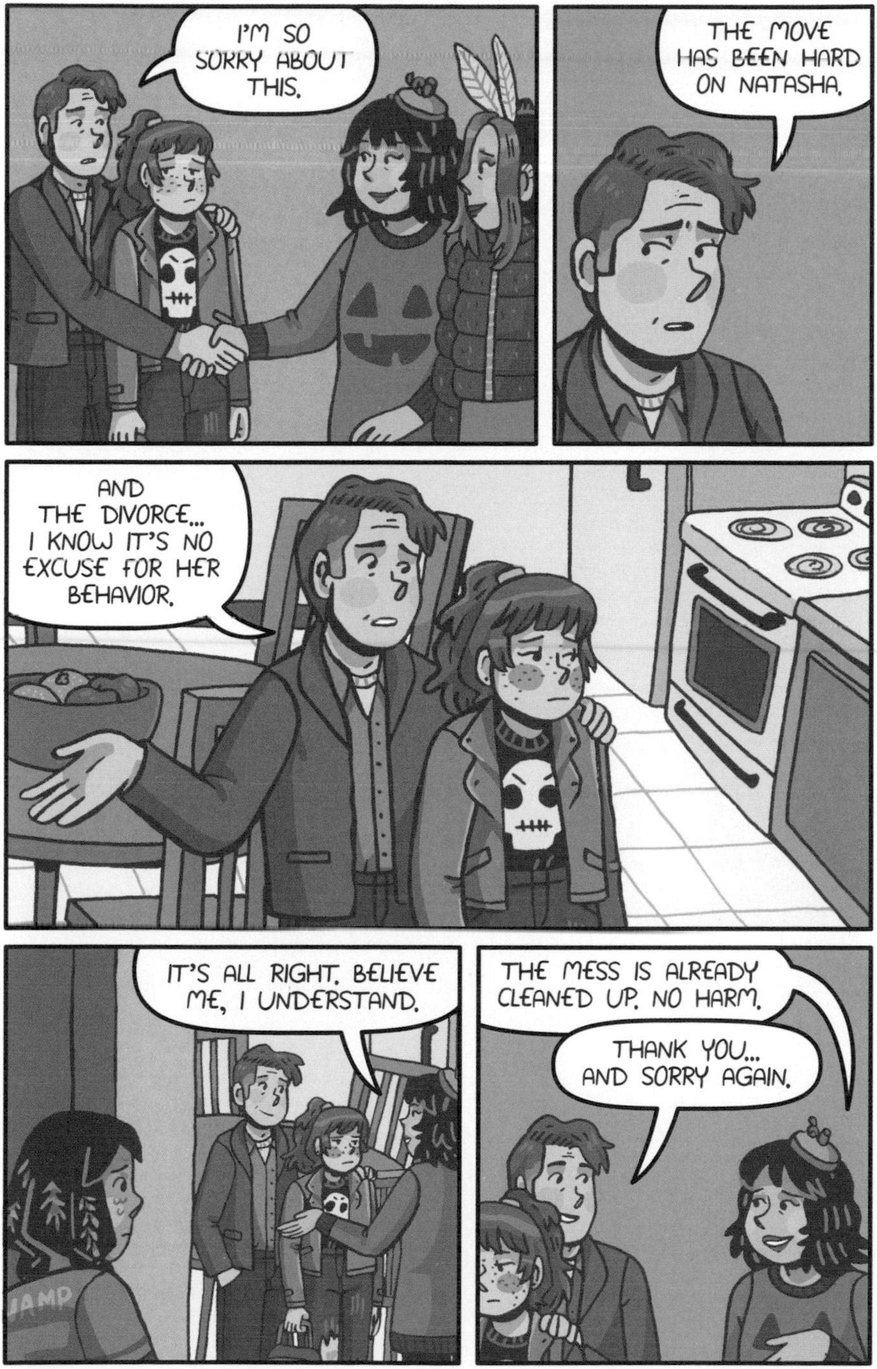
I'M SO SORRY ABOUT THIS.
THE MOVE HAS BEEN HARD ON NATASHA.
AND THE DIVORCE... I KNOW IT'S NO EXCUSE FOR HER BEHAVIOR.
IT'S ALL RIGHT. BELIEVE ME, I UNDERSTAND.
THE MESS IS ALREADY CLEANED UP. NO HARM.
THANK YOU... AND SORRY AGAIN.

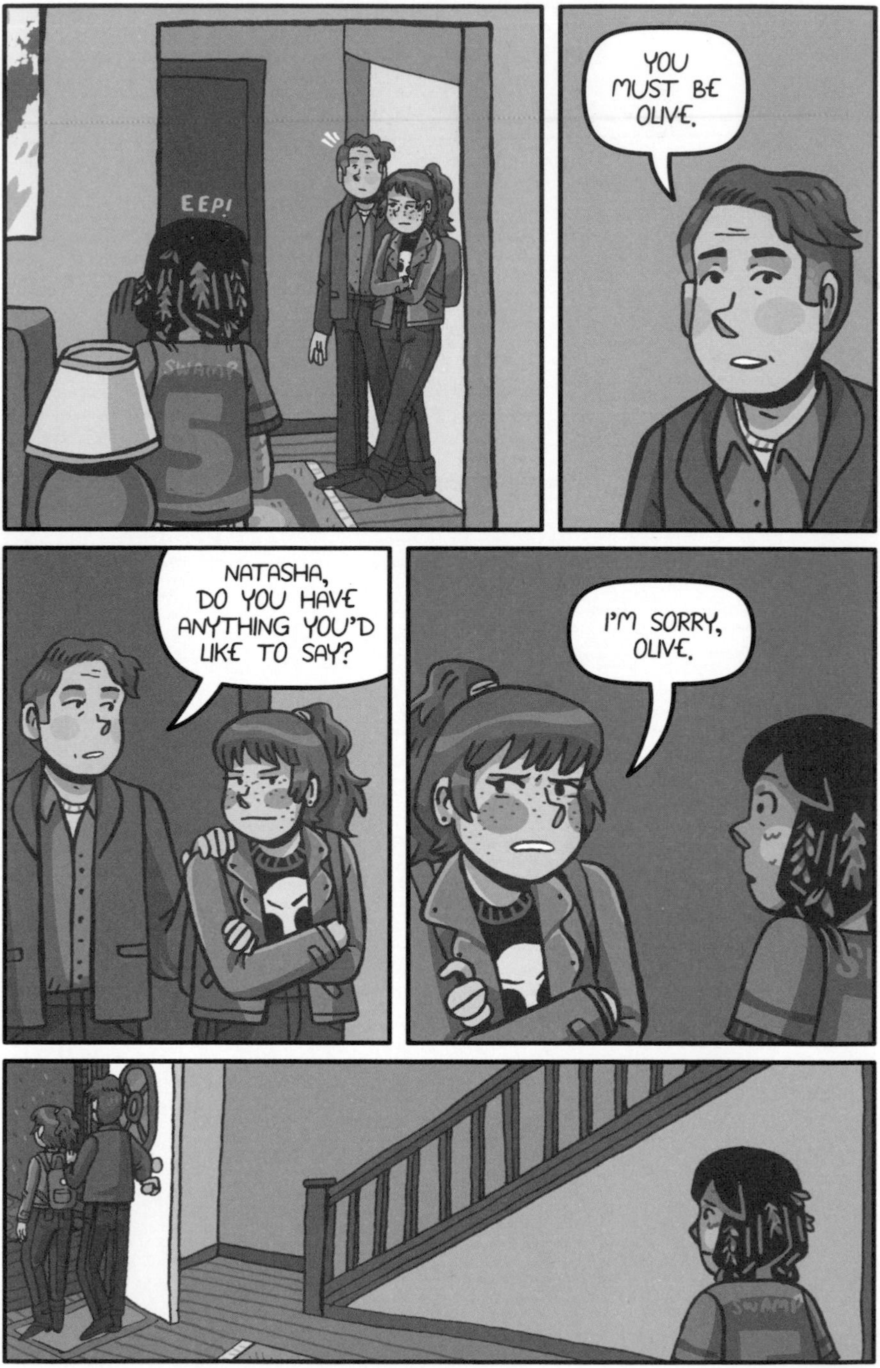
EEP!
SWAMP
5
YOU MUST BE OLIVE.
NATASHA, DO YOU HAVE ANYTHING YOU'D LIKE TO SAY?
I'M SORRY, OLIVE.
SWAMP

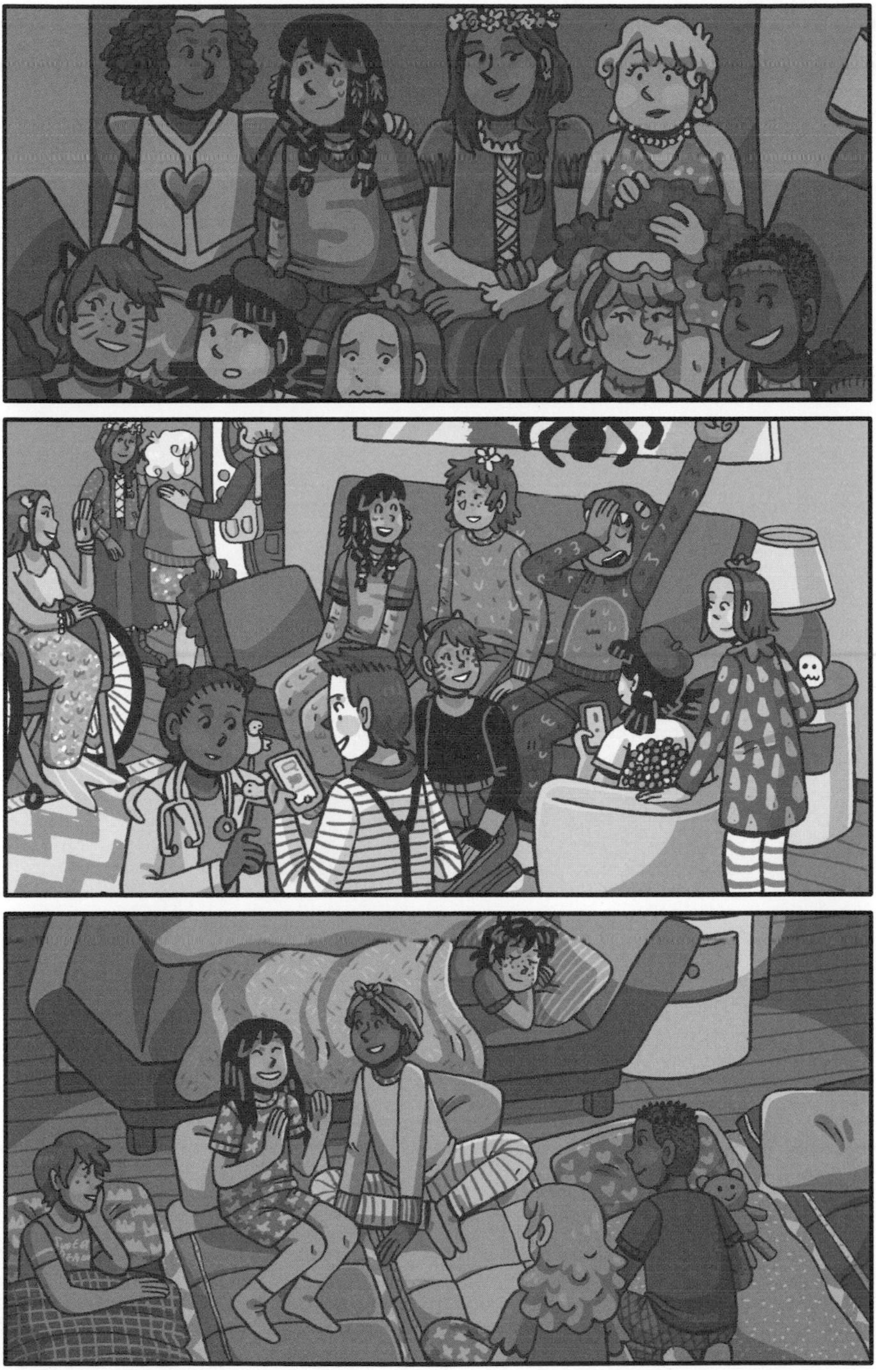

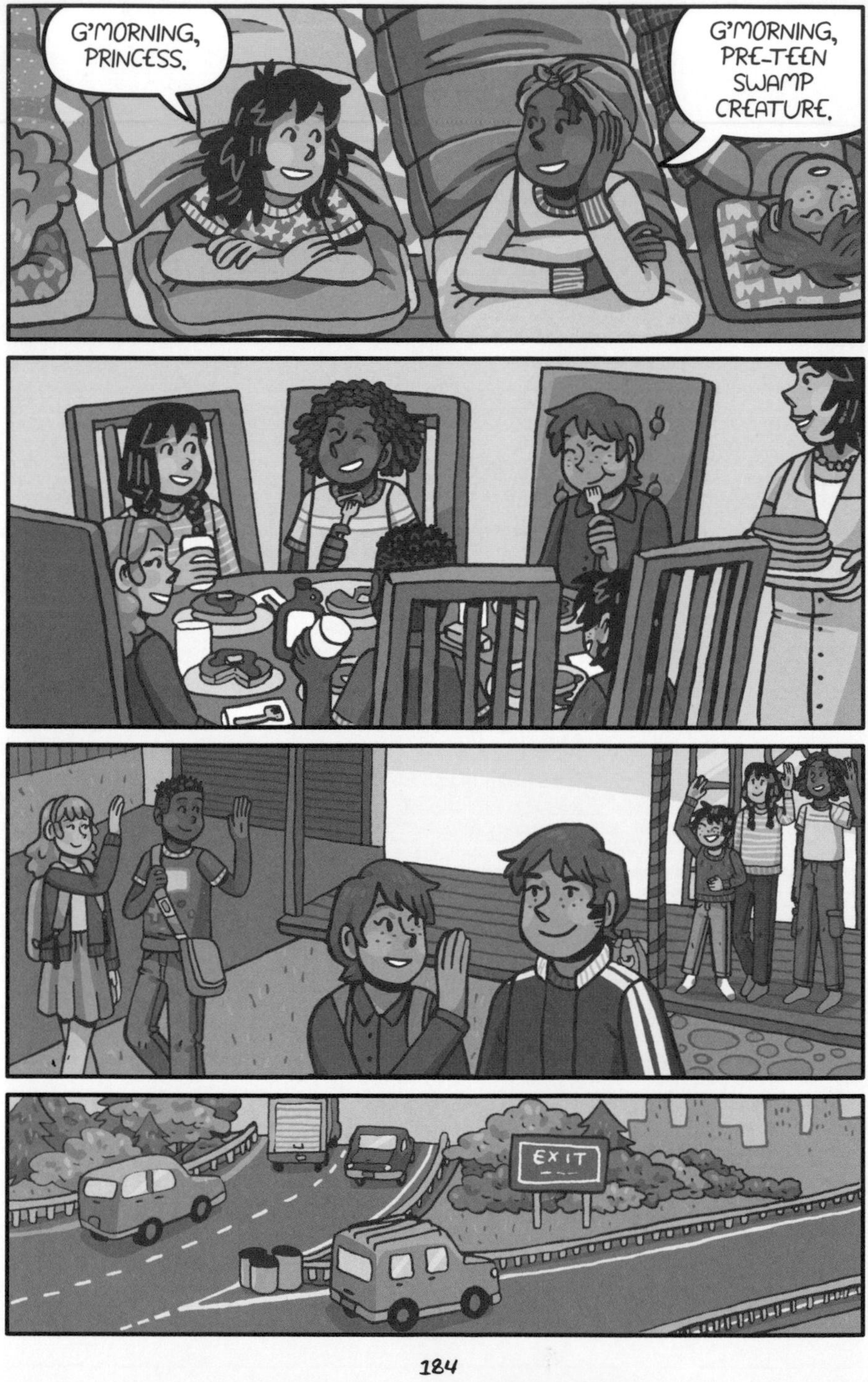
G'MORNING, PRINCESS.
G'MORNING, PRE-TEEN SWAMP CREATURE.
EXIT

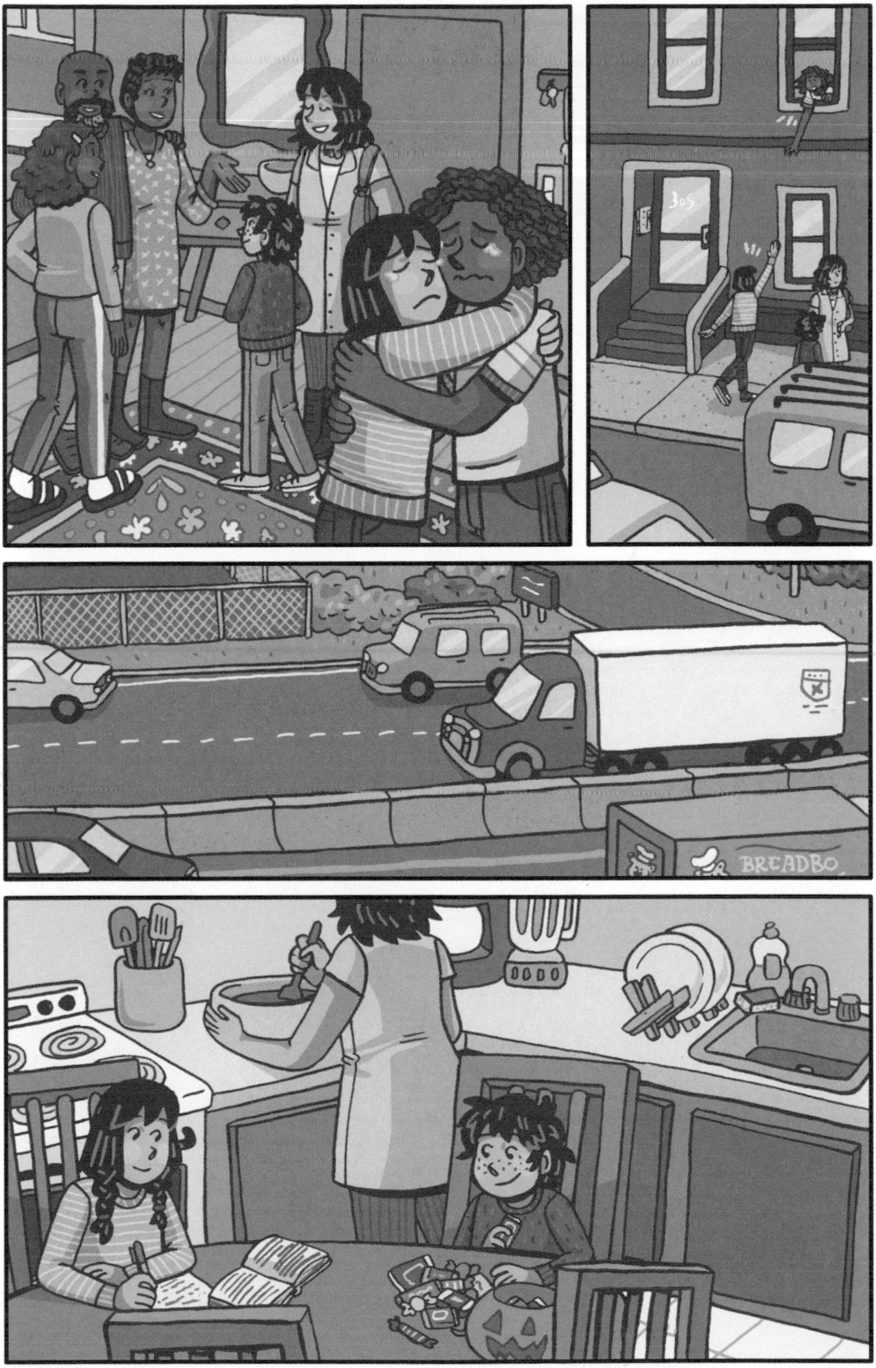
305
BREADBO

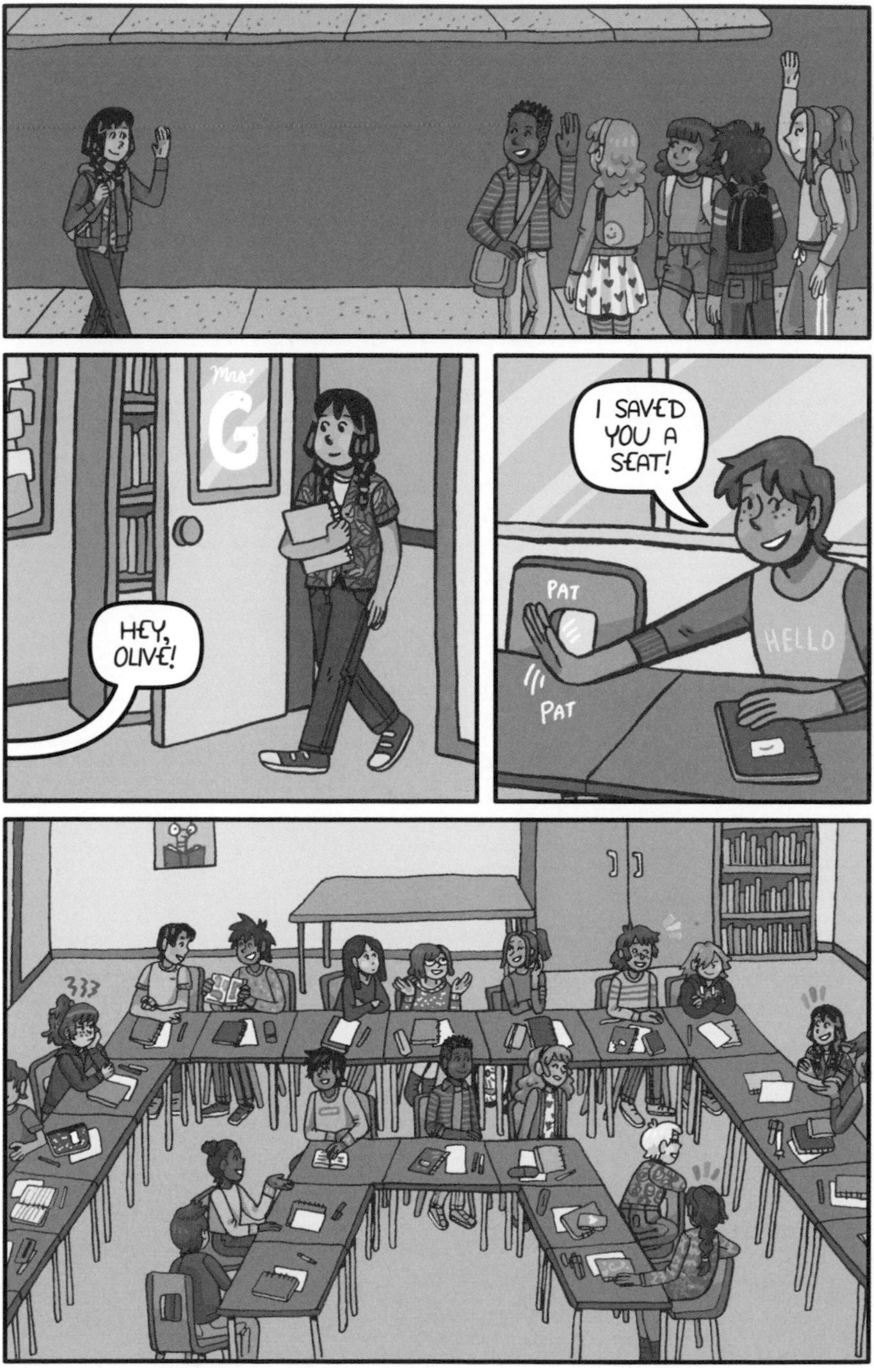
HEY, OLIVE!
I SAVED YOU A SEAT!
PAT
PAT
HELLO

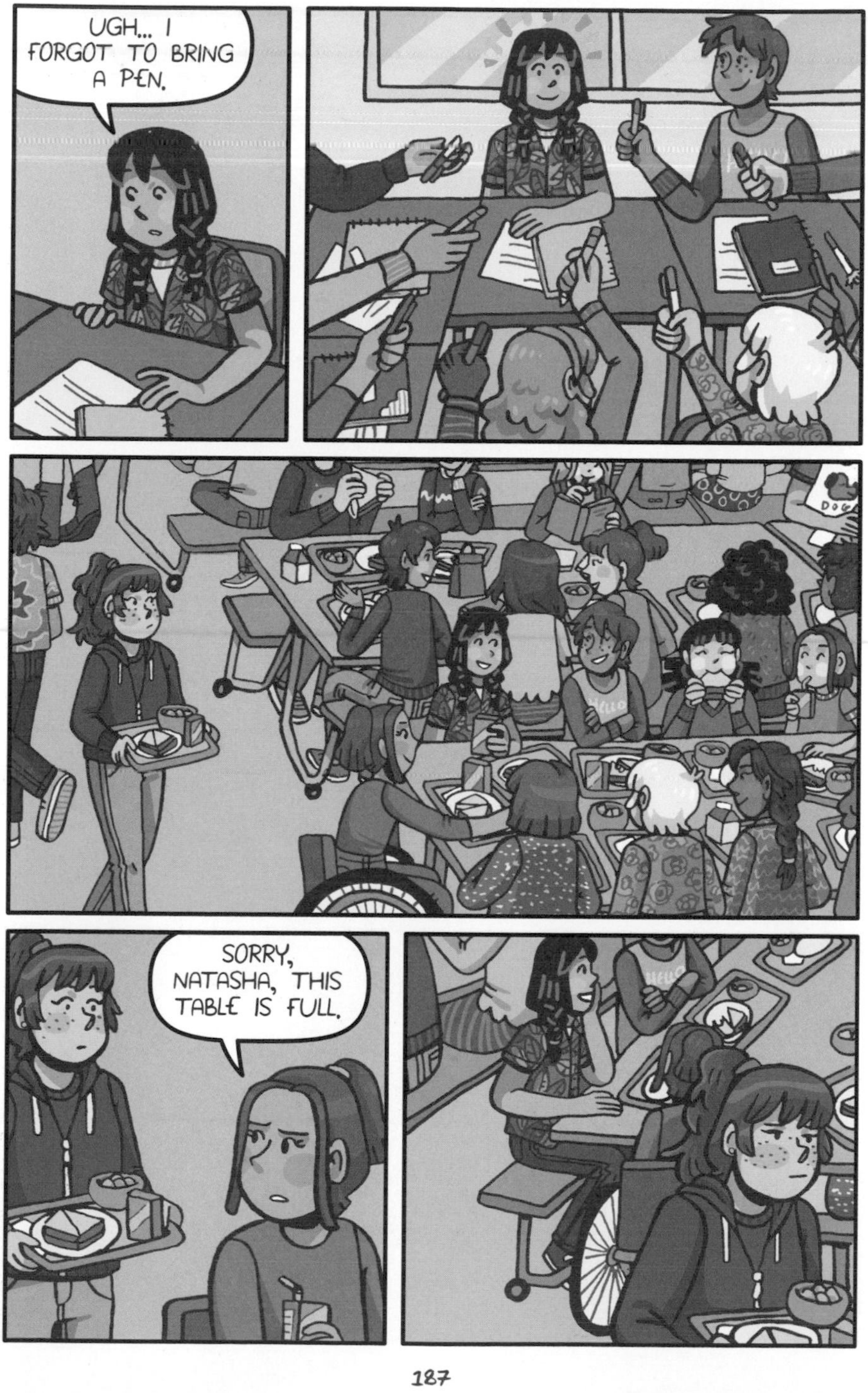
UGH... I FORGOT TO BRING A PEN.
SORRY, NATASHA, THIS TABLE IS FULL.

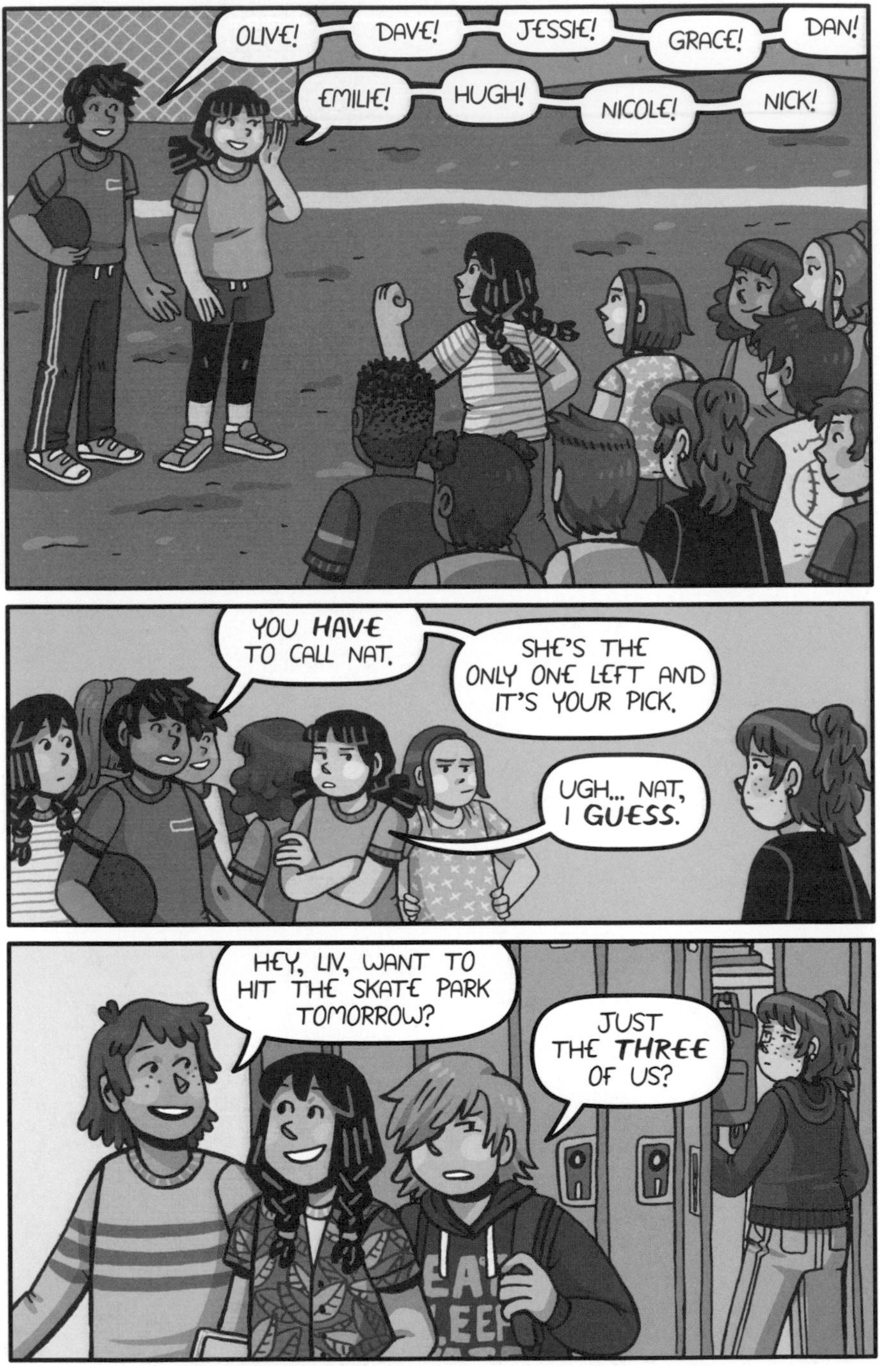
OLIVE!
DAVE!
JESSIE!
GRACE!
DAN!
EMILIE!
HUGH!
NICOLE!
NICK!
YOU **HAVE** TO CALL NAT.
SHE'S THE ONLY ONE LEFT AND IT'S YOUR PICK.
UGH... NAT, I **GUESS**.
HEY, LIV, WANT TO HIT THE SKATE PARK TOMORROW?
JUST THE **THREE** OF US?

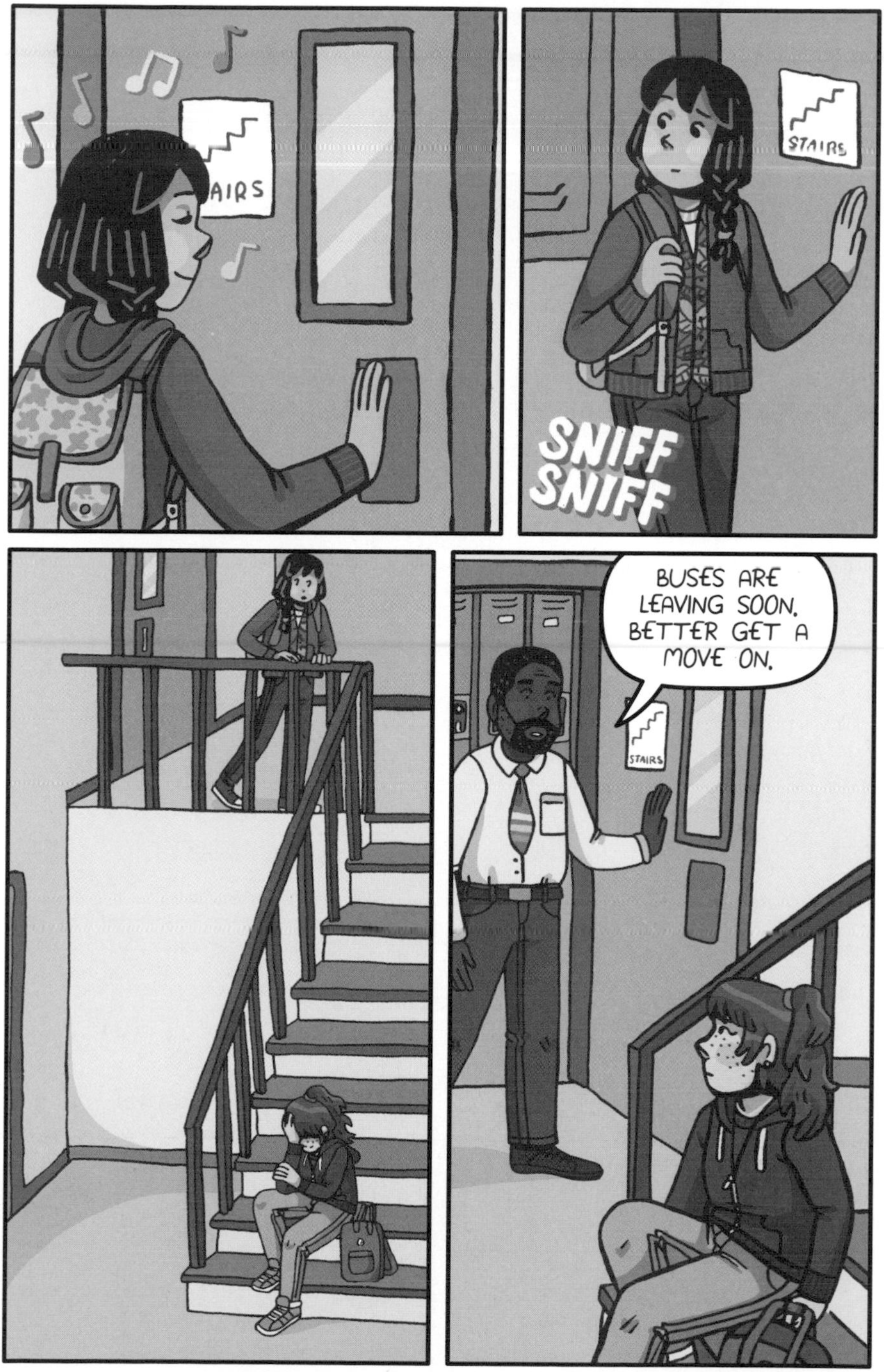
AIRS
STAIRS
SNIFF SNIFF
BUSES ARE LEAVING SOON. BETTER GET A MOVE ON.
STAIRS

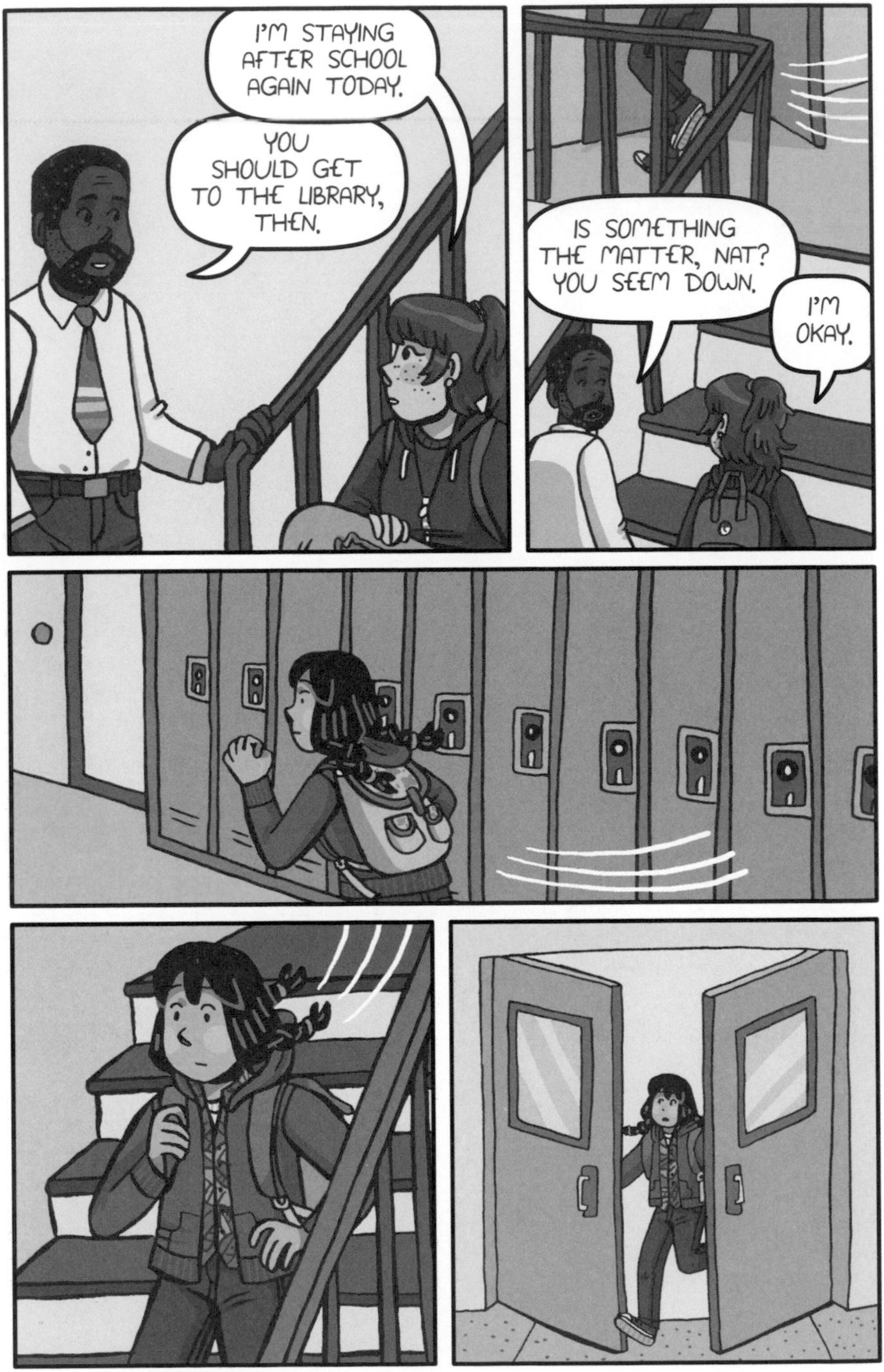
I'M STAYING AFTER SCHOOL AGAIN TODAY.
YOU SHOULD GET TO THE LIBRARY, THEN.
IS SOMETHING THE MATTER, NAT? YOU SEEM DOWN.
I'M OKAY.

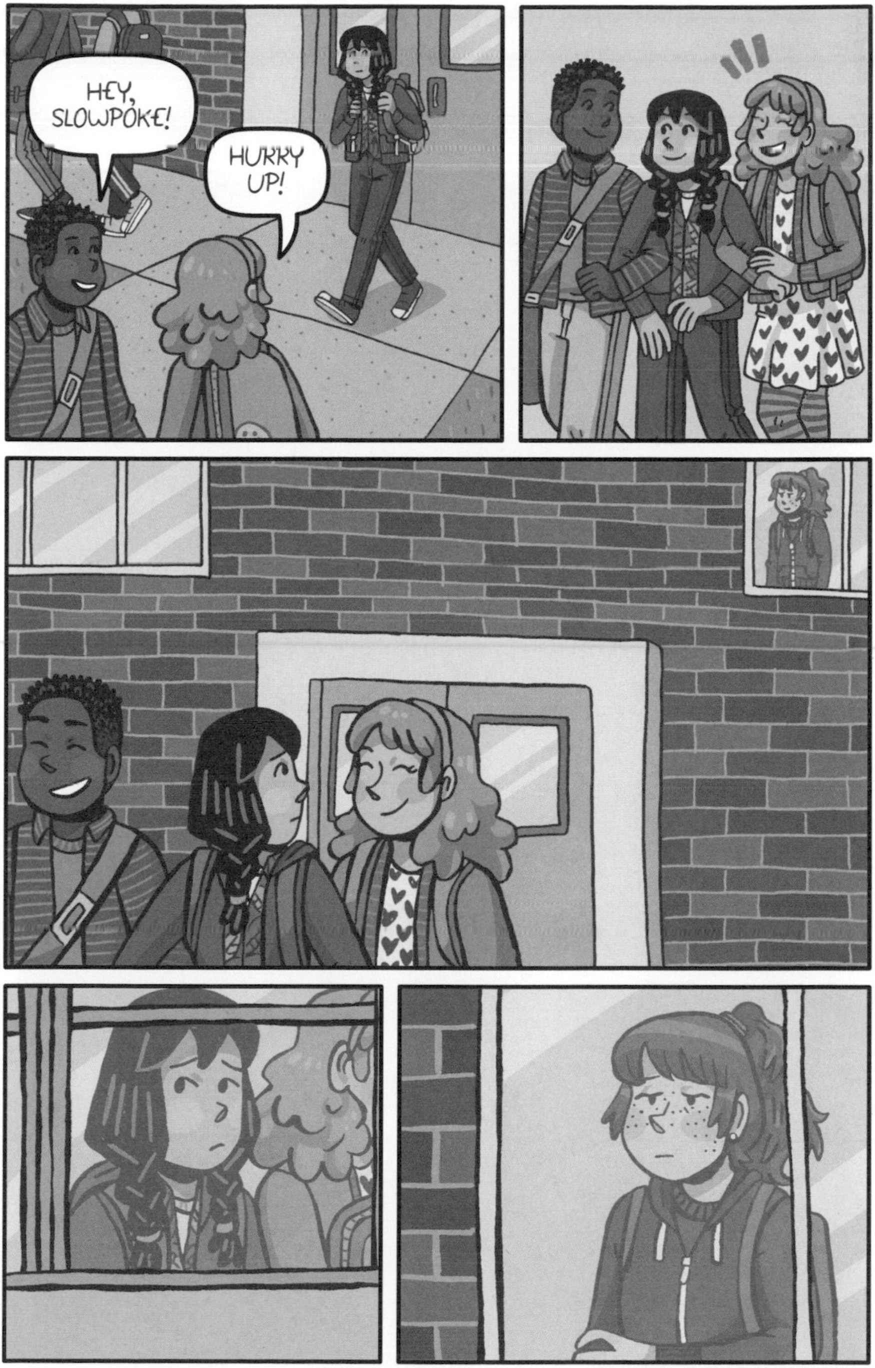
HEY, SLOWPOKE!
HURRY UP!

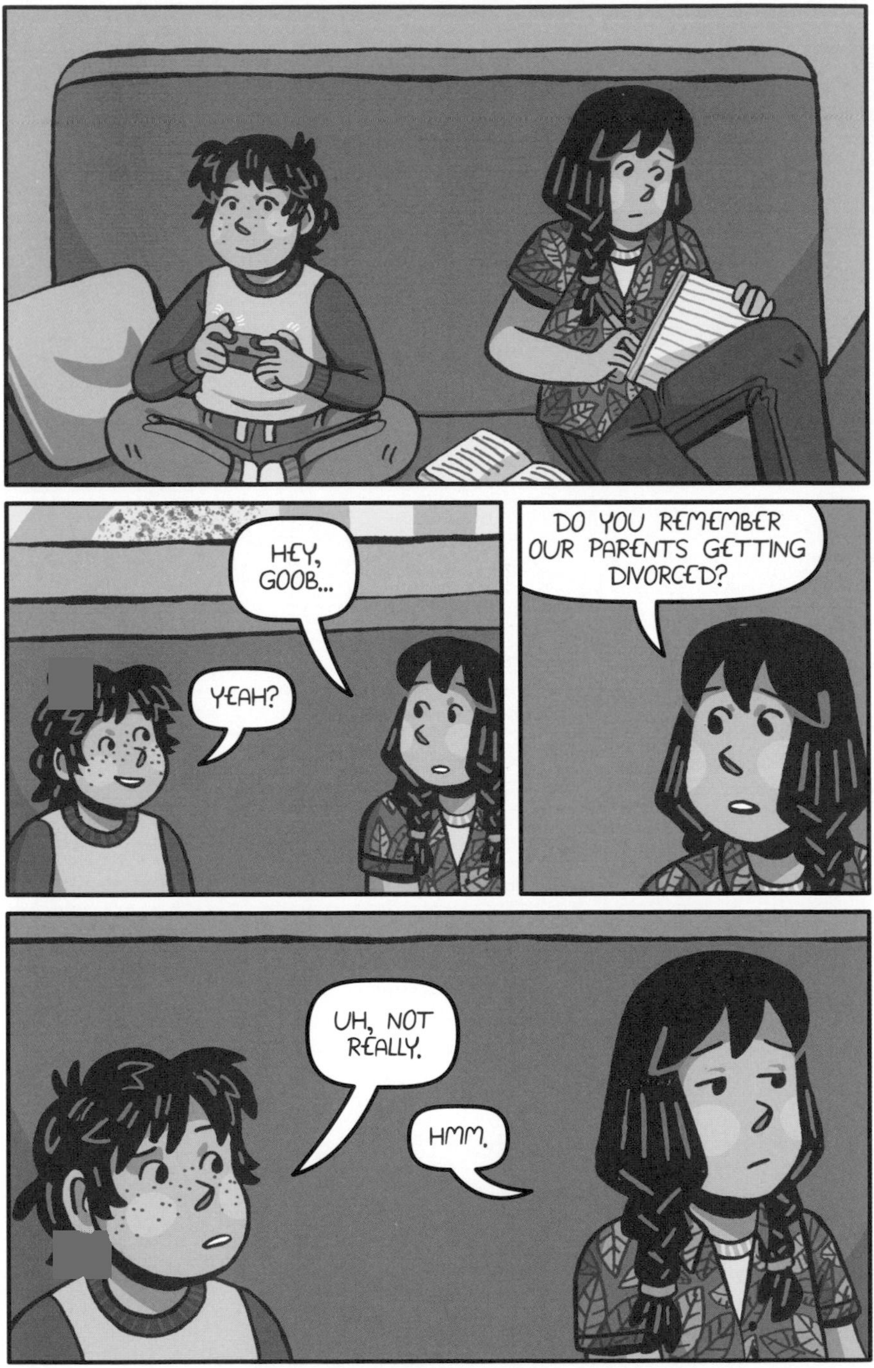
HEY, GOOB...
YEAH?
DO YOU REMEMBER OUR PARENTS GETTING DIVORCED?
UH, NOT REALLY.
HMM.

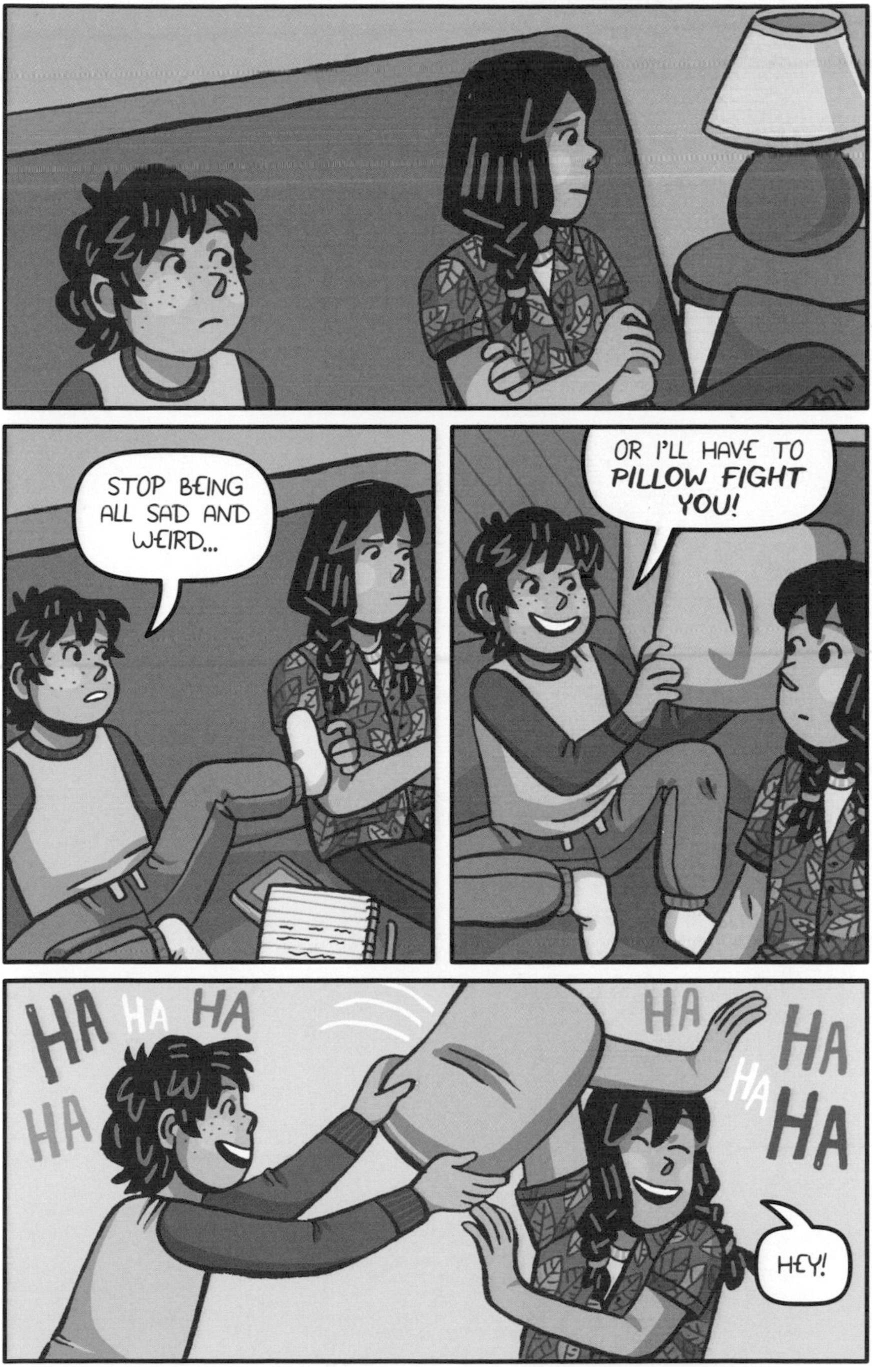

STOP BEING ALL SAD AND WEIRD...
OR I'LL HAVE TO **PILLOW FIGHT** YOU!
HA HA HA HA
HA HA HA HA
HEY!

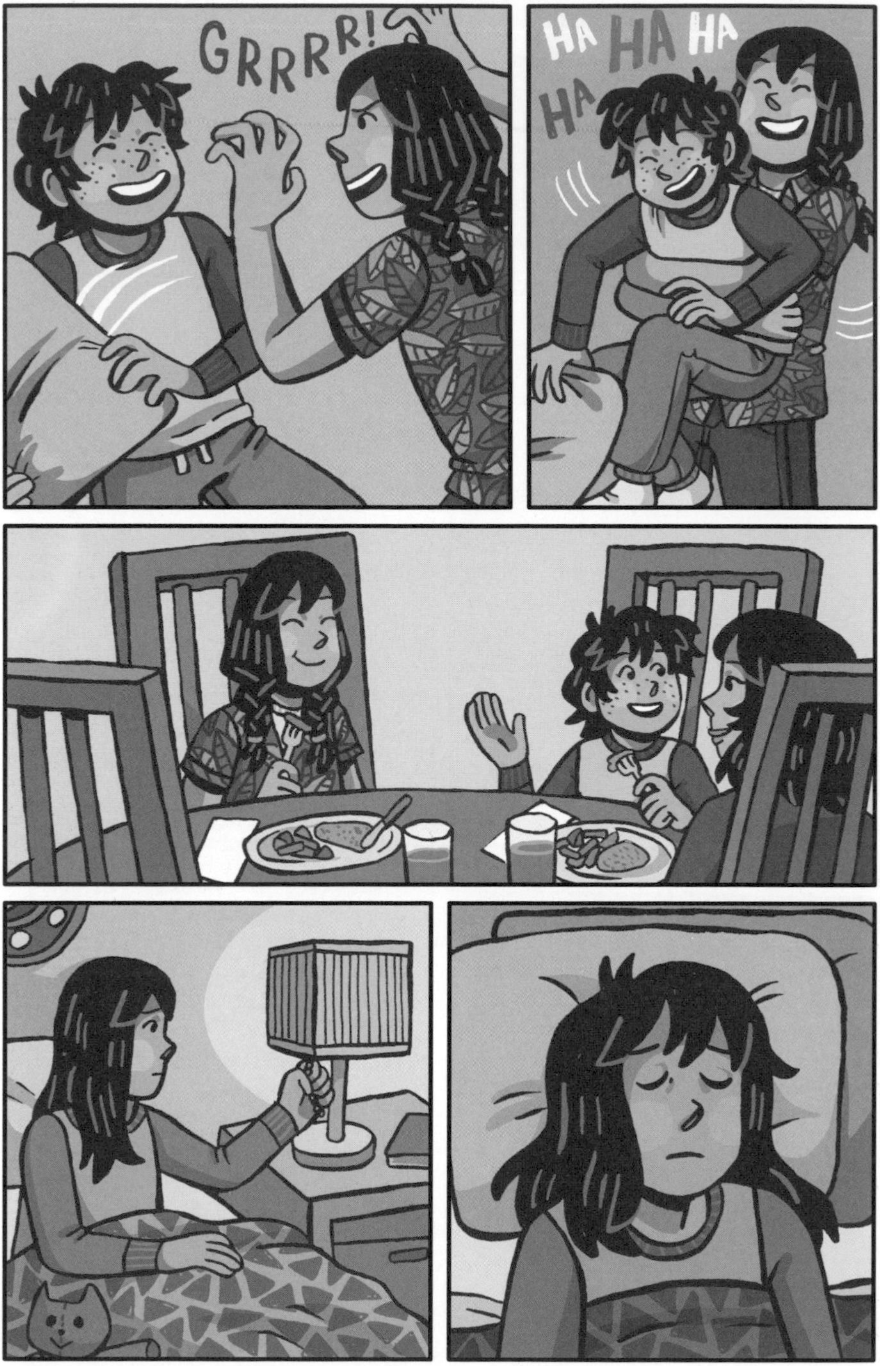
GRRRR!
HA HA HA
HA

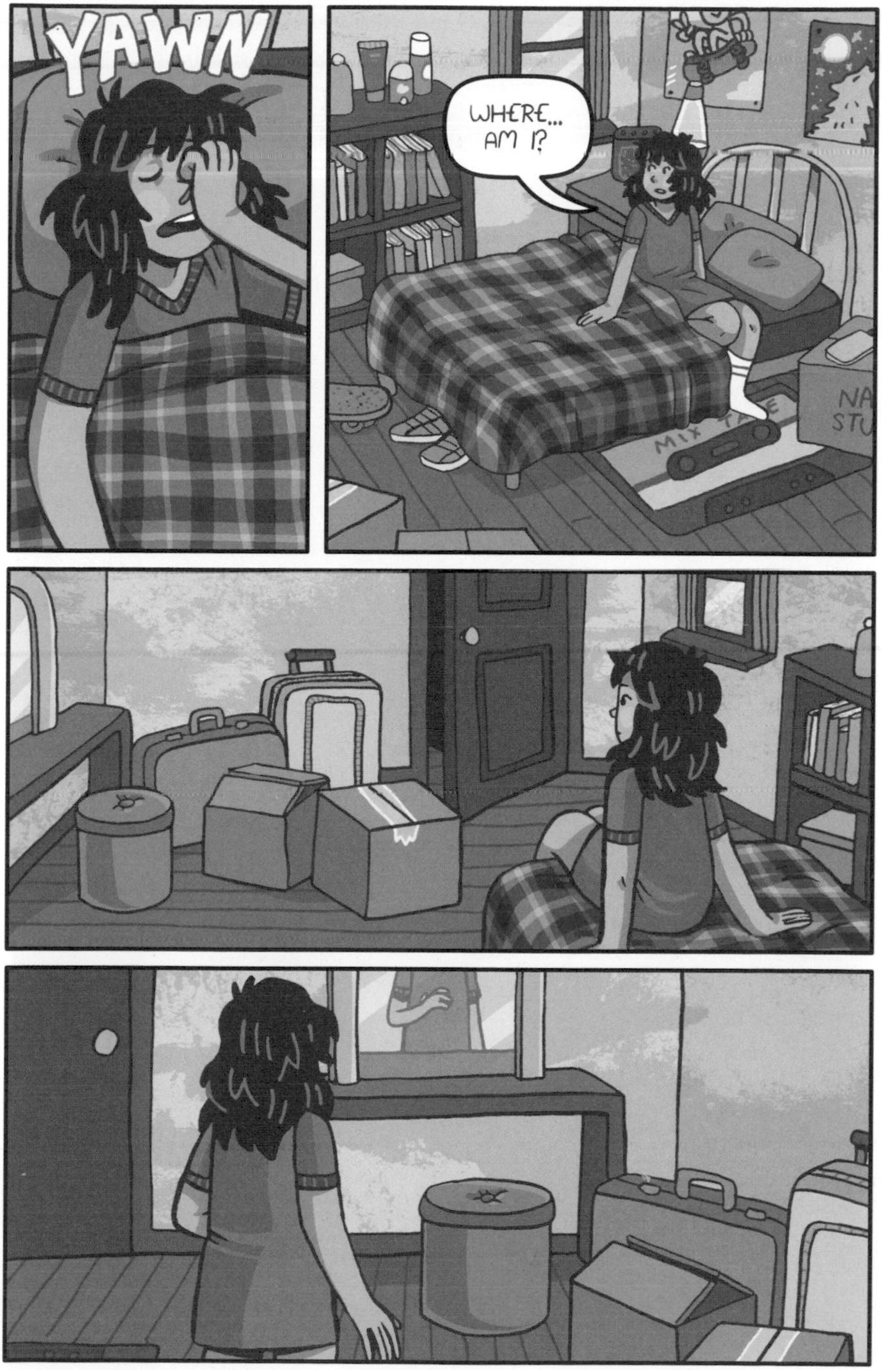
YAWN
WHERE... AM I?

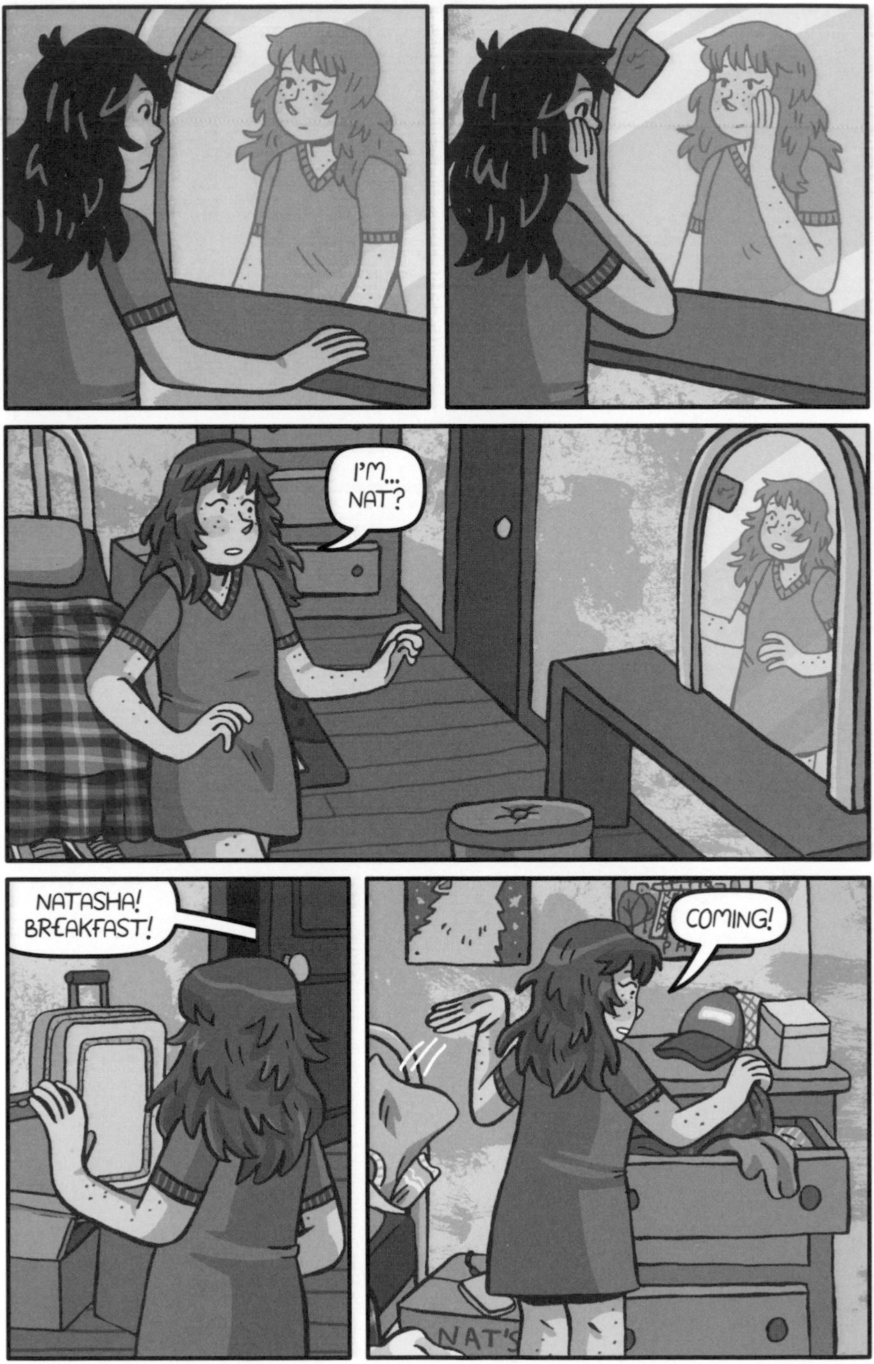
I'M... NAT?
NATASHA! BREAKFAST!
COMING!
NAT'S

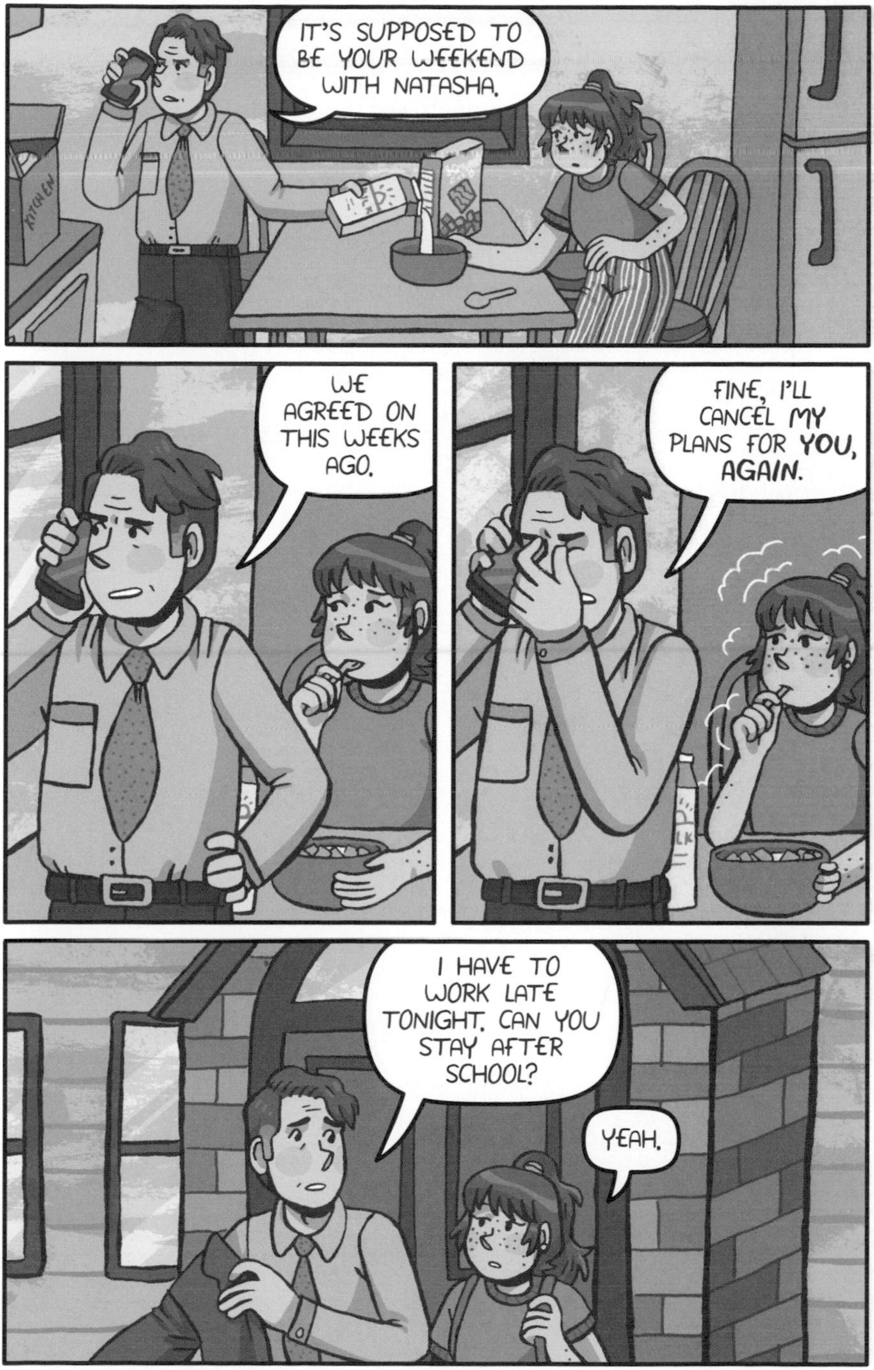
IT'S SUPPOSED TO BE YOUR WEEKEND WITH NATASHA.
KITCHEN
WE AGREED ON THIS WEEKS AGO.
FINE, I'LL CANCEL **MY** PLANS FOR **YOU, AGAIN.**
I HAVE TO WORK LATE TONIGHT. CAN YOU STAY AFTER SCHOOL?
YEAH.

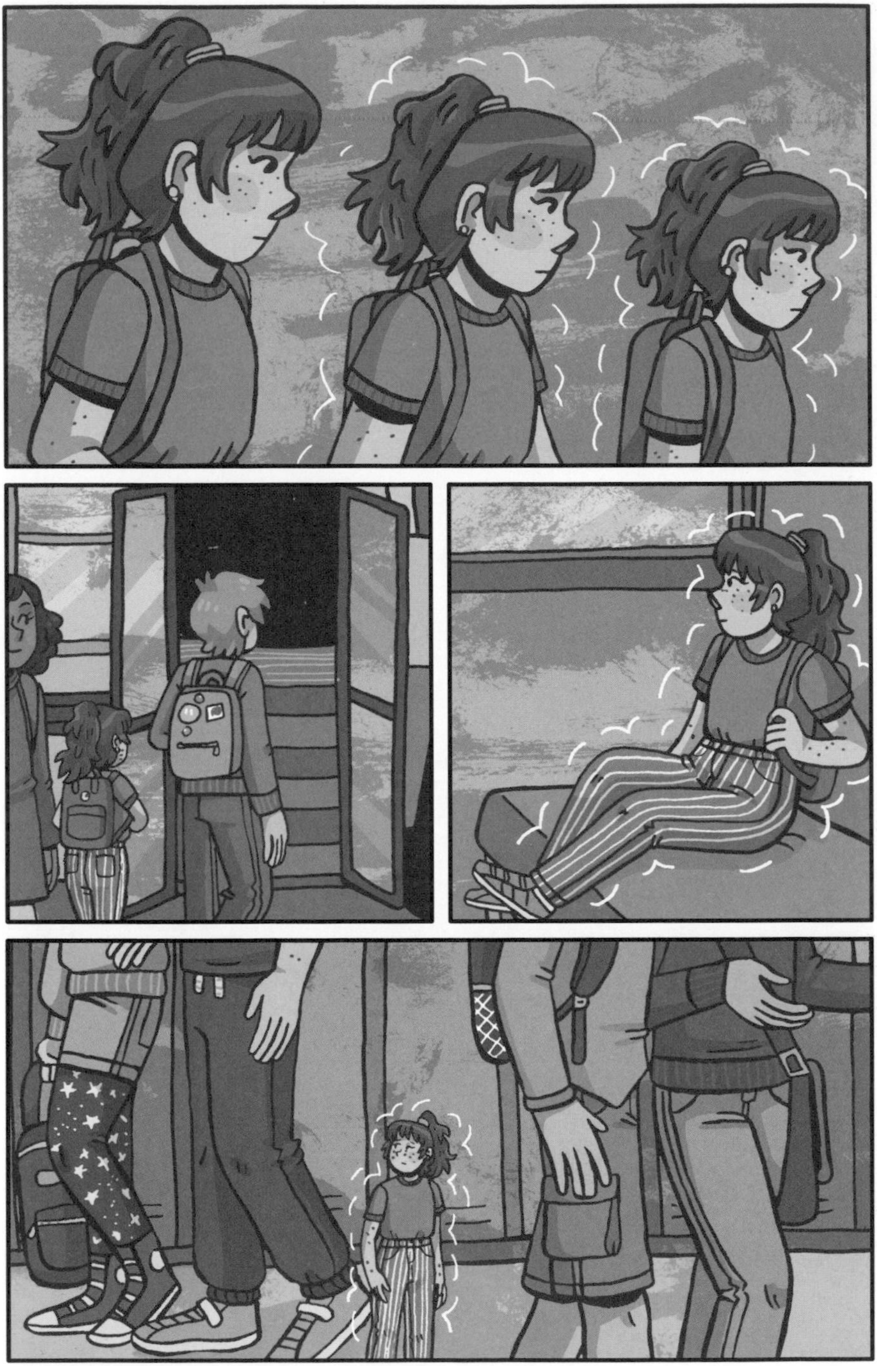

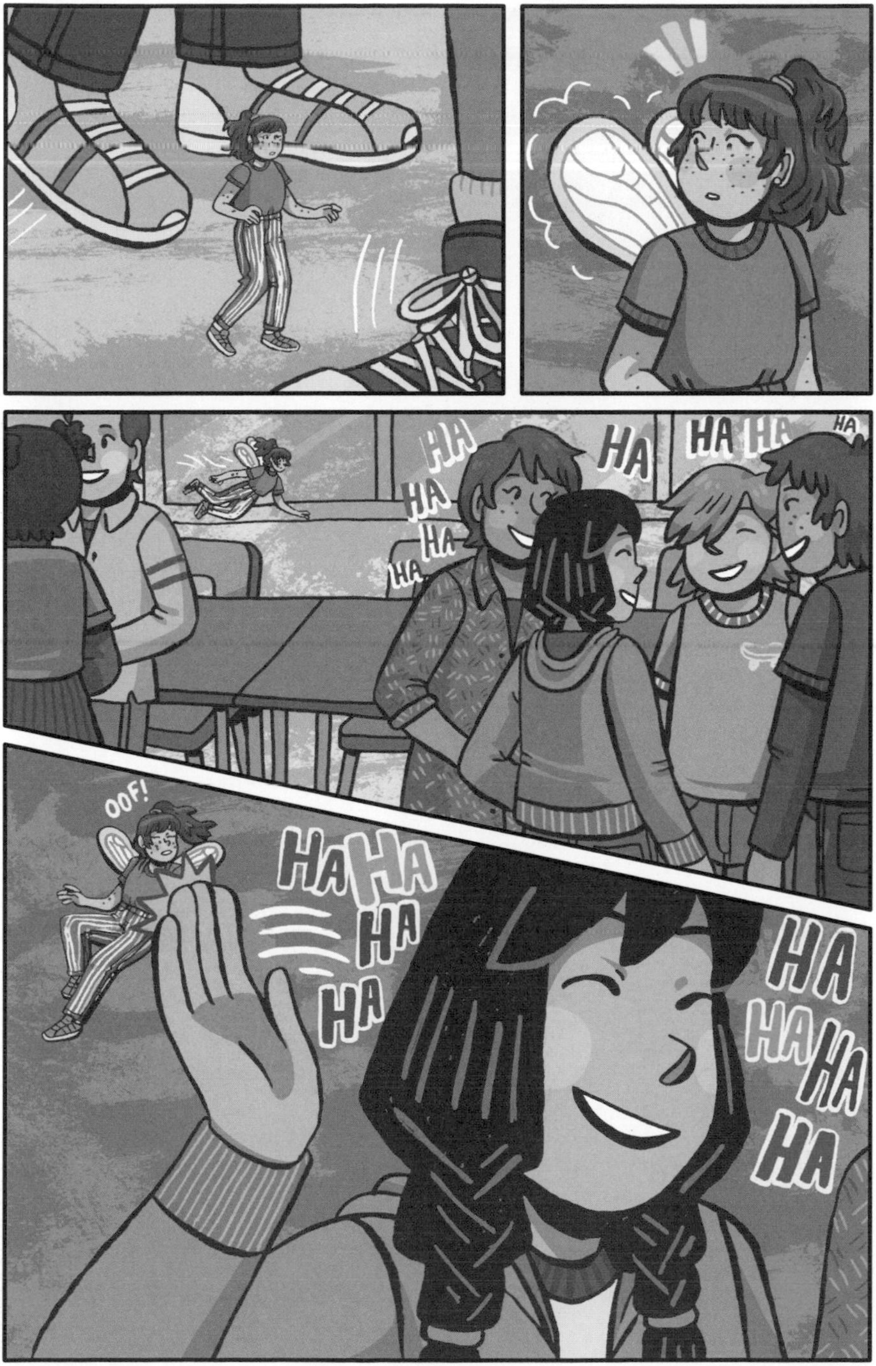
HA
HA
HA
HA
HA
HA HA
HA
OOF!
HA HA
HA
HA
HA
HA HA HA
HA

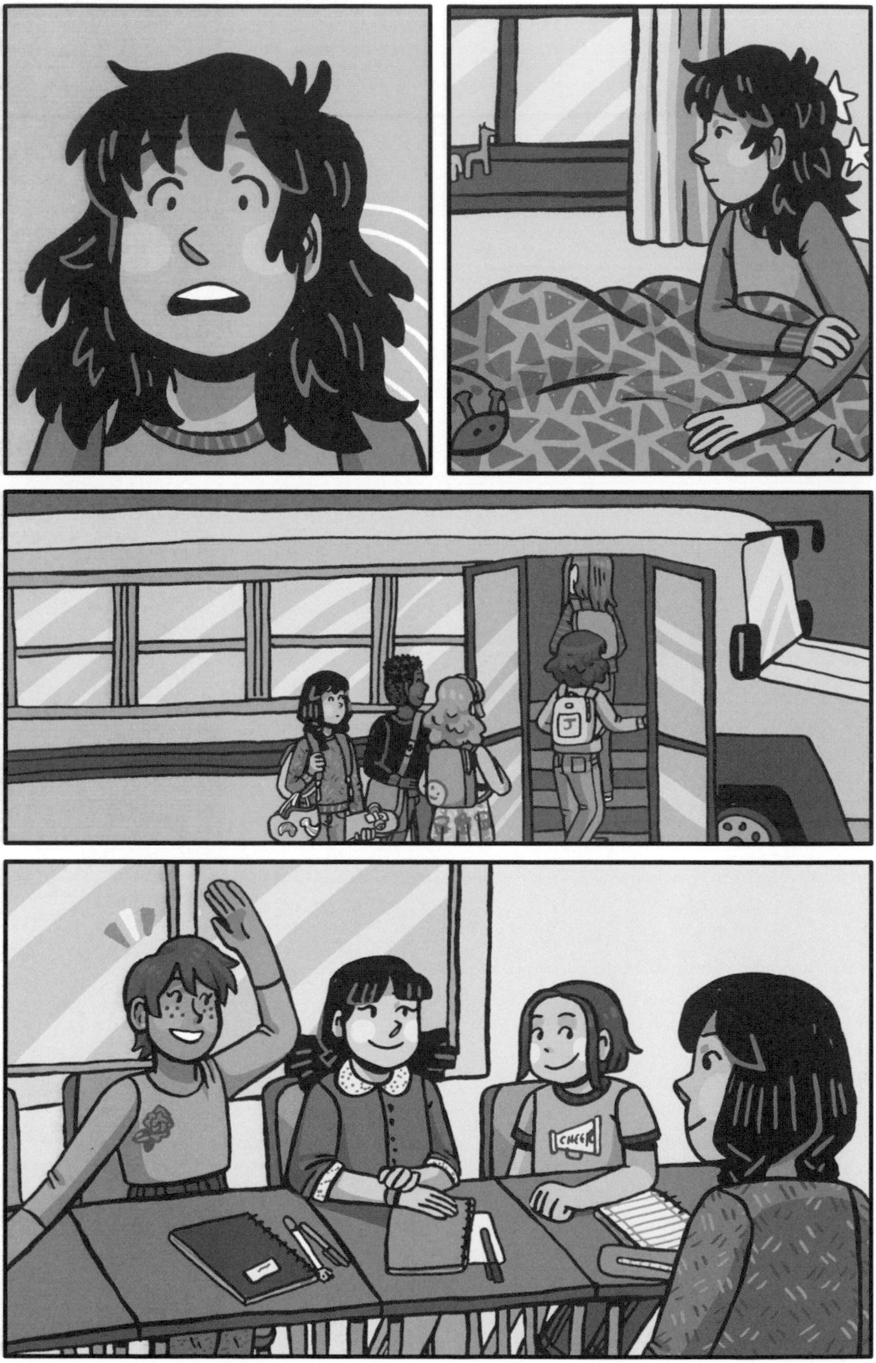

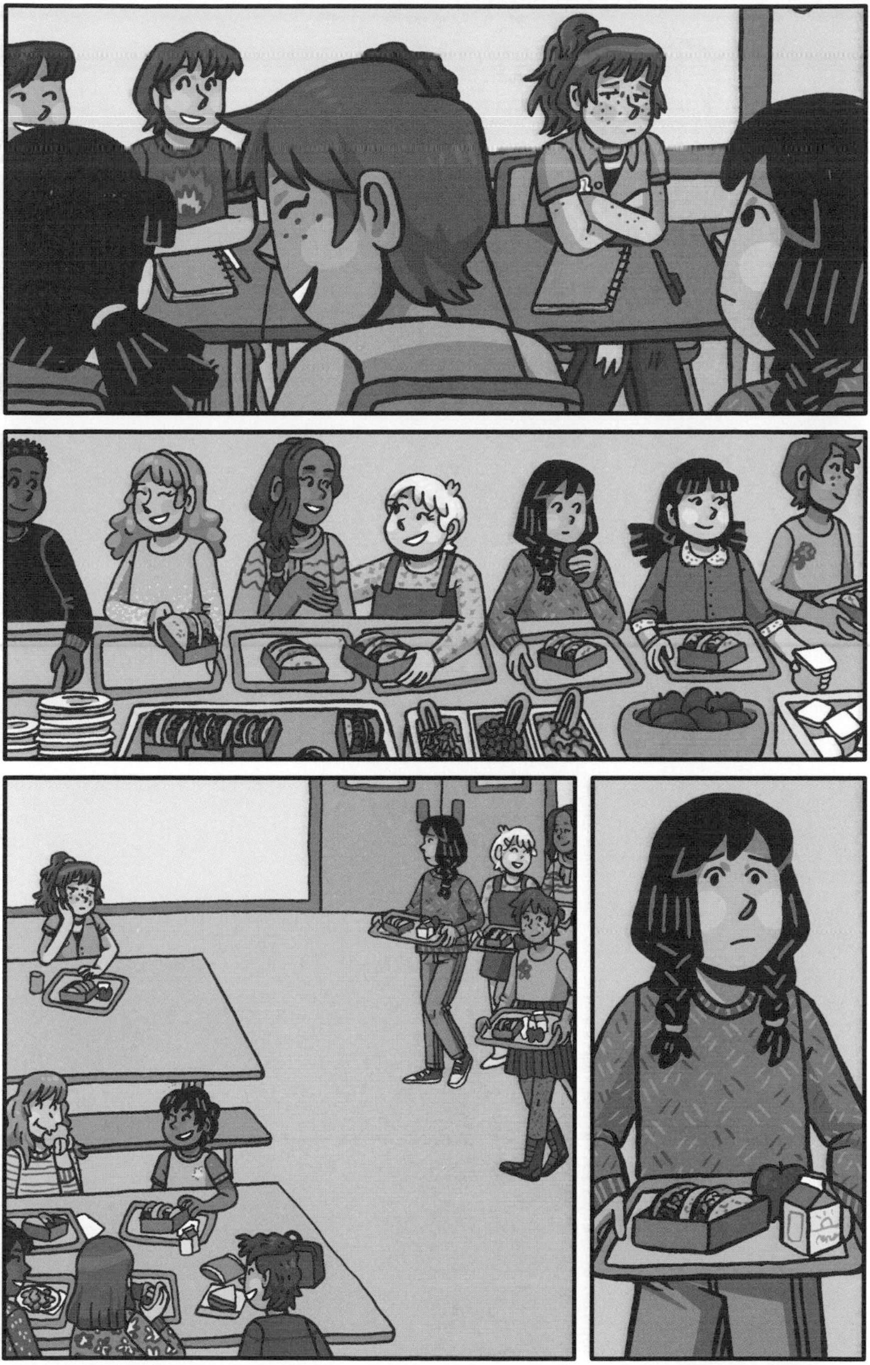

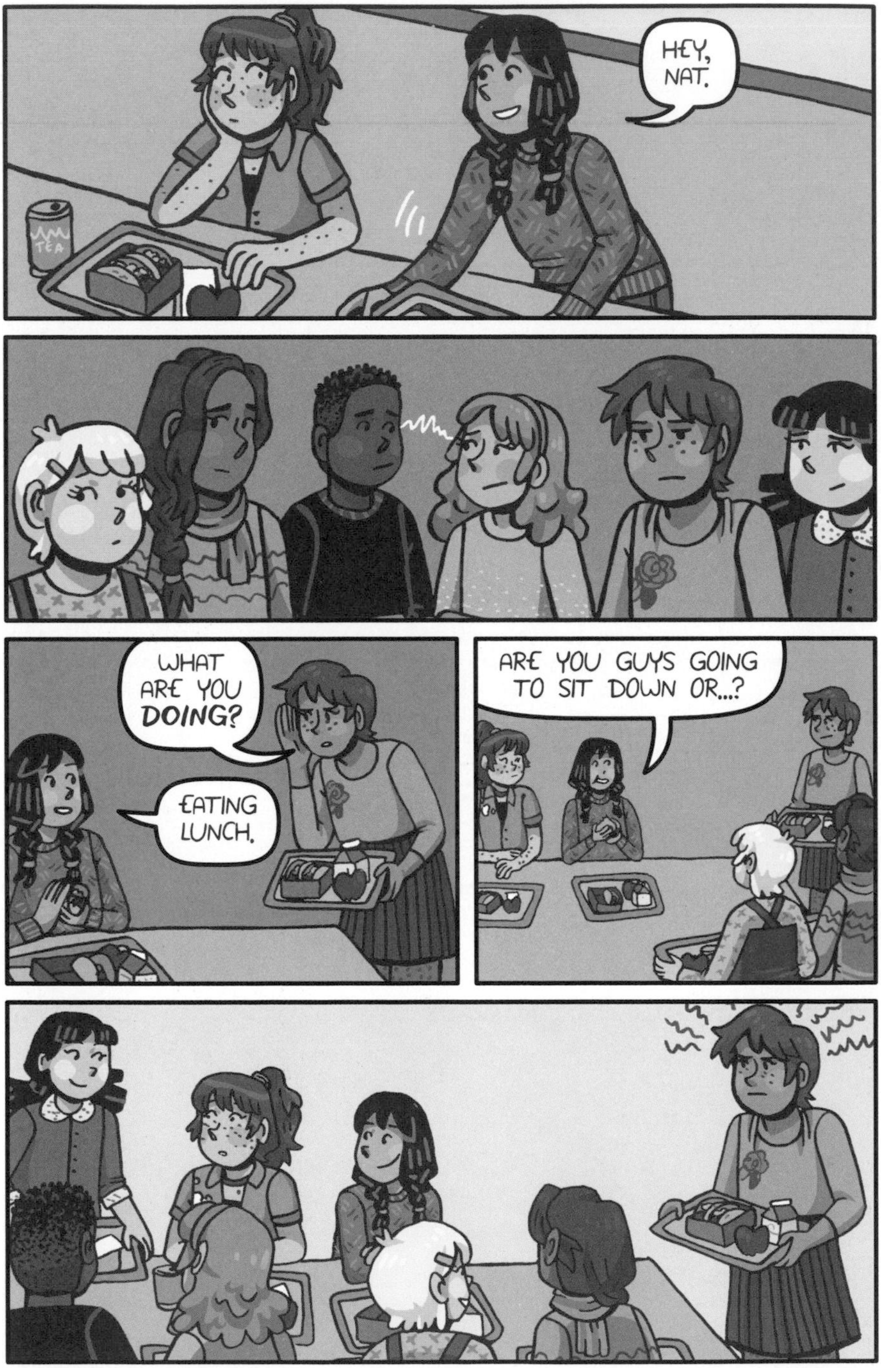
HEY, NAT.
WHAT ARE YOU DOING?
EATING LUNCH.
ARE YOU GUYS GOING TO SIT DOWN OR...?

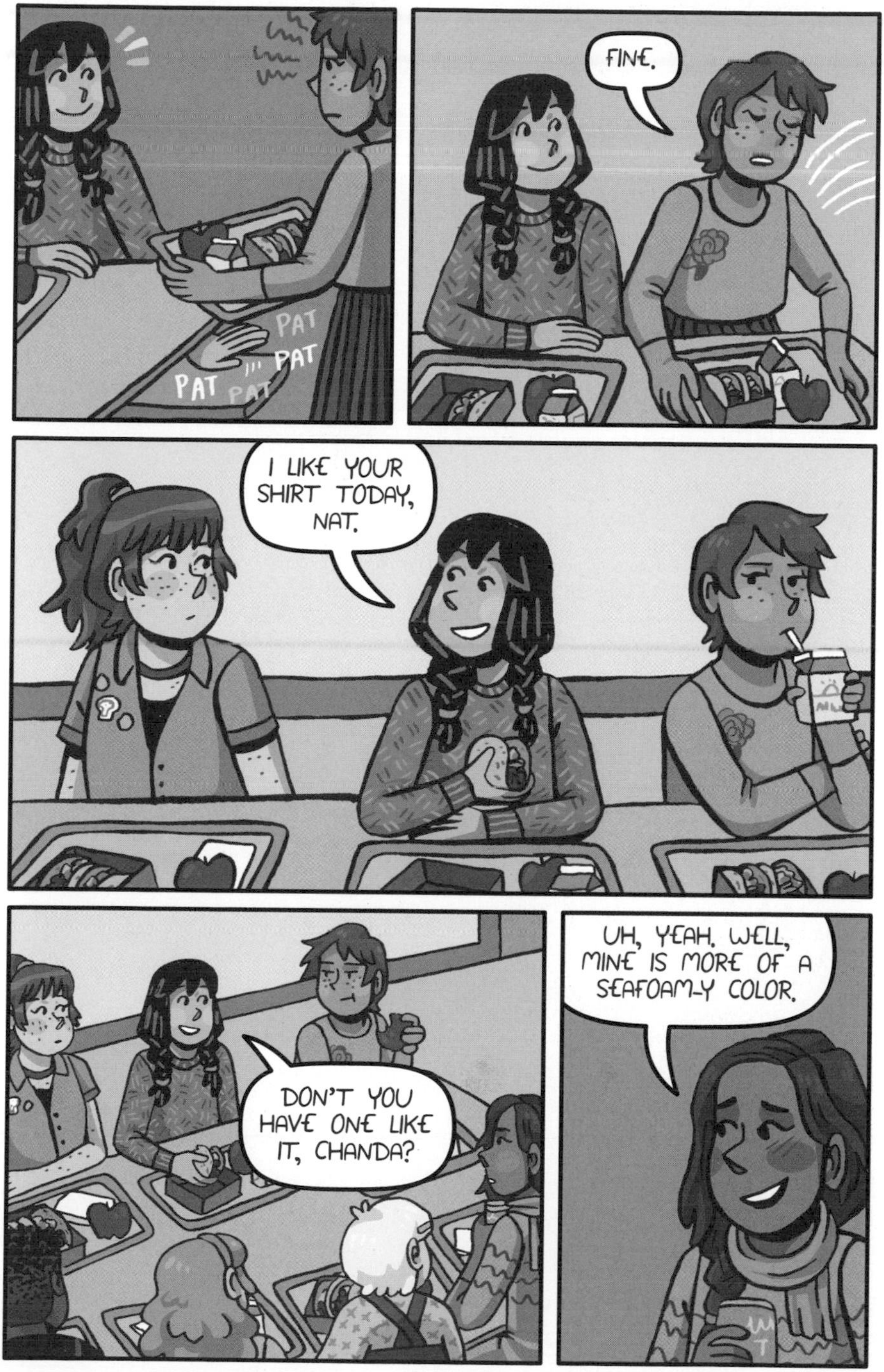
PAT
PAT
PAT
PAT
FINE.
I LIKE YOUR SHIRT TODAY, NAT.
DON'T YOU HAVE ONE LIKE IT, CHANDA?
UH, YEAH. WELL, MINE IS MORE OF A SEAFOAM-Y COLOR.

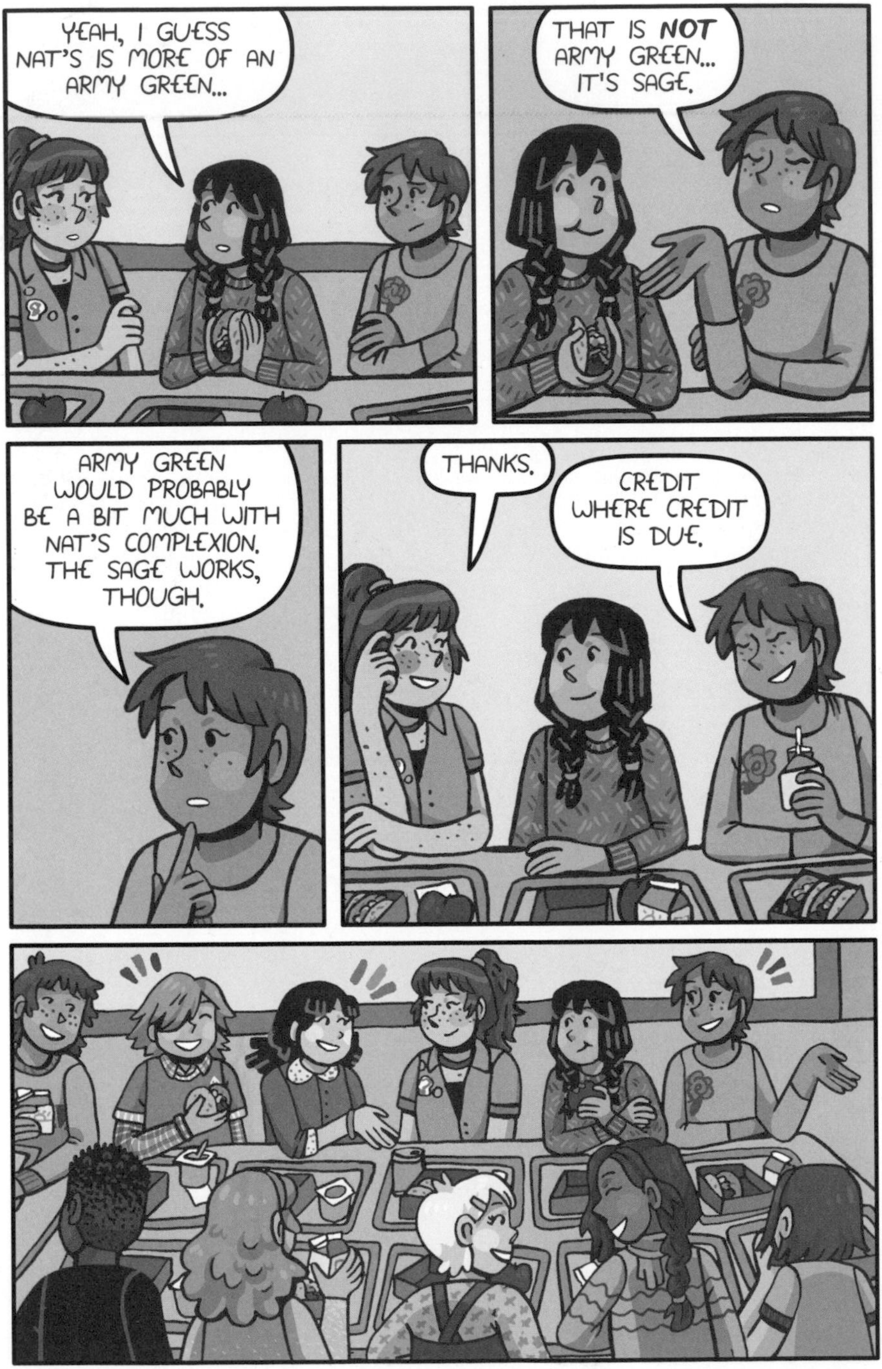
YEAH, I GUESS NAT'S IS MORE OF AN ARMY GREEN...
THAT IS **NOT** ARMY GREEN... IT'S SAGE.
ARMY GREEN WOULD PROBABLY BE A BIT MUCH WITH NAT'S COMPLEXION. THE SAGE WORKS, THOUGH.
THANKS.
CREDIT WHERE CREDIT IS DUE.

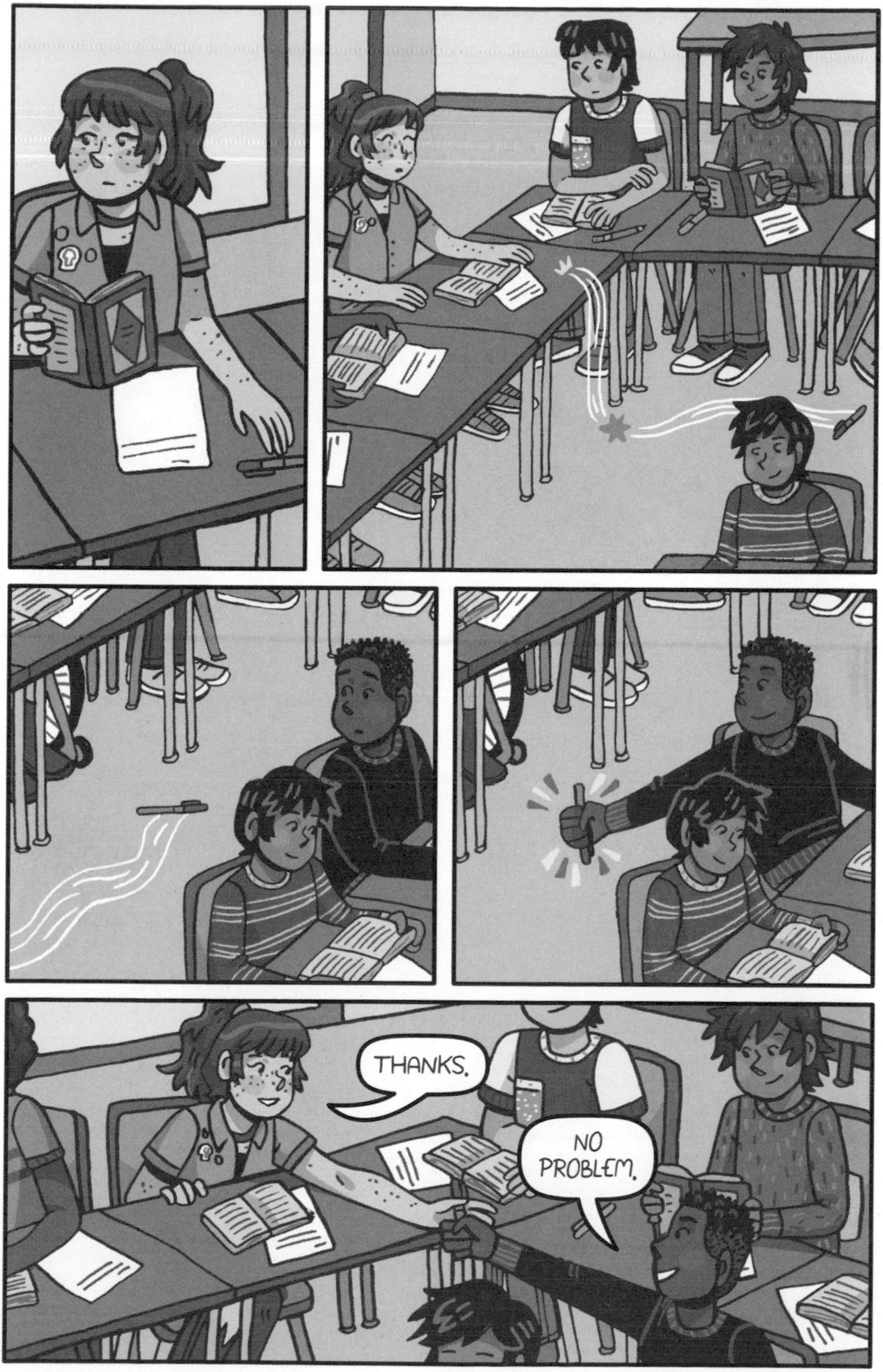
THANKS.
NO PROBLEM.

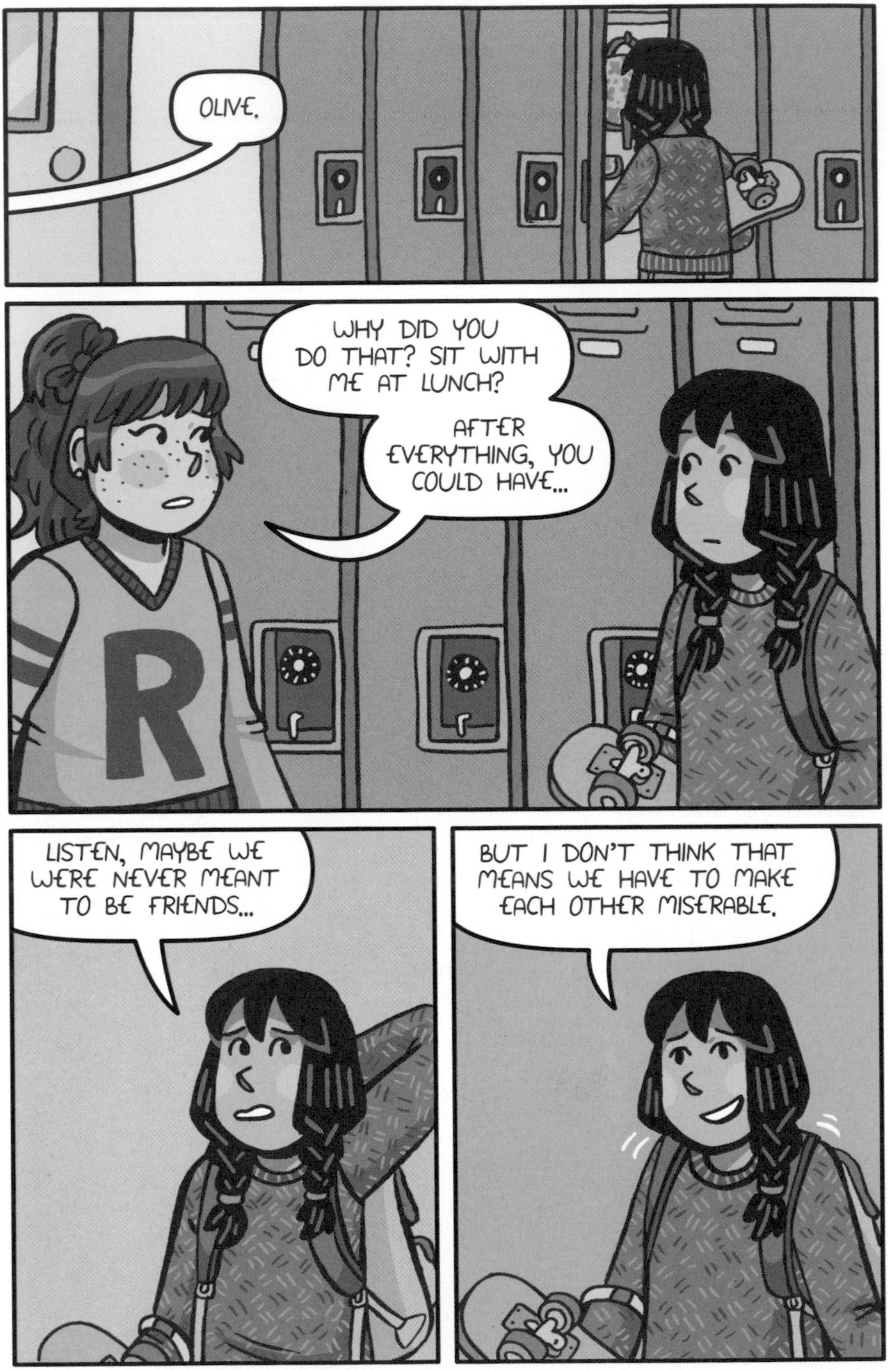
OLIVE.
WHY DID YOU DO THAT? SIT WITH ME AT LUNCH?
AFTER EVERYTHING, YOU COULD HAVE...
LISTEN, MAYBE WE WERE NEVER MEANT TO BE FRIENDS...
BUT I DON'T THINK THAT MEANS WE HAVE TO MAKE EACH OTHER MISERABLE.

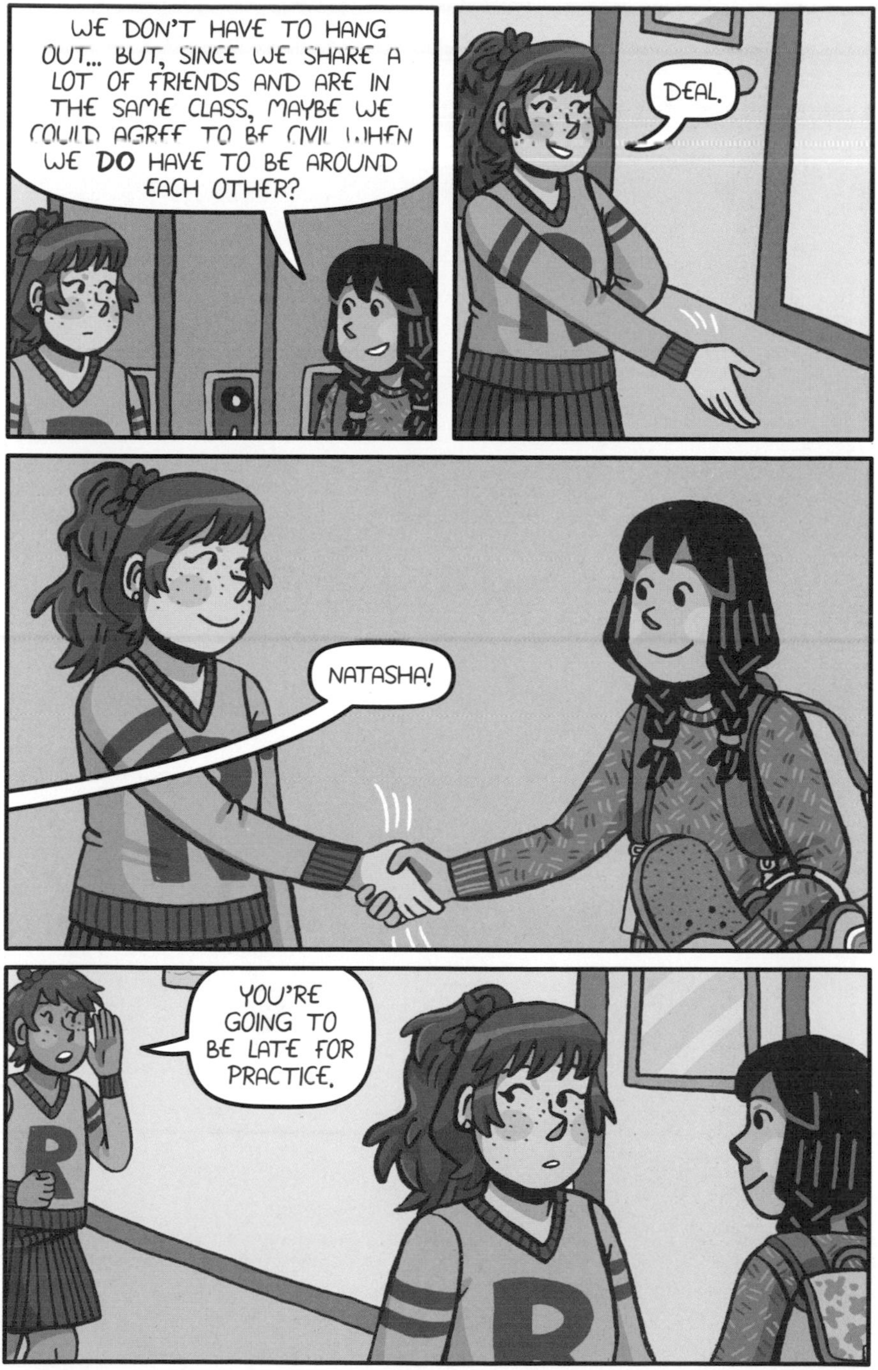
WE DON'T HAVE TO HANG OUT... BUT, SINCE WE SHARE A LOT OF FRIENDS AND ARE IN THE SAME CLASS, MAYBE WE COULD AGREE TO BE CIVIL WHEN WE **DO** HAVE TO BE AROUND EACH OTHER?
DEAL.
NATASHA!
YOU'RE GOING TO BE LATE FOR PRACTICE.

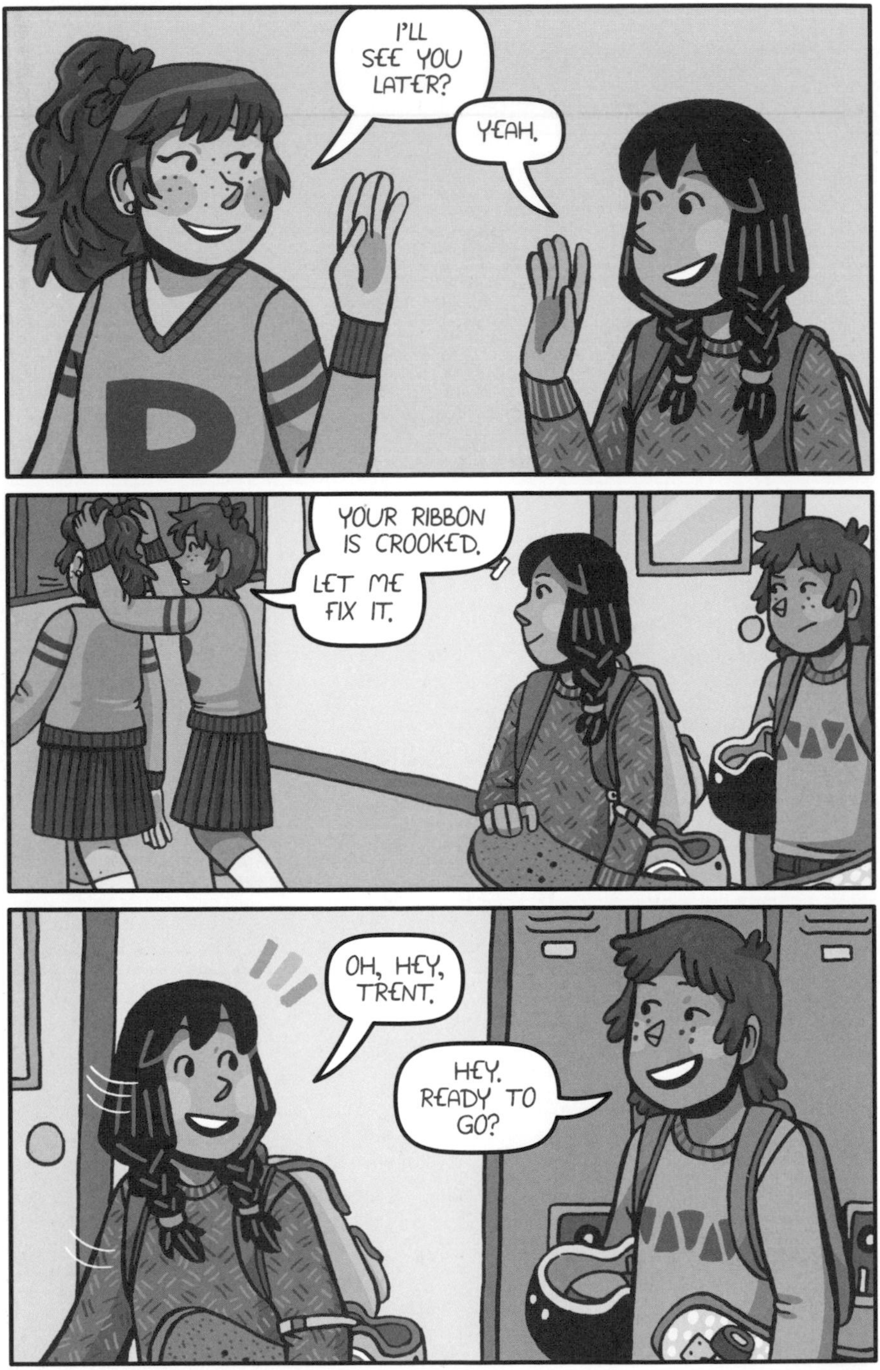
I'LL SEE YOU LATER?
YEAH.
YOUR RIBBON IS CROOKED.
LET ME FIX IT.
OH, HEY, TRENT.
HEY. READY TO GO?

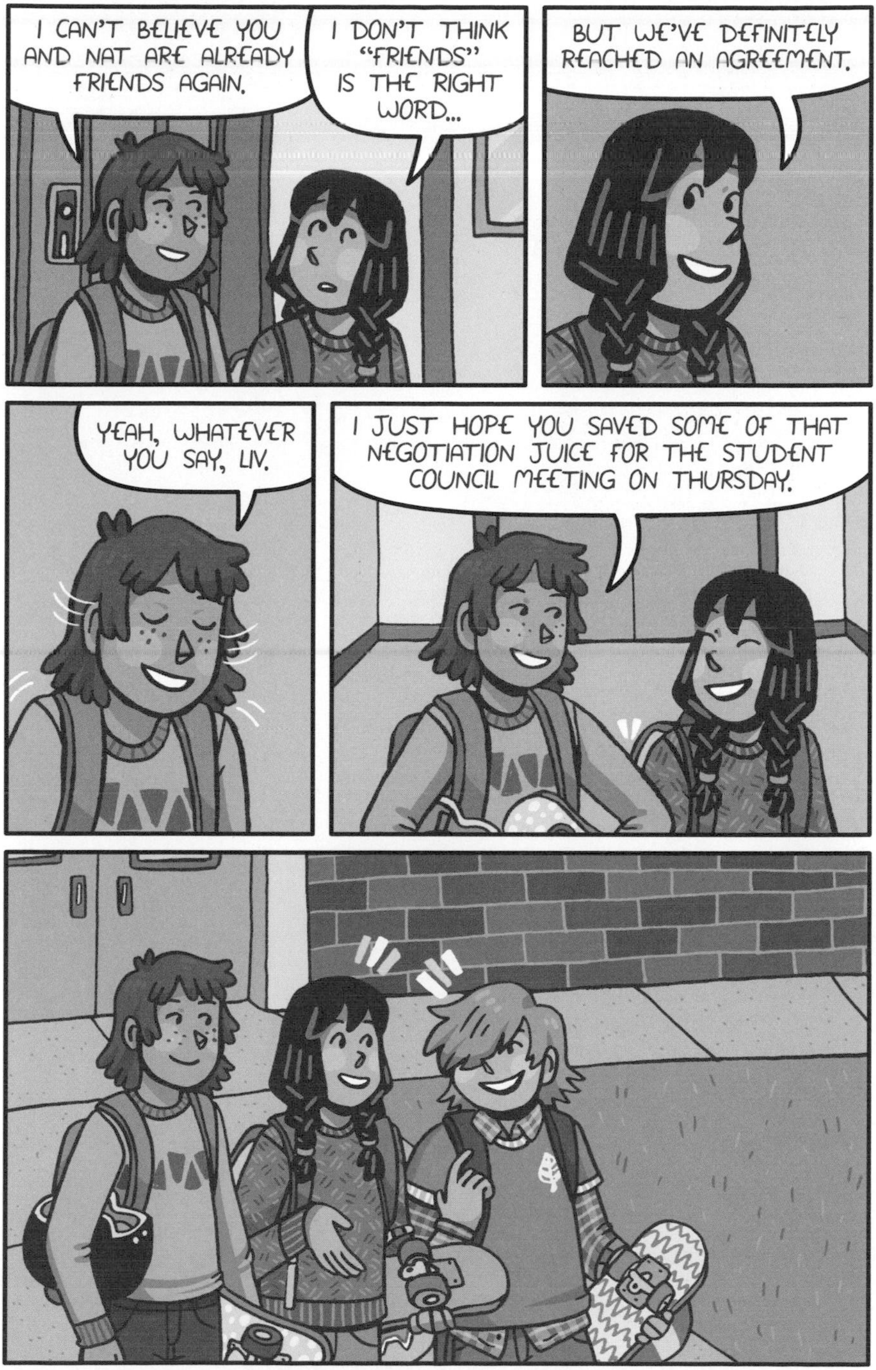
I CAN'T BELIEVE YOU AND NAT ARE ALREADY FRIENDS AGAIN.
I DON'T THINK "FRIENDS" IS THE RIGHT WORD...
BUT WE'VE DEFINITELY REACHED AN AGREEMENT.
YEAH, WHATEVER YOU SAY, LIV.
I JUST HOPE YOU SAVED SOME OF THAT NEGOTIATION JUICE FOR THE STUDENT COUNCIL MEETING ON THURSDAY.

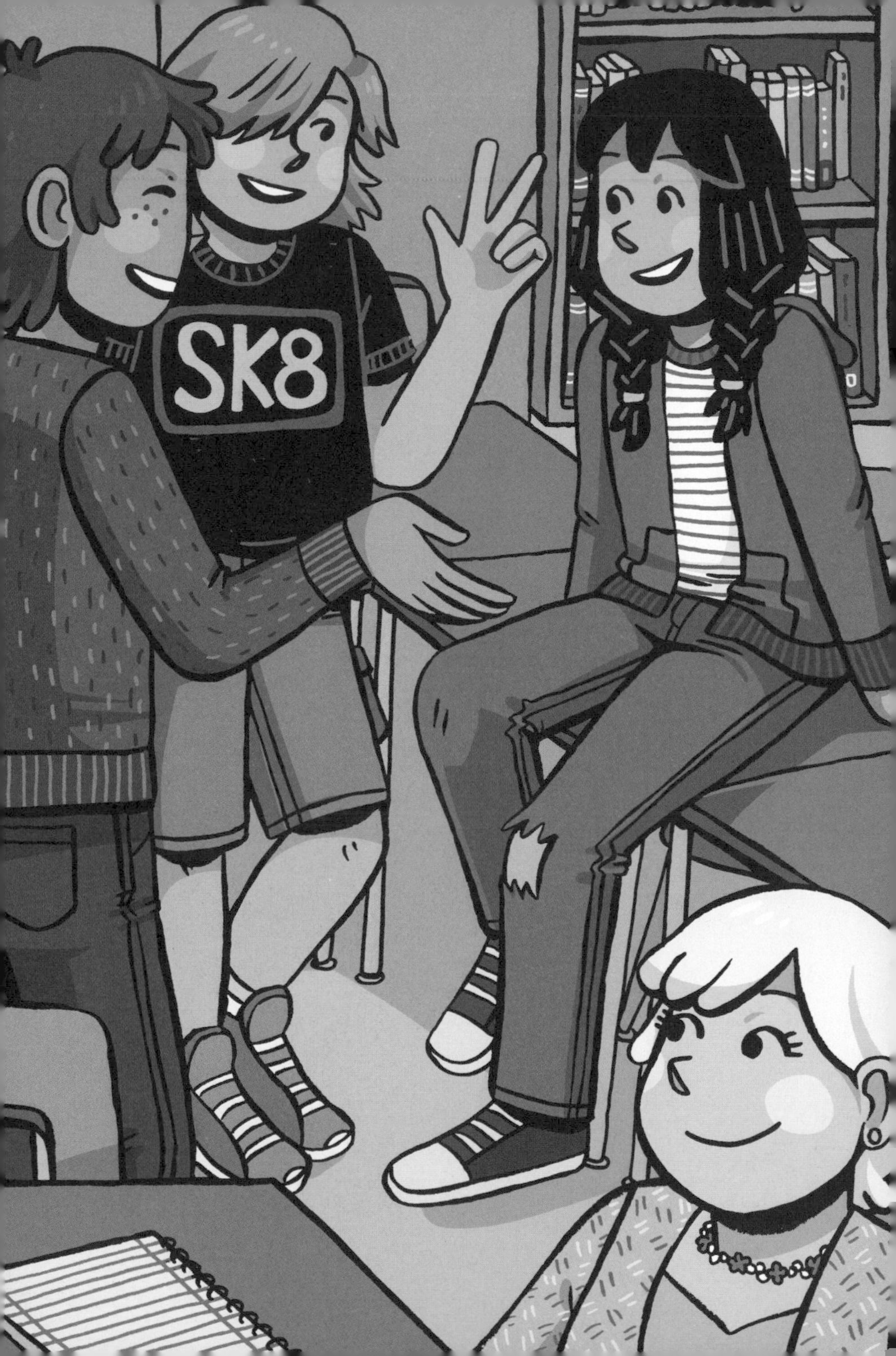
SK8

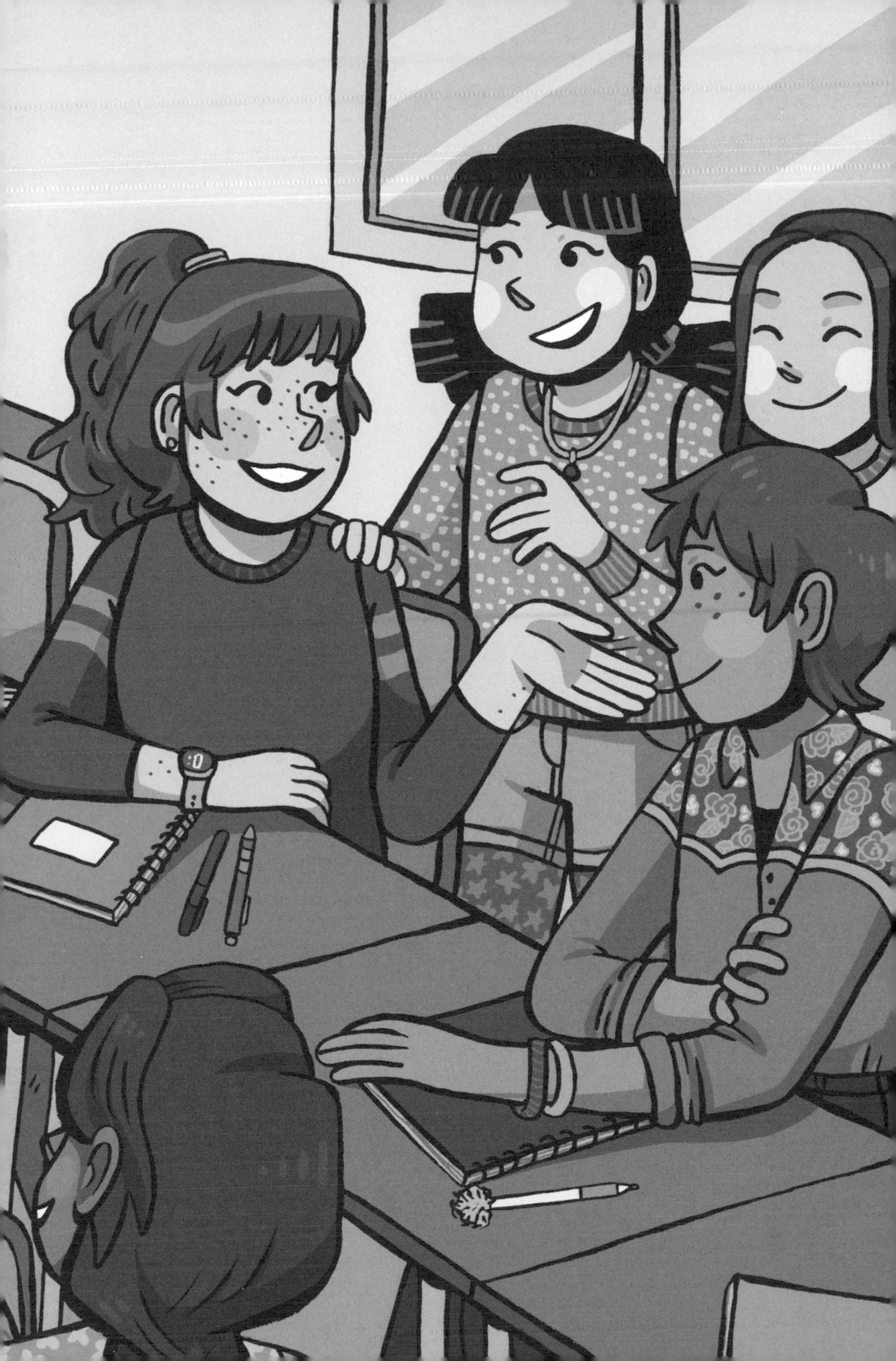

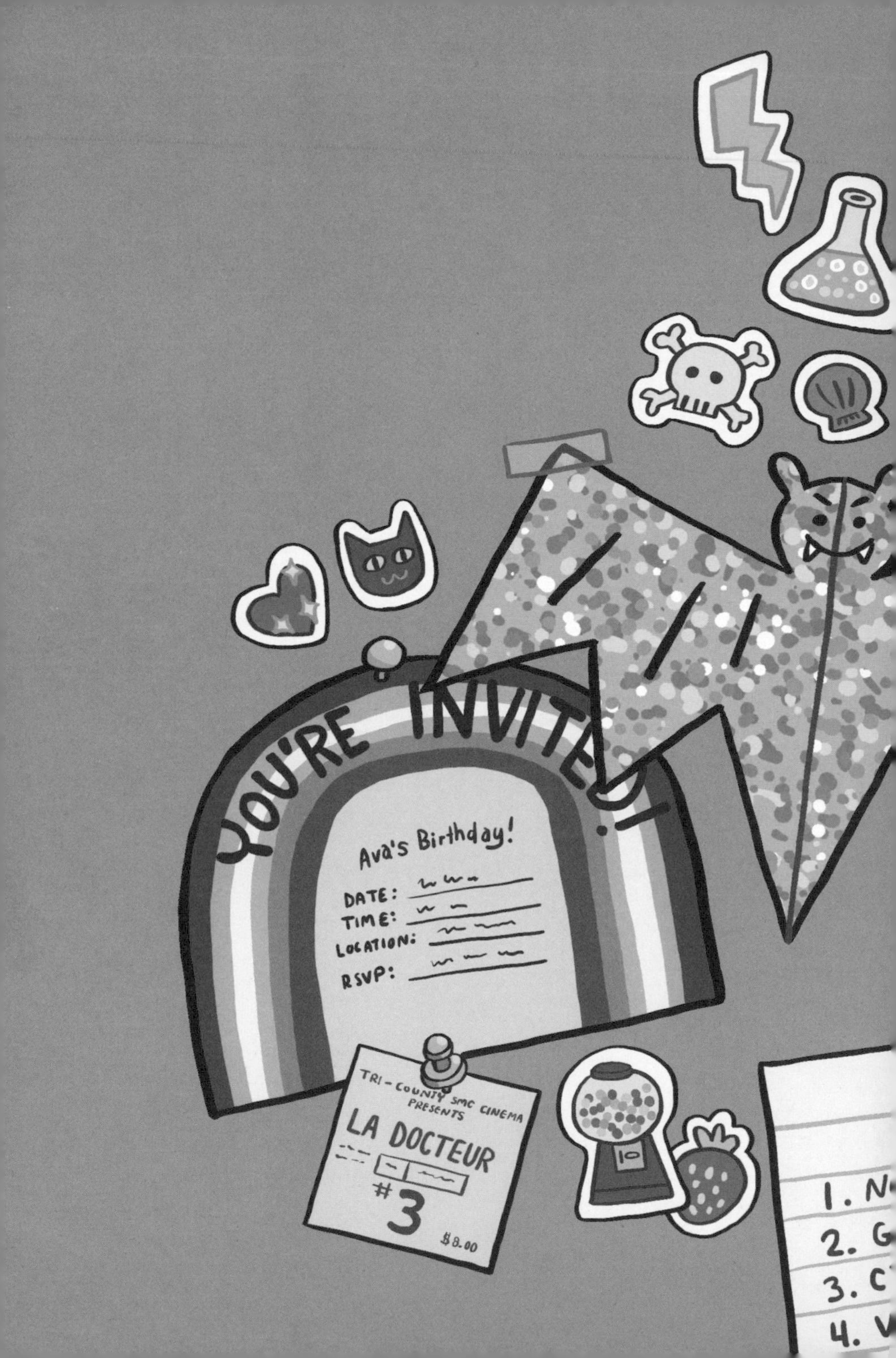

YOU'RE INVITED!
Ava's Birthday!
DATE:
TIME:
LOCATION:
RSVP:
TRI-COUNTY SMC CINEMA PRESENTS
LA DOCTEUR
#3
$8.00
10
1. N
2. G
3. C
4. V

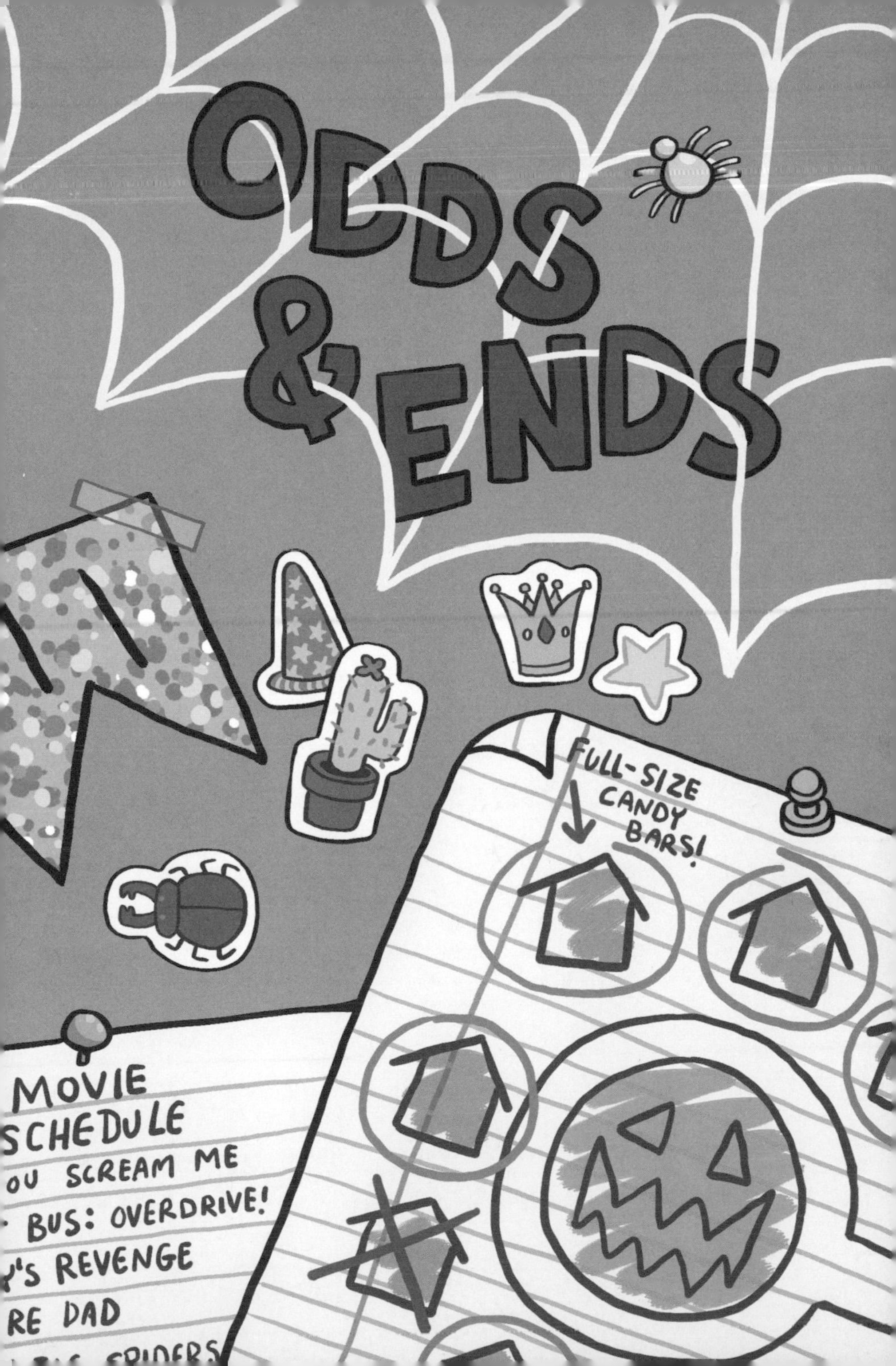

ODDS & ENDS
FULL-SIZE CANDY BARS!
MOVIE SCHEDULE
OU SCREAM ME
BUS: OVERDRIVE!
'S REVENGE
RE DAD

CRAFTY COSTUMES

You don't have to spend a ton of money or know how to sew to make your own cool costumes! Here are some quick and easy costume ideas from Olive's friends that use some items you might already have.

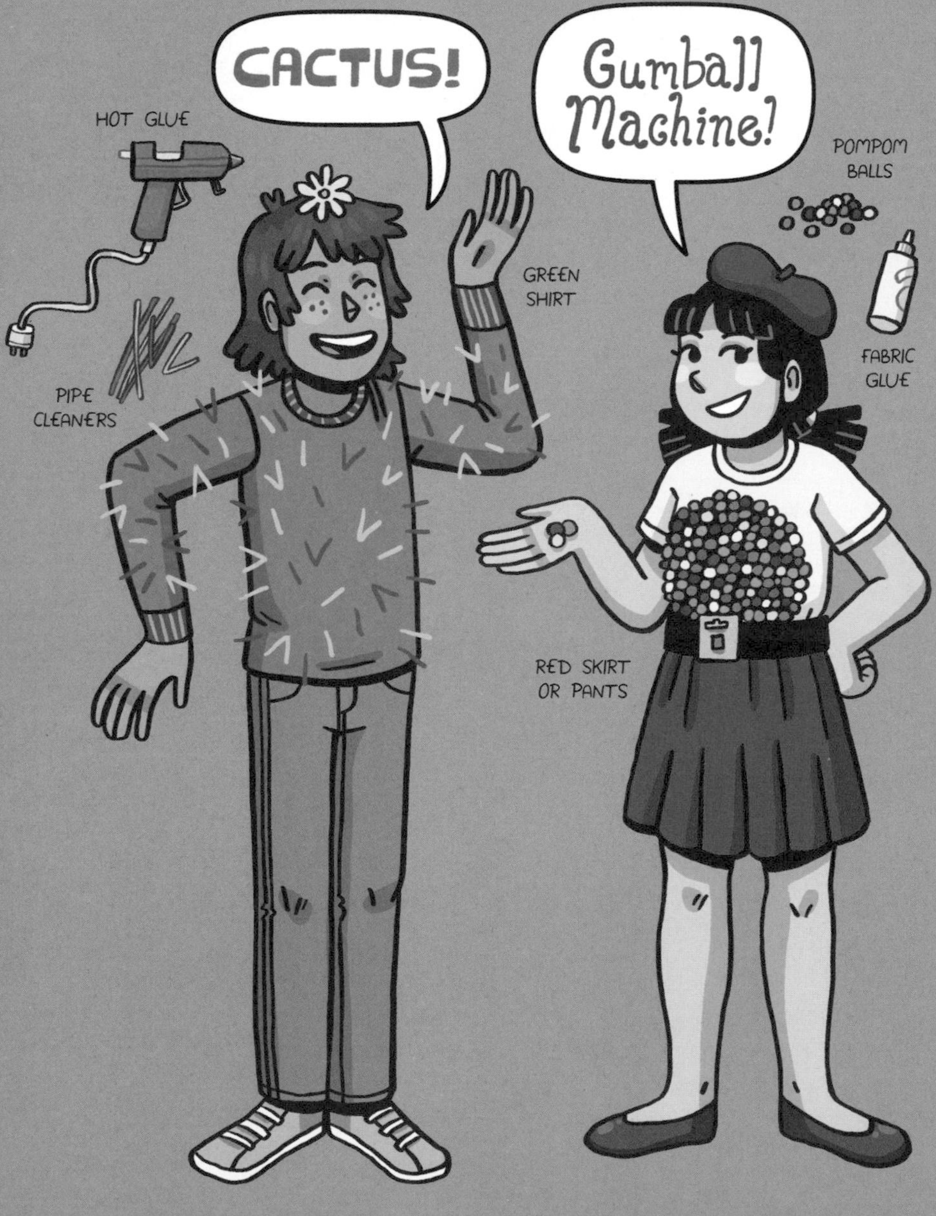

CACTUS!
Gumball Machine!
HOT GLUE
PIPE CLEANERS
GREEN SHIRT
POMPOM BALLS
FABRIC GLUE
RED SKIRT OR PANTS

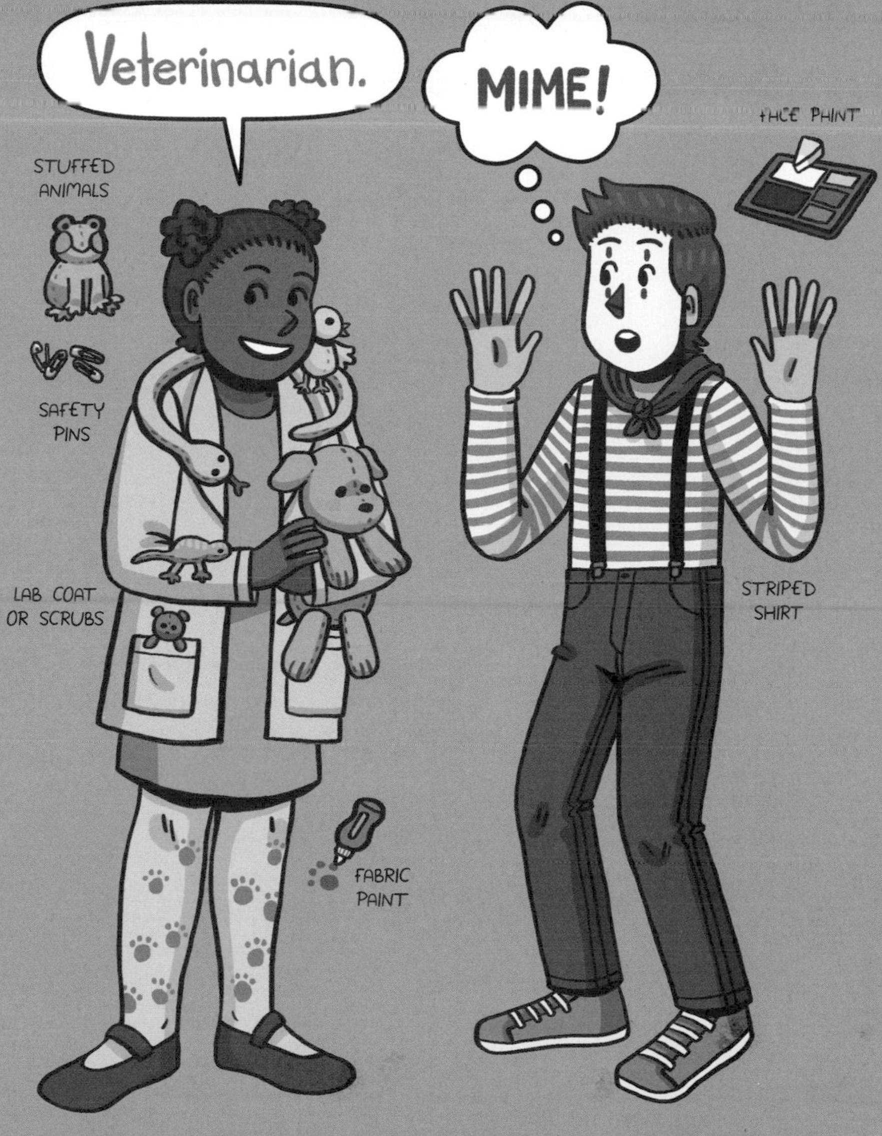
Veterinarian.
MIME!
FACE PAINT
STUFFED ANIMALS
SAFETY PINS
LAB COAT OR SCRUBS
STRIPED SHIRT
FABRIC PAINT

What crafty costumes can you come up with? Here are some ideas to spark your creativity.

PRETZEL: Brown clothes, cotton balls, and fabric glue
ROBOT: Cardboard boxes, tin foil, and duct tape
SCARECROW: Flannel shirt, hay, and face paint
GRAPES: Purple balloons and green paper (for the leaf)

Q & A

Q: With *Clash*, we join Olive in her fourth book...and her friendly nature is challenged like never before! What drew you toward exploring this story?

An early sketch of Natasha!

KAYLA: Olive is a people person, and we see her make friends easily in the other books. I thought it would be interesting to write a story where she didn't get along with someone, since that would be a first for her. In our lives we all meet people whom we don't connect with or don't interact well with, and a lot of the time they're going to be people whom we have to spend time with, whether we like it or not. I wanted to show Olive finding peace with this sort of situation, even if it doesn't end with them becoming best friends.

Q: Have you ever dealt with a situation like the one in *Clash*?

KAYLA: Yes, sort of! When I was Olive's age, there was a kid who really got under my skin—and we saw each other constantly since we had all the same friends and participated in the same sports and activities. We tried to be friends, but our personalities were just too different and all we ever did was rile each other up over nothing. We were never mature enough to talk things out like Olive and Natasha do. I wanted to write a story where someone handles that difficult situation in a healthier manner.

Q: You get a lot of feedback from your readers either at the conferences you attend or on social media. What are some things that you hear most often from readers?

KAYLA: I get a lot of feedback about the characters that readers like (or don't like) and whom they'd like to see more of in future books. For a lot of readers, I think the characters are the element they connect with.

The feedback I get most often from parents is about how graphic novels have gotten their reluctant readers into reading—reading for fun and reading on their own! These kinds of comments are super important to me. I think everyone should enjoy reading and be able to read the kinds of books that make them happy.

I try to fit four pages of inks on each sheet of Bristol board—two on the front and two on the back—but that's still a hefty stack!

Q: Do you have any favorite parts of being an author-illustrator?

KAYLA: I like everything about it. I love entertaining people. I was always a jokester and a ham as a kid, so when I hear that people find my books funny, that part of my brain lights up. I also really love meeting new people, so I feel very lucky that I have the opportunity to travel around and talk with readers, librarians, teachers, parents, and other creators as part of my job.

Q: Can you speak to the way you develop characters, in words or in pictures?

KAYLA: Usually, I think about the characters' personalities first, and then what they look like will come to me later. Their appearances might change from my initial idea as I start to draw them and realize what works and what doesn't work, but it's sort of an organic process. With Olive, I decided right away that I wanted her to have dark hair and a signature hairstyle so she'd be recognizable and stand out if she was in a big group of characters. Then there was a conscious choice to make Olive's family have the same dark hair to link them all together.

Q: Is there any advice that you give to aspiring authors and illustrators?

KAYLA: I usually give the same advice to anyone who is interested in writing, art, or illustration, and that's just to *start!* Kids and teens especially can get paralyzed with the idea of being "good enough" to start a project, but you're never going to get better unless you start putting in the work. It's like learning an instrument or a new language or any sort of skill—at first you're not going to be great at it and you might have some missteps along the way, but the best way to get better at something is to practice and not let doubt or hesitation get in your way.

Olive in *Clash*...inking all the emotions!

Acknowledgments

First, I'd like to thank my readers. The year 2020 was stressful for a lot of people, myself included. There have been days where it's been hard to get motivated or stay focused, but the kind words I've received about my first three books have helped to brighten even the dreariest days. I'm so grateful for the chances I've had to interact with readers digitally, through virtual visits and social media. So, thank YOU!

I'd also like to extend gratitude to everyone whose hard work went into bringing another Olive adventure into existence! Thank you to my excellent editor, Mary, for your insights and guidance. My amazing agent, Elizabeth, for your support and wisdom. Micah, for your lettering work. Jess, for breathing life into the pages with your coloring skills. Andy, for the multitude of tasks you perform to keep things running smoothly and looking fabulous. And everyone else at HMH who works behind the scenes to get these books printed and in front of readers.

Last, a big thank-you to my family and friends. I'm very lucky to have so many supportive people in my life. Mom, Dad, and Grandpa—I wouldn't be able to do what I do if you hadn't believed in me from the start. And Jeffrey, I could fill the rest of the page thanking you for the various ways you help me to be my best as a writer, artist, and person—but hopefully by now you don't need me to spell it out for you.

—KAYLA